REBECCA ST. CLAIRE

Oracles of Whispering Crows

First published by Cursing Raven Books 2024

Content Warning: This book contains graphic depictions of realistic and fantasy violence; body horror; sexual situations between consenting adults; foul language

First edition

This book was professionally typeset on Reedsy.
Find out more at reedsy.com

To Kris and Markie,
For all the advice, love, and support throughout this process, and many, many others.

Chapter 1

Towering buildings of old wood and crumbling gray stone, bounded by wrought iron fences lined the narrow cobblestone streets of Czarnenburg's Old Town. Once the city's thriving heart, the district's age alone suggested it was, in fact, the original settlement just west of the Zirzig Hills in the northern part of the Atharian Empire. The mechanomagical illumination so common in the Empire's cities, Arcanyx crystal street lanterns, was largely absent from this district. The few that were present flickered at uneven intervals from their positions on the corners of the winding, narrow streets, resulting in long, heavy shadows being cast by the decrepit architecture. Now, the perpetually clogged storm drains and rusted sewer pipes kept the streets moist and reeking of shit and death.

On any given day, the Old Town district teemed with life. Rats scurried from the sewers, popping into the streets through holes in the sewer pipes or through storm drains in search of food scraps dropped by pedestrians eating on their daily travels.Dogs and cats, scrawny and flea-ridden, limped along the streets, feasting on the bodies of dead rats and birds. Heavily populated by the bouerin, the empire's unwashed and impoverished debtor class, shuffled about in their unkempt and dirt-stained clothing of black, gray, and white fabrics and their tattered footwear with rotting, holey soles.

City constables in their gray wool suits, imperial soldiers in their gold-trimmed green wool uniforms, and humanoid-driven and driverless mechanomagical mobile wagons were rare sights in Old Town. Wooden carts, often pulled by children, hauled goods from one location to another as urchins, charlatans, and swindlers peddled wares and picked pockets on the narrow, sun-starved streets.

On any given night, prostitutes, pimps, and purse-snatchers wandered the streets, plying their trade. They emerged after the last faint tolling of the bronze bell rang from the tower of St. Casimir Cathedral, a marvel of early Tshípogothic architecture. Peeking through a window's tattered curtain after the sky turned black might reveal body snatchers or grave diggers trudging toward a cemetery.

On this night when black clouds hid the moon and stars, however, the first in the month Kieliah in the year 1787 Age of Arcanum, only one figure walked the streets of Czarnenburg's Old Town. She was tall for a Human woman, with long black hair pulled back and slicked into a pompadour, brown eyes, and olive skin. The puffy sleeves of a cream-colored poet shirt flounced from under the sleeveless black leather vest with gray pinstripes. A small lantern, a flintlock pistol, and a long, single-bladed knife with a silver-edged blade hung from the belt over her hips. She wrapped herself in a black leather trench coat, secured over her shoulders with an old Atharian cloak broach.

Though the first of Kieliah placed the year's movements early within the spring season, Czarnenburg was far enough north that a chill filled the air. White clouds wafted toward the sky from the woman's mouth and nostrils. A shiver raked down her spine. The woman gasped, and then she slid her arms into the coat.

Small splashes of fetid, yellowish-brown sewer water splashed as the woman's riding boots sloshed through the cobblestone streets. Red and gold undertones emerged from within her brown eyes as she surveyed the silent, empty streets. Her nose twitched. The streets reeked of death, fresh and violent death, but that was why she was here.

Earlier that day, the woman stepped off the Crystal Rail, the lightning fast train that connected the major cities of the Atharian Empire. A few blocks from the Old Gehrman Bahnhof in the Market District, she found the Golden Lion Inn, acquired a room, and saw a notice board. There, she found a curious request for aid.

To All Would-Be Monster Hunters and Self-Styled Adventurers,

By the authority of Hertzoch Reinholdt Kratescu, the Office of the High Constable of Czarnenburg offers a reward of one hundred torbal for any who can provide proof the they have slain the beast that, for the past week, has stalked the Old Town district. Reports indicate this beast stands upright on its hind legs and is twice the height of a Human or an Elf and may or may not have thick fur covering its body.

Interested parties should approach the constables manning the barricade entrance at Hemlock Charnel Lane after sunset and present to them this flier. They will brief you on the information known at this time. May the Lord of Sky and Storm light your path.

"I doubt that." The woman scoffed in a husky voice as she snatched the flier from the board.

Night fell, and the woman turned onto Hemlock Charnel

Lane. Refuse, rat and bird carcases swarmed with flies and maggots, and human excrement dumped from chamber pots in the tenements looming along the sides of this narrow road. The barricade stood two blocks ahead, an iron frame wrapped in barbed wire, guarded by four city constables armed with powerful search lanterns and muskets. A gate hinge was visible in the flickering street lights. They eyed her with suspicion as she approached.

When she reached the barricade, the oldest of the four constables, a haggard Human male with long wisps of gray hair and stubble lifted his gloved hand to halt her progress. "Purpose, miss?"

Miss? Did he not know who she was. The woman stuck her chest forward, and then remembered she wore only a nondescript leather vest and not the leather jerkin marking her as a member of the Holy Order of St. Arnulf Ironhand. *You are unworthy to wear this*, her father, Grand Master Caspar Richter, had said to her only three days ago. She winced, and her chest fell. She nodded. Of course, this man wouldn't know who she was.

She handed him the missive. "Something needs hunting. I've got experience."

The constable snatched the missive as he eyed her. He snorted. "What experience is that?"

"One vampire, a handful of ghosts, and over a dozen Ashfodellian fiends. I had help for some, but not the vampire and half the fiends. What lies beyond the barricade?"

"Death." He turned and peered into the darkness. Without looking back at her, the old constable asked, "You sure about this?"

"Tell me what you know."

He shook his head and sighed. "You read the flier. We know that. The residents here aren't terribly helpful, most of them being thieves and whores. Can't trust them. It all started ten days ago when an outbreak of Veigt's Laughing Death spread. The barricades were originally for quarantine. About a week ago, things changed. The station got reports of this thing stalking them. All descriptions said it was big and walked on two legs, except when it ran. Then it switched to four. Some say it had fur. Some said it didn't. They say it eats people. None of us have ever seen it."

That was unhelpful. It could be anything from a lycanthrope to a halgul to half a dozen fiends. Laughing Death complicated matters. Unlike its name, the bacterial disease was serious. It mimicked influenza throughout most of its course, but right before the infected died, the skin around their lips receded, giving them the appearance of a broad, creepy smile. And then their last breath came in a warbling laugh, spreading the bacteria to those nearby. The woman surveyed the area. In cramped conditions of Old Town, that had devastating potential.

She nodded. "Doesn't tell me much. A lot of things fall into that description."

"No shit," the constable said. "Why do you think we fucking called for you lot. Fucking Holy Order of St. Arnulf's has refused to send someone. Guess they got more important things to do now than protect us."

She winced. This wasn't the first time someone had accused her former order of that. "Well, I'm here now. Where has this creature been sighted?"

"All over." He paused and clicked his tongue against his teeth while thinking. "The first four reports were near the old well in the center."

"Looks like it drinks water."

The old constable made a disgusted face. "Not that the well is much cleaner than the rest of the shit-filled muck water, but I suppose."

"That provides a place to start."

The old man snorted. "First fucker to come since we posted those two days ago, and it's a woman. No offense, you look like you've got some beef on you, trained a bit. Weapons look in good order from what I see. Are you sure? You go in there, and you might not walk out."

"That's fine if it happens."

The constable blinked. "Oh. Okay then. Yes, miss. Name? That way we can inform your next of kin, or if you succeed, spread the word?"

"Karina Ri—Karina Skejik. I'm Karina Skejik."

He nodded. Turning to the other constables, he said, "Open up. First hunter's coming through."

Karina wince as the gate screeched upon opening. The old constable gestured with his hands and a nod. Karina returned the nod and strode through the gate, drawing her pistol as she crossed the barricade. The gate closed behind her, and the lock slammed closed.

As she walked through the heavy shadows of the flickering street lamps, the old constable said, "Lord of Sky and Storm light you path, miss. You'll need it."

"I believed that." Karina paused before she added, "Once. Now, it's only a hope."

Hemlock Charnel Lane snaked ahead of Karina's sloshing footsteps. Alone in the dark, she switched on the lantern she had bought secondhand for a handful of torbal earlier in the day. It flickered and buzzed, came to light, and then faded to darkness. Two slaps and a grunt later, the lantern illuminated. Courage would have it fixed in an hour.

Karina winced in pain at the thought of Courage Faern'doln, the budding technomagus she befriended while assisting the Society for Afterlife and Arcane Research. She rubbed her neck, which still bore the scars from the simulated bite the vampire terrorist Marius Bedwyr inflicted upon her. What did he do to Courage? Was he still in that windowless building in Iszenstadt? Did the Crimson Fangs move him somewhere else? And was he safe? This hunt's reward would give her funding to search for him. But how?

And what of Gwyn? The moment in the SAAR headquarters where Marius Bedwyr, masquerading as SAAR Director of Operations Ambrose von Harenheim, revealed that the Elven woman Karina knew as Gwynarra Caoilfhionn was Hertogia Gwynarra Vandiamante, the last heir of the vampire family with whom her family had feuded for centuries. Karina had confessed her feelings for Gwyn to Gwyn earlier in that day, but when the revelation emerged, Karina drew her pistol and attacked. Of course, the vampire survived the fight, but why didn't she fight back? Gwyn would be an asset—no. Karina shook her head. Her cousin Garrus was wrong. Gwyn would not speak to her again, regardless of the circumstances of their next meeting.

A dog's mournful yowl snapped Karina back to the moment. She wiped the single tear that had formed in her eye. That was the past. Finding Courage was her future. The hunt was her present.

What remained of the old well sat at the heart of Old Town. Once a proud structure of stone and wood that served as both a provider of fresh water for consumption and usage as well as a place for gossip and news delivery, only a crumbling stone circle remained in the center of graveyard of broken cobblestones and dilapidated shanties that served as a reminder of what was once a vibrant open-air market. Off in the distance, thick boards covered the doors and windows of the only tavern and inn serving the district.

Karina dropped to her knees and searched the ground around the well. The lantern allowed her to see only a few feet around her. She missed the technology once available at her disposal in the Holy Order. A creature of the size reported should have left tracks or blood trails in the area. The area was higher than the surrounding streets, so no brackish, fetid water from the sewers pooled around the well, but the soil protruding from the cracked and uneven cobblestone was moist.

On the north side of the well, Karina ran her fingers along the cobblestones and felt a slight dampness. She held her fingers in front of her lantern. A thin layer of blood that had yet to dry coated the tips. The creature was here recently. She unhooked the lantern from her belt and held it close to the cobblestones. She squinted as the mechanomagical illumination pushed the thick shadows of night back. The trail of blood was faint and hard to spot, but Karina found trickles in a discernible pattern.

With her pistol in one hand and the lantern in the other, Karina followed the trail of blood as it moved north through the old streets. Gaunt faces glared from windows as she tracked her prey. They hid behind tattered curtains or shutters if she looked in their direction. The night was cold, and the people, gripped by fear and illness, were colder. Aside from Karina's footsteps and the squeaking shrieks of rats who scurried away from her approach, silence filled the night air.

The trail led her to a small, two-story townhouse that served as a butcher shop. Only a few jagged bits of splintered wood remained of the shop's door. Karina tensed her muscles before returning the lantern to its place on her belt. Switching her pistol to her left hand, she drew the long knife with the silvered blade. Closing her eyes, she said a quick prayer for divine sight to help her sense her prey.

"Light shine in the darkness. Show me my foe." Listening for the voice from within, only a quickened heartbeat emerged. Nothing more. *Perhaps there's nothing to sense. That's what it has to be,* she thought as she stepped into the shop.

The butcher shop was in shambles. Broken glass and wood littered the floor. The remains of display cases had either been thrown or had fallen onto the floor. Gnaw marks dented the bones once belonging to the large primal cuts on display. The butcher's cleaver had been lodged into the wall. A layer of dried blood had been splattered over everything in a manner similar to a pretentious child imitating an modernist painter's style. As Karina stooped to examine what appeared to be a thigh bone from a large animal, possibly a cow or a deer, her fingers brushed against a small tuft of bristly reddish-brown fur matted into the blood.

"The beast has fur," she said in hushed tones. "That rules out a halgul, but between the various species of lycanthrope and the dozens of fur-covered fiends, I still know little about my quarry."

Two staircases, one ascending and one descending, emerged from the small hallway beyond the archway that had formerly served as a door frame. As with the shop's front door, the splintered remnants of the door lay on the floor of the hallway beyond.

Kneeling to examine the floor, thick splatters of blood ascended the staircase, and within those dried splatters, were foot prints—two sets of foot prints. One was humanoid, and the other set of prints were not made by Human—or even humanoid—feet, but they were neither lupine nor canine. They were shaped like tripartite, or double-cloven, hooves. Karina nodded.

The first rule of hunting was to know your quarry. Unless her training in the Holy Order was incomplete, and she dismissed that thought with haste, the tripartite hooves could only belong to a Buok'gnoula, a carnivorous fiend, humanoid in appearance, that was covered in thick, rough fur and had a head that resembled a cross between a leopard and a hyena. These fiends roamed the ashy sands of the Crematory Wastes in packs, hunting those damned to the domain of Yehngarbaal, the fiendish lord of insatiable hunger and violence.

Karina released a breath she forgot she held. She had trained for this. Though some may have found the Holy Order's methods callous and cruel, family arcanists summoned various types of fiends for the young hunters to train against while the elder and more experienced hunters observed, stepping into the fray only if it proved necessary to save a life. But why had her request for divine sight to sense the presence of this fiend not granted?

She ascended the stairs, taking care to be as silent as possible on the old wooden steps. Karina's nose wrinkled as she ascended. Even through the reek of Old Town, the rancid stench of death grew stronger. Her breathing slowed, as she held her breath in an attempt to block the reek. The stairs creaked beneath her boots. Halfway up the stairs, a pair of adult-sized hand prints found their way into the blood trail. Karina swallowed hard.

Karina's heart quickened as she neared the landing at the top of the stairs. The butcher's flat would be beyond the door, but as she continued her ascent, this door as well had been shattered. The butcher, or someone in the shop, attempted to flee up the stairs, but Karina knew the wouldn't survive long. Buok'gnoula were relentless hunters, agile and strong. With a deep breath, she steeled herself for what she feared she would find.

A wave of nausea washed over Karina as she reached the landing. The combined stench of recent—but not fresh—death and the reek of animal shit thrust its horrendous odor into her nostrils. She sputtered and coughed. Karina gasped and then covered her mouth. Making noise was not good.

Death greeted her. A humanoid carcass lay on the floor of the small flat's den, picked clean of all but the last bits of flesh by the Buok'gnoula and the swarm of flies that buzzed about the room, seeking sustenance from the corpse and the massive piles of shit the fiend had left in its wake. Karina covered her nose with the back of her left hand and swatted the flies away with her right hand as she examined the room. The corpse appeared to have been killed recently, either earlier this night or last night.

The room had been ransacked. Perhaps the corpse put up a fight while it still lived, or perhaps the fiend ripped the flat apart in search of loot to bring home to its pack leader. Karina gritted and gnashed her teeth. Buok'gnoulae were pack fiends. They didn't leave Ashfodell alone unless summoned. But who would summon one? And why?

A twenty minute search revealed the butcher's small flat was mostly empty beyond the possessions one would expect such a person to have. Nothing in the flat suggested any connection to dark magic and fiend summoning. Karina held her nose as she left the flat and descended the stairs. The Buok'gnoula apparently spent a lot of time here, given the amount of shit on the floor. She paused after four steps. Assuming the fiend had set up a camp here, remaining in the butcher's flat would mean her quarry would return.

"But someone else might die." Karina lowered her head. *Gwyn wouldn't allow that.* Her eyes widened. Why had she thought that? She shook her head and quickened her pace as she descended the stairs. Hertogia Vandiamante's opinion no longer mattered.

Karina paused as she reached the ground floor landing. Her gaze turned from the butcher shop to the stairs descending to the basement. Why was that untouched? Buok'gnoulae were scavengers and looters. Every other door in the in the building had been destroyed. Why was this door spared? After another look into the storefront, Karina descended the stairs.

The door was locked. Courage could pick the lock, but he wasn't here. Karina gritted her teeth and mentally kicked herself. She should have gone after him, wherever the Crimson Fangs took him. But she went north toward Froam, where Gwyn was born, and ultimately, toward Florescia, where Gwyn was likely to return. She had to make things right. And she needed the vampire if she were to rescue that gadget-loving Ashbourne from the vampire insurgents.

Karina kicked the wooden door. The maple cracked and buckled. She grunted and kicked again. The door splintered around her heel. After another kick, Karina was able to slip her hand through the door, feeling an unexpected rush of wintry air, and turn the locking mechanism on the other side of the knob.

A meat freezer stretched out before her. Karina shivered, and her breaths trembled as they slipped through her chattering teeth. She hadn't felt a cold this sharp since the night she and Gwyn shared a bed, and the vampire's frigid body temperature shocked her awake, thinking her ally had died. Huge slabs of animal carcass hung from the ceiling, untouched by the fiend. Beyond the butchering table, another door, a wooden door loomed in the center of the wall.

Buok'gnoulae are carnivorous and have a terrifying sense of smell. The fiend should have sniffed this room and devoured it. Why was this room spared?

The door on the far wall was unlocked, and Karina stepped through it into a storage room filled with stacks of wooden boxes that rose to uneven heights as they leaned, balanced in a precarious fragility. The acrid scent of brimstone cut through the cool, stale air. Karina tilted her head to the right and squinted. A butcher's basement shouldn't smell like brimstone.

She moved through the basement toward the source of the brimstone smell. Halfway through this basement room, the towering stacks of boxes ended, and an open workspace with an artisan's workbench stood against the north wall. Two books, a fountain pen and its ink pot, and a handful of tallow candles lay atop the workbench. A large stain the color of dried blood and the size of a medium dog or a child lay on the floor. Karina's face twisted in disgust.

The first book was a journal of sorts. Upon scanning

the first few entries, Karina surmised it to be a journal of grievances. A few of the grievances were against public figures in Czarnenburg, such as High Constable, who did nothing to curb crime in the district, and against Bishop Walburga, for refusing to hear last rites for those afflicted by Veigt's Laughing Plague. The butcher held grudges against many in Old Town who criticized his butchery in public, which hurt his business and for which he blamed his wife leaving him alone with their infant son. He swore vengeance on each of them in turn.

Karina gasped. She turned her attention back to the stain on the floor. *A father wouldn't—couldn't—do that to his own son. This one was an infant. I don't want to know.* She closed the journal.

The other book had been printed on low quality paper. Karina frowned and then nodded as she read the title, *The Theory and Practice of Magick* by Alazor Crol. The butcher had suffered a fate appropriate for one who dabbled in Ashfodellian magic. That explained the Buo'gnoula's appearance. Now all that remained was to find the fiend.

Deciding not to wait for the fiend to return, Karina walked through the basement toward the stairs. She ascended the stairs and turned into the storefront. As she stepped beyond what remained of the counter, a woman's scream pierced the silence. Karina jerked her head toward it, and then a barking howl cut through the night. Karina narrowed her eyes and smirked. Her quarry revealed itself.

Weapons drawn, Karina raced into the streets, following the sounds of the screams and howls. She darted through the serpentine maze of winding streets, fetid sewer water splashing around her boots. The woman's screams grew more frantic. Karina's heart thundered, and her breath burst from her lungs in growling pants, pushing white clouds into the cold night air.

The fiend's howl was hungry and vicious. The woman's screams turned to pleadings for her children's lives. Karina slipped as she turned a corner onto a narrow alley. Children crying soaked the night. Karina steadied herself and continued her push toward the sound, turning from the alley into a crossroads.

Three children covered in a corner, trembling and crying. Their mother, a matronly woman with slight Sun Elf features, stood before them, her hands crossed in front of her face as she screamed for help and begged the fiend to leave them alone. Blood and spit drooled from the Buok'gnoula's rotting yellow fangs as it towered over the woman.

The flintlock flashed and thundered as Karina fired. The fiend's howl shot up two octaves as the shot struck its left shoulder. Thick, black blood oozed over the reddish-brown fur dotted with black patches. As the fiend gnashed its teeth and spun around, Karina hastily reloaded the pistol.

"Run," she shouted to the woman and her kids.

The woman nodded and guided her children away from danger, saying, "Thank you, miss. Gods protect you."

The Buok'gnoula charged Karina, still reloading the flintlock, with a frenzied intensity for which she had not accounted. Its rancid breath reeked of hot death and shit. A massive paw slammed into Karina's jaw.

She grunted and staggered, shaking her head as rushing blood warmed her jaw. The fiend rushed her, but a quick shot at the fiend's knee halted it. As the fiend howled, Karina scurried back a few paces. She grabbed at her neck, but the holy symbol of the Lord of Sky and Storm wasn't there. The memory of hurling it onto the floor of her bedroom as she home on her father's orders. No god would help her end this fiend.

The fiend limped as it rushed her. The two traded blows with blade and claw. Blood splattered and flowed, covering both in dark crimson. The Buok'gnoula slammed its shoulder into Karina. She staggered until building's wall stopped her.

The fiend pummeled her, its fists slamming into her chest, stomach, and face. Karina grunted. Tears mixed with the blood, and both streamed down her face. The Buok'gnoula grabbed Karina's head in a single paw and pounded the back of her head into the brick repeatedly.

The world spun around her. Karina peered through a veil of bloody tears. She was tall, but the Buok'gnoula loomed over her. A small glimmer of light twinkled against the fiend's fur beneath its left armpit. As the fiend reared back for a haymaker of a claw slash, Karina swung wildly with her long knife. The silvered blade lodged itself in the fiend's flesh between two of its ribs. The Buok'gnoula yowled in agony.

Karina fought through the haze before her eyes. Her training in the Holy Order had become muscle memory, and a series of fast slashes across the chest caused the fiend to reel. With a flick of her wrist and a shift of her stance, she thrust the point of the blade through the fiend's chest. It's final howl ended in a rattling gasp as it slumped and fell. As its furry face hit the pavement, Karina panted and wiped the blood from her face.

Karina surveyed the scene. One kill without the aid of any mechanomagical devices. How many of her family could say that? She grabbed the fur on the top of the Buok'gnoula's head, and with four hacks, she cut through the neck, severing the head.

A few moments later, Karina returned to the barricade gate on Hemlock Charnel Lane. The constables recoiled at the sight of her. She approached the old constable, held up the fiend's head, and dropped it onto the cobblestone at his feet. He grimaced as he looked over over. An approving smile crossed his face. He nodded.

"Fuck me, miss Skejik. I didn't think you'd return with that *thing's* head. You've earned the damned reward. I'll tell the High Constable, and you'll have it in the morning. Your address?"

"The Golden Lion. I'm in room twelve."

"Someone will see you in the morning. You go rest and take a bath."

Karina nodded. She returned to the Golden Lion. The modern renovations adorned the exterior. Wrought iron finials topped the steep gables on the roof, and gables topped the massive windows on the street-facing wall. Entering the hotel, the bellhop eyed her with curiosity until her glare caused him to avert her gaze. She trudged through the inn's restaurant and sat at the bar.

The bartender whistled and grimaced as she approached. "Rough night? What are you having?"

Karina chuckled. Her father's words echoed in her mind. *Strong drink dulls the senses, making the hunter vulnerable to the beast and makes men cowards.* Courage always drank black beers, so Karina thought for a moment and said, "Give me a schwartzbier, the strongest you have."

"Understood." The bartender nodded. "Charge to your room?"

She nodded. "Twelve."

The bartender poured the beer and handed it to Karina. It smelled of hops and coffee, rich and strong. She sipped the beverage, and it was heavy, thick, and bitter. Karina winced. She didn't expect the thickness and the frothy head that gave her a mustache until she wiped it off. She tasted chocolate notes, which she didn't expect from what others had told her of beer's taste.

Halfway through the beer, a pleasant fog filled her head. For the first time since she kissed Gwyn on the train to Schwarzfeld, Karina smiled. One beer turned into another and then a glass of whiskey and water followed. Once she finished that, Karina staggered a winding path through the restaurant and up the stairs to her room. As she crashed onto the bed and fell into a snoring, drunken sleep, a fog descended upon Czarnenburg.

Chapter 2

Nearly five days after the steam ship departed Clérmontán in Froam, it docked in the Sapphire Harbor, the westernmost district of the city of Ristarad on the southernmost of the Zyntarian islands, San'Irinna. White sand beaches greeted passengers who stood on the deck as the ship pulled into the delta, through an arch formed by the Gigantos, a colossal bronze statue of an armored warrior whose feet balanced atop the red clay of the coastal cliffs. Children waved to the ship as it passed, and those on the terraced city's lowest levels sat on the edge of the cliffs, allowing their feet to dangle over the edge as they watched the sun set over the Palriniir Ocean.

Gwynarra Caoilfhionn emerged from her cabin only after the bell to disembark had sounded. Though the salty air was warm on this spring evening, her black cloak remained draped over her shoulders, concealing the white blouse with its lace jabot that peaked from beneath her long, black leather vest. As the setting sun painted the sky in shades of purple and orange, she still wore the octagonal sunglasses with the enchanted red lenses Courage had made to help with her day-walking sickness. Her fitted trousers, riding boots, and tricorn were all of the same black leather. A small sword and a flintlock hung from her belt.

Her pale skin and white bob contrasted with the warm, olive to umbra skin tones and thick, curly black hair of the Zyntarian Humans and the bronze skin and henna hair of the Sun Elves who walked the streets. Born to a Froamian Snow Elf family, her skin paled further after she was embraced by the Vandiamante family. People smiled, waved, and even greeted her and the other travelers as they traversed the dusty stone streets that ascended and wound through the districts.

When docking, she was able to reserve a room for herself and a stable for her horse Siobhan at the Elysian Havens Inn for two nights. Her horse was sent ahead of her, but since she only carried her travel pack, that remained on her person. A hunter traveled light, and one needing to flee at a moment's notice traveled lighter.

Gwyn passed row after row of white stone houses adorned with roofs and doors painted blue and trimmed in gold that glinted in the sun's last rays. Many had small herb, flower, or vegetable gardens. As she neared the Laurel Gardens District, home to the city's wealthy and elite, jasmine's fragrant scent mingled with the fresh sea air. Jasmine was her mother's favorite scent, and Gwyn smiled.

Shadows lengthened on the dusty white stone streets. Gwyn turned onto a narrow alley scrunched between the back wall of the temple dedicated to the Lunar Huntress on the higher terrace and the back of the Academy of Philosophical Arts and Sciences on the lower terrace. Wind whipped through the alley, pushing her cloak and hair forward. Gywn's slender fingers brushed against the rough stone until she found a place that resonated with familiar energy.

Gwyn pressed her fingers into the wall and whispered, "The

hunger fills me. Open the way."

A shimmer of crimson light glowed from within the stone where it met Gwyn's ring finger. A line of crimson light traced a rectangle upon the stone, and then blood dripped from the top of the rectangle down to the stones on the street. The blood congealed and then transformed into sheer satin curtains that parted in the middle. Gwyn pulled the curtains apart, stepped through them, and the wall returned to normal behind her.

Beyond the mysterious curtain, a room where women lounged on crimson and purple satin and velvet cushions around a central fountain from which blood wine flowed from the mouths of the snakes sprouting from the head of a nude gorgon. The gorgon's face had been carved to resemble the transcendent calm that followed an orgasm. The women who were clothed wore sheer dresses patterned after the traditional chiton. Seated at the base of fountain, a lyrist strummed soft, melodic minor music that filled the crisp air.

Gwyn removed her hat and ran her fingers through her hair. As one of the servers approached her, the whispers filled the air. "Is that her?"

"Yes, it's the Silver Scourge who slew the Dread Wight of Colgaran Pass. Poor dear, what happened to her family."

"Such a shame."

And then a turn in the whisperings made her wince. "Have you heard the news from Athar?"

"No, what?"

"She was seen with one of the Richters."

"A Richter? Her? After what they did to her family—to so many of us? No, that can't be true. Has she betrayed us?"

"We'll find out."

A young woman with tendrils of wavy black hair framing her face approached. She smiled and bowed before handing Gwyn a bronze amphora painted with black scrollwork. "Good evening, mistress. What is your desire?"

"I just want a drink and a doll. I'll be gone once I've fed."

The servant nodded. "The wine from our fountain is complementary. The doll will be fifteen drachmari. Does the mistress have any requests for her doll?"

Someone I thought wanted me, Gwyn thought. She sighed and then shook her head. "Female or first available. I'm just going to feed, and then go about my business." Gwyn handed over the coinage. "There's an extra five for you and five for the doll. Thank you."

The servant bowed before returning to the back rooms. Gwyn walked over to the fountain and filled her amphora with the blood wine. Feeling the eyes of every woman on her, Gwyn found an empty cushion away from the crowd where she reclined and sipped. The wine's notes of cedar, fig, and clove provided a warmth and sweetness that Gwyn enjoyed. She closed her eyes, remembering the yearly holiday to either Ristarad or Asta'Ir to procure three dozen barrels of wine.

As the lyrist strummed, the women lounged, drank, and conversed. Gwyn drank in silent contemplation, lost in the bittersweet world of her memories. A dozen bars passed and one of the older women, a statuesque brunette with bronze skin and emerald eyes looked across the room and spoke in a commanding voice. "You have great nerve, Hertogia Vandiamante, if the rumors are true that you, the Silver Scourge, has aligned with the Holy Order of St. Arnulf Ironhand."

The lyrist stopped on an unresolved movement. The crowd

gasped and stared. Gwyn sipped her wine. Without saying a word, she tilted her head down and returned the woman's gaze, making eye contact by looking over the rims of her sunglasses. *I should've expected word would get around,* she thought. She sipped her wine once more.

And then Gwyn's words sliced through the thick silence as she spoke in a measured and remorseful tone. "She was not who she led me to believe she was. The story is over."

The woman smirked. "So, even the Silver Scourge can be fooled. What hope is there for us then?"

"Avoid the Atharian Empire. I don't think you'll have anything to fear." Gwyn sipped the wine.

The woman leaned forward. Her smirk turned into a frown accompanied by a glare. "And what of you, hunter? How are we to feel safe in your presence?"

Gwyn sipped the wine once more. "I came for a drink and a bite. My sword has remained in its sheath, and my pistol has not left its holster. I won't be in Ristarad long enough to visit again."

"And who—or what—are you hunting?"

Rage's seething venom dripped from the corners of Gwyn's words. These interactions had grown stale and frustrating. "Answers. I came to make offering to the Sythrokli in exchange for wisdom. Something you might consider obtaining before uttering your next question."

The woman had struck a nerve. Six years ago, the Holy Order of St. Arnulf Ironhand stormed the Vandiamante villa and slaughtered Gwyn's adoptive vampire family, but due to the quick thinking of one of the servants, Kiernan Valfrido, she was able to flee. After a stint training in the fighting pits here, she earned the moniker of *Silver Scourge,* and she then used those skills to aid others beset by monsters, both humanoid and not. The praise she earned from the living paled in comparison to the sting of the mistrust from her own kind, as they eyed her with suspicion, wondering when—and not *if*—she would hunt one of them.

The woman chuckled. She licked her lips, and her voice slithered. "Did I strike a sensitive spot behind your fang? It must be so lonely knowing none of us trust you."

Gwyn drained the amphora and then set it on the floor beside her cushion. Her jaw clenched. She rose to her feet and placed her slender, gloved hand on the hilt of her sword. The assembled crowd's jaws dropped, and even the antagonistic woman shrank into the throng.

"One grows accustomed to solitude quickly if one is to survive." Gwyn turned her attention to the staff. "Keep the coin."

She stormed from the sanctuary into the night-darkened streets of Ristarad. Stars flashed in the blackened sky. Gwyn winced as she clutched her growling throat. She had not had a proper meal in over a week, and the alchemic blood potions she made only staved off the hunger for so long, and when under duress, the potion's impact was lessened. At her age, she could stave off the hunger's feral rage by eating mortal food, but once she had been a vampire for a century, she would only taste ash when eating such foods.

A rat scurried by her feet. Gwyn's gaze followed it, and her ears picked up the thumping of its heart. Every muscle in her body tensed. She was to be crowned Sezara of the Midnight Court in Florescia upon her return, but this would not be the first rat she fed on to survive. Giving in to hunger presented a less desirable option than feasting on undesirable food.

A whispered hiss slid through Gwyn's lips as she bared her fangs. Her vampiric celerity allowed her to overtake the rat with minimal effort. The rat screeched, and its screech intensified as Gwyn's fangs pierced its side. It twitched and whimpered as Gwyn drained it of blood. A few moments passed, and the twitching stopped.

Gwyn kneeled and placed the rat's carcass on the ground. "Thank you, little one."

The Elysian Haven wasn't far, and that was the inn the Vandiamantes always stayed when visiting Ristarad. As she walked toward the Laurel Gardens district, she chuckled and shook her heads. Memories flooded the mind when least expected.

Three drunken Human men stumbled from the door of the Leopard and Lyre, a tavern frequented by Academy students, shortly after Gwyn passed. They whistled and called out to her, but Gwyn rolled her eyes and ignored them. Their pace quickened. What could three drunks do to her? Gwyn continued along at her normal pace.

One of the drunks grabbed her shoulder and yanked her toward him. As she spun around with fangs bared and eyes glared, the drunk spoke with slurred words. "Hey, we're trying to talk to you. It's rude to ignore people who just want to be friendly."

"Yeah," one of the others said. "And when someone pays you a compliment, you're supposed to thank them and not be a stuck up bitch."

Gwyn offered a sweet and gentle smile, practiced in aristocratic courts. "A lady speaks when and to whom she desires. Her wishes are to be respected."

With a swiftness the men wouldn't have expected while

sober, Gwyn struck. Her boot slammed into the chest of the man who grabbed her shoulder, dropping him onto his ass with a grunt. She punched the second man in the face, knocking him back.

The third man rushed her, but she spun around him and kicked his ass, knocking him forward. The first drunk cursed her and threw a punch. Gwyn blocked it, slid forward as if riposting with her sword, and wrapped her hand around his throat. He sputtered and gasped from as much from a lack of oxygen as from the shock of this slender woman's strength.

Gwyn lifted him off the ground and slammed his back into the wall of one of the buildings. He grunted. Gwyn closed the distance between them. His blood thundered as it flooded through his veins. Gwyn moaned in hunger. And then her nose wrinkled at the emergent stench. Her eyes dropped to see a wetness grow on the man's trousers as he pissed himself.

Gwyn slammed him against the wall again and then growled into his ear. "I bet I'd get tipsy draining you. You're nothing, but you do not consent." She tossed him away, and as he hit the ground with a grunt, Gwyn said, "A rat saved your life tonight. Learn from that."

The drunks stumble-scurried away. Gwyn turned around to continue on her way. A handful of steps later, she paused. Her eyes met those of a young woman dressed in a gold-trimmed blue chiton-inspired dress. She was Human with skin of burnished bronze. Thick black curls framed her face and cascaded over her shoulders. Bite marks pierced her skin in multiple locations.

Gwyn nodded, and the woman dropped to her knees. "Good evening, mistress. This one asks if you hunger."

Gwyn lifted her right eyebrow as she approached the

woman. She looked around. No one else walked the streets. Still, she kept her tone hushed. "A doll outside the sanctuary is off the clock. You are under no obligation to offer."

"This one maintains a small townhouse, as do many of the other dolls." She pointed to a two-story white building with a balcony protruding from the second story. "This one heard the scuffle from her window. Forgive this one, if she was presumptuous, mistress, but your anger resembled that of hunger's rage. Thus, this one offers you sustenance."

"What is your rate? And do not dance around the question. I will pay what you charge, and consent will be discussed indoors."

The woman nodded. "Yes, mistress. This one charges ten drachmari."

Gwyn nodded. "Accepted."

The woman rose from her knees and led Gwyn to her townhouse. After ascending the stairs, they entered the woman's bedroom. Lavender curtains adorned with fragrant jasmine blossoms framed a circular bed. She opened the curtain and sat on the bed, patting the spot beside her.

Following ancient customs, blood dolls never told vampires their names. Gwyn loathed this tradition and the formality of speech that surrounded the practice, but she was in no place to demand changes. She presented the woman with the ten drachmari. A favorable exchange rate blessed her as she left the Atharian Empire, giving her more drachmari than she expected.

The woman accepted the payment. "What does mistress wish of me?"

Gwyn exhaled. The exchange with a blood doll often included some form of sexual gratification, and the vampire's bite often induced orgasmic spasms in the mortal they bit. Her voice was gruff—huskier than she expected, which called Karina's voice to her mind. "I hunger. I only wish to feed."

The woman spread her legs. Her thick thighs jiggled. "Does mistress wish to drink from this one's neck, her arms, or her thighs."

"Your neck will suffice."

Gwyn sat on the bed beside the doll. She leaned forward. The doll smelled of lavender and sweet wood. Scars decorated the woman's neck where she had taken repeated piercings. Gwynarra moistened her lips as she leaned forward. Her young fangs glistened in the light provided by the silver Arcanyx lamp. The woman leaned in, offering no resistance. She moaned and grunted as the vampire pierced her skin just above the point where her neck met the right shoulder. The blood flowed around Gwyn's fangs as she held the wound open for a moment before releasing the bite. Warm blood seeped from the two puncture wounds, she suckled and lapped at the sweet blood. After a few moments, she pulled her lips away and dragged her tongue across the wound to encourage coagulation.

"Thank you," Gwyn said, rising from the bed. "Enjoy your night."

"This one thanks you, mistress, for allowing her to be in your service. There is room if mistress wishes to remain for the night?"

Gwyn shook her head as she reached the door. "No. That would not be proper. Thank you again."

After leaving the woman's townhouse, Gwyn grunted and kicked the dirt. While she partook of sexual relations with blood dolls on occasion—and only when stressed, as she was at present—the woman's skin and thick black hair reminded her of Karina, whose olive skin and black hair were an unusual combination among Atharian citizens. None of the Ricthers Gwyn remembered storming her home as a child had such features.

They must come from her mother, Gwyn thought. She then cursed under her breath as she walked toward the Laurel Gardens. *Why am I thinking about her? After all we'd been through together, as far as we came toward each other—all of it—undone with Bedwyr's fucking revelation of my identity. Did she give me a chance to explain why I didn't tell her who I was? No. The moment it was confirmed, she attacked. She shot at me. She drew that fucking silvered blade they all carry. I could've killed her. I'm sure that's what he wanted, but I didn't want that. I should have.*

An expansive district populated by the city's wealthy and elite, the Laurel Gardens had fewer buildings than any district other than the Agora Heights. Expansive gardens with laurel and olive trees, burbling fountains, and blooming jasmine and lavender perfumed filled the empty space, providing a fragrant tranquility to the area. Oplitoi, the city-state's military guard force, patrolled the streets in uniforms of bronzed military weave, a stiff fabric treated with alchemical concoctions to be blade and shot resistant while allowing full range of motion. They noted her appearance and nodded. She was a foreigner, but she wore the traveling clothes common to Florescian nobility, allaying suspicion of her intent.

Her father led the attacks that killed both of my families. I should want revenge, and I did. Six years ago. She had never met any from my family until she met me, and yet she hated us with a vitriolic passion simply because she was told to do so. And then we connected, and I saw the person she was behind the uniform. I thought she saw the person I was, but blood ties knots even the gods cannot unravel. Gwyn sighed. *I should've fucked the doll, get my frustrations out, and move on. Ah, here we are.*

The Elysian Haven Inn was a large building whose suites all faced the district's central gardens. A row of six fluted columns supported the second floor balcony and provided the building with the appearance of an ancient temple. Marble tiles lined the interior floor, and vibrant frescoes depicting scenes of heroes in battle, villagers in celebration, and gods contending with monsters adorned the walls. After checking in, Gwyn drifted into the dreamless death-sleep of the vampire.

The next afternoon—Gwyn wasn't even a morning Elf and certainly wasn't a morning vampire—she ate a light lunch in the inn's dining hall before walking to the open air market in the Agora Heights to purchase a goat and scented oils for her offering at the temple. Her head throbbed, and her stomach churned. Day-walking sickness was no treat. The sunglasses lessened the severity of the symptoms but did not eliminate them.

That task completed, she mounted Siobhan and left Ristarad. Heading northeast, they traveled for an hour before reaching a small but dense copse. Thick-trunked fir trees and towering blacksap pines sprung from the thick underbrush. They followed the well-worn trail travelers' feet had beatete into the foliage on their way to the Sythrokli Oracle beneath the Sylvan Temple of the Lunar Huntress.

The copse opened into a small grove, bounded by nine fluted columns of white marble. Each column had been carved into the shape of the moon's progression from a hollow column representing the dark moon to a full circle to another hollow column. A stone altar adorned with a pair of antlers holding a censor attached to each corner stood in the grove's center, and a cavern's mouth opened just beyond the column marking the full moon.

She tied Siobhan to a post and scritched the horse's mane. One of the priestesses dressed in their ceremonial white chitons that fluttered above the knee greeted her. Gwyn presented the sacrificial offerings, and the priestess led her to the altar. After placing the goat and the oils atop the altar, the priestess snapped her fingers. The censors sprang to life. White plumes of perfumed smoke spiraled through the air with the sweet and earthy scents of incense they contained. She gestured for Gwyn to approach the altar. After removing her hat out of respect, Gwyn did so.

"Lunar Huntress," Gwyn said, "She who presides over the moon, its mysteries, and those who hunt in the wilds, hear my prayer and grant my request. Though my kind does not normally pray to you, I come to your temple with a simple request. I ask your guidance through your Oracle that I might find my friends." She paused. Yes, she still counted, or wanted to count, Karina among her friends. "Or to at least know they are safe. Grant me this, and the next hunt, I dedicate to you."

Gwyn took a single step back from the altar. The white plumes blackened, causing Gwyn's unbeating heart to sink in her chest as her shoulders slumped. She nodded. She donned her hat and turned to leave.

Sparks burst from the censors, and Gwyn spun around. Smoke rose from the goat and the oils as the sparks from the censors ignited small but growing fires upon them. Gwyn removed her hat once more and returned to the altar. The smoke whitened, and the plumes straightened as they rose to the heavens. A hopeful smile crept across Gwyn's face as fire danced across her offering.

"The Huntress accepts your offering, traveler," the priestess said. "Go now to the Sythrokli and ask your question."

"Thank you." Gwyn bowed to the altar and then descended into the cave, returning her hat to her head only after she was beneath the surface.

The cavern's path spiraled down for six concentric levels until one reached the lowest level. The cool, damp air had a faint sweetness that cut through the earthiness of the soil and rock. Two bronze doors upon which ancient Zyntarian verses had been etched stood at the end of the circular chamber at the cavern's bottom. Gwyn had walked through tombs with less silence than the antechamber of this sacred space.

Gwyn approached the doors. Metal grinding on stone sounded through the antechamber, and the doors opened with a resounding clang. Gwyn stepped through the doors into a subterranean temple arranged like the one above with one difference. Instead of an altar, a large silk cushion sat, and atop the cushion, the Sythrokli Oracle, dressed in white with a veil covering her face rested, flanked by two masked Oplitoi. The air buzzed with an energetic headiness that caught Gwyn off guard.

The Oplitoi focused their gaze upon Gwyn who raised her hands to show they were empty and that she came in peace. They nodded, and she approached the Oracle. When she reached a small cushion in front of the larger one, the Oplitoi spoke with a single, deep, resonant voice. "Kneel."

Gwyn removed her hat once more and kneeled on the cushion. The Oplitoi then said, "Request."

Gwyn nodded. "Sythrokli Oracle, I come with a request more humble than that to which you are accustomed. An altercation and explosion separated me from my dearest friends, and I fear they are in danger. I don't know how to even find them. Please, tell me where they are, or if you cannot, tell me they are safe."

Silence filled the chamber once more. The Sythrokli Oracle sat upright and then slowly began swaying. Guttural moans soaked in a rich vibrato poured from whatever lips lay behind the veil. The swaying became writhing, and the guttural moans became choked gasps for air. Without warning, the Oracle collapsed onto her cushion. And there was silence.

Minutes passed. Gwyn's eyes darted around the room. Was she supposed to say something? Should she just leave?

The Oracle shot upright. "Deep beneath the mountain black, the horned one, chained, toils with iron and liquid fire, giving new life to the damned that have earned the red king's ire. The orphaned childe with shattered heart quests to earn her blade, black or white. Where she walks is beyond my sight."

Gwyn nodded. The rumors were true. The Sythrokli Oracle spoke in riddles. "Thank you."

As Gwyn bowed, the Oplitoi said, "Depart."

Gwyn left the Oracle's temple. As she rode back to town, her mind turned over the riddle's words. *They're alive. That's good. What's the black mountain with liquid fire? That's got to be a volcano, but there are none on the continent. Where did Bedwyr take Courage? And Karina's not an orphan, and she's not a child. And what sword is she looking for that she moved somewhere an oracle can't see? What does "Where she walks is beyond my sight" even mean?*

Gwyn stabled Siobhan and then returned to her room. As she walked through the inn's lobby, the desk clerk called her name. Gwyn turned and approached the check in desk, and the clerk held out a sealed envelope. "Miss Caoilfhionn, forgive me, but a courier deposited this letter for you, addressed by a different name?"

Gwyn took the letter addressed to *Gwynarra C. Vandiamante.* She nodded and frowned. The use of her adopted family's name meant whoever sent this knew she was a vampire. The Midnight Court would've sent a representative who wold have waited for her, and they would either have addressed it to *Hertogia Vandiamante* or *Sezara Vandiamante.* The handwriting was unfamiliar to her, but someone knew she was here. And she didn't know who that was.

Gwyn walked with a quickened pace to the mechanomagical elevator powered by Arcanyx crystals. Her shoulders relaxed when she the doors closed, leaving her alone inside it as it rose. When it stopped on her floor, she wrapped her hand lightly around the hilt of her sword. Her muscles tensed, and she exited the elevator.

She walked to her room and examined the door. All looked normal, and the door was locked. Her eyes darted about the hallway. No one was present. She pressed her ear to the door and heard nothing but the hum of the mechanomagical electric lighting. Gwyn nodded.

If someone's waiting to kill this vampire, she thought. *I'm going to be hard to kill—even in the sunlight.*

After a final confirmation of the hallway's emptiness, Gwyn shifted her form into a pale mist and floated through the space between the bottom of the door and the floor. The mist wafted into the room, allowing Gwyn to observe with her senses but not interact. No one was present unless they were on the balcony.

Taking the chance, Gwyn shifted back into her Elven form with her back to the wall that opened into the balcony. She drew her sword and used her free hand to slide the door to the balcony open while standing out of sight. Neither sound nor movement greeted her. Gwyn slipped onto the balcony and found herself alone. The vampire exhaled, relaxed her muscles, and sheathed her sword.

Gwyn returned to the room, closing and locking the balcony door behind her. She sat on the bed and popped the unfamiliar seal on the envelope. A different, more feminine, hand wrote the letter itself. The letter was brief, and it was wrapped around a travel voucher from Ristarad to Rotzendam.

Hertogia Vandiamante,

Forgive my intrusion into your affairs, but a situation has emerged that has necessitated this communication. You may not remember me, but we met on the last holiday your family took to Ristarad before their untimely deaths. My name is Willymijn Sazkyeerts, daughter of Countess Sazkyeerts of Rotzendam. A friend of mine told me she saw you in the sanctuary in Ristarad, and that is how I knew how to get a message to you.

Our family has fallen victim to a series of mysterious disappearances, and the local politzi have had no success in finding them. The details I will spare you in this message, but should compassion not fail in you, I will provide details upon your arrival. Please, we are not asking this as a favor based upon former alliances forged between our families. I am asking this as any who seeks your aid. Your fee will be paid, and upon my honor, my family will be in your debt.

A travel voucher has been provided to you. Forgive the urgency, but we ask that you leave this night. Though of different lineages, we are sisters by the Will of the Blood. Please be swift.

Rotzendam was the southernmost city on the island nation of Amydzeen, a politically neutral nation north of the midpoint of the Myddean Sea. Gwyn's goal was to return to Florescia, and Rotzendam was about halfway between Ristarad and the port of Grachtovia. From Gractovia, she planned to head to Utrezzo to check on Mathias and her family estate, and once she secured home, she would head to Delfia for her coronation.

Her eyes widened. Gwyn's muscles tensed, and then she exhaled. Running her fingers through her hair, she said, "Fuck, I'm about to become a Sezara."

Chapter 3

Iszenstadt was a large industrial city located at the southern edge of the Shunkrir Peaks in the central part of the Atharian Empire. Connected to the rest of the empire by both the Crystal Rail and the Wyntra River, Iszenstadt supplied much of the iron and steel manufacturing needed by the Grand Imperial Army. Thick clouds of smoke rose from refineries and factories, filling the air with a pungent reek and causing the mechanomagical air purifiers to work overtime.

In the direct shadow of the mountains, stood the Imperium Center for the Rehabilitation of Traitors. Bordered by a tall wrought iron gate, this imposing windowless building of black stones loomed as a glaring gargoyle angrily surveying the town below it. No smoke rose from its towers. No one emerged during the day to keep the grounds manicured. And no civilian vehicles beyond a single black carriage pulled by two black mechanomagical horses was ever observed entering or leaving.

On the top floor, in a well-appointed office with ornate purple, silver, red, and black paisley Kalamashi rugs atop the red oak floor board, Marius Bedwyr sat in a mahogany leather chair behind the matching desk. The earthy scent of the leather bindings from the old books on the shelves lining the walls mingled with the rich, smoky scent of his Cavendish tobacco.

Tall and broad-shouldered with fair skin, hair the color of gilded rust, and what were considered handsome features for a Froamian Human man, the vampire who walked among mortals under the name Ambrose von Harenheim directed the operations at this rehabilitation center that converted the bodies of traitors into monstrous automatons called Dieneryn that were designed to perform one task while inspiring fear and disgust in those who saw them. He dressed in aristocratic but unremarkable clothing save for the silver pendant six small golden Arcanyx crystals set along its edge.

On this afternoon, the day after Karina completed her first hunt after being exiled from the Holy Order of St. Arnulf Ironhand and shortly before Gwyn disembarked at Ristarad, Marius Bedwyr sat in his office, poring over financial reports as the mournful dirge, "The Last Waltz" by Cordelia Arenfroi played through the crystal speakers.

The communication console on the desk buzzed. When Marius answered, the masculine baritone voice emerging from the crystal speaker said, "Lord Bedwyr, I've the update you requested on the necro-evocation core and the spectro-conjurational resonant transformers, Sir."

"And that update is?" Bedwyr's tone was calm and expectant.

"Well, they are still charging, Sir. It's been slower since that Ashbourne we apprehended from your office found and drained one of the stored energy from the children's suffering."

"I am aware. Will the mana bomb still be ready to detonate

on schedule?"

"Doubtful but not impossible, Sir. He drained that transformer completely. Took us longer to return it to operational condition. We returned it to the orphanage, but by the time we accomplished that, St. Hiltegardt's was under new management and the basement had been emptied of the punishment devices. Also, Sir, are you aware that your heir at the orphanage has vanished without reporting his whereabouts?"

Marius stroked his chin. He shook his head. "Unfortunate, both of those incidents. However, we will continue with this plan while I accelerate the backup plan. How soon can we regain the power lost by the Ashbourne's interference?"

"If we up the level of pain to those here, we might be able to return to the scheduled date, Sir, or within one week of it."

"Push the traitors to the edge before we begin their rehabilitation. Let their suffering in life and in service bring glory to our empire."

"Yes, Sir. Over and out."

Marius Bedwyr sat in silence as the call ended. He turned in his chair to stare at the map of the continent of Deomoht on the wall behind him. A black push pin adorned with a red crown was positioned atop Iszenstadt. A white push pin with a black horse had been positioned atop Czarnenburg. And positioned in the middle of the Myddean Sea was a black pin adorned with a silver crown.

Where is that little vampire? I need her dead, he mused. *We lost track of her five days ago in Clérmontán. She could have traveled anywhere from that port. Logic dictates she would return to Florescia for her little coronation, but she's too smart to head there directly. She knows the ports will be watched. She knows the roads will be patrolled. If I were her, where would I—ah! That's where she's headed.*

He spun in his chair again and dialed a number on the communication console. When the voice, a gruff and deep masculine voice answered, Marius said, "Caspar, old friend, it's Ambrose von Harenheim. How are you this day?"

"I am well, as well as can be given how I have lost my daughter to sin and debauchery."

Marius nodded and grinned. "Yes, terrible what that Florescian vampire did to her. That does, however, bring us to the reason for my call. I have information on the vampire's whereabouts you may find beneficial."

"Tell me. I long to end their line and avenge my family."

"Good. Well, she's too smart to travel back to Florescia directly, knowing we're watching her, but she does desire to return home. And her birthplace, her true home, is the ruined village of Fáchrives in Froam. Given where we last saw her, it makes sense she would travel to that home for a time. As it was abandoned when you sought to root out that vile traitor Marius Bedwyr, no one would be there to inform on her, a perfect hiding place for a time."

There was a snort and a chuckle over the comm line. "Those damned monsters do love their drama, and the dead should remain in the ruins, buried under the earth."

"I agree," Marius' voice purred with dark hunger. "I suggest sending someone to patrol the ruined city. That Severus boy was quite skilled at obtaining information. He would do well for this. She deserves his brand of mercy."

Caspar Richter paused for a moment in thought. "Yes, I can spare him at present. Thank you, Ambrose. You do great service for the empire."

"As do you, old friend. Farewell."

A wicked smirk snaked across Marius' face, and he chuckled. His voice, which resounded like the crashing of ocean waves against the surf, became lean and hungry in tone. "The empire. Our empire. No, *my* empire. Once I take revenge on those who stole my crown from me and carted so many of my people to that torture pit of an orphanage, why should I not turn my sights on the imperial throne? Has Zanguis not blessed me? Why should I not become the next Blessed Emperor and usher in an empire powered by the Will of the Blood?

"Oh, Caspar, I had hoped your daughter would rid me of that Florescian nuisance and her popular heroism, but alas, she did not. And so I had to force my hand. Her outcome was unfortunate, dear friend, but what I have done to her will pale in comparison to your fate. The game is already begun, and while the black knight moves his king's forces against the lone white queen, the red king will snatch the black throne from beneath them all. Checkmate."

Eighty feet beneath the floor of Marius Bedwyr's office was a massive chamber carved into the mountains that served as both mechanical factory and mechanomagical workshop. Molten steel poured from huge, heated vats into smaller molds that moved along conveyor belts. The steam they produced filling the air with a pungent humidity. Screams capable of transmuting wine to vinegar cut through the whirring din of the machines and the screams of those strapped to the work tables.

Humans and Elves lay on steel tables, stripped naked and secured with leather and iron restraints. They were linked to Health Preservation Units, mechanomagical devices that facilitated the infusion of alchemical concoctions through tubes inserted into their veins via long, thin needles. Clad in black robes and expressionless masks, physicians marked their bodies, subjecting them to painful procedures without any anesthesia. The surgeries involved extracting parts of their spines, brains, and even one or more eyes. In some cases, fully functional limbs were amputated, while the alchemical infusions kept the victims painfully conscious and alive.

A rusty mechanical claw transferred the tables and these poor victims from the medical bay to the technomagical workshop. There, skilled technomagi cauterized the wounds and grafted a plethora of mechanomagical apparatuses to their bodies, including blades, saws, axes, battering rams made of skulls, or flamethrowers. Each of these unfortunates had their own brains, eyes, and spinal cords replaced with mechanical ones. Some of the victims suffered even more drastic modifications, with half of their bodies, or everything except their heads, being removed. The remaining body parts were then refitted with mechanical replacements, powered by a series of rune-etched Arcanyx crystals.

As one moved farther into the mechanomagical workshop, armed guards stood outside a small chamber separated from the rest of the workshop by a thick iron wall and windowless door. The chambers interior walls, ceiling, and floor were painted white, and aside from the crystal ceiling light, the only other fixtures in the room were a workbench in the center of the room, a simple cot in the corner next to a toilet, a mechanical chute in the wall to the left of the door and a large crystal eye embedded in the other walls and in the corners of the ceiling.

Chained to the workbench was a teal-skinned Ashbourne, Courage Faern'doln. Tall and lanky, this young technomagus had two dark teal springbok style horns sprouting from beneath the matted mop of black hair atop his head. Burns, scrapes, dirt, and grease stains covered his face, his white shirt, and his tattered trousers. A torn trouser leg revealed a mechanomagical prosthetic leg whose power crystal was not illuminated.

The wall chute opened, and an iron slide, stained with oil and blood, slid through the opening and attached itself to work table. "Fuck," Courage said in his Edriu brogue as he kicked the work table's leg. "Another one's coming. Wonder what this one did."

A series of mechanical parts and a box slid onto the desk. One of the parts was a blade, and another was a flintlock. This one would be a weapon of sorts. The box contained the Arcanyx crystals and other mechanomagical apparatuses Courage was to affix to the damned soul who would be sent along shortly. Squeaky feminine whimpers and crying echoed down the slide. Courage winced. The poor soul was still alive, and that meant he'd have to see the consciousness, the humanity, and the light die in their eyes as he worked.

And then the body slid through. She was an Elven woman. Her fair skin marked her as a Snow Elf, but her hair was one of the rarer colors, an iridescent purple. An Arcanyx Life Stabilizer was attached to her chest. Its power crystals dimmed as they moved into view of the eyes in the walls and floor. As Courage looked over everything, including the brown leather goggles with the blue crystal lenses to replace the eyes that had been carved out, leaving bloody sockets in their wake, he gasped.

"Miss Assistant Director Mueller, what are you doing here?"

"That…that voice?" Alyriana Mueller, former Assistant

Director of Operations for the Society for Afterlife and Arcane Researcher, spoke in a strained, tear-soaked tone. "Mister Faern'doln, is that *you*? Why are you here?"

"So, anyway, Gwyn and Karina got in a fight when Marius Bedwyr, the guy you thought was your director, outed Gwyn as a Vandiamante vampire. I tried to stop them, but I accidentally overloaded and crossed energy streams on my wandvolver, and it exploded. Next thing I knew, I woke up in a cell, and then that Marius guy kind of threatened to make sure I never got to see my mum before she dies if I didn't help him. So, here I am, in a room with all of these arcane dampening eyes in the walls and ceiling." He pointed. A moment passed before he blushed in embarrassment. "Sorry, I forgot they cut out your eyes. Anyway, they seem to be attuned to my arcane signature, because I can't use my magic and because the crystal powering my prosthetic leg won't work."

"And that's why I'm here. The Holy Order of St. Arnulf Ironhand raided our headquarters, killing all who stood up and asked what was happening, and arresting the rest of us. We were tortured, convicted of treason, and brought here. What's to become of me? Be honest."

Courage looked over everything. "Seems you're going to be some kind of Kriegsdieneryn. There's a sword and a pistol to attach to your arms—oh. They already cut off your hands. Ouch. Sorry about that. Anyway there's also this—what the fuck is this contraption?"

The Ashbourne picked up a small device with a series of Arcanyx crystals swirling with pink, orange, green, and pale blue lights. He muttered a few things under his breath as he looked at the schematic drawn on the back of the metal casing. A small copper antenna protruded from one side.

"Huh. Interesting. Looks like some kind of control switch that connects remotely to the primary motor apparatus. Oh, there's a kill slot, so this thing is a remote override of the PMA. Not a terrible idea, given if any of you break free of your controller, you'd be right to be fucking pissed, and you'd probably—oh. Shit. I'm sorry, Miss Assistant Director. This is probably torture, since you know what I've got to do."

"Please, don't make me suffer any more." Her voice was a weak whimper.

Courage nodded. "I'll be quick. Promise you."

True to his word, Courage worked with swift diligence, transforming Alyriana Mueller into a Kriegsdieneryn. He winced and gnashed his teeth as she screamed, an inevitable response as he cut into her body to remove her brain, spine, heart, and lungs before replacing them with the appropriate mechanomagical counterparts. Blood spurted from her body, drenching him in the thinned sanguine liquid. Courage choked and sputtered as blood shot into his mouth, but he'd done this enough over the past four days to no longer vomit from the blood and the reek of bile, shit, and encroaching decay. He installed the PMA override circuit and then sewed up her chest cavity. He attached the weapons and then the goggles. With a heavy sigh, he pressed the button that signaled the collecting conveyor to emerge through the chute, which caused the table to tilt so the newly built Kriegsdieneryn would slide onto the moving belt, exiting Courage's work cell.

"Goodbye, Miss Assistant Director Mueller," he said in a hushed, reverent tone. "Please ask the Corvidiae to forgive me for doing this to you and everyone else. I'm so sorry."

Courage lowered his head. He hobbled over to his cot

and sat in the corner of the room, his knees pressed against his chest. As he wrapped his arms around his bent legs, he lowered his head to his knees. Courage wept.

Chapter 4

With a small piece of copper wire strangled between her right thumb and index finger, Honor Faern'doln uttered a swift string of guttural words. The wire vibrated and eventually glowed with a reddish orange light. The teal Ashbourne nodded, and her jagged white bob waved in rhythm.

"Courage Anders Faern'doln, where the fuck are you? You answer me right this fucking instant, or I swear to the gods, I will shove your—"

The light at the end of the wire faded, stopping her from finishing the message she was sending to her younger brother. With a screamed string of utterances, she slammed her fist on the white ash writing desk in her solarium. She stared out the window as the sun rose over the city of Al'Adara.

The largest city-state on the Indigo Coast and beyond the southeastern edge of the Atharian Empire, wealthy traders from Khal'Dara in Kalamash founded the city as a trading post in 837 Age of Iron. Over the following millennia, the city grew and flourished, blending Kalamashi culture with that of the southeastern corners of Deomoht. To the north, the Bazaar Plaza opened, teeming with life as merchants, customers, sailors, children, and animals moved about in the open air, perfumed by exotic spices. To the east the gargoyle-topped white walls and towers topped with minarets adorned in tiles of gold and lapis lazuli of the Alcazaba Citadel, the fortified heart of the city and location of the ruling Zul'atun.

As Honor's gaze shifted, she saw the labyrinthine streets winding with a graceful elegance through the mix of homes and businesses surrounding courtyards, pools, and open-air gardens. Colorful mosaic tiles of azure, emerald, ruby, and gold depicted scenes from the myriad of mythologies and religions of those who joined together to make Al'Adara home. Glowing runes illuminated the street signs, allowing all to know the names of the streets in their own languages.

She turned her attention to her work atop her desk. A half-finished lyric sheet for a ballad of the legendary Edriu hero Caerdon Naclaer stared back as she tapped the butt of her ivory fountain pen on the desk. Honor sighed. The words stopped flowing five days ago when her brother stopped responding to her magical attempts at communication. She wrung her hands and growled, tensing the muscles in her arms.

With a growl, she slammed the pen onto the desk. The ink pot bounced, splashing the black liquid onto the dark beige paper. Placing her elbow on the desk and her face in her hand, she rubbed her temples.

I need to find that fucking butthead, she thought. *He never ignores my magical communication. If he's busy doing some weird little tinkering, he'll tell me so and ping me later. This isn't like him. I can't even find him with that damned magical detection spell I learned. I should've paid more attention in those basic magic classes I took, but no, I had to drop out and head to the conservatory. Maybe I'll stop by the university and pay one of the perpetually broke arcanist students to craft me a "Summon Butthead" spell.*

Honor lifted her head. A single chuckle escaped her lips. "That's it."

She rose from her chair and grabbed her sword belt and rapier. After wrapping and knotting the belt over the cream blouse she wore over fitted black leather trousers, she grabbed her coin purse. Her plan required a fair bit of coin. As the words *Let's do this* entered her mind, she left her home.

Honor Faern'doln hurried through the labyrinthine streets, her boot heels clicking on the stone streets, joining the din of humanoid, animal, and mechanomagical sounds of city life. The air smelled of the salty water of the Elsivian Gulf, warm spices and meat grilled over coals, the yeastiness of bread baking, blooming jasmine and lavender, and the stench of animal excrement.

The streets of the Arcane Enclave district were narrow and serpentine. The towering walls and the long shadows that shifted faster than expected during the middle of the day combined with the pungent smokes of dozens of smoldering resin and cone incenses dizzied the head of pedestrians. Imps, pixies, falumps, and owlcats—all either pets for various residents or familiars for arcanists—darted about the streets seeking food or on various errands. The district had an otherworldly ambiance.

At the end of a narrow alley widened by the rows of arches, Honor found an arched purple door with a crescent moon at eye level. Her nose wrinkled from the earthy scent of patchouli and the reek of rotting animals. She looked around and saw no one in the alley. She opened the door and coughed while walking through the thick haze of perfumed smoke that wafted from the building's interior.

Beyond the haze of incense smoke, Honor brushed aside the curtains of glass beads and bells in the darkened room. Oil lanterns and white candles flickered ahead. Incense smoke curled and swirled through the darkness. Honor coughed as the smoke pushed into her nose and mouth.

"Come in. Come in. Sit. Ask the spirits." A resonant voice whose harmonics sounded like three voices in one emerged from the darkness.

Following its sound, Honor reached a circular table where a sphere of clear Arcanyx crystal sat between two flickering candles. She sat in the chair. Opposite her was a Human woman with dark olive skin pulled taut against her bones, thick eyebrows and curls of black hair, and sparkling green eyes. Wrinkles on skin and dark circles beneath her eyes told the tale of a long life. She dressed in sumptuous purple and red silk adorned with golden jewelry and bells that tinkled when she moved.

"Yes, ma'am," Honor said. "My brother Courage hasn't responded to any magical communication in almost a week, and I can't detect him anywhere with magic either. I know I'm not that powerful, so I hoped maybe you could find him with your magic?"

The old woman chuckled, nodding, as she ran her index finger along the width of her face and over the curve of her upper lip. "The spirits tell me many things when I speak to them. Those who have crossed into the Shadowfields see with eyes we cannot possess. Their aid, however, does have a price of twenty-five zitakyi. You do understand, dear. Don't you?"

Honor nodded. She handed the crescent moon-shaped silver coins to the woman. "Here you go, Madame Atoel. Please, I need to find my little brother."

Madame Atoel's bony fingers curled around the coins as she took them from Honor. She smiled through her thin, dried lips. She took a deep breath and closed her eyes and held her hands on the sides of the Arcanyx crystal ball. Honor rolled her eyes.

Green light flashed within the crystal. Madame Atoel hummed in rhythm with the flashing of the light as it strengthened into a small sphere of light in the crystal's center. The flickering sphere swirled counterclockwise around the sphere's interior, and Madame Atoel's body swayed along with it. Her humming became moaning that deepened into hoarse, guttural growling.

The mystic threw herself against the back of her chair and then slumped forward onto the table, motionless. The shadows behind her darkened into visible forms as three shadowy figures emerged. A young woman, slender and fair, stood to the left of the unconscious mystic. A mature woman with a full figure stood to her right, and behind the chair loomed an elderly woman with a hunched back. All three wore white masks shaped like a corvid's face and beak.

"Fuck, it's them—it's *you*," Honor said as the Corvidiae appeared before her. "Look, I'm not a religious person, but my brother put his trust in you. If you know where he is, please tell me."

The young woman, Maiden Magpie, spoke first. "In shadows' dance, the tale unfolds, The Red King strikes, the Black Knight folds. White Queen weeps, her kingdom cleaved, In cryptic realms, a code perceived."

The mature woman, Mother Crow, spoke next. "Reforge the shards, a quest divine, Where broken pieces intertwine. Seek the place, of iron's glow, And fires fierce, where whispers go."

And then the Raven Crone spoke with a voice that harmonized in triples. "Where damned souls pace, a grim encore, To walk once more, on desolate floor. In riddles veiled, the truth lies deep, The secrets held, their secrets keep."

The Corvidiae faded into shadow and disappeared. Madame Atoel remained motionless, but her voice emerged. "Your answer they have granted. You may now leave."

"Thank you." Honor nodded. "Thank you, Corvidiae."

Honor left the mystic's parlor. As she walked through the Arcane Enclave, she mulled over the cryptic riddle offered by the goddesses of death and magic. *What the fuck does any of that mean? Red king, white queen, and black knight? What the fuck crazy game of chess was Courage playing? I'm going to need help on this. I can't ask the family, not with mum's condition worsening because of that dingus' distractable nature. Who can I get to help?*

Honor paused. A moment passed, and an idea formed in her head. She smirked. "I think I need a cinnamon roll."

The Zahra Oasis sat just north of the towering mansions in the Sapphire Quarters. This massive park and urban green space featured tree-shaded walking paths that wound around natural springs and lakes where children fed ducks while university students, always male, played the same three chords on the guitar and lyre with varying degrees of proficiency while singing insipid lyrics of love written by another who, unlike them, had experienced it. In other parts of the Oasis, ornate gold and marble fountains, surrounded by benches and public chess board tables, stood, water burbling from openings in the statuary atop them.

At the edge of the Zahra Oasis, where the Sapphire Quarters

connected to the Grand Souq where artisans plied their crafts and created art and artifice, sat Xrissa's Pies and Pastries, filling the air with warm spices, yeasty doughs, and citrus-tinged sweetness. Through the arched, floor-to-ceiling windows, passersby saw display cases filled with cinnamon rolls the size of a child's torso; pies filled with nuts, fruit, and a variety of custards; cakes sized for a person's hand and for an entire table; sweet and savory hand pies; and a varied assortment of cookies, candies and other sweets all set atop the pink and lavender tiled floor.

Behind the mechanomagical door that opened and closed by proximity, lay the kitchen. While most kitchens weren't anything to speak of, this shop's owner, Xrissa Kosol, had designed specialized mechanomagical automatons to stock, measure, mix, and bake with only minimal supervision. She didn't always use them, but when foot traffic or large orders filled her queue, she activated them to lessen the strain on her two employees.

On this particular day, a handful of patrons sat and dined at the bakery's tables. Xrissa flitted about the front of the store in the pink and lavender checkered apron that covered the white and silver dress she wore. Though she had the midnight purple skin and white hair that characterized Moon Elves, her height was closer to that of a Dwarf. She kept her white hair in an elaborately braided bun, a hair net, and a lavender toque with pink flowers made from repurposed gears.

As Honor stepped into the shop, a bell tinkled at a high pitch. Its vibrations pushed a fan attached to a thin wooden stick. The stick fell forward, pushing a ball bearing along a track where it bounced on a series of tonal blocks, producing the melody of a lullaby Moon Elf mothers sang to their children. The ball came to a stop when it slammed into a wall, pushing a button to sound a buzzer. As the buzzer ended, an Arcanyx crystal glowed with yellow light, and the ball bearing disappeared and then reappeared in its spot by the door. Honor shook her head and laughed.

Xrissa spun around. Her voice was a high, swift, staccato. "Welcome to Xrissa's Pies and Pastries! What can I get for you? Oh, hi, Honor! Here for your regular? Got some fresh."

Honor smiled. Xrissa was a ball of perpetual energy. Honor replied, "Business good, Xrissa? Yeah, I'll take an apple turnover and one of your specials."

The Moon Elf beamed and nodded. "Sure thing! Just one special? Not buying one for your brother? How is he? Haven't seen my best customer around in over a month. Guess he's off on one of his treasure hunts, huh?"

As Xrissa moved to get the pastries from her display case, Honor followed her, leaning close. Worry drenched her voice. "Kind of what I wanted to talk to you about. You able to join me at a table for like five minutes?"

"Give me one ticky-tick." Holding the pastries in a parchment pouch, Xrissa walked to the door connecting to the kitchen. As it opened, she called out, "Hey, Aldina, can you watch the front for a bit? Switch on BAXTER if you need help back here."

"Yes, Miss Kosol."

A young woman of Kalamashi ancestry with dark brown skin and thick black hair tied a clean apron around her waist and slid out front. "We're ready to go, but BAXTER is helping Atticus monitor the ovens."

"Good." She and Honor walked to an empty table near the back of the bakery's storefront. As they sat down, Xrissa said,

"So, what's up?"

Honor took a bite of her apple turnover in an effort to collect her thoughts. "Okay, so my stupid genius of a little brother was on one of his treasure hunts when he got sidetracked. You know how easily he gets distracted."

Xrissa responded with a series of swift nods. "Yeah, it's really cute when he tells his stories and goes in spirals. He really should consider switching from coffee to Crimson Minotaur Stamina Beverage. That's what I use to keep my brain focused for work and tinkering projects. If he'd let me go with him, I'd keep him stocked. What's he been doing?"

Honor shrugged. "Not entirely sure. He was pretty vague about it when I caught up with him in Sonnenburg, but it seemed pretty important. Anyway, last time I got a hold of him, he was on his way to Schwarzfeld. Haven't been able to get a hold of him through magical or mundane communication."

Xrissa frowned. "Do you think something happened?"

"Not at first." Honor shook her head. "You know what a butthead he can be. I figured he was ignoring me to be an annoying little shit, but then it kept happening. And then today, I went to see Madame Atoel. The Corvidiae showed up and gave me one of their bullshit cryptic riddles. There was some weird shit about a black knight, a red king, and a white queen, but Mother Crow said I needed to reforge the shards and seek the place of iron and fire or something like that. I figure it's some place in the Atharian Empire, because that's where he was, but beyond that, I don't know."

Xrissa scratched the nape of her neck. She nodded. "I can think of a couple of places it could be, at least a couple of cities, based on where most of the iron gets mined in the empire.

They're big cities, though. Lots of places he could be."

"Fuck! I was afraid of that." Honor chomped into the turnover and devoured half of it, filling the air between them with silence. And then she added, "I know this is asking a lot, but I don't think I can find him by myself. So, what I'm asking is—"

"For us to go on a treasure hunt where Courage is the treasure?" Xrissa bounced in her seat as she asked. "Of course, I'll do it! I've been wanting to go on a treasure hunt with Courage since he started talking about them, but since you're the one who asked, I'll go with you."

Honor smiled, and then the smile turned into a smirk. Should she say what entered her mind? She thought she should, and so, she said, "Well, he's great at talking about his gadgets or history, something like that, but he's right shit at talking to people. If he could get over his shyness on that front, he'd have asked you a long time ago."

Xrissa's eyes widened, and her smile broadened to match them. "Then it's settled. After I close up today, I'll go home, pack, and ready SAAMy. We'll meet you at your place and head into the empire."

Chapter 5

The sun had just set when the Ocean's Spear, a mechanomagical passenger ship renowned for its speed and luxury, pulled into Rotzendamn's harbor. As Gwyn stepped onto the deck, she saw the bustling Harbor Quarter spring to life, with traders unloading exotic goods from distant lands and sailors preparing to dock for the evening. The distant calls of seagulls echoed through the air, and the aroma of fresh pastries from nearby bakeries mingled with the salty sea breeze, filling the air with an inviting scent. Her stomach growled and hissed.

Her gaze shifted toward the Windmill Heights where the silhouettes of the windmills turned gracefully in the evening breeze, their sails painted in hues of crimson and gold. Charming brick buildings with large windows, steeped gables, ornate carvings, and color facades, architectural stylings popular during the Amyzdeenian Golden Age, came into view. Small garden plots from which tulips would soon bloom framed their doors. These tall and narrow structures stood proudly along the plethora of canals, which served travelers and residents alike. Along the edge of the canal through which the Ocean's Spear traveled, quaint cafés and taverns opened their doors, their mechanomagical lanterns beginning to glow softly as daylight faded away.

Pedestrians, cyclists, and motorists milled about the cobbled streets. Some residents and travelers stood upon the stone bridges that crossed over the canals, observing the sunset. Artists painted and sketched outside the cafés. Impressionist watercolors were popular among residents. Joyful music burst from the open tavern doors. The city exhibited a calm acceptance of itself, and Gwyn smiled.

"Hertogia Vandiamante!"

Gwyn spun toward the source of the voice calling her by her family name and title. Her hand rested on the hilt of he small sword until she recognized the speaker. Gwyn smiled and waved as Willymijn Sazkyeerts scurried over to hug her. Willymijn smelled of tulips and fresh grass, and her long brown tresses bounced as she moved. Two men in dark suits stalked toward them but maintained a respectful distance, their frock coats bulged in a manner consistent with a concealed flintlock.

They must be her guards, Gwyn thought.

Willymijn looked her over and smiled. "You cut your pretty white hair. At least you're safe. I'm so sorry about what happened to your family. And I wish our reconnection occurred at a more joyous time."

Gwyn nodded. "I thank you for your sympathy, and I extend that same sympathy to your family in your hour of need. What is it I may do to assist?"

Willymijn nodded. "Mother is beside herself with fear and grief, but we will speak on those things at the manor with her.

"However, you must be famished from day-walking. Come. We will dine at my favorite of the city's sanctuaries, and before you speak the words, you will not be beset by the horrid fears regarding your professional activities over the past few years."

"My horse," Gwyn said with a nod. "Siobhan is still on the ship. I need to get her."

Willymijn snapped her fingers and pointed toward the doors opening in the hold. "Standar, collect Hertogia Vandiamante's horse and stable it alongside ours." She turned her attention to Gwyn and smiled. "Your horse will be cared for as if it were one of our own. Now, come. You will also spend the next day with us, so you are rested for what the night will bring."

As they walked, a wistful smile wafted across Gwyn's face. She chuckled. "It's been years since I've been able to sleep through the day. I won't say no to that pleasure."

Willymijn giggled. "Well, if the other rumors are true, you will return to a more proper schedule of rest and waking, Sezara."

Gwyn nodded, and then she exhaled. *I'm heading home after this, and my coronation will occur. This is my last hunt. It's a bit out of the way, but I should stop by Fáchrives and visit the mass grave where her family buried everyone they murdered.* And then Gwyn whispered, "I'm about to be Sezara."

Willymijn wrapped her arm around Gwyn's. "And we will all be in attendance to celebrate your ascension."

Willymijn Sazkyeerts led Gwyn to a red carriage pulled by four brown and white mechanomagical horses. Willymijn entered a destination onto the keyboard inside the carriage, and the driverless carriage rode along one of the city's narrow streets. It turned into an alley and passed through a brick wall, pulling into a garage where six other carriages had been parked.

"We are here," Willymijn said. "Hertogia Vandiamante, I

welcome you to Bleeding Tulips Café and Blood Bar."

As they stepped into the sanctuary, soft, ambient lighting from floating chandeliers cast a gentle glow over the space, creating a cozy ambiance. A beautiful mosaic of polished white and black marble tiles lined the floor. Rich, dark wood paneling lined the lower half of the walls, while the upper part was painted in a soft, muted red, contributing to the cafe's refined and soothing feel. Tasteful artwork by Amyzdeenian masters of the baroque period, framed by gold, adorned the walls, interspersed with tall shelves stacked with old leather-bound books, decorative antique teapots, and ceramic plates.

In the center of the room, blackened mahogany chairs with plush cushions of muted red velvet sewn with golden threads surrounded small, intimate tables made of the same wood, each elegantly set with polished silverware and fine crystal glassware atop gold-trimmed white cloths. Potted plants and fresh tulips in red, white, and yellow were tastefully arranged throughout the space, infusing a sense of nature and life into the elegant setting.

The rich, earthy aroma of freshly brewed coffee from the coffee bar at the back beside the door leading to the blood doll rooms, the warmth of spices and spiced fruits, and the gentle sweetness of baked goods permeated the air. Gleaming brass accents adorned the coffee bar with its steel equipment whirring, steaming, and percolating. Upbeat, syncopated, jazzy music played softly in the background, allowing patrons to tap their feet and even dance, as a handful of couples did, while not overpowering the hum of pleasant conversation.

The hostess, a youthful Elven vampire with her blonde hair in plaited braids, approached them and curtsied. "Welcome back again, Lady Sazkyeerts. I see you've brought a guest.

Will you be dining in your private suite?"

"We shall. I believe Hertogia Vandiamante would prefer the quiet, yes."

Gwyn surveyed the room. A few eyes blinked as they stared, their faces darting into another direction upon making eye contact with her. She nodded. "This sanctuary is nice, but, yes, I would."

The hostess escorted them along the hallway that led to the doll rooms. At the end of the hall were four rooms with golden nameplates, each having the name of one of the noble houses holding power in or around Rotzendam engraved into the gold. They entered the Sazkyeerts family booth where red and gold cushioned couches surrounded a central black mahogany table.

As Gwyn sank into the plush cushion with a dreamy smile, the hostess bowed once more. "There is a wine rack in the table, and a server will be along shortly to bring an assortment of sweets and to collect your doll requests."

She departed, and Willymijn opened the cupboard within the table's single support and produced two bottles of blood-infused wine and two crystal glasses. She removed the cork from the first bottle and poured Gwyn and herself a full glass, leaving only a hair's breadth of empty space at the top of the glass. Gwyn recognized the vintage and took a long, slow sip. She sighed with contentment as the Florescian Pinot Noir slid down her throat.

"I thought you might want a taste of home, Sezara," Willymijn said with a smirk. "And besides, Mother won't wake for another two hours. She's no sunset person like I am."

"This is lovely," Gwyn said as she looked about the large

private room. "I've never seen a sanctuary serve food as well, and I remember Amydzeenian pastries from my younger days—not that I'm terribly ancient."

The two women laughed. "Yes, the Bleeding Tulips caters to those of us who have yet to lose their mortal sense of taste—both for music and for food. And you will find the dolls here quite a different experience. But I will not spoil that surprise for you."

They passed a few minutes in idle conversation before the promised server entered the private room. He carried a silvered tray covered in small plates containing a chocolate fondue pot heated by Arcanyx crystals and assorted fruits, cakes, and small cookies for dipping. The tray also carried a selection of pastries and pies, breads and cheeses, and caramels for enjoyment. He then asked their preferences for a blood doll. Gwyn bounced happily as she ate. Willymijn requested her standard, Yerant, a muscular Human male with black hair and a deep tan, and then she turned to Gwyn. "Would you like me to request one for you?"

"Do I need to know their names," Gwyn asked. "I've never been able to get one to tell me their name. My standby has been an Elven woman or first available."

Willymijn guffawed until she snorted. "Sezara, you've spent too much time in the old countries. Things are different here. Bring her Illyria. I think that will be the best choice."

After a few moments, the requested blood dolls arrived. Illyria was a red-haired Wood Elf with skin bronze skin with red and gold undertones and a subtle silver glow in her green eyes. She wore a mustard yellow blouse with a red walking skirt. She sat beside Gwyn and bowed her head.

"Welcome to the Bleeding Tulips. My name is Illyria, and

I offer my blood to you for sustenance and my company for conversation."

"Call me Gwyn." Gwyn smiled.

The four of them talked for hours about literature, art, and music. The blood dolls in Rotzendam all possessed a university education, and saw their role as more than a mere food source. They were entertainers, providing pleasant conversation to the vampires who fed upon them.

As the carriage traveled to Sazkyeerts Manor, Willymijn leaned close to Gwyn and asked, "It seemed you did not miss the formality and licentiousness of the old ways."

Gwyn smiled and shook her head. "I've never been a fan of the stilted, formal observance of feeding from a doll. And I've only fucked them when I was frustrated or angry—only a handful of times since I accepted the Vandiamante family blood. When I fed in Ristarad, I declined the offer of sex from one of the most beautiful Human dolls I've ever seen. It just wasn't the right time."

Willymijn lifted an eyebrow and licked her lips. "Why is that? Is there someone your heart is set on?"

Gwyn winced. She shook her head. Gwyn sighed. She turned her gaze to the carriage window and watched the nocturnal street. "Not any longer. She'd rather make her father proud than be with me. Nothing more to say."

As the moon rose in the star-speckled sky, the family carriage passed through the iron gate that opened in the stone fence surrounding the Saskyeets family estate. An intricate hedge maze, pruned to perfection, formed an intricate labyrinth of greenery, beckoning guests to explore its secrets. Opposite the hedge maze and within the heart of a garden of fragrant tulips, roses, and daffodils stood a magnificent fountain, adorned with intricately carved white marble figures of dancing women that came to life as water cascaded from their hands into the crystalline basin below.

The carriage wheels rolled gently on the cobblestone path as it came to a halt, the mechanomagical horses snorted oil-soaked smoke from their nostrils, and their tinny whinny announced the carriage's stop. As the door opened, the soothing sound of water burbled through the night sky. As Gwyn, Willymijn, and the remaining guard stepped from the carriage, the majestic sight of the manor house greeted them with its soaring turrets, gabled roofs, and arched windows. Ivy crawled up the brick walls with the grace of a master ballet dancer, hinting at the rich history held within the manor's walls.

Countess Emilja Sazkyeerts met with them in the sitting room. Red wallpaper with a burnished gold filigree pattern covered the walls. Elegant antique furnishings of black mahogany and chocolate brown leather adorned the room while still providing enough space for none to feel claustrophobic. Arcanyx crystal lanterns pulsed with gentle undulations, providing both soft light and purified air that smelled of spring wildflowers. The Countess had reached middle age before becoming a vampire, and the gentle wrinkles on her face, framed by her silvering black hair, displayed both gentility and kindness. Her husband had passed a century earlier, but she still donned the black attire of mourning.

She rose to greet them, offering Gwyn a warm and welcome smile as they shook hands. "Welcome, Hertogia Vandiamante, to my home. All warmth and hospitality I extend to you, that there be friendship and alliance bonding our houses. And I extend to you my heartfelt sympathies and condolences regarding the deaths of your family."

Gwyn nodded. "Thank you, Countess Sazkyeerts. It is my hope that the bonds between our families become only stronger throughout the coming centuries. I too offer my sorrows that our meeting is not a moment of joy but of sorrow. Please, how may I be of service to you?"

The three women sat on the couches surrounding a low table. One of the servants brought each a glass of blood-infused wine in a crystal glass. Countess Sazkyeerts sighed. "I have little to tell you, and whether it was by chance or the Will of the Blood that alerted us to your proximity, I hope that same force guides you."

"Willymijn's note had few details, mentioning only something about disappearances?" Gwyn sipped her wine.

The countess nodded as a flattened smile crossed her lips. "Yes, for two weeks now, we have noticed several of our clan not returning to their homes and being unresponsive to communication both mundane and magical."

Gwyn's gaze lifted as she nodded in thought. "A hunter, perhaps? That is something we all find concerning."

"That was our first thought," Willymijn said. "But we have found no evidence in the homes, and there have been no sightings of hunters or suspicious individuals in Rotzendam."

A dark chuckle danced through Gwyn's lips. "Not all hunters dress as I do." And then her voice darkened as she said, "Or as the Holy Order of St. Arnulf Ironhand do. A hunter would leave evidence—a stake—but you both have said disappearances. Hunters don't abduct. They kill."

"Yes, that they do." Countess Sazkyeerts said. "And my clan members were all in public when they were last seen—all from the Shraff-Van Dyke Memorial Library."

Gwyn tilted her head to the side. "A library is a strange place to disappear—unless you get lost in a book."

The three women laughed. Countess Sazkyeerts sighed. "I've not laughed so heartily since my dear Aryld fell to betrayal. But that is where all were last seen. I apologize for having no more to offer."

Gwyn sighed and nodded. "Nothing similar about the missing vampires? Anything that might explain the choice to disappear or be abducted? I like to at least have some idea of what I'm hunting."

The countess shrugged and shook her head. "They were artists, former soldiers, courtesans, a professor of techno-mancy, and a gambler. Men and women in equal number."

"One, Darys Van Hoernin, is non-binary, Mother."

"Yes, thank you, Willa. One was—is—non-binary."

"They were all old too. Don't glare at me, Mother. They were all like six or seven centuries, and they looked it. Well, Alysira didn't, but she's a Sun Elf. She may be like a thousand for all I know."

Gwyn nodded. "Well, I'm not that old, and I'm none of those things. But I suppose I'll be visiting a library for the first time in years tomorrow night."

Willymijn leaned forward. "What are you going to do? Do you want us to send a decoy for you to use as bait?"

"No." Gwyn shook her head. "I will endanger no one on my hunts if I can avoid it. If someone or something abducted them, the fact that I am a vampire should be temptation enough. Perhaps I will go before night."

"You shall do no such thing, Hertogia Vandiamante," Count-ess Sazkyeerts said, speaking with a voice full of motherly authority and compassion. "You are a guest in our home, and as a fledgling, you need your rest. Since those damned Richters murdered your loving family, you've been forced to walk in the sun. Here, you will walk beneath the stars and allow the moon's gentle light to caress your skin."

Gwyn smiled. "That does sound lovely. It's been so long since I was able to sleep in the day."

Countess Sazkyeerts nodded. "Then with that settled, Willa, escort Hertogia Vandiamante to her room. I know that after a night of traveling, a hot bath is what I desire more than anything."

"Yes, Mother."

Chapter 6

The wind howled through the streets of Rotzendam, rattling the windows and shaking the roofs on the buildings. As thunder screeched and lightning flashed, the rain beat against the cobblestone streets as Gwyn stepped from the Sazkyeerts family manor and pulled the hood of her cloak over her tricorn. Siobhan hated storms, and so the vampire hunter of monsters stalked her unknown prey alone.

The streets were deserted, save for an occasional carriage, pedestrian hurrying to shelter, or pair of constables walking their beats. The Arcanyx streetlamps flickered in the wind, mimicking the gas lanterns of previous centuries and casting eerie shadows on the wet cobblestones. The only sounds the living could hear were the howling of the wind and the crashing of the rain. No longer limited by mortality, Gwyn's sharpened ears discerned rats scurrying in an alley to her left and a crying baby—likely teething from the timbre of its screams—from a window above her.

She smiled. Though walking in the rain was not always pleasant, the cool spring night air comforted her skin. Gwyn woke at sunrise as had become her custom of necessity, but the recognition of her safety in the Sazkyeerts manor allowed her to return to the death-sleep, remaining there until the sunset and Willymijn woke her for the evening's breakfast, which she followed with another hot bath perfumed by oil of Zyntarian rose. After another glass of blood-infused wine, Gwyn set out on her hunt.

A bittersweet smile drifted across Gwyn's face. *This will be my last hunt before my coronation—my last hunt. After six years, it's fitting I end my adventures protecting vampires.*

The Shraff-Van Dyke Memorial Library was a large and ornate library located in the university district. Designed in the Amyzdeenian Baroque style popular in the 1300s of the Age of Arcanum, the exterior of the library was made of white marble and features a large portico with six fluted columns. The interior of the library is decorated with frescoes, sculptures, and stained-glass windows. The windows were unique in that instead of depicting religious scenes, as was common during the time of their construction, they depicted scenes of daily life among the various social circles in Rotzendam.

As Gwyn stepped through the double doors and into the lobby, blue and green Arcanyx crystals flashed, drying her clothes in a matter of seconds. Gwyn doffed her hood and hat, brushed her fingers through her hair, and donned her tricorn before approaching the mechanomagical door opening to the General Collection Hall. The door slid open as she stepped on the mat before it, and the vampire stepped into the maze of shelves on the ground floor of a vast room with high ceilings and towering shelves that reached all the way to the top. The walls were lined with books, and the air was thick with the smell of dust and leather.

A handful of patrons milled about the library on this dark

and stormy night, searching through the thousands of shelves for knowledge, enlightenment, or entertainment. Stairs and ladders moved on command, remaining dormant until needed. The occasional flash of light from a magical tome opened by one unskilled to control the powers within it burst through the gentle light of the floating crystal chandeliers, and the faint whispers of spirits trapped within the pages of ancient grimoires danced around Gwyn's ears.

The library's map, a scaled three-dimensional replica of carved marble set atop a maple table. A door on the fourth floor led to the Encantarium, a special collection of strange and wondrous artifacts enchanted to allow children to experience the stories they read as reality. The Hall of the Makers, a series of rooms and studios for artists in need of privacy, spanned the third-floor corridor connecting the tawdry Baroque bodice-ripping romances and the ancient history collections. And at the far end of the hall on the ground floor, a staircase led to something called the Necrotorium.

"Are you looking for something specific?"

A feminine voice slipped through the silence over Gwyn's left shoulder. She spun around to see an elderly woman with bluish-white hair bound in a severe bun. Half-moon spectacles rested on the tip of her upturned nose. A high-collared burgundy blouse and black walking skirt covered her body. She smiled.

Gwyn nodded. "I'm new here, and I—"

"I am aware of that," the woman said. "I recognize the faces of everyone who has stepped into this library, and I've never seen yours. So, are you looking for something specific?"

How should I answer this, Gwyn thought. *I don't know how to ask what I need to ask, but I've no reason to assume she knows anything. She would have spoken to the constables if she had.*

Gwyn shrugged. "I've had little time for reading since leaving home, but I'm here on behalf of Countess Sazkyeerts."

The librarian frowned and then pursed her thin, dry lips. "I thought as much from your...*foreign* clothes and the fact that you willingly walked through the storm at night. Well, I shall tell you what I told her servants and the constable detective. It is an unfortunate coincidence that those souls were last seen perusing the books in our care; however, we bear no responsibility for their deaths or disappearance beyond allowing them to get lost in a book. Now, is there anything related to the function of this library that I may help you with?"

Gwyn responded with a rusty but practiced aristocratic smile and a single nod. "Thank you, but I am familiar with libraries, and this map is quite clear."

"Then I shall leave you to it." The librarian bowed. "But I shall watch to ensure you get into no trouble, given your stated association."

The librarian walked away. Gwyn rolled her eyes. *Well,* she thought with a chuckle. *This will be my final hunt, and this will be my first hunt inside a library.*

Gwyn walked in the opposite direction as the librarian, and she ascended the moving staircase to the second floor. As she perused the rough-edged pages of a copy of *Heroes and Haunts: Legends from the Bards of Edrium and Froam* bound in tattered but soft brown leather, she glanced, on occasion, over the railing to the ground floor. Nothing out of the ordinary transpired, but the libriarian routinely lifted her gaze to hurl a stern gaze in Gwyn's direction. Gwyn cocked an eyebrow in thought. That was odd, but then she shook the feeling away.

The fourth floor buzzed with the energies leaking from the magical tomes chained to the shelves. Many floated a finger's width above the shelves. The fine hairs on Gwyn's arm and neck stood at attention. The whispers swelled, increasing in number, into a dizzying cacophony of sound. *Visit those who have fled the grave.* Some promised power for those connected to the energetic threats of the Awtkha. Gwyn brushed it aside. Were she to learn magic, her nature demanded she draw power from Shtakre Ngkushúché, the Will of the Blood, as undeath severed one's connection to both the weavings of arcane energies and the Wheel of Souls.

Bound, chained, inscribed deep within the page. Gwyn stopped and stood at attention. Her gaze shifted from side to side. Were the books telling her to look in them?

Gwyn walked to the nearest book, a torso-sized volume bound in charred brown leather with bronzed fittings. The black ink spanned the width of the parchment pages. As she riffled through the pages, Gwyn whispered to the book, "Show me where I need to go to find what I seek."

Silence screamed through the chattering cacophony of arcane whispers. Gwyn narrowed her eyes. She slammed the book back onto the shelf. It whimpered and slunk into the corner before floating again. The whispers turned to brittle, mocking laughter. Gwyn stormed off toward the stairs.

As she descended, the whispers joined in harmony, singing a song Gwyn hadn't heard since childhood. *So close your eyes and let us go, down to the land of the faeries below. Where dreams are real and magic true, and you'll be safe and loved nevermore.*

Gwyn's ears perked as she listened to them repeat the repeated stanza. She shook her head. *That's not the lyric Mum used to sing. It was "safe and loved forevermore." Why are they singing it incorrectly?*

No one wandered the third floor shelves or in the Hall of the Makers. The whispers continued singing the lullaby with the incorrect refrain. Gwyn's eyes narrowed, and she growled, baring her fangs momentarily before remembering that the living were present.

Gwyn continued her descent. The voices grew louder and more resonant as she descended to the second floor. Gwyn clenched her trembling fists and sucked in a breath and tensed her muscles. The whispers got more and more lyrics incorrect as Gwyn reached the ground floor. Rage built inside her, and the urge to scream burbled in her throat.

And then she passed the library's map and paused. What was that? There was a stairway descending to the Necrotorium. Gwyn didn't know what that room contained, but reaching it required a descent, as the lullaby suggested. Earlier whispers mentioned something about those who fled the grave. Gwyn shrugged. Glancing toward the desk revealed the librarian was elsewhere. Since she had no better lead on her quarry, Gwyn headed toward the Necrotorium.

No mechanomagical staircase assisted her descent. The roughness and narrowness of the stone stairs told of their age, and the air acquired an earthier scent the farther down one descended on the spiraling path. The stone walls grew progressively more damp to the touch during the descent. After thirty-seven steps down, Gwyn glanced over her shoulder. No one was behind her. She then resumed her journey.

Iron slats reinforced the arched wooden door at the bottom of the stairs. Gwyn lifted an eyebrow. Doors like that had gone out of fashion fifteen centuries ago, remaining common only in Tshípogothic-style cathedrals and manors in the

Atharian Empire. The door was locked, but these hinged doors always had slivers of space between the door and the frame.

"The Necrotorium is closed to the public, accessible only by arcanists and clergy. And you, young lady, appear to be neither."

The librarian's stern voice echoed through the narrow staircase. Gwyn turned to find the elderly woman standing behind her, arms folded across her chest and a frowning glare on her face. Gwyn smiled and bowed at the waist. "You are correct, my apologies. I was merely curious as to what a Necrotorium was, as none of libraries in Florescia have such a room—even the one in my family's estate."

The librarian laughed. "You can read all about the Necrotorium in the history books on the first floor. Come along. I will show you."

She lifted a pointed eyebrow and gestured up the stairs. "Is there no option for a guided tour? Money is no object."

The librarian narrowed her eyes further. "And what was your name, you who are so wealthy?"

"Gwynarra." Gwyn smiled. "Vandiamante, or Hertogia Vandiamante, if one were to use my title."

"Come along, Hertogia Vandiamante. We do not offer tours to the public—even those with peerage doing favors for others of their kind." The librarian scoffed. "Besides, the lighting is malfunctioning. We can't have you tripping over things that might fall and hurt your delicate frame."

Gwyn tapped her right ear with her index finger and winked. "My Elven eyes are accustomed to low light that I can see in all but the blackest of darkness without difficulty. Oh, and speaking of the Sazkyeerts family's need, are you certain what I seek is not beyond that door? I can easily take a quick peek and be gone in a matter of minutes."

"Why would the Necrotorium be connected to a string of vampire disappearances?"

A faint smirk flitted across Gwyn's lips. She hadn't mentioned vampirism yet. And then she gasped. "Vampires? Are you saying the Countess is a vampire?"

The librarian blinked, coughed, and sputtered her words. "It's a well-known fact they are vampires. It clearly speaks to your ignorance and deceitfulness of intention that you did not know such a fact that all in Rotzendam know."

The librarian's nervous laughter answered Gwyn's next question, and her unexpected dash to situate herself between Gwyn and the door confirmed suspicion. Gwyn feigned surprise, smirked, and then said, "I'll just be a minute, thank you."

Gwyn transformed into mist and shifted through the crack between the door and its frame before reforming. Shelves filled with books rose to the ceiling, creating a series of narrow, intersecting corridors. The books were stacked on their sides, spines facing forward, in columns of four or five volumes tall. Book leather, sawdust, old paper perfumed the air, but Gwyn's nose crinkled as she detected a metallic smell. Silver and gold didn't have *that* particular smell, but iron did. The iron in blood did, to be precise. Gwyn drew her weapons and ducked through a break in the shelves to hide in another corridor as the door opened behind her.

"Disobedient little vampire, I'll add you to our collection."

The librarian's voice grew raspier and darker. The door slammed and then locked. Light flashed, and Gwyn peeked around the corner of the shelf. The librarian's flesh melted into her musculature, and her hair fell from her head. Beneath the illusory layer of skin was an amalgamated form of stitched parts. One half of her skinless face had Elven features, but the other had Goblinoid features from the cheek down. From the cheek up, a draconic skull with a single horn emerged, uncovered by flesh and muscle. Eyes of differing colors and sizes bulged from the sockets. Rotting yellow teeth filled her mouth. Lines of uneven stitching grafted together the neck, shoulders, and arms that ended in bestial claws, but all were from different creatures.

A flesh grafter, Gwyn thought. *Fuck! It's not using the vampires for its body, is it? But the smell of blood...*

Flesh grafters were the souls of necromancers damned to Ashfodell who grafted bodies for themselves from fiends, monsters, and foolhardy adventurers in an attempt to claw their way out of perdition. Arcanist scholars reported the process of body creation and perdition escape to be a grotesque experience that scarred the created body, twisted the mind, and warped the soul of the grafter until only splintered fragments of their humanity remained.

The flesh grafter chuckled a growling laugh as she stalked Gwyn. "Your floral perfume gives you away. As if such a delicate scent would occur in a place such as—Ouch!"

The thundering flash of Gwyn's flintlock interrupted the flesh grafter's mocking speech. She staggered as the shot shattered her left cheek. A mixture of necromantic ichor and blood gushed from the wound. Gwyn rushed the flesh grafter, flipped her pistol around, and slammed its butt into the flesh grafter's jaw. The fiend grunted.

"A delicate rose still has painful thorns."

With a shrill, feral screech, the flesh grafter's claws extended by the length of her hands. Slash after slash, punch after punch, the flesh grafter pummeled Gwyn. The vampire didn't expect the fiend's swiftness. A swift kick to her stomach slammed Gwyn into one of the shelves. She grunted. A large tome fell onto her head. The flesh grafter raked her claws across Gwyn's face, drawing blood from each scratch.

The flesh grafter thrust her sharpened claws into Gwyn's side. The vampire screamed. The fiend responded with a dark laugh as she purred in Gwyn's ear. "No one will hear you down here—well, no one except those vampires you won't save."

Gwyn looked around the room, and her heart sank. She was alone. Karina wasn't there to chant her exorcism prayer. She was alone, as she had been for the six years before she met Karina and Courage.

Courage! She didn't lack courage, but she had to know he was safe. Where was he? Blood trickled down Gwyn's face, creating a curtain over her eyes that dimmed her vision.

The flesh grafter continued its assault. Blood stained the tattered remnants of Gwyn's vest and blouse. The vampire cried, screamed, and grunted from the fiend's speed. Gwyn's head spun, and she staggered and reeled like a drunk leaving the Vermillion Oaks. The flesh grafter licked her blackened lips.

The flesh grafter curled her fist and punched. The reeling vampire's head bobbed, avoiding the fist as it slammed into the outer support of the shelf. The flesh grafter hissed.

Gwyn wiped the blood from her face as the flesh grafter's fist recoiled from striking the shelf. The vampire shook her head and then lunged. Her small sword's point pierced the fiend's stomach. The flesh grafter winced and sputtered.

Gwyn twisted the blade and flicked it to the fiend's left. Blood poured from the wound on the fiend as the earliest wounds on Gwyn's face began healing.

The flesh grafter backed away with a swiftness equal to her attack. She kept her eyes on the vampire who pursued her as she darted through the labyrinthine catacombs of books. The fiend pushed a freestanding shelf onto the ground, obstructing Gwyn's path. The vampire followed, but as the shelf crashed and splintered and as the books tumbled to the tile floor beneath their feet, the flesh grafter turned her back to Gwyn and fled.

Chapter 7

The flesh crafter left a trail of blood as it fled through the Necrotorium. Though it overturned shelves upon the floor in an attempt to disguise its movements, Gwyn's vampiric senses made following the blood's scent easy. Traversing the terrain, however, was far less simple. The scent of blood strengthened, but old and dead blood darkened and soured its aroma. Whimpers, hissing moans, and the occasional anguished scream limped through the air. As the shelf-lined labyrinthine passages opened into a chamber, Gwyn paused and reloaded her flintlock with one of the cold iron and blessed salt core balls Assistant Director Mueller had assigned to her.

The sources of the anguished sounds huddled in iron cages. A garden irrigation system hung above the cages, spraying a mist of some liquid upon them. With each spraying, those imprisoned twitched, hissed, winced, and screamed as their flesh reddened and blackened. In the room's center loomed an iron surgery table with an unclothed woman bound by leather straps. Her pale skin was reddened and scarred. She turned her bruised and gaunt face toward Gwyn. Salty tears had dried around her crimson eyes.

"Watch out," she said.

Gwyn turned her head as the flesh grafter emerged from behind a workbench and tossed a clear liquid at Gwyn, splashing her raised arms and neck. The vampire screamed as hot pain shot through her body. Her skin reddened and blistered. The flesh grafter laughed. "You won't heal so quickly from holy water, will you?"

Holy water felt like acid on a vampire's skin. Gwyn's wounds burned and throbbed, and the open skin from unhealed claw marks bubbled and blistered. Its burns healed, but they remained longer than most wounds, and that explained why the vampires in the cages remained imprisoned. They were weakened from the prolonged exposure—probably starved too.

The flesh grafter's claw slashed Gwyn's shoulder. The vampire winced and slashed at the fiend. Back and forth they fought, each pressing the other with minimal advantage. The vampires in the cages whispered and murmured about the Silver Scourge not forgetting her own kind amid their screams as the holy water scalded their flesh.

A succession of claw slashes to the face and torso staggered Gwyn. She reeled, and the flesh grafter pounced. Gwyn grunted and winced, baring her fangs, as her back slammed into the floor.

The flesh grafter slithered onto Gwyn's chest, setting her thighs atop Gwyn's upper arms. A flurry of punches pounded the back of Gwyn's head into the tile. Blood streamed into her mouth.

The fiend reared back and opened her clawed hand. Acting on instinct, Gwyn flicked her off-hand wrist upward and fired her flintlock. The flesh grafter shrieked as the shot lodged itself in her ass. She clenched her cheeks and shifted her weight.

Gwyn shifted to mist form and then returned to her natural Elven form behind the flesh grafter. She thrust her blade through the fiend's torso, running her through. As a sanguine-soaked gasp rattled from the fiend's lips, Gwyn unleashed a flurry of slashes and then grabbed the flesh grafter by the back of her neck before slitting her throat. The rattling weakened and fell silent, and Gwyn shoved the flesh grafter to the floor.

The weakened and wounded vampires cheered as best as they were able. After surveying the room, Gwyn located the controls for the sprinklers and shut them off. As she worked to open the cages, one of the vampires said, "You…you haven't forgotten your own kind. The rumors were false"

Gwyn smiled and nodded. "What happened here? What…is this place?"

The vampire who was bound to the table, a Human woman with fiery curls who appeared to be around Gwyn's age, responded. "The Necrotorium is a place where the dead have their consciousness transferred into parchment that is sewn into book leather made from their own flesh. This…*thing* was using it for her own purposes—whatever they were."

"What will you do now," another vampire asked.

Gwyn shrugged. "Help you all return home in safety. Then, either Countess Sazkyeerts or I will discuss the matter with the constabulary. Given a flesh grafter had taken up residence here, I'm certain they'll keep this quiet, which is good. We don't want any vampire hunters getting wind of, well, any of you."

"What of you?" The redhead found and donned clothing as she spoke. "You too are a vampire."

Gwyn nodded. "Another of our kind who hired me to

handle a matter for him and his organization betrayed me to the Holy Order of St. Arnulf Ironhand. It's only a matter of time before other hunters find me."

The clocks tolled two o'clock in the morning before Gwyn returned to the Sazkyeerts family manor. The vampires she escorted home alive had already called to let their clan matriarch know what had transpired to the best of their abilities. Thus, Countess Sazkyeerts and her daughter Willymijn stood in the garden awaiting Gwyn's arrival.

After the exchange of formal greetings, a servant brought each woman a glass of blood-infused wine. The countess sipped and then smiled. "Thank you, Hertogia Vandiamante, for doing what none have done for my clan. The tales told of you are true without fail. But tell me, what was it that entrapped them? My people spoke in uncertain words."

Gwyn drained half of her glass and sighed. "The librarian—or the creature impersonating the librarian—was a Fleischphropfen, a fiend who was once mortal. Specifically, they are necromancers damned to Ashfodell who then graft together bodies out of the flesh and bones of various creatures in a bid to escape perdition. From what your people told me, they went to the Necrotorium to visit the books of deceased friends and family, but the Fleischphropfen, who had taken on the form of a librarian, decided to use them as a renewable source of parchment and grafting parts."

Countess Sazkyeerts pursed her lips. "Unpleasant. However, you have our gratitude for ending this threat before it became even more dangerous and troubling."

"What will you do now," Willymijn asked.

Gwyn sipped more of her wine. "I'm heading home. First, to whatever's left of Fáchrives to visit my parents' grave and then to Utrezzo. From there, Delfia for my coronation. My time as a hunter for hire is over. Such things are unbecoming of a sezara."

A mother's knowing smile drifted across Countess Sazkyeerts' face. "Sorrow darkens that statement. Do you not wish for your crown?"

Gwyn sighed and then shrugged. "I'm too young. I've only been a vampire for nine years, but the Midnight Court has sent messenger after messenger begging for my return. I thought I'd have a few centuries before assuming this responsibility."

The countess leaned in and placed her hand atop Gwyn's. "We all wish for more time before the burden of responsibility falls upon us. For some, the burden arrives in nature's timing. For you, others forced it upon you, but it is still yours to bear." She paused and offered a warm smile. "Do not let sadness add to your crown's weight. Your travels have undoubtedly given you the wisdom to rule with justice and kindness. But the night draws to a close, and you must be exhausted from the ordeal."

"And I could definitely use a bath, and I'll need to rise early enough to go shopping. My clothes are in tatters."

"Yeah, you are kind of grody," Willymijn said.

"And concern yourself not with clothing, my dear," Countess Sazkyeerts said. "I will instruct a servant to take your measurements before you rest, and our tailors will have both your clothing repaired and a new ensemble for you to wear that befits your status both as protector of all peoples and as Sezara of the Midnight Court of Florescia."

"I thank you, Countess Sazkyeerts, for your generosity and hospitality." Gwyn paused and sighed. "I hate the stilted formality of aristocratic discourse among our people, but your actions this night demonstrate that the bonds of fondness and familiarity between our two houses has remained strong. May the bonds our houses enjoy now only flourish and prosper in the perpetuity of night."

The countess smiled. "By your actions, Hertogia Vandiamante, and by my words this night, I swear both alliance and friendship will flourish and prosper between our houses. Now, it is late, and all of us need our rest."

A servant brought Gwyn another glass of wine to enjoy while she bathed. After her bath, another came and took her measurements as well as taking her damaged clothing for repair. Alone, Gwyn curled up in the plush armchair in the bedroom of the guest suite and stared at early morning sky as the storm let up before drifting to sleep.

The next night was a whirlwind of activity. The constable detective arrived for Gwyn's statement before sunset and before the tailors arrived, thus Gwyn answered their questions while wearing a white dressing gown. True to the countess' word, the tailors had worked tirelessly to repair Gwyn's traveling clothes, and they brought with them another outfit for her as well. The white silk blouse had a detachable lace jabot and dramatic lace handkerchief cuffs. The vest resembled her leather vest, but it was made of a tone-on-tone black satin brocade, and the fitted trousers slid under a walking skirt that detached with the push of a button, should she find herself in need of a quick change to fend off an assailant on this last leg of her journey as the Silver Scourge. After the first meal of the evening, they bid each other farewell in the both formal and informal styles, and Gwyn rode back to the port, as Countess Sazkyeerts had purchased her passage from Rotzendam to Liffecienne, the port city nearest the ruins of the town of Fáchrives.

Two days passed before Gwyn arrived at the ruins of Fáchrives. In its heyday, the town was little more than a glorified village on the border between Froam and Edrium. Originating in Hammer Bay, the Starflow River cut through the town's center, and the Donaugh Marsh bordered the town to the north. The air always smelled of wildflowers and fresh bread. Ewain Donal, the owner of Silver Leaf Toys, performed marionette shows for the children every Suraelsday in the town square.

Gwyn sighed, as the sight that greeted her this sunset held none of the joy of those memories. The marsh had crept its way into the town, soaking the soil and filling the air with the peaty scent of rot and decay. The thatched roofs of the small cottages had rotted, and the walls had started to crumble as a result of weather's assault and a lack of maintenance.

A fetid lake swarming with insects and snakes rested where the town square once stood. No puppet shows would be performed this Suraelsday beneath the shadow of the church devoted to the worship of the Lord of Sun and Song, but given that Sister Adaire, the last priestess, married a priest devoted to the Lord of Sky and Storm, that deity was worshiped as well.

Gwyn sloshed through the square and ran her fingers along the mossy exterior of what remained of the town well. She smiled, remembering accompanying her mother on the daily walk to collect water. Plumbing and irrigation supplied the homes and business, but the women often collected water at the well to share news and bond. But the womens' conversations had died, and even the wind was silent as she stood here.

Gwyn removed a single torbal from her pouch and clutched the square coin tightly in her hand. She looked up at the moon. By her estimation, fifty days remained on Courage's new bargain with the Corvidiae. Where was he? And who was this red king who had cheated them that they demanded he kill? Was Courage even alive?

Tears of watery blood formed in the corners of her eyes as she said, "For all I would love, my wish, should any of the spirits hear me, is for Courage to do what I can't. I wish for him to see his mum, his dad, and his family again, all alive and well."

She tossed the coin into the well and headed north to what remained of the Vermillion Oaks. Weeds and shrubs pushed through the foundation. Gwyn's mind flashed back to the inn and tavern former glory, a blend of Froamian and Atharian architectural styles. Half-timber panels framed by gray and black stone, maple floorboards, and circular windows once defined the building's exterior. Little more than a charred husk remained of the once-lively common room where townsfolk and travelers would gather at sunset for storytelling, song, and supper. Three steps of the staircase that ascended to the dozen rooms for guests and to the family's residence remained. The beds, dressers, and appliances had long ago crashed into the ground floor.

One final memory had seared itself before Gwyn's mind, a memory she once relived in dreams night after night until the gift of vampirism meant dreamless sleep. As she walked to an area south of town infested with thorny vines, she recalled the Richters in their black uniforms marching the adults, bound in iron chains, to this spot where one after another, the

Atharian Empire's treason hunters who doubled as witch and vampire slayers pronounced a sentence of guilt for the crime of harboring the traitor Marius Bedwyr and then murdered them. Guns fired. Axes and swords removed heads from necks. And nooses strangled necks. The bodies were dumped in a hastily dug mass grave next to the killing field.

As the sky darkened and the stars peeked through the night's curtain, Gwyn set up a camp at the edge of the field. She built a small fire to keep Siobhan warm on the spring night, and as the horse ate from her feedbag, Gwyn walked into the field and sat among the thorny bushes, weeds, and the occasional wildflower that marked the area where all of the adults she knew as a child had been buried.

Tears choked her words, and her voice cracked, as Gwyn spoke to the unhearing dead. "Hi, Mum. Hi, Da. It's me, Gwynarra. I'm home. I look a bit different than when you last saw me. I've been through a lot without you. I'm sure you'd be worried, but you'd also love to hear the stories. Maybe one day soon I'll come back and tell you.

"Things have been hard without you. The orphanage was a right hellhole where we all got to see the worst of the empire, but a really nice family from Florescia came by and adopted me. They're nobles in the court. Well, they were until those fucking Richters killed them too. I'm the last of my families, and thanks to them, I'm going to be crowned sezara. I may be a Florescian noble, but I'm a Froamian girl at heart. I've not forgotten you, the lessons you taught me about being a good person, and the love you showed me. I've been blessed to have the good fortune of two loving families. Speaking of, there's someone else I need to talk to. I'll be back before leaving tomorrow. I love you both."

Gwyn's accent thickened with each syllable. She moved a few paces over, hoping she was in the right place. "I'm not sure if you're right here or not, but Missus Greely, Mister Greely, I just wanted to let you know Mathias is still alive—well, he's not *alive* alive, but he's undead like me. You'd be right proud of him, protecting the kids at the orphanage we were beaten and humiliated at. But, given he was in Sonnenburg, it would only be a matter of time before the damned Richters got wind of him. I convinced him to come live on my estate in Utrezzo. I promise you, we'll take good care of each other. I'm sure he'd like me to send his—Fuck!"

Holy water's familiar acidic burn shot through Gwyn's body as the liquid splashed on her arm. She spun around and drew her sword as a man with black hair wearing the familiar black uniform of the Holy Order of St. Arnulf Ironhand emerged from the ruins. He wore the night vision goggles Karina had worn, and a cocky smile snaked across his face. Seven white and gold Arcanyx crystals glowed on the flintlock pistol he had pointed at Gwyn.

"Now, now," he said. "Kindly remove your hand from that blade, you fucking monster. Let's not make a mess of things any more than we need to. Fitting, Director von Harenheim was right about you, the serpent who corrupted my impressionable cousin came back to its den. Now, you'll get to join your treasonous parents. You earned this death sentence the moment you accepted Vandiamante blood. And now I, Severus Richter, have the honor and privilege of ending your foul line."

And then the thunderous shot of a flintlock pistol tore through the night.

Chapter 8

While Gwyn traveled to Rotzendam and Karina slept after her successful hunt, Courage Faern'doln remained chained in his cell beneath the Imperium Center for the Rehabilitation of Traitors. On this morning—afternoon—evening—-he wasn't certain of the time of day, as time in his windowless and clockless cell moved without demarcation. He had grown gaunt during his imprisonment, fed only a single bowl of flavorless, sludgy goulash twice per day. And the tracks caused by his tears had stained his teal skin and the thin shirt he wore.

Regardless of the time of day, Courage stood at his worktable, finishing the required modifications to another damned automaton. This poor sod, a doctor working in a free clinic for the impoverished, begged for mercy. He had a wife and three children. He had done nothing wrong. Courage believed him, but the Ashbourne only shook his head. The only mercy he could offer was a death as swift and relatively painless as possible. Too swift a death would make the body unusable as a Kriegsdieneryn. Too slow a death would add another nightmare to the collection that haunted Courage.

As Courage affixed a necrotic energy enchantment chamber

to a repeating flintlock rifle appendage, he looked at the wires connecting the appendage to the nervous system of the host. The rifle's barrel pointed at one of the magic dampening eyes on the wall. The guards outside the cell would hear the weapon fire, but how long it took them to respond, how they would respond, and how long it took to repair the *accidental* damage were unknowns. Thus, this would be an experiment, of sorts.

And so, Courage manipulated the electrical synapses in the host's brain, sending direction through the arm and into the gun appendage. With a flash of fire and a puff of smoke, the appendage fired. Courage shouted a curse as the shot burst from the barrel and struck the crystal in the center of the eye on the wall opposite the body chute.

As the eye shattered, Courage smirked. He hobbled over and stood in front of the blinded eye. The power crystals on his mechanomagical prosthetic leg flickered and illuminated. He tested its movement, and it behaved as it had previously. Courage smiled. This part of the experiment proved successful.

Courage winced as the door to his cell opened. Four armed guards, all pale-skinned Froamian vampires wearing the red cloak of the Crimson Fangs, stepped into the room. Courage lifted his arms and opened his hands to show he had nothing usable as a weapon. One of the guards narrowed his eyes and barked a question. "What the hell happened? We heard a shot."

"Yeah," Courage said, panting. "I was attaching the repeating shot appendage to the host body, per the instructions on the form accompanying it, and I accidentally sent a signal to the appendage that initiated the firing apparatus. So, the mechanisms work. That's good at least. Made a bit of a mess in the wall. That's not so good."

The guard snarled and growled. "Stupid technomagus." He turned and pointed at two of those who accompanied him. "You two, stay in here and watch the little Ashbourne. Make sure he doesn't try anything funny. I'll go find someone who can fix that fucking eye. Can't have him getting an escape attempt in his mind."

The two guards grunted but nodded. He and the fourth guard exited the cell, closing and locking the door behind them. The two guards stood on opposite sides of the door. With stern expressions and narrowed eyes, they observed Courage as he finished his work and summoned the conveyance to remove the automaton.

I expected a swift response from these bastards, Courage thought. *But, once they send someone to repair the magic-dampening eye, I'll observe the repairs and learn how to remove them with a bit more subtlety. Then, I'll send word to Gwyn and my sister—and maybe Karina. That might be a problem if Gwyn comes. I hope she'll help me. If she's still alive, that is.*

As Courage learned the swiftness of the Crimson Fangs' response to gunfire within one of their strongholds, Karina's head throbbed in time with the screeching alarm clock. She groaned as every muscle in her neck, back, shoulders, and arms ached, rebelling against her command to roll over and silence the shouting mechanism that inflamed every blood vessel the front of her head. Three slaps of her right hand later, Karina succeeded in this task.

And then Karina's stomach churned. An acrid, acidic burn thrust its way from her stomach to her lips. Then it dissipated.

And then it thrust its way up again. And then it dissipated again, and again, and again. Each time the feeling thrust into her lips, a choked and gurgling cough pushed spit forward. Her eyes watered, and she covered her throat.

Karina rolled over and grunted as she fell onto the floor of her room. She lifted her head, and the room span around her, circling her vision and then turning upside down. Her stomach lurched again. Karina rose to her knees but fell forward from the dizziness and nausea. With a lurching grunt, Karina crawled to the bathroom of the rented room in the Golden Lion where she buried her face in the toilet bowl and vomited up everything she'd eaten for the past three days.

She smacked her lips as a cottony dryness filled her mouth. Karina whimpered and groaned as her muscled ached under the strain of lifting her svelte body upright, using the toilet for leverage. Once upright, she staggered three steps to the lavatory and turned on the cold water. Karina splashed the water on her face and then cupped her right hand and drank water while resting her forehead in the palm of her left hand.

"Why do people drink this poison if this happens the next morning?" She gazed upon her reflection in the mirror, noting every cut and every bruise on her face, neck, and shoulders.

Karina's already husky voice was an octave lower than usual, and phlegm building up in her her throat gave her voice a growling timbre. Her heart shoved blood through her veins, increasing the frequency of throbbing pain stabbing her head. Her breaths came heavy, ragged, and forced.

Karina took a quick shower, dressed, packed her mostly empty rucksack, and descended the stairs. As the hostess sat her at a small table, her stomach churned again. The server, a young man with slicked black hair who wore a white dress shirt and tan trousers, winced when he saw the pallor on her face. "Rough night? Hope it was a big celebration."

Karina squinted from the painfully bright lights. "Yes, it was a rough night. I just want milk and porridge."

"I can do that, ma'am," the server said. "But if I may make a suggestion, you may want some labskaus."

"What is that?"

"Old sailor's meal. It works like magic for a hangover or upset stomach too. It's salt pork, corned beef, a bunch of pickled vegetables, fried potatoes and onions, all topped with a few fried eggs that are still runny when you cut into them. It's a lot of food, but trust me, you'll feel better in a few hours after eating it."

A cold wave of nausea washed over Karina. "I don't know, but I've got a long trip ahead of me, so a large breakfast might be prudent. I still want the milk."

"Yes, ma'am. And I'll keep your water glass full."

The server was correct, as the labskaus was the largest plate of food Karina had had outside of the Midwinter's Eve feast. Halfway through her meal, two men wearing constable uniforms approached her. After identifying themselves, they set a sack of torbal on the table in front of Karina.

The tall, lanky constable with red hair, a lazy right eye, and a goatee that aged him by seven years and who identified himself as Assistant High Constable Walker said, "On behalf of the Office of the High Constable and of Hertzoch Reinholdt Kratescu, we thank you, Karina Skejik, for your service in slaying that *thing* stalking the Old Town district of Czarnenburg."

She sipped her milk. Through her hoarse voice, she said,

"No one deserved to die—especially not being eaten alive. It was a happy coincidence I was here."

"You look roughed up," the other constable said. "And not just from the fight."

Karina stabbed the salted pork, onion, and potato and took a bite before responding. "It's been a rough week."

The two constables nodded. Assistant High Constable Walker said, "Reports from the field said you fought like a Richter. You traveling off-duty?"

Karina's cheeks flushed. She sighed and shook her head. "Not part of that family." And then mentally, she added, *Anymore.*

"If you're looking for work," the Assistant High Constable said, "we could use someone of your skills."

Karina offered a faint smile. "I'll consider it, but I've got to find someone first. Once I find her and that situation goes as the gods allow, then I may return for work."

They nodded and left. Karina finished her breakfast and then checked out of her room. As she left the Golden Lion Inn, she noticed a thick fog obscured her vision. Even the street lamps provided little assistance. The streets were empty and silent. No mechanomagical carriages, horses, or wagons moved about the street, and no pedestrians milled about. Odd.

I'm unfamiliar with the city, she thought. *I need to get to the Old Gehrman Bahnhof and take the Rail to Bellecairn. That's the closest stop to Florescia. From there, I suppose I'll walk to Utrezzo and hope she'll listen to me. Not that I deserve that after—wait. What? That? How can that be?"*

A shadow moving through the fog drew her attention as it danced at the edge of her vision. It was a woman with olive skin and long black hair with curls cascading to the small of her back. The golden coins on her bracelets, headscarf, and belt jingled in the day's unexpected silence. The lace cuffs of her white blouse floated in the air as she danced in the margins between light and shadow, and her pleated red skirt billowed, rising and falling like a cloak as the woman moved.

Her warm brown eyes met Karina's. The woman smiled and danced away into the fog, fading from sight. Karina gasped again. "Mother? Mom! How?"

Karina raced after the woman who resembled her deceased mother. She followed the dancing woman through the fog-darkened streets. The mysterious figure danced and flitted as if the fog were of no concern to her.

The hangover impacted Karina. That was why she felt the fog's thickness more than ever before. The buildings seemed taller, more angular, as if they leaned at unusual angles with sharply rounded edges. And the street breathed beneath her, rising and falling in uneven pulsing waves. Yes, this was all caused by the hangover, but that was her mother dancing through this thick fog. And why was she wearing the traditional dress of her people—clothing she only wore when Karina's father wasn't around?

Karina chased after the dancing figure as the streets narrowed and descended. One hundred seventy-five steps down, Karina descended into a place where the streets grew narrower than they were in Old Town. No signs marking the names presented themselves, and the crystal street lamps had been replaced with gas powered flames that flickered and danced in time to the unheard rhythm of the strange figure's movements.

One hundred seventy-five more steps Karina descended. The angular buildings gave way to crumbling buildings of gray stone whose walls rose to meet the arched ceilings. The lights in the windows flickered and died in a manner befitting eyes closing for the last time. The wind whimpered as it shambled through the air, carrying with it an earthy but slightly fetid reek of decaying leaves. The mysterious woman danced on.

One hundred seventy-five more steps Karina descended. Each step became narrower and steeper than the last. A single church bell tolled in the distance as the arch-roofed buildings gave way to crumbling walls and hollowed structures that intermittently emerged from the sides of the narrow streets. The fog thinned to gauzy wisps that wrapped around the crumbling structures and the scattering of leafless trees with blackened, gnarled branches as the mysterious woman continued her dance.

A final one hundred seventy-five steps Karina descended. The fog thinned to the wispy thickness of crepe paper. A single, arched gate towered before her, looming at an unnatural and unholy angle. The figure turned toward Karina, beckoned with a smile and a graceful hand motion, and then darted through a crack in the wooden doors of the gate.

This was foolish. Karina *knew* that. Her mother had been dead for years, but Karina had never once dreamed of her like this. This couldn't be her mother, but she looked exactly as Karina remembered her mother looking when she was alive. She smiled as brightly with as much warmth and love in her eyes as Karina remembered.

Karina turned and glanced behind, but only the visually impenetrable thickness of the fog greeted her. She turned back to the towering gate. There was a crack between the two doors large enough for her to slip through.

"I'll just see what's on the other side," she said, justifying her curiosity to herself. “It won’t take long. Czarnenburg is a city on the Crystal Rail. There can’t be anything too dangerous outside of its gates. I’ll be fine.”

And with that, Karina stepped through the gate into that which was beyond.

Chapter 9

A twisted forest of gnarled, leafless trees with bone white bark surrounded Karina as she passed through the gate. The gate? Karina spun in place, but the gate was no longer behind her. Black stars shone against the night sky. When did it become night? It was before noon when Karina left the Golden Lion Inn. Her heart quickened its pace. Black stars set in a black sky, but she could see? The dim glow of the phosphorescence of the lumen flowers sprouting from the black soil must have provided the illumination she needed to see. Yes, that had to be the reason.

The air was cool and dry. A dusty and musky earthy smell dominated it, but competing notes of various incenses that ceased to smolder in previous ages poked through. The whimpering wind carried the tear-soaked reek of decay to Karina's wrinkling nose. The gray sere grass rustled silently in the whimpering breeze. When the sorrowful wind fell silent, no sound emerged from the darkness.

"Hello?" Karina peered into the darkness. "Mother, are you here? Where is here? Where am I? Mother, or whatever I saw in Czarnenburg, went through that gate, so she must've gone through this forest. Courage would know where I am." Karina sighed. "And Gwyn would know what to do. I know she would. Together we could—but I have to do this alone now. That's how things are."

As Karina surveyed the forest surrounding her, the wind wailed a keening dirge that chilled her and sent a shiver snaking up her spine. The leafless trees rattled and shook, and suddenly a passage—a tunnel bordered above by the touching tips of the gnarled branches—revealed itself. Karina shrugged. A bit too fortuitous, but she had no other clear passage. Thus, Karina readied her weapons and set out along the path.

The claw-shaped twigs at the end of the low branches of the leafless trees scratched at Karina's clothes and skin. The lumen flowers flickered as Karina moved past them. The ground was soft, but no sounds emerged as Karina stepped on dirt, on branch, or on flower.

The wind wailed, and that wasn't a metaphor. Karina's heart thundered. Her breaths were quick and shallow, and she saw them drift in white clouds from her lips in the chill of the night air. Was it night? It should have been midday. But the sky was black, and the stars were blacker but shining in their blackness. No, the wind brought the only sound, the sound of wailing, weeping, crying. It trudged through the air with the solemn pace of a funeral procession.

Karina used the light of the lumen flowers to peer through the trees. There were no animals, no tracks, no gnawed bones, and no shit on the forest floor. No tracks sank into the soil. No birds flitted through the air or flocked in the leafless, lifeless trees.

What kind of a forest is this? Karina's mind flitted from thought to thought as she looked around while following the path. *There's nothing here but trees, soil, and the wind. Even my feet aren't making a sound as I walk. And why does the wind sound like it's in mourning? Did someone die?*

Karina stopped. A horrible realization widened her eyes, and her jaw went slack. She gasped and then covered her mouth. Her shoulders slumped. Her voice emerged in a strangled whisper. "I'm dead, aren't I? I drank myself to death at the Golden Lion's restaurant. Father would be even more humiliated if—but I gave everyone my mother's last name. And her family travel from nation to nation without telling anyone where they go next. That's why it's so silent here. They tossed me into an unmarked grave. I died alone."

A sigh plummeted from Karina's lips. She gave three solemn nods and resumed following the path through the forest of lifeless trees. "The holy books tell us after death the Corvidiae judge the soul based upon its actions in life. I betrayed the teachings of my faith with Ailinya, and I almost betrayed them again with Gwyn. Gwyn…no god will take me for loving one willingly cut off from the Wheel of Souls. The fiery mountains and crematory ash wastes of Ashfodell await. I hope Mother isn't going to see me damned. Oh, Lord of Sky and Storm, I pray you—where am I?"

Karina blinked three times and then turned to observe the land around her in all directions. The forest was gone, existing now at the edge of her perception on the horizon behind her. When had she exited the forest? How long had she walked in this vast expanse of sere grass stretched before her in all directions. No lumen flowers guided her, but the moonless black sky with its blacker stars cast no shadows.

Could the dead see in the dark? Of course they could. Ghosts moved about with ease. And as a dead soul wandering the Shadowfields, this was to be the daylight to which she would grow accustomed until the Corvidiae bound her in molten chains and handed her off to the Ashfodellian Gaolers.

Better to continue and get my judgment over with, Karina thought as she trudged through the gray sere grass.

How long Karina trudged through the vast plain, which had she remembered all of her religious training, she would have known to be the plain of Hali. The black sky remained fixed and unmoving. Minutes, days, weeks, hours, seconds passed. Time meant nothing in the silent blackness devoid of all other sentient beings, and yet strange moons circled the black sky, reflecting no light as they passed from south to north. Neither hunger nor thirst assailed her, and exhaustion never weighed upon her body.

The plain of Hali gave way to the Haïthan Desert whose charcoal sands stretched alongside the cloud waves of the Hyades Sea. The waves gave a gentle roar as they pulsed in time with the movement of the slowest of the moons. Karina's feet crunched as her black boots stomped through the sand. A forceful wind kicked up from behind her.

A shadow darkened the sand as it moved over Karina. From behind and overhead, she heard what sounded like a barred owl's screech cutting through a lion's roar. Karina spun toward the sound and shrieked as a massive black-scaled dragon, a beast she knew of only from artistic renderings in collections of ancient lore, flew toward her at a speed comparable to the Crystal Rail.

No cover presented itself, and Karina froze as the great wyrm barreled toward the ground. Clouds of sand burst into the air as the dragon landed, shaking the ground with the force of its descent. Karina staggered.

Trained instinct overtook her, and Karina fired her flintlock into the dragon's side. Dark green blood seeped from around the wound. Karina tensed, readying her blade. The dragon stirred, then curled into a ball like a giant cat, and drifted to either sleep or death.

Not wanting to chance its rage or hunger upon waking, Karina bolted through the desert sands. The ground rose at a steepening angle, slowing her pace as the Haïthan Desert gave way to the Hastrui'in Mountains.

Karina paused, resting her hands on her knees as she panted. A small rock bounced against the worked stone of the mountain after her boot brushed against it, setting it into motion. Karina snorted.

"There was sound just there. I heard sound." She stomped on the stone, and her boots thudded. "I heard that too. I didn't hear my own movement in the forest. Did I hear anything in the desert or the grasslands? I remember the ocean and the dragon but not my own sounds. I'm hearing my own sounds now!"

A brief smile crept across Karina's face as she looked around. The mountain path was made of worked stone. It wasn't brick, and it wasn't cobblestone. These stones had a roundness to them and were of a size too large for bricks or cobblestones. None were vertical in their placement, but all protruded at an angle. Whatever they were, they were, however, the right size for headstones.

Ahead in the distance, perhaps five hundred paces, stone walls like those protecting a city from the wilds loomed. Karina smiled. A city meant others, which meant she wouldn't be alone any longer as she wandered this sunless, shadowy wasteland. She quickened her pace in bursts, as tiredness began to overtake her as she ran over the tombstone-shaped path markers. Karina burst past the iron gate and realized it wasn't a city's boundary but that of a large estate, or what remained of one. Dying trees, a withered garden, unblooming flowers greeted her as she approached the decaying remains of a once proud estate. As she moved, her eyes fixed on the opening double doors of the manor, she passed a statue of a woman holding a pistol and a healer's caduceus without taking note of it.

As the doors opened, six men, carrying gas lanterns of rusted iron, pulled a long cart containing three stacked coffins. Little of the men's faces beyond the four-day stubble on their chins was visible beneath the shadows cast by the tattered wide brims of their hats. As they moved along the path, their eyes had a lifeless sorrow but remained focused on the path ahead.

Karina approached. "May the storm protect you and the light guide your way. Please, I'm lost. I don't know how I arrived at this city, and I don't know where I am. Please, what city is this?"

The cart continued on its way. One of the men stopped and turned to face Karina. His lifeless eyes gazed upon her with confusion, pity, and a fear arising from understanding. He responded in a gruff voice, speaking a harsh language Karina did not know. When she tilted her head in confusion, the man offered a solemn nod, turned, and rejoined the other men.

From the remaining structural elements, the manor once stood as tall as a cathedral with three stories, arched windows, and multiple gables on its room. How many there were in the manor's prime, Karina did not know. She paused to reload her flintlock, readied her weapons, and stepped inside.

What remained of the ground floor was a pile of rubble that spanned from the exterior wall on Karina's left to the grand foyer's wall on her right. The floors above had crashed. Much of the wood paneling that remained had rotted away. Scorch marks blackened the walls. Some of those scorch marks took the appearance of terrified people—adult, child, and infant. Shattered glass littered the floor. What appeared to be a hastily dug and covered grave bulged at the base of the grand staircase that ascended to the higher floors. Energies dark and ancient pulsed in the air, and the entire place, though open to the elements, reeked of sorrow, fear, and death.

"What happened here?"

The one standing door turned to dust as Karina touched the knob to open it. What was once a well-apportioned library stood beyond the now-empty door frame. The rich mahogany and leather furniture, the shelving that rose to the ceiling, and the rolling ladders remained untouched. Dust and ash filled the shelves. Whatever lore, knowledge, science, and philosophy once filled this proud bastion of the written word, nothing remained but a single book on the armrest of a worn leather chair in the far corner against the back wall.

With hesitant, testing steps, Karina approached the leather chair. Patches of various upholstery patterns in numerous shades of brown spoke of its age and love by at least someone. She smiled. This chair reminded her of the chair in the family library where she would sit on her mother's lap while being read stories as a young girl. A tear formed in the corner of her right eye as she sank into the soft cushion.

Opening the book to the page marked by a golden ribbon, Karina soon realized she was reading someone's diary. This felt wrong, but it might be the only way for her to learn what happened here—wherever here was. The handwriting was elegant and feminine, and the language was that of the

Atharians, making reading easy.

I can hardly believe what has happened. My beloved fiancé, Antonio, brother of Hertogius Gyocomus Vandiamante, is a vampire. I learned this truth one week ago, on the night before our wedding, when he came to me in the moonlight, his eyes glowing red and his fangs bared. He told me the truth of his family, his lineage, and his nature. I should have killed him. Father would have wanted that of me, but I love him with a passion bordering upon sin.

And yet, I knew that I had to tell my father, but I was afraid of what he would do. I didn't want to lose Antonio, but as the daughter of the Grand Master of the Holy Order of St. Arnulf Ironhand, saying nothing would bring shame upon my family. In the end, I decided to tell my father everything.

Father was furious. He called off the wedding and placed me under arrest in my own chambers. My cousin, Albrecht, told me father has declared me afflicted with "vampire madness" and that he planned to send me to the St. Tymphania Asylum. None committed to that place leave before death.

My heart is shattered. I don't want to be sent away from Antonio. I know that he loves me, and I love him. I am going to miss Antonio so much. He is the only one who understands me. In his arms, I felt safer than in any of the Lord of Sky and Storm's holy places. But I also know that my father is right. After all, how could we who hunt monsters continue to protect the innocents if we share a bed with that which we kill?

But a Richter must be strong and must be brave. I have to find a way to get out of this asylum and be with Antonio again. I will not give up hope. I will not let my father win. I will find a way to be with the man I love.

Karina dropped the diary onto the floor. Her jaw fell

open. Three panting, shock-filled breaths burst from her open mouth. “This…this can’t be. Antonio Vandiamante killed Karolinya Richter’s fiancé on the eve of their wedding. Father told me…” Karina paused and slumped into the chair. She nodded. “Father also told me Hansel von Duessel was a member of the Crimson Fangs when all evidence pointed the opposite.”

Karina leaned forward and picked up Karolinya’s diary. “The feud was based on a lie. My family lied to protect its name. My family killed Gwyn’s family twice on wrong information. I…I attacked the woman I loved to earn my father’s love. We’re no better than common murderers who lie and steal and kill to get what they want.” She clutched the book tightly against her chest. “I have to find Gwyn. If nothing else, I must apologize for what I’ve done, for what I’ve said, and for what I’ve thought.” And then Karina wept.

When the tears ceased flowing, Karina placed the book in her rucksack, stood, and looked around. *If Karolinya’s diary is here,* she thought. *Then is this my family’s home? How did it become so rotten and burned? What happened here? Where is Grand Cathedral of Ullin’s Heart? And, how do I leave? Do I just retrace my steps?*

Karina walked through the library once again. As she stepped through the door frame, she found herself in an open field of ash gray dust. The rotting remains of the Richter family manor were nowhere in sight. No black stars, no strange moons, and no never-warming suns moved about the heavens. Nothing was around her save for a rectangular pit dug into the soil.

Curiosity won. Karina peered into the pit, an open grave. Its size spoke to the towering stature of the person—the man—

to be buried once the pit had been filled in. This man was not resting in a coffin, but he lay atop a pile of branches and dried leaves. He wore a blue tunic and brown trousers and boots. His wavy hair was red on one side and blond on the other, and gems of gold and blue adorned his well-groomed beard. He held a hammer shaped like a storm cloud and a spear shaped like a lightning bolt in the hands crossed over his beer barrel of a chest.

The hair. The beard. The thunder and hammer! Karina gasped. "The Lord of Sky and Storm! But, he's a god. How can he be dead?"

Laughter fluttered in on scavenger wings. Three women dressed in black and corvid masks appeared around the grave. Each carried a torch.

Maiden Magpie laughed. "Those on earth and in the sky, this is true. All things die."

She tossed her torch into the grave. Mother Crow then laughed and said, "Men die swift. Gods die slow. Love dies before they ever know."

She tossed her torch into the grave. The flames ignited the kindling beneath the Lord of Sky and Storm. Smoke, perfumed with sweet funerary incense, rose from the pit. The Raven Crone cackled. "The sun will dim. The moon grows dark. Belief too dies without life's spark."

She tossed her torch into the grave. The smoke grew thick and heavy. Karina coughed, covered her nose, and backed away. "Why? Why show me this? If everything dies? What's the point? What matters? What is eternal?"

In unison, the three women laughed and said, "Life is eternal, set in stone, always giving. Life does not die, for it feasts on the living."

The three cackled and danced about the pyre. The flames burst into the air. Karina shielded her eyes from the blaze as the heat reached a crescendo. And then all was silent.

Karina blinked again. She was alone. It was night. The stars were bright pinholes in the black sky, and a single moon shone overhead. The air reeked like a swamp. A small campfire flickered in the distance, not too far but not close enough to see anything beyond the shape of a single person and a horse. Karina walked toward the fire.

The person at the fire screamed. It was a woman. The horse whinnied in fear. Through the fire's light, Karina made out the form of another person pointing a gun at the woman. Karina quickened her pace. As her heart hurled the blood through her veins, Karina heard nothing else. Once close enough, she lifted her flintlock and fired.

Chapter 10

The Fish and Fowl Inn and Tavern was the only public house, restaurant, and inn located in the small fishing village of Vulgren, located west of the Volg Woods on the Atharian Empire's western coast. The Fish and Fowl only had a handful of rooms on the second floor, but few visited the isolated hamlet on any given month. On any given night, the tonwsfolk gathered in the common room on the first floor to drink, eat, and dance. On this night, the night Gwynarra Vandiamante sailed from Rotzendam to Liffecienne, the Fish and Fowl hosted another gathering as well as the townsfolk.

Beneath the Fish and Fowl, was a secret sanctuary for vampires, specifically for the organization known as the Crimson Fangs. Behind a blackened steel door upon which the face of a ravenous wolf encircled by bat wings had been etched where one must speak the pass phrase, *Zanguis, our Mother,* to enter, sat a sanctuary arranged in mockery of the Lord of Sky and Storm's cathedrals. Red tallow candles hung from crystal chandeliers. Able to see in complete darkness, vampires needed no light, but they enjoyed the dramatic ambiance provided by the flickering flames. Arcanyx crystals circulated fresh, perfumed air and controlled the climate. They were undead and immortal, but vampires, however, were also creatures of comfort who craved the world's sensual pleasures.

One hundred vampires, almost the entire organization, gathered in their private, hidden sanctuary on this night. Waiting for Marius Bedwyr's arrival, many sat at the assorted blackwood tables and leather sofas, drinking and conversing. Others danced to the sensual music from a string quartet seated before the altar on the far wall. Two identical statues of a beautiful naked woman with full breasts, long curving horns protruding from her forehead, and a long tail curling elegantly about her leg flanked the altar. The confessional boxes where vampires drank absinthe diluted with human blood that dripped from ornate crystal fountains were full.

One of the vampires in attendance asked, "You think he'll be early tonight?"

"You know Marius," another said. "Froamian punctual as always."

"Ah, so Don't expect him until twenty-three thirty."

They laughed. At twenty-three twenty-seven, the door behind the altar opened, and Marius Bedwyr and his three Nozy bodyguards with their hairless, ratlike features emerged from the room beyond. Marius wore a cloak of crimson velvet and a crown of iron set with rubies. Every vampire fell silent, stood at attention, and saluted. Marius returned the salute and gestured for everyone to return to their seats. A female vampire brought him a snifter of blood-infused cognac, which he swirled in his hand, sniffed, and then sipped.

"My comrades in arms, dearest friends, and beloved childer," Marius began. His voice was calm but powerful, and his tone sounded like the crashing of waves against the shore. "Thank you all for trusting me to lead you in this, our great struggle. All of us were stolen from our homes in Froam and Edrium as the Atharian Empire marched through our homes, slaughtered our parents, and took that which was our birthright. But here we are, all united, all striving together toward that common goal, all prepared to sacrifice for the greater good of ending the Atharian Empire and the oppressive stranglehold their *blessed emperor* seeks to hold over all our lives for perpetuity."

The crowd murmured. Some cheered. Others booed and hissed at the mention of the Blessed Emperor. Marius raised a hand to quiet them. "I understand your feelings. These past decades I have toiled to gain that monstrous man's ear, and as we now move from the middlegame to the endgame, my seat on the High Holy Council is assured."

"How will you earn that?" The vampire who shouted that stood to be noticed. "That society you headed has been raided by the damned Richters, and everyone who worked there has been executed for treason or turned into your bloody war abominations."

Marius nodded. "Yes. That they have. However, during the process of distracting the Richters with this little salvo, our creation of the Kriegsdieneryn has endeared me to the emperor. He has praised my vision, which were it not for those of you who toiled and experimented upon those poor criminal wretches, that would not have been possible." He held up a remote control device that was small enough to conceal in his hand. "And this, the device that controls the override switches installed within the newer models, will bring those same damned Richters before the imperial executioners."

Another voice from the crowd, a woman's voice, called out

and asked, "Is that how you plan to deal with those monsters who killed our families and sent us to that torture house of an orphanage? What about the mana bomb we've all heard rumors about?"

The elder vampire chuckled. He bared his fangs in a feral, lupine smile. "Oh, I've not forgotten about that. First, we plant evidence that the High Exarch has taken a bribe from the Crimson Fangs to assassinate the emperor. Then, the mana bomb shall destroy the Richters, their manor, and the Grand Cathedral of Ullin's Heart. Should that fail, or should a situation present itself beforehand, the override switch will allow me to manipulate the Blessed Emperor's perceptions of events and then save Imperial dignitaries from Caspar Richter's shocking treason."

The crowd cheered at the thought of revenge on the Holy Order of St. Arnulf Ironhand. The Richter family of witch, monster, and traitor hunters had marched on their homes, killed their parents, and carted each of these vampires off to St. Hiltegardt the Open-Armed's Orphanage where the staff took great pleasure in beating, burning, and starving the treason out of these, and other, children. For many, the nightmares only ceased once they became vampires. None had forgotten the sight of the black-uniformed Richter family as they lined up parents and adult siblings and then by blade, axe, or gun, executed them without trial.

"Now," Marius said as the crowd quieted down. "You may have noticed that our Blood Wolf Division is absent. They have taken the Grand Imperial Army uniforms and weapons our successful raids have procured and are prepared to launch a midnight raid on Milmigua, straining diplomatic relations with the independent city-states on the Indigo Coast and distracting the military from other actions we have planned to take. Rest assured, victory is close at hand. The emperor's bloodless corpse will hang on a stake before Kieliah's end."

One in attendance asked, "And then what, Marius? Will you return to Froam and rule from your throne in Clérmontán?"

"Yeah," Another vampire added. "You talk of the emperor's fall but not the empire's. You're not planning to take the throne for yourself? I thought we were destroying this damned empire and going home."

The crowd began to murmur. Many voiced similar concerns about Marius' intentions and rumors, fears, and concerns that had spread throughout the ranks. Marius narrowed his eyes and growled. This was not needed now—or ever.

"My dear ones," he said. His voice blended sorrow with a predator's threat. "Your words wound me more than a stake dipped in hallowed water ever could. If ever I have done anything to cast doubt on your soul as to the honor of my intentions, I beg your forgiveness with contrition and remorse reserved for the most sacred of pilgrimages. As my comrades, my countrymen, and my children, allow me to bury these fears. Now, we know that an ill word's spread is swift, but sacred speech is slow to move.

"Now I stand accused of ambition beyond that which I have stated, and to that, I now state my desire to be only that which I know I am entitled. The throne stolen from my upon the Atharian march, none would deny me. And yet, I can see how the temptation, were I of lesser stock than that of Froam, to take vengeance and then ransack and pillage the lands of those who so ransacked and pillaged ours.

"This temptation I understand, and were I less than an honest man, I would deny ever having such emotions. For

I did, as a young man and even as a fledgling, such lusts inflamed my soul and moved me to strive to become the man of honor and honesty I am this night. I have grown. I have reflected. And now, I can say to you that I only desire that to which is mine.

"Victory after victory, have I not commanded? The spoils of which I have shared with each of you in equal measure. Is there lie to this? Is this what one who seeks the imperial throne would do? Does the emperor share with all who serve him, or does he toss crumbs from his table—crumbs of the bread and meat taken by force to pay the ever-rising taxes—to those who have labored that he may live in luxury. Think no longer on these fearful rumors. I have not changed my goal, and I have not changed my loyalty to you, to Froam and Edrium, and to the children of Zanguis."

With a snap of his fingers, Marius ordered wine and blood brought to all vampires present. The murmuring slowed and then fell silent. Marius' honeyed words accomplished their task of quelling the growing fears from his ranks. He smiled as merriment and pleasure became the topics of conversation for the remainder of the night.

Chapter 11

The Crimson Fang vampires began gathering beneath the Fish and Fowl an hour after sunset, the same hour that the Crystal Rail carrying Honor Faern'doln and Xrissa Kosol stopped in Schwarzfeld. The train station sat on the border between the Old City's Wartheimer Square and the Merchants' Quarter. Looking to the Old City, they saw towering buildings of stone and timber lining a serpentine maze of narrow streets where the statue of the first emperor, Albrecht Wartheimer, whom imperial historians honored with the moniker of Great Liberator, pointed to the massive cathedral devoted to St. Florian that towered over this district. Gazing to the Merchants' Quarter revealed organized squares of half-timber houses, their lower floors often serving as the storefronts.

As the streetlamps powered on to combat the growing darkness, the lights in the storefronts throughout the city faded into darkness. The lights of the taverns, the restaurants, the inns, and the houses sprang to greater life. The air was cooler than in Al'Adara, and a gentle northern breeze carried the faint smell of industry from the Artisans' Quarter through the air. Residents, travelers, and armed imperial soldiers walked along the sidewalk as the honking of mechanomagical wagons and carriages overtook the sounds of conversation and footsteps.

"So," Xrissa said in her chipper squeak of a voice. She took a swig from a large flask she carried. "It looks a bit late to visit some of the artisan shops. Courage would probably have been there. He showed me the blueprints for that wandvolver he planned to make when I last saw him. I wonder how it's coming along."

Honor shook her head. "Knowing that dumbass, that invention of his probably got him in trouble. He'd almost completed it the last time I saw him. Honestly, given our family's love of beer, we need to find the inn nearest the best brewery in the fucking city. They'll know something about my little brother. Where are you going?"

Xrissa's traveling attire was a sleeveless black leather jerkin and matching fitted trousers. An oversized wrench and hydrospanner hung from her hips, and goggles with a wheel of lenses and six glowing Arcanyx crystals rested on her forehead. SAAMy, a massive crossbow with a series of vials filled with powdered Arcanyx crystals and two large googly eyes that flanked the opening for the bolt between the two bow limbs skittered along after her on six spindly legs.

Honor cursed under her breath and chased after Xrissa who had skipped off toward the nearest Atharian soldier in his dark green uniform. Standing nearly two feet shorter than the soldier, the short and curvy Moon Elf stood on the steel toes of her boots and waved her arm wildly. "Hi! Hi! Hey! Excuse me! My friend and I are looking for her little brother. Where's the best place to get a good beer here?"

The soldier stopped and stroked his handlebar mustache. His dark green uniform with its golden trim and ornate epaulets had been recently cleaned and pressed. He nodded and muttered thoughtful grunts before saying, "That's a personal preference, isn't it? Schwarzfeld has many breweries, but for my torbal, you'll find no beer better that the pils from Black Forest Brewery."

"Could we get directions to there?"

And then Honor added her question to Xrissa's. "They wouldn't happen to have a schwartzbier, would they? My little brother likes those."

The soldier nodded. "They do. He an Ashbourne like you?"

Honor nodded.

"He's much more handsome," Xrissa said. "He has messy black hair, bright golden eyes, and straighter horns than her. I think he's about your height, maybe a little taller with his horns. They're very pointy. Any chance you've seen him?"

The soldier balked. He shook his head. "No, sorry. I haven't seen him. Can't say I've seen any Ashbournes in the last month."

"Can you at least point us to this Black Forest Brewery," Honor asked. "If there's an inn near it, I know my brother would've stayed there. They might know something."

"Yes, ma'am. I can do that. You'll be looking for the Black Boar in the Old City. It's a bit small, but it's a paper ball's throw away from the brewery." He then pointed and them directions before the two women thanked him and walked off.

"Really? He's more handsome than I am?"

Xrissa responded with a vigorous nod. "Well, first of all, you're not a man, so you're not handsome. Second, he has such an adorable face, like a lost little puppy. And have you never noticed how his eyes light up like the candles on a

Midwinter tree when he's talking about history, artifacts, or inventions?"

Honor smirked as they walked. "It is hard to ignore how excited he gets. And someone needs to put a collar on that lost little puppy—might make him easier to get a hold of."

"That'd be easy to do. All you'd need to do is tool some black leather to match his hair into a collar and affix a golden clasp to match his eyes. Then you would need to affix a signal-coded electro-charged crystal to it—you'd want low power, of course, because you want to shock him but not hurt him—and then fashion a remote-control relay device." She paused to take another swig from her flask. "Oh! And you'd also want a leash to connect to the collar to help guide him. I don't think I've ever seen him walk by the bakery without him taking a wrong turn."

Honor chuckled. That's because his dumb ass thinks he looks nonchalant doing that, she thought. Doesn't want to make it seem obvious he's there to see you. And then she said, "Please tell me that's whisky in there and not—"

"Crimson Minotaur Stamina Beverage!" Xrissa thrust the flask into the air, turned it upside down, and let the reddish-yellow liquid cascade into her open mouth. After swallowing, she added, "Take the day by the horns! It's the only thing my alchemical flask produces. Fifty-four liters a day."

Honor shook her head. Fifteen minutes of walking and pleasant conversation later, they arrived at the Black Boar Inn and Tavern. Sandwiched between the Black Forest Brewery and an attached livery, the inn was tiny, but the tavern on its ground floor was a large open room with four communal tables. A handful of guests and residents sat at either the tables or the long bar, eating and drinking. There was minimal conversation. An Elvish bard with a soft and sweet voice sat beside the hearth and played her Froamian harp.

From behind the bar, a Human woman smiled as they entered She wore a traditional Atharian dirndl of with a floral apron over the white blouse and green dress, and her blonde hair was in plaited braids. As they approached, the slight pointedness of her ears suggested partial Elven lineage.

She greeted them. "Hallo. Welcome to the Black Boar. I'm Isla." She paused and scanned Honor. "Have I seen you before? You look familiar. Cut your hair?"

Honor shook her head. "Never been here, but my brother might have been a few days ago. We're looking for him."

"He's tall with messy black hair, the handsome face of a lost puppy, golden eyes, and pointy horns," Xrissa interjected. "His name is Courage. Have you seen him?"

"Before you answer," Honor held up her hand. "Do you mind a little magic? Nothing violent or flashy, promise. Just a small illusion to show you his face."

Isla nodded. "Sure, I guess."

With a quick finger curling pattern and a handful of ancient words, Honor produced an image of Courage's face that floated above her upturned, open hand. Isla leaned forward and observed the detailed image. She ran her fingers along her braided hair and nodded. "I think I remember him. He was here maybe two weeks ago with an Elven woman, white hair. What was her name? We've changed ledgers since then, or I'd look to see if I remember. I think she was Froamian. She carried a harp like Teluria does."

She pointed to the bard who was singing a slow, mournful dirge about fallen heroes. Honor nodded. "Yeah, he mentioned something about doing a job for some arcane society or mystical order. Would you happen to know of any here?"

Isla gasped. "I don't know of any arcanist order, but about a week ago there was an attack by the Crimson Fangs on the Society for Afterlife and Arcane Research. Newspapers and local gossip pointed to an Ashbourne assisting them with one of the Richters and the Silver Scourge."

"The Richters? The Crimson Fangs? The Silver what?" Honor scratched her head. "Who the fuck are those what-nots?"

"The Ricthers are a family of vampire hunters who tend to hunt traitors and terrorists, like the Crimson Fangs. They're some terrorist organization run by a vampire named Marius Bedwyr, if you can believe that. Like anyone disloyal to the empire would tell you their name. Anyway, apparently, the society called to the Richters—the Holy Order of St. Arnulf Ironhand—for aid, and they sent one member of the family. I didn't see this happen, because I was working—the Society's headquarters is on the southern side of the city—but rumor says the Silver Scourge, an Elven woman from Froam who hunts monsters to help anyone was seen walking alongside the Holy Order's representative, and there was an Ashbourne man trailing behind them."

Honor nodded. "How much is a room for the night?"

Isla winced. "We just raised prices due to new imperial taxes. Eight torbal."

Honor fished into her pocket and handed her ten torbal. "The other two are for your help. We need a place to rest for the night."

Isla smiled. "You're most kind." She handed Honor a rusted key. "Room six. Enjoy your stay. The bar will serve until two in the morning, and our kitchen is open until twenty-two bells."

"Thank you," Honor said. "We'll probably be back for a drink in a bit. Just need to freshen up."

Honor and Xrissa walked up the stairs to room number six, locking and closing the door behind them. The small but homey room had rustic oak furnishings and quilted bedding resembling something a grandmother would gift their grandchildren. Xrissa flopped onto the bed that was too large for the room and rolled onto her back. "So, taking a shower or a bath?"

"Neither," Honor said. She fished around in the small leather pouch on her belt and pulled out a piece of copper wire. Holding it up, she added. "Don't have a proper name, but this *Silver Scourge* seems to be a singular enough person that I should be able to send her an arcane message. We'll go from there."

Xrissa nodded. "And then we get her, and we can find Courage."

Honor nodded and sighed. *Here goes nothing,* she thought. Holding the wire between her fingers and thumb, she uttered the incantation. The wire vibrated and then glowed with the familiar reddish orange light. "Silver Scourge. I'm Honor Faern'doln. You know my brother Courage. Please help me find him. Tell me where you are. We'll come to you. Please."

A few moments passed in tense silence before a Froamian voice responded. ""Not now. Gunpoint. One hour."

Chapter 12

The shot from Karina's gun lodged itself in Severus Richter's throat. His eyes shot wide, and blood poured form his mouth. His jaw trembled as his gaze moved from Gwyn to Karina behind her, and as he slumped forward and fell to the ground, he spoke his last word in a rattling whisper.

"Traitor."

Siobhan whinnied loudly. Gwyn spun around and gasped. Karina, holding her smoking flintlock in a firing position, walked toward her through the wet grass. Gwyn leaped to her feet, drew her own weapons and pointed her pistol at the woman she once considered a friend and something more. Her voice trembled, but her weapons pointed with steel's unwavering resolve as she spoke.

"Don't. Don't come any closer. I won't hesitate. Not this time."

Karina nodded. Gwyn's response was neither unexpected nor undeserved, given that the last time they were together, Karina attempted to kill Gwyn. Karina stopped walking. She tossed her flintlock toward the corpse of her cousin, and then she repeated the process with the blade she carried. Unarmed and at a tactical disadvantage compared to the vampire before her, Karina lifted her arms and displayed her open palms.

"I mean no harm, Hertogia Gwynarra Vandiamante. I am not here to kill you."

Gwyn winced as a voice pierced her head. Her eyes shot wide, but seeing Karina respond with curiosity, Gwyn narrowed them and snarled. Under her breath, she whispered, "Not now. Gunpoint. One hour."

Gwyn took a single step closer to Karina. The former vampire hunter's clothes had slash marks on them from claws and stains of dirt, blood, and sweat. Gwyn sniffed at the air. The blood was fresh, perhaps a day or two old, but it wasn't a vampire's blood. Her clothes were different. The black uniform of the Holy Order of St. Arnulf Ironhand was replaced by a cream, puffy-sleeved poet's shirt and black leather trousers beneath a black leather vest with gray pinstripes and a long leather coat.

Karina's heart pounded in her chest. Sweat beaded on her forehead. The white clouds of her breath carried silent prayers toward the black sky as Gwynarra Caoilfhionn Vandiamante, the vampire—the *woman*—she had befriended, had learned to trust, and had grown to love, circled her the way a lion stalked its prey.

Gwyn's fangs were bared. She no longer had a need to hide her nature from Karina. Marius Bedwyr saw to that. Her lips twitched into a smirk as she glared into Karina's eyes and, for the first time, saw fear. "Then why the fuck are you here, *Richter?*"

Karina winced. The venom that soaked Gwyn's voice when she spat Karina's last name stung worse than it ever had before. Karina sighed and nodded.

Now what, she asked herself. *I've earned her hatred—not my family, not my father, but me. Who was she talking to? How do I convince her to at least listen to me? Why did Severus—of all my cousins—why did Severus have to get here before me? Maybe I could...*

As she finished her thought, Karina dropped to her knees. She lowered her gaze so she no longer met Gwyn's glare. Karina tensed every muscle in her body and sucked in a sharp breath. Without releasing the breath, she said, "I came to beg."

Gwyn snorted. "Then beg."

Karina swallowed hard and then nodded. "I, Karina Alyxandra Skejik Richter." Her voice trembled in a mournful warble as she said her last name, the name she no longer used. "I came to beg your forgiveness for my words spoken against your family and my actions taken against you. I came to beg your forgiveness for the lies my family has spread about yours that led to their murders. And I came to beg your aid. Please, I need you to help me free Courage Faern'doln from the Crimson Fangs."

Karina lowered her face to the dirt and then whispered, "And I need you."

Karina winced. Did she really utter that last statement? Well, there was no point in being dishonest now. Everything needed to be laid bare if she had any hope of survival, success, anything. Karina slammed her eyes shut. Her muscles tensed. And without rising from her prostrate position, she waited.

Gwyn's boots sloshed and crunched on the soggy grass. She continued circling Karina, but the Human hunter felt the vampire's presence draw closer. The circles were smaller, quicker. And yet, beyond the sounds of her steps, Gwyn remained silent.

"Everyone seems to need me to find Courage. If I fucking

knew where he was, I'd have gone after him already. He's probably in the fucking heart of the godsdamned empire, protected by your bloody fucking family. What am I supposed to do?"

"They're not my family anymore."

Karina's voice trembled, and tears welled in her eyes. Her body shook as it lay prostrate before Gwyn. The vampire snarled. "So, you throw away your weapons. You take off the murderers' uniform. You change your clothes. And suddenly, you have a revelation? Is that it?"

Karina whispered her response. "No."

Gwyn stiffened. Through gritted teeth, she asked her next question. "Then what happened?"

Karina lifted her face and torso to look at Gwyn. Soupy mud dripped from her face. She removed her vest and loosened the collar of her shirt. After all this time, the two wounds Marius inflicted upon her neck remained vibrant an visible.

Gwyn's eyes widened and then burned. Her cheeks flushed as she growled. "Who did this to you?"

She recognized those marks, their spacing, and their location. A vampire had claimed Karina's body—at least for a meal. That was all it was. Karina would *not* give in so easily. Rage enflamed Gwyn's body. That meant—no. No vampire would violate *that* law of conduct. To do so would mark one as anathema among society.

"It's not what you think, but it's supposed to look like it."

"Then explain it to me."

Gwyn's tone was sharp like her blade—like her fangs. Karina nodded. "Marius took me to a building in Iszenstadt—a medical facility. He has another office there. In his office, he used some sort of mechanical device to burn these scars into my neck. He convinced my father you did it, and when I protested too much, father expelled me from the Order and threw me out."

Sorrow choked Karina's words with progressive intensity as she spoke. The tears that had welled in her eyes streamed down her muddy cheeks. Snot dripped from her nose onto her mouth. Karina sucked in the snot and then wiped her face with the back of her sleeve.

Gwyn struggled to return her face to a neutral expression. Her mouth complied, but sympathy and sorrow darkened her green eyes. The only reason Karina turned on her so quickly was because she thought it might earn her favor in her father's eyes. Their conversations around campfire, across the bed in Kaltbrück, and on the train to Schwarzfeld flashed before Gwyn's mind.

So, Gwyn thought. *Her father listened to her speak the truth as well as she listened when I spoke it regarding her family's atrocities. I want to be mad. No, I want to hug her, kiss her cheek, tell her everything can be made right. But it can't. Her family won't listen.*

The silence gnawed at Karina's soul. She held up her hands. "Please, let me get something from my rucksack. It's not a weapon. You'll want to see this. I swear."

Gwyn extended her sword, pointing the blade at Karina's throat. "Remember, I'm much faster than you are. If you try anything, you won't see me strike."

Karina nodded. She wriggled her arms around so the rucksack fell to the ground in front of her. She opened the flap and pulled out the leather journal. Karina gasped and fell backward as the journal crumbled to dust in her hands.

"What the fuck was that?" Gwyn waggled her sword toward the dust in a performatively threatening manner.

"That was—how?" Karina looked at her hands. Dust from the journal remained in her palms. "I held it. I read it. How?"

"What was it?" Gwyn grew insistent.

"Karolinya Richter's diary." Karina narrated everything that happened from the moment she woke up after the hunt, followed her mother—or a ghost who took her mother's form—explored that strange landscape, and then came upon the ruins of what she now thought was her family manor. "And the only room I could enter was the library, but it was in the wrong place. The diary was there, and I read the entry from the night before she was sent to die alone in St. Tymphania's. She confessed that your uncle, Antonio, didn't kill her fiancé. He was her fiancé. It was all a lie. The feud, the hatred of your family above all others, the push to find and kill *you*, the last heir, all of it stemmed from a lie."

So that was why Uncle Antonio always mourned the one who got away, Gwyn thought. Then she nodded. "He never knew what happened to her. That was centuries ago, and until the day he was murdered, he mourned for her."

"Everything I said to you about your family was based on a lie. When Marius Bedwyr outed you, it burned that you didn't trust me—that you *couldn't* trust me—with who you were. I loved you. I *still* love you, but then my feelings for you collided the shame Father heaped upon me when I was caught kissing Ailinya. I acted out of hurt and shame instead of understanding."

Gwyn nodded, and Karina continued. "And then I saw the Lord of Sky and Storm's open grave, and then the Corvidiae set the body on fire. The fire flash blinded me for a moment, and when I regained my vision, I saw someone pull a gun on a screaming woman. I didn't know it was my cousin

Severus threatening you. I acted on instinct, remembering you scolding me for allowing innocents to suffer when I had the power to aid them."

She remembered that, Gwyn thought as a smile crept over her face. *I did scold her. She ran off on our mission for the Society but then came back to "save me" from the werewolves. She knew I was there. She didn't know I was here. Maybe she's changing.*

Karina offered a faint smile in return before lowering her gaze and replying, "I listened to you. I learned. I've had a lot more to learn. And you don't have to forgive me or love me, but please, I beg of you, help me free Courage."

Gwyn placed the flat of her blade under Karina's chin and lifted it. Karina's eyes widened, and her mouth went dry. Her breath stopped. Gwyn said, "I was right about you."

Karina closed her eyes. She swallowed hard and lowered her chin, pushing the blade toward her throat. This was it. This was how it ended.

"That night we shared a room in Kaltbrück and I watched you pray." Gwyn flicked her sword away, rushed forward, and caught Karina's chin in her hand, forcing Karina to meet her gaze. The vampire's voice purred took on the timbre of a panther's purr as she said, "I said you looked good on your knees, and I was right."

Before Karina registered Gwyn's words, the vampire claimed Karina's mouth with her own. Gwyn's lips were cold but soft, and the floral scent of her perfume overpowered the swamp's decaying reek. Gwyn's breath was hot and humid. Karina felt warmth building within her, and she moaned, leaning into the vampire's kiss.

Their lips danced, and Gwyn slid her tongue between Karina's lips and teeth. She teased the Human's tongue with her own before pulling back and gently biting Karina's lower lip. Gwyn broke the kiss, and Karina released the breath she'd been holding for most of the conversation with a relieved sigh. Her chest heaved in heavy panting breaths.

The women smiled at each other. As Gwyn held Karina's face in her delicate hands, she licked her lips as her eyes looked Karina up and down. The vampire then said, "My knight needs new clothing, but I like this look on you."

Karina blushed as a grin burst onto her face. At that moment, Honor Faern'doln's voice burst back into Gwyn's mind. "Shit. You'd better be alive. Will you fucking help me find my dumbass of a brother?"

Gwyn chuckled. "That's two asking for my aid. Meet us in Clérmontán, the Moonlit Rose. We'll plan there. I hope you have a destination or a direction."

Karina tilted her head. "Why Clérmontán? Who are you talking to?"

"Courage's sister, Honor, wants my help finding her brother. I figure Courage is somewhere in the damned empire, but I need to send letters to Delfia and Utrezzo, and Clérmontán is safer than Dornbach, in case more of your family is watching me. We'll meet with Honor and formulate a plan."

Karina nodded. Her gaze turned to her cousin's corpse. Ravens had begun picking the flesh from his bones. She walked over and grabbed his weapons and ammunition. "No sense in letting good weaponry go to waste."

Chapter 13

The capital city of the Atharian Empire, Sonnenburg, sat on the southern edge of the Zwarbeil Forest. was a massive city of towering buildings of ancient gray and black stone with soaring spires, gabled roofs tiled in blackwood and red oak, and stained-glass windows gazed down upon the long, narrow cobblestone streets. Imperial soldiers patrolled the streets in armored mechanomagical wagons as pedestrians dodged mechanomagial brooms sweeping the sidewalks of the shops and restaurants.

At the city's center sat the Imperial District, and at the district's center was the Cathedral Square, where the St. Victus Cathedral's spires towered above the cobblestone streets, and the rose window looked down on those milling about the square like the all-seeing eye of the Lord of Sky and Storm. The sweet, earthy scent of frankincense, myrrh, and copal remained in a perpetual haze around the cathedral. At any hour between sunrise and the moon reaching its zenith, the sounds of prayers and chanted choral song could be heard from within the cathedral, and on each hour, the great bells tolled.

Fourteen bells tolled. On the day that Gwyn and Karina began their travels to Clérmontán, rain pummeled Sonnenburg's cobblestone streets. Thunder's roar drowned the rumbling of the mechanomagical engines, and the frequent flashes of lightning joined with the crystal street lamps in providing illumination for those moving beneath the thick, swollen gray clouds.

A young Human man walked through the Cathedral Square, staying in the shadows cast by the towering buildings as he moved. His skin was pale, not an uncommon trait among Atharian Humans and the many Snow Elves living within the empire's borders, and his hair was dark. Even though the rain-soaked black cloak that shielded him from the worst of the weather was weighted down by rain, its hem lifted with each step, revealing crimson lining.

The man passed through the massive oak double doors. He winced and shielded his eyes as the bright lights from the golden chandeliers reflected off the polished white marble floors and walls, adorned with golden accents and painted statuary of St. Victus, St. Hiltegardt, St. Hurud, St. Pyetros, and St. Arnulf Ironhand. Located in the apse behind the altar, the cathedral's castrati choir—the only remaining castrati choir on the continent—chanted hymns in their angelic, feminine voices. Once he crossed into the nave, two red crushed velvet carpets, trimmed in golden cord, lined the central aisle between the rows of kneeling benches. No one sat while worshiping the Lord of Sky and Storm here, but all were expected to either stand or kneel in reverence.

Fewer worshipers stood on the southern side of the cathedral. Even fewer prayed at the altars in the southern alcoves. Thus, the man chose that side to walk along, his downcast eyes cared not to see the ceiling painted to depict scenes from the life and miracles of St. Victus.

A priest in gold-trimmed white robes followed the man as he moved toward the transept. The hooded man stopped at the last alcove and folded his hands in the appearance of reverence. The priest observed the silent observance. He approached the man and said, "Most remove their hoods out of reverence when in this holy house, and they voice their requests in this most hallowed house of worship for the Lord of Sky and Storm. There is no need to fear judgment for your request. Speak your desire for holiness, and it will be granted."

The hooded man nodded. He removed his hood. "Forgive me. I am pressed for time and wanted to make my request as quickly as possible."

The priest nodded. "All is well. We cannot forget decorum and respect in the house of our god. Shall I pray with you?"

"No," the man said. He turned and locked eyes with the priest. And then his brown eyes flashed red. "It would be best if you forgot I was here."

"Yes."

The priest nodded and then walked off. The man watched the priest return to his station before the man stepped closer to to the transept wherein the staircase that ascended to the Exarchial Palace, allowing a pillar to shield him from the priest's line of sight. The man donned his hood once more, took one step back, transformed into mist, and floated underneath the door.

A vampire's mist form did not trigger automatic lights to illuminate, allowing the vampire an easier time skulking through shadows. This allowed for an easy ascent to the fourth floor of the cathedral. The vampire stopped on the landing. Only one floor, the Exarchial Palace, remained, but reconnaissance informed him the entrance would be guarded. Observing his surroundings, he noted the stained glass windows were sealed, leaving no hope of passing through a crack.

He thought for a moment. A flash of lightning illuminated the window. He bared his fangs in a feral smirk. After stretching his arm and opening and closing his gloved fist a handful of times, the vampire punched the window. He brushed away the shards of colored glass that had embedded themselves in his leather glove, transformed into mist once more, and using the storm as cover, floated to the roof of the Exarchial Palace.

Once atop the cathedral, the vampire crawled to the massive glass window over the temperature controlled pool and garden. He then flicked the ring on his right index finger. As the small crystal illuminated, he said, "The Black Gardener is in position atop the Exarchial Palace. Eyes on the Prize, all good? Over."

A few moments later, the response came. "Eyes on the Prize reporting, Black Gardener. The mark just entered the High Holy Council Chamber with the Red King right behind him. Plant the seeds. Over and out."

The Black Gardener shifted to mist and slid through a crack between the window's hinges. The vampire glared and snarled. The pool and garden room was larger than the flat he lived in. Were it not for the temperature control and the magically empowered pots, none of the palms, pink falump ears, golden ginger flowers, lunar dwarf hibiscuses, and fly needle succulents would have survived in this climate. Gold leafing covered the bamboo frames of the rattan furniture surrounding the pool. Before leaving the pool room, he produced a vial containing a viscous dark green liquid into one of the pots containing a palm.

Pocketing the empty vial, the Black Gardener moved the massive apartment that served as the High Exarch's residence until he found the executive office suite. Once there, he opened the top right drawer on the white marble desk and placed a series of papers and the empty vial into the drawer, taking care to ensure the pages weren't on the top but close to it. His mission accomplished, the Black Gardener opened a window, crawled onto the wall, closed the window behind him, and scurried down the side of the cathedral.

Once he reached the street, he activated the comm ring and said, "Black Gardener has planted the seeds. Water them three times. Over and out." And then, under the cover of the storm, he disappeared into the city.

While the Black Gardener planted papers and a mysterious vial in the High Exarch's residence, the High Holy Council gathered on the opposite side of the Cathedral Square inside the Imperial Palace. As the members of the Council arrived, they passed the throng of filthy, unclean peasants with scabrous and pock-marked faces wearing tattered and hastily patched mismatched clothing that surrounded the gate and begged for coin. Ignoring the presence of children among the throng and knowing that without any doubt these drains on society who chose to beg over work would spend the coin on only the most deviant of vices, none on the Council had torbal to spare.

Once beyond the gold-plated iron gates that towered over the two-story wall of gray and black stone that bordered the palace grounds, the Council members who turned their gaze to their left saw the Imperial Grove, the last remaining old growth red oak and blackwood trees within the borders of the empire that had been transplanted here and arranged into what bore only the faintest resemblance to a natural forest. Those who glanced to the right saw the Imperial Game Field and Gardens, an express of manicured lawn where the Blessed Emperor oversaw games of living chess, croquet, and boccie. Beyond the Game Field sat a massive garden of flowers, ferns, and other plants from across the empire, arranged by geographic location.

With its towers rising higher than the spires of St. Victus Cathedral, the Imperial Palace was a masterpiece of white and gray stone construction. The arched windows, buttressed construction, and gabled roof marked it as a masterpiece of the Tshípogothic revival in the early centuries of the Age of Arcanum. The palace's interior, however, was made from the same gold-adorned white marble as the St. Victus Cathedral.

As the Council members entered the palace, they passed through the Grand Promenade, an expansive foyer whose white marble floor had been lined with a gold-trimmed carpet of green velvet. Statues of former emperors and High Generals of the Grand Imperial Army lined the marble walls. Glancing upward as one walked toward the double staircase that spiraled upward at the far end of the foyer revealed a ceiling enchanted to always remain as bright and warm as the sun at noon. And yet, the air inside the palace remained crisp, cool, and perfumed with roses.

Stepping onto the third floor, one passed through the Hall of Reflection. Mirrors in ornate golden frames adorned with diamonds and emeralds lined the walls. The arched golden doors at the hall's far end opened to the Imperial Receiving Suite. This four-room suite included the formal dining hall, a reception hall, the chamber where the Blessed Emperor and the High Holy Council met, and the throne room.

When the Blessed Emperor Josyph Hapfsburgh met with the High Holy Council, four Imperial soldiers and four agents of the Holy Order of St. Arnulf Ironhand stood guard. The soldiers stood outside the chamber, and the Richter agents stood inside. The chamber itself was a smaller version of the throne room. A red oak table, shaped like a half moon sat at its center. The four chairs of the High Holy Council were around the curve, and atop a dais behind the flat side stood the Blessed Emperor's chair.

The Blessed Emperor sat upon the green velvet cushion of his throne. He had grown lean and frail with age, but in his youth, his broad shoulders and prodigious strength signaled to all that his morality would be unyielding. Thin wisps of gray hair protruded from beneath the golden circlet at the base of his diamond and emerald-laden crown. Clouds darkened his sapphire eyes, and a long beard hid the wrinkles on his face. He wore a charcoal suit beneath a robe of soft ermine fur as white as the marble in his palace. On his lap rested the golden sword and scepter, symbols of his office and of his roles as guide and guardian of the people.

The Grand Master of the Holy Order of St. Arnulf Ironhand, Caspar Richter, sat on the Blessed Emperor's left hand. Like the emperor, his hair had thinned and silvered with age, and wrinkles and scars had adorned his stern, tanned face in the areas not covered by his trimmed silver beard and bushy eyebrows. He wore his order's dress black uniform, trimmed in gold and adorned with the symbol of the Lord of Sky and Storm on the right breast.

Beside him sat Augustus Krank, the High General of the

Imperial Army. This middle-aged man had slicked back his blond hair and shaved his angular face that had not cracked a smile in five years, according to soldiers who worked closely with him. His piercing green eyes matched the hue of his wool dress uniform with the oversized, ornamental epaulets and trim all made from the same golden cord.

Next to High General Krank sat Marius Bedwyr, Director of Traitor Rehabilitation and the former Director of Operations for the Society for Afterlife and Arcane Research. Using the name Ambrose von Harenheim and wearing a life's aura pendant beneath the crimson ascot around his neck, this vampire hid his nature and identity from those who wanted nothing more than his arrest and public execution.

And next to him, at the emperor's right hand, sat High Exarch Klauz Bohnoepfer. This rotund man with over-gelled black hair and an aquiline nose donned the immaculate gold-trimmed white robes common to the priests of his faith, but he adorned his neck, wrists, fingers, and waist with gold jewelry encrusted with diamonds, citrine, and yellow topaz. Atop his head was a golden mitre with three lightning bolts protruding from the point at its top.

Amid the din of multiple conversations, the Blessed Emperor tapped his scepter on the table three times. A brief fit of coughing followed. The men of the High Holy Council, their attendants who stood against the wall, and the Richter agents flanking the emperor and the door focused their attention on the oldest of the men in the room. For a man with as frail a body as his, the Blessed Emperor's voice's voice had a commanding power to it. "We trust the unfortunate business with your former organization has been dealt with, Lord von Harenheim?"

Marius allowed the smile to vanish from his face as he nodded. "Yes, Your Excellency. It appalls me that I saw no evidence of their collusion with the Crimson Fangs, and while I still mourn the lives damaged and lost by their infidelity to our glorious empire, I would like to extend my gratitude once again to Grand Master Richter for the aid his noble order of hunters provided in quelling the uprising and mitigating the damage they could have caused."

Caspar Richter nodded. "Had your new project, the Dieneryn, not proved so effective, we would have had a much more difficult time. As distasteful as I find the idea, making those who betrayed us useful in our defense in a way that spares the lives of honorable citizens is acceptable. And according to my agents, their performance exceeded all expectations in both efficacy and efficiency."

Marius nodded and allowed the smile to return to his face. The gruff bass voice of High General Krank broke the momentary silence. "How long before you've enough of these *things* to form a proper division?"

"Now, I must protest," High Exarch Bohnoepfer said, raising his left hand. "Though the bodies used in the creation of these automatons are those of traitors, heretics, and criminals, they are still sentient, living beings, and as both Saint Hurud and Saint Hiltegardt have taught us in their meditations, all life is sacred, being breathed into existence by the souls of the gods. The Lord of Sky and Storm demands they be respected as such."

"They are." Marius Bedwyr extended his left hand toward the High Exarch in a calming, conciliatory gesture. "The choice is laid before them. They may choose to be executed, have their corpses hung from the streets of Sonnenburg, and allow their souls to be forever damned, or they can choose the path of service, knowing that the suffering they experience during their transformation works to purge their soul of impurity and redeem it upon the eventual cessation of function."

He then turned to High General Krank and added, "To answer your question, High General, given the current production time, three months."

"We'll need to speed that up," Krank said.

"Again, I must ask," Bohnoepfer's tone grew more insistent as he spoke "I must ask how long will they exist in this limbo between life and death?"

Marius paused in thought. "My technomagi estimate that the power cores on the Kriegsdieneryn alone could last for ten years, but without the Society for Afterlife and Arcane Research providing a supply of Ashfodellian fiends to bind to those crystals, additional empowerment crystals must be added, thus slowing production."

"Ashfodellian fiends?" The High Exarch gasped, his face awashed in horror. He turned to the emperor and pleaded, "Your Excellency, as the leader of our church, I must protest the use of such entities in official capacities. While this may be efficient and efficacious, we must think of the spiritual ramific—"

The Blessed Emperor raised a single finger on his right hand and hurled a scathing glare at the High Exarch. "We are aware of the spiritual ramifications of this, and we have considered it. Our own meditations with the Lord of Sky and Storm have led us to believe it to be acceptable to our holy god. We would also take time to remind the High Exarch that he is but the second highest ranking member of our church, after ourself. Yes?"

Shame flushed the High Exarch's face. He lowered his gaze and nodded. "Yes, Your Excellency, forgive me."

The comm ring on Marius' left hand buzzed and flashed three times. The emperor turned his steely but tired gaze toward the vampire and said, "Lord von Harenheim, is that private communication more important than this meeting?"

Marius feigned shock at the message, hiding his left hand in the pocket of his trousers but moving it in a way to accidentally brush the High Exarch's pen off the table. "Pay it no mind, Your Excellency. It is merely a requested update that our newest batch of construction Dieneryn have been completed and are ready to be shipped to their destination." He looked down at the floor. "Oh dear. It seems I've made a bit of a mess. Allow me."

Marius snapped his fingers. One of his attendants moved forward, sliding a hand into his pocket. The attendant dropped to a knee while leaning over to hide the High Exarch's pen from view as he removed his hand from his pocket—taking care to conceal the pen hidden by his downturned palm—and picked up the High Exarch's pen. He then rose to his feet, placed the pen from his pocket onto the table, and pocketed the High Exarch's pen.

As he backed away from the table, Marius nodded and smiled. "Thank you, Stefan."

The High Holy Council Meeting continued as normal. The final order of business was the ratification of an increased sales tax to fund an increase in spending on military weapons to replace those recently stolen by the Crimson Fangs and to increase production of the Kriegsdieneryn through the formation and funding of a small Imperial Order of Arcanists, to be headed by Ambrose von Harenheim. For his part, Marius begged the emperor to strike that line from the declaration, claiming such an honor was too tempting of misuse. The Blessed Emperor, with counsel from Grand Master Richter and High General Krank refused Bedwyr's request. High Exarch Bohnoepfer voiced notable opposition, but he was voted down.

The Blessed Emperor then placed the declaration on the table, signed it, and requested that all sign as well. Richter, Krank, and von Harenheim signed without incident. As the High Exarch leaned forward to sign reluctantly, Stefan pushed a button on a small remote hidden inside his pocket.

As Bohnoepfer reached the final syllable of his name, a thick cloud of pungent green gas seeped from the pen's nib. The Blessed Emperor coughed and gagged. The High Exarch dropped the pen and gasped in surprise.

Grand Master Richter and High General Krank leaped to their feet. Caspar pointed to the agents flanking the emperor. "Garrus, Reinholdt, apprehend the High Exarch. Ambrose, you have arcane training. Do you know what happened?"

Marius pointed to the pen. "May I?"

The emperor nodded, and Marius scooped the pen in his hands. He examined the nib, and then he took the pen apart. Thoughtful and contemplative sounds slipped through his closed lips. He nodded and then said, "I can't be certain of the substance without a full alchemical investigation. However, inside this pen is a mechanism designed to allow a small amount of poison, likely contained inside the ink, to seep through the nib when enough pressure is applied. There are several poisons that, when exposed to air, will transmute into gaseous form. Fortunately for us, this one was neither colorless nor odorless."

One of the attendants offered the Blessed Emperor a glass of water. As he drank, Grand Master Richter turned to the other two agents and said, "Search the St. Victus Cathedral—including the Exarchial Palace. If you find anything, bring it here at once."

They nodded and left the chamber. Sweat beaded on the High Exarch's forehead. "Your Excellency, we have had our philosophical differences, but I have never wished anything but honor, glory, and eternal praise upon you. Please, you have to know this is a misunderstanding caused by one who wishes me gone."

"We shall reserve our judgment, Klauz Bohnoepfer, for the presentation of evidence. Until then, we will all wait here, and you will be bound."

The two Richters who now flanked Bohnoepfer produced handcuffs and snapped them around his wrists. The High Exarch nodded, slumped into his chair, and stared at the floor.

An hour later, the two agents sent by Caspar Richter returned and presented him the empty vial with green ink residue and the papers. The Grand Master read the papers and then sighed. "Your Excellency, these papers here are letters from Marius Bedwyr to High Exarch Bohnoepfer, both decrying the use of the Dieneryn and thanking the High Exarch for his willingness to join their cause against us. They also detail a specific plan for the High Exarch to use poisoned ink to assassinate you." He tossed the papers and the vial onto the table. "I am certain that, when examined, the poison will be in that vial, and it will be the same as was inside the pen."

The High Exarch screeched. "Your Excellency, you can't believe this. This is false. I would never side with those abominations, and never would I betray you. Please, continue to investigate. Your wisdom will unlock the true treachery at work."

The Blessed Emperor sighed. "We shall assume full control of our holy church. Klauz Bohnoepfer, the evidence recovered from your residence aligns with behaviors we have witnessed in this room today. With our heart heavy and burdened with sorrow, we find you guilty of treason and heresy against us and our empire. Our love for you will stay the executioner's hand. You will not hang in the streets."

Bohnoepfer sighed in relief. "Thank you, Your Excellency. You are truly merciful."

"Instead, you will be delivered to the Imperium Center for the Rehabilitation of Traitors. Lord von Harenheim will determine how, as one of our servitors, you will earn your absolution. Take him away."

Amid the screams and pleads by the former High Exarch, the two members of the Holy Order of St. Arnulf Ironhand led the condemned man from the chamber. Caspar Richter and Augustus Krank shook their heads. A faint smirk twitched on Marius Bedwyr's lips, baring the tiniest hint of fang.

Chapter 14

Two days passed since Gwyn and Karina left the ruins of Fáchrives and traveled south to Clérmontán where they were set to meet with Honor Faern'doln and Xrissa Kosol and then plan Courage's rescue. Clérmontán was the capital of Froam before the nation became a vassal state of the Atharian Empire. Brightly painted pastel townhouses with white oak trim lined the cobblestone streets, which were illuminated by wrought iron crystal lamps. The growing heat did little to calm or silence the vendors in the central market, who shouted their wares to customers huddling under the shade of colorful umbrellas.

Karina's arms were wrapped around Gwyn's waist as they shared Siobhan. A harsh breeze blew the salty air of the Myddean Sea against their faces. Few mechanomagical conveyances traversed the cobblestone streets. Karina looked around, noticed only a handful of local constabulary patrolling the streets, and asked, "Why haven't I seen the Grand Imperial Army?"

Gwyn chuckled and pushed the red sunglasses up from the tip of her nose. Her Froamian brogue grew stronger as she spoke. "Don't take this the wrong way, my dear knight, but Clérmontán, a city known for its university and theater scene, is a bit too rough and tumble for your empire's finest to handle. Don't worry. I'll protect you."

They laughed. Karina kissed Gwyn's cheek. "What is our plan for the day, my princess?"

"Well, it's almost thirteen bells. We'll check into the Moonlit Rose, and then since you need to eat and since I can still taste food, we'll grab lunch. Then, we'll get some shopping done."

Karina leaned in and whispered into Gwyn's ear. "But don't you need to eat, *you know*?"

"Blood?" Gwyn smiled. "I can go a few more days without fresh blood, maybe a week once I brew some of the alchemic blood I always have with me."

"Is that how you survived when we worked together?"

Gwyn nodded. "That and vampiric sanctuaries—hidden taverns where we can drink blood-infused spirits and..." She paused in thought before finishing the sentence. "Feed off of blood dolls."

"Blood dolls?"

"Mortals who get paid to provide consensual services. We don't drain them, and they can revoke consent at any time." Gwyn felt Karina's energy shift and darken. "If it makes you uncomfortable, I can find other ways to get sustenance."

"What about me?" Karina's voice came in a soft, terrified whisper. She removed one hand from Gwyn's waist to rub her neck.

"After what Marius did to you—and what he almost did to you—I was not going to ask." She licked her lips, circling the tips of her fangs with her tongue. "Not that I don't want to know how you taste, but he transformed the act of feeding from one of sensual survival to one of torment and suffering. I will promise you this, if you ever think you wish to offer your blood to me, you will have total control over the frequency, the location of my bite, and the length of my feeding. This is new to both of us."

Karina jerked her head back. "*You* have never been with another? Even I have, but you know that."

Gwyn guffawed. "Not since I became the last Vandiamante. I've had a doll for an hour or a lover for a night, but I've never stayed in one place for long. And I've been with no mortal since my turning. There are things we will need to discuss before my coronation."

"Coronation?"

Gwyn gasped in mock surprise. "You didn't know? My grandfather, Gyocomus Vandiamante, was a Hertogius in the Florescian court, but he was also Sezar of the Midnight Court that governs all vampires. When I became the last of my line, I became the next in line for that throne. That's where I was headed when we met, both times."

"You are a princess." Karina's voice rose from shock to excitement and then fell to a more personal concern and fear. "Where will that leave me?"

Gwyn signaled for Siobhan to slow her pace. The vampire leaned back and wrapped an arm around Karina's neck. Her tone was gentle. "Wherever you decide to be. We've options, but I know there's a lot about me that will take you time to grow accustomed to. Well, here we are."

Built during the heyday of the Froamian theater scene during the thirteenth century of the Age of Arcanum, the Moonlit Rose was a three-story building of white stone with a facade meant to evoke the ancient grandeur of a Zyntarian temple from the Age of Faith. Four fluted columns supported the second floor balcony, designed with a sculpture of the great Froamian hero Cu'Chlaran slaying the Arenthian Boar set in the triangular pediment.

Illuminated by crystal chandeliers, the interior was one of warmth and elegance. Hand-woven rugs adorned the oak floorboards. An elegant filigree of pink roses with their thorny stems stood out on the pale yellow wallpaper. The lobby had a stone hearth that flickered and warmed a small cauldron of oil scented with the essences of rose, violet, and gardenia. Leather furnishings surrounded the hearth, providing places of rest for those waiting for their rooms to be ready or for hired carriages to arrive.

Karina froze and stiffened. This place looked expensive. Sure, Gwyn was a princess, and her family had aristocratic title—not that she remained in the line of succession after being expelled from the Holy Order that demanded austerity and frugality. The twenty torbal her father provided for her first, and only, solo vampire hunt was little more than enough to cover the reserved hotel room and porridge for breakfast. Her breathing quickened, but she followed Gwyn to the reception desk.

"Welcome to the Moonlit Rose Inn, I'm Janelle. How many nights?" The receptionist was an attractive Human woman with black skin and curly hair.

Gwyn smiled. "Thank you, Janelle. We're meeting someone here, and I'm not sure if she's arrived. Has an Honor Faern'doln checked in?"

"Let me check." She scanned the guest book and shook her head. "I don't see anyone in that name. I'm sorry."

"Don't be." Gwyn shook her head. "I'll reserve her a room too, but I'm not sure when she'll arrive. So, that'll be two rooms for four nights—just to be safe. Can you keep the key for her at the desk?"

Janelle checked the books. "That's not a problem. We can easily accommodate that. That will be four hundred torbal for the two rooms. Is that okay?"

Karina's eyes bulged in her head, but Gwyn simply slid the rectangular coins across to the receptionist. Janelle smiled as she accepted the money and then handed Gwyn two keys to room twenty-seven.

As they ascended the stairs, Karina sputtered her words. "This place—you just paid—The stipend for my one hunt Father provided me wasn't enough for one night here. How?"

Gwyn shrugged. "I make good coin doing what I do, and on those nights I get to rest, I choose to do so with at least a modicum of luxury." Using her full strength, Gwyn pushed the taller woman against the wall and then purred into her ear. "You won't complain about the bed."

The vampire spun on her heels and continued walking. Karina released a breath she didn't know she had sucked in. She swallowed hard as she watched Gwyn's hips swaying as she walked. Her eyes widened, and she gasped. Karina blushed, then smiled, and then followed after Gwyn.

Room twenty-seven was a massive three-room suite with a sitting room, a bathroom, and a bedroom. The blue wallpaper was a tone-on-tone robin-egg blue filigree. Both the sitting room and the bedroom had full-length windows behind midnight purple curtains that opened to the balcony. The sofa and chairs were fog gray leather with golden accents, and the desk and coffee table were of varnished oak. The bedding on the canopy bed was fog gray and midnight purple, and at the far end of the bathroom and situated within a raised alcove and beneath a skylight sat a claw foot bathtub of white marble large enough for two people.

Karina sat on the bed, and as she sank into the pillow top mattress, she allowed herself to fall onto her back. A soft moan escaped her lips. "This bed is like a cloud. It's like sitting in Mother's lap as she hugged me. Even my parents' bedroom isn't this massive and opulent."

Gwyn slipped off her riding boots and trousers, folded them, and placed them on the dresser. Standing only in her vest, blouse, and bloomers, she sauntered over to the bed and peered through the curtains. "Wait until we reach Utrezzo. It'll probably need to be repaired and cleaned, but you'll grow accustomed to this." After she finished, she added mentally, *if you stay*.

Karina rolled over. "I thought we were going to have lunch. Why are you removing your clothes?"

"You've never eaten naked?" Gwyn smirked, baring her fangs and laughing. "I'm changing into something clean."

She slipped into the walking skirt that transformed into trousers that Countess Sazkyeerts had commissioned for her and then slipped back into her riding boots. The skirt swished ever so slightly as Gwyn spun to fix her hair in the mirror only to frown at her lack of reflection what was likely a silver-backed mirror. With a sigh, she ran her fingers through her hair and then donned her hat once more.

Karina stared with a slacked jaw as her heart rate increased. "I—wow—You look—This makes me want to see you in a gown."

Gwyn grabbed a menu from atop the dresser, sauntered to the bed, and sat beside Karina. As the former vampire hunter rolled over to lay her head in Gwyn's lap, Gwyn stroked the woman's black hair. "You'll get the chance. Riding trousers are practical for riding and hunting, but I'll soon be wearing dresses and gowns again." She tossed the menu onto Karina's lap. "Here. Let's order lunch."

Without moving, Karina opened the menu and scanned it. "You don't want to go to the restaurant?"

Shaking her head, Gwyn continued stroking Karina's hair. "Bad Galenic—wait, why am I still saying that? Look, we can walk around in the day, but day-walking sickness is a lot like a Galenic. Oh, and the sun is fucking bright today. I'd like to rest a bit before we get our shopping done."

"You mentioned purchasing alchemical supplies. Will you be purchasing the reagents to make the ones to help with your condition?"

"Nope. I won't kill a unicorn."

"What?" Karina rolled over, sat up, and looked into Gwyn's eyes.

"It's a required reagent," Gwyn said. "I have two left from the six Deputy Director Mueller supplied us with, but I won't use any of those until we find Courage. And beyond a damned riddle the Sythrokli Oracle told me when I asked where he and you were, I don't know where to begin."

"Even I don't know where I was. What did it say?"

Gwyn shrugged. "She said you were off questing for a blade but were beyond her sight."

Karina tilted her head. "I wasn't looking for a blade. I wanted to find you and apologize. What did the oracle say about Courage's location?"

"Something about beneath a mountain with iron and liquid fire and giving life to damned souls."

Karina scratched the back of her neck as she thought. "The first part of that suggests Courage could be in Dornbach or Iszenstadt—maybe even Ullinburg—as they're all near the Shunkrir Peaks. The Crimson Fangs have a facility in Iszenstadt. That's where Father collected me, and..."

Karina's voice trailed to silence. The scene in Marius' office flashed before her eyes where he mockingly said, *Your little Ashbourne is safe, for now. He has skills I have a use for and information I need.*

Gwyn wrapped her arms around Karina, holding her tight. The vampire kissed the Human's forehead. "What is it? Do you know?"

Karina gritted her teeth and kicked the bed. "I was so close. The facility I was in was a medical facility of some sort—a black building—but Marius said Courage was safe because he had skills and information. After I left home, I could have gone after him."

"And you would have died. Fuck, we still might, but we fought off an army of angry spirits and Ashfodellian fiends before Marius fucking outed me. That won't happen this time. Unless you've got a family secret, he won't be able to use that against us."

Karina thought for a moment. "My mother was a Putnici wanderer. It was something Father said to hide to be marriageable."

Gwyn planted a gentle kiss on Karina's lips. "That won't be an issue. Now let's order lunch."

They dined. After lunch, they deposited their traveling clothes to be laundered before leaving the Moonlit Rose for shopping. After purchasing Gwyn's needed alchemical supplies from the Apothecary's Attic, the vampire allowed Karina to choose the clothier who would provide her new outfits. After Karina balked at the offer of both choice of clothing and of multiple outfits, she selected the Hunting Gentleman. She selected a practical outfit that resembled the one she was wearing, but this leather vest was longer and had a tone-on-tone filigree pattern. For her traveling attire, she chose a cream shirt with a detachable jabot, black leather trousers with a gold tuxedo stripe, a red vest with gold buttons and trim, a black leather frock coat with gold buttons and trim, and a black opera coat with red lining. Gwyn smiled in approval of each choice.

They exited the Hunting Gentleman as the sun neared the western horizon. Unaware of the hooded man who followed them for a short distance before turning into an alley, the smiling vampire said, "You've done your research, Miss Skejik, selecting the colors on the Vandiamante coat of arms."

"Well, *Hertogia* Vandiamante, I was hoping my first solo hunt would be to find the last heir. We are all trained to recognize your scarlet wildcat holding a golden fasces at the center of a black field."

Gwyn slid her arm inside Karina's. "And you found her. Let's get back to the inn, have supper, and then—"

At that moment, Honor Faern'doln's voice protruded into Gwyn's head. "The godsdamned fucking train broke down just outside of Czarnenburg. We won't get to Clérmontán now until the day after tomorrow."

Gwyn nodded. "Honor, we've reserved you a room at the Moonlit Rose. The key is at the reception desk. All is paid. Wind-backed travels." Gwyn smiled and returned her attention to Karina. "The night and tomorrow are ours."

Gwyn and Karina dined at the inn's attached restaurant. Once they returned to their room, Karina wrapped her arms around Gwyn's waist and spun the vampire in a circle, causing her to squeal and then giggle. Gwyn placed her arms around Karina's neck, and the pair danced a brief but proper dance. Karina leaned down and planted a tentative, gentle kiss on Gwyn's lips, which the vampire joyfully returned.

As Karina broke the kiss, she said, "I never forgot how brightly you smiled when you danced while enjoying your food."

Gwyn flashed a smile as she sat on the sofa in the suite's sitting room. "I swear vampirism has made every sensation more powerful. Shame this is tinged by the fact that I'll lose all sense of taste for mortal food in just over nine decades. Won't get any nourishment from it either."

Karina sat next to her, leaning back into the leather cushion. Gwyn slid over and rested her head on Karina's shoulder. Karina brushed Gwyn's cheek with her left hand while kissing her forehead. The vampire sighed in contentment.

"Will you lose the ability to taste other things as well?"

Gwyn nuzzled into the crick of Karina's neck, inhaling her spiced and woodsy aroma. She nibbled Karina's earlobe and purred, "I hope not. If my family's behavior is any indication, the only issue will be a partner with enough stamina to keep up."

Karina nodded. Why was she hesitating? Her heart quickened its pace. Gwyn would notice that. Hesitation cost her a chance in Sonnenburg. Pray? No. Prayer took too long even when the gods answered.

"Your heart is thundering, Rina." Concern softened Gwyn's words. "Are you well?"

Something twitched inside Karina's body as Gwyn slipped a nickname—not her first name, not her knight in black leather, and not the distasteful *little Richter*—but a nickname, a pet name that was, or could be, just between them. Her body flushed with heat, and she uttered a quick, sharp gasp.

This is it, Karina thought.

"I am not well. No, I'm—no. From the moment in that vile orphanage where you spoke to me as *Karina* and as *your knight* and not as a Richter, I've wanted nothing more than to touch you, to hold you, to kiss you. That moment revealed that what I wanted more than all I've wanted—more than my father's love and praise—was to be by your side. And during my exile from my family, from my god, from you I told myself my search for you was because I needed to apologize for my actions. That was not true."

Karina shifted, and Gwyn sat up, confusion widening her eyes. Gwyn nodded. Her words came in a whisper only a breath's volume above silence. "Okay. I see."

Karina closed her eyes for a moment and took one deep breath. She clasped Gwyn's hands in her own and stared deep into the vampire's trembling green eyes. "I wanted to apologize to you, but I needed you to forgive me. And I craved you to love me. Each waking moment I spent as I traveled from Ullinburg to Fáchrives was half agony, half hope. And then I found you. And now..."

Karina paused. She dropped to one knee before Gwyn. As she lifted her gaze to meet the Elven vampire's slightly confused expression, Karina said, "I give myself to you with a heart that is more yours than it has ever been mine. I will be your knight if that is all you wish of me, but I beg you to know that I love you."

Tears welled in the corners of Karina's eyes. Her voice trembled and cracked as she spoke, the cracks growing in frequency and intensity. And she sat and waited.

Gwyn nodded. "I love you too. After we separated, I cursed myself for being unable to not think about you, unable to relieve stress with a blood doll because *you* were the one I wanted, and unable to stop loving you. I want you by my side, and it should be obvious, I want you in my bed. And I had hoped when you appeared two days ago that we could pick up where we left off.

"But as much as I want that, you betrayed me. Yes, I wasn't forthcoming about my identity, and I wanted to tell you—eventually, after realizing I cared for you. But you betrayed me. You weren't upset at learning my last name is Vandiamante. You pulled your pistol and attacked me without hesitation. That's not something we can just pretend didn't happen."

Karina nodded. A heavy lump filled her throat, and swallowing did not remove it. Her cheeks burned with shame, and her muscles tensed. This was how it felt when hope died.

And then Gwyn leaned forward and brushed the back of her hand on Karina's cheeks. A faint, gentle smile drifted across the vampire's lips, and both love and compassion filled her eyes. "I will promise you this—and this arises from my own selfish desires—we will start again. This time, let there be no secrets between us. A queen cannot rule if she deceives those closest to her, and a knight cannot serve with honor if she deceives her queen. I love you, Karina Alyxandra Skejik. I probably always will. This is what I can offer in honesty."

Karina relaxed and released the breath she held. She nodded. "I accept." And she kissed the back of Gwyn's hand.

Chapter 15

While Gwyn and Karina had an important conversation inside their suite at the Moonlit Rose, a red crystal illuminated on the communication device in Marius Bedwyr's office on the top floor of the Imperium Center for the Rehabilitation of Traitors. He looked up from his book and lifted an eyebrow. Crimson Fang business. Folding the corner of the page he was on, Marius closed the book and set it on the table. He lifted the handset and pressed the answer button.

"Lord Marius," the masculine voice that emerged through the handset's speaker said. "We have eyes on the Vandiamante heir. Agents have spotted her in Clérmontán, walking the streets alongside that Richter girl."

Marius snarled. "Are you certain it was her?"

"Yes, sir. The report says she's even going by Vandiamante now. Not hiding who she is."

The leader of the Crimson Fangs scoffed. "Either Severus Richter has failed, or this bitch is taking her time returning to Florescia."

"Shall we engage, sir? We can make it look like the Richter girl killed her and then offed herself."

Marius shook his head. "No. I need her dead, but a

disgraced Richter's actions will not have the needed impact of the Holy Order slaying a beloved hero of the people. Do we know their current location?"

"Not with any precision, sir. The report has them in the vicinity of the Moonlit Rose Inn."

"Of course." Marius nodded. "Florescian nobles have long chosen that inn when visiting my old home. Unfortunate news, but thank you. Keep eyes on them, and report when you have a precise location."

"Yes, sir."

The call ended. Marius rose from his chair and stood before the map on the wall behind him. Glaring at the movement, he moved the white queen and the black knight to Clérmontán. Tapping his index finger against his chin, he sighed. "I need her dead, and I need imperial forces to kill her during a moment we might spin to gain public sympathy and evoke rage in Florescia that leads to war. If I can convince the Grand Army to conquer Florescia, then my throne can be on Clérmontán—in the center of my empire. This may be the last chance."

He returned to his chair and dialed a line on the communication device. When a familiar Atharian male voice responded, Marius said, "Caspar, it's Ambrose. I hope all is well, but it is with a heavy heart I contact you."

"Have you an update on Severus' location, Ambrose? He has not responded to attempts at communication."

Marius bared his fangs in a smirk. He then removed the smirk with a heavy, performative sigh. "It is with great sorrow that I must assume he has died, Caspar. Word has reached me from those abroad that the Vandiamante heir has been spotted in Clérmontán and that your poor, deluded daughter is by her side."

Caspar's audible growling sigh slid through the communication line. "She has made her choice. I will send agents to kill them."

"Might I make one request, old friend?"

"Ambrose, I cannot let them live. I don't want to hear about love or whatever nonsense my daughter might put forward about this abomination being a good person."

"Quite the contrary," Marius said. "I ask for you to make one final attempt at forgiving your daughter. Go yourself. Show her the contrast between a father's holy love and the unhallowed charms of the vampire. Break the hold the bitch has on her. Return your daughter to the flock of the righteous, and together, slay the beast."

There was silence as Caspar Richter considered the request. After a moment, he said, "Her mother would want that. Do you know their location in the city?"

"Not with precision, but reports place them in the vicinity of the Moonlit Rose."

"I can be there by late morning. Can your sources keep me abreast of their movements?"

Marius smiled. "Oh, yes. Yes we can." He ended the call.

The night passed without incident, but in the morning, an icy jolt raked across Karina's back. Her eyes shot wide, and she sprang into a sitting position only to find herself in the soft bed in the Moonlit Rose with the sleeping body of Gwynarra Vandiamante falling over, her slender pale arm draped across the bed in a manner that reminded Karina Gwyn slept with an arm wrapped around her. Karina smiled a wistful, pained smile.

At least she didn't send me away—or kill me, Karina thought. *I would have deserved either for what I did. And I have a chance to make it right.*

Karina brushed her fingers over Gwyn's icy cheek. The vampire didn't move, didn't smile, and didn't moan—the way Ailinya did. The death-sleep would require adjustment. Karina leaned over and kissed Gwyn's cheek before rising and taking a bath.

After her bath, Karina styled her hair in the pompadour style both she and Gwyn preferred. Karina frowned. She needed a trim. Perhaps she would slice off her hair down to her shoulders or something else less Richter. She donned her trousers and cream traveling shirt.

Karina's nose wrinkled as she walked into the sitting room and saw, and smelled, Gwyn's alchemical equipment. She didn't want the stench in the bedroom, and their conversation lasted well into the night, so she allowed the final phase, the coagulation of the serum, to continue throughout the night and the morning as she slept. The dripping liquid reeked of flaming rotting onions, but it looked and moved like blood. A thought crossed Karina's lips, but she winced as the wounds on her neck burned for an instant.

Kneeling in the center of the room, Karina grasped at her neck. She shook her head. The holy symbol she once wore was likely discarded by the family's servants—or it remained on the floor of her childhood bedroom. Karina shook her head, clasped her hands, and lowered her gaze.

Her voice trembled as she spoke. "Lord of Sky and Storm, hear my plea. I've not spoken to you in weeks, and for that I beg forgiveness. These last few weeks have been difficult, and I have been and felt alone. What happened defies all I know how to explain, but somehow, my journey brought me to the woman I sought. She's granted me a second chance I…I am uncertain I deserve. If you had any hand in that, thank you. Now, I ask—I don't know how to ask this—but I ask…help."

Karina rose, returned to the bedroom, and finished dressing. She walked over to the desk and penned a quick note that she placed atop Gwyn's clothing. *Running two quick errands and unsure when you'll awaken. Wait for me. Love, K.* She reached the bedroom's door, paused, and then turned back. Thieves and criminals exist in all cities, she thought as she grabbed both her pistol and the silvered long knife.

As Karina approached the door, she paused and listened. A familiar masculine voice, muffled by the wall between them seemed to say, "We should knock. It's polite. There's no reason to barge in like we're trying to—" Thunderous knocking on the suite's door interrupted him, but Karina heard an audible sigh as the man said, "To wake the dead."

Karina stood near the door and spoke in a commanding tone that dropped her already husky voice half an octave. "Who is it? Speak your business."

Her eyes burst wide, and she staggered back as her father's voice responded in an equally commanding tone. "Karina Alyxandra Richter, do not take that tone of voice with me. Open the door this instant."

Karina tensed and sucked in a breath. She narrowed her eyes and then opened the door. Her father, Caspar Richter barged into the suite, flintlock in one hand and wooden stake in the other. His narrowed eyes scanned the room. Tottering after him was the first voice, Karina's cousin Garrus Richter, a tall man with warm brown hair and an unexpected trembling at the corners that threatened to sour the perpetual smile on his face.

"Father, Garrus, what are you doing here? How did you know I'd be here?"

Caspar wrapped his daughter in a long, tight hug. Karina looked confused. As he pulled away, the eldest of the Richters smiled and sighed. "Even after your insistent slander, Ambrose von Harenheim wants nothing but the best for you, my daughter. He received word that you and that Vandiamante whore were seen together, but instead of retribution, upon his counsel, I offer you a father's love and forgiveness."

Karina pushed away from him. "Marius knows we're here," she whispered, perhaps too loudly.

"Why do you persist in spreading lies about one of the High Holy Council?"

"Hi, Karina," Garrus waved from behind his uncle.

"I'm not lying, father." Karina growled her words. Her nostrils flared, and her cheeks flushed. "Ambrose von Harenheim is Marius Bedwyr. He is the man who did this to me." She pointed to the wounds on her neck. "Not Gwyn. And as far as your love and forgiveness, where was that when you expelled me from our Holy Order and our family?"

Caspar lifted a paternal finger in warning. "Karina, you need to understand the stress of hearing your daughter, who is barely an adult, was almost killed in—"

"I am twenty-five, father. I am not barely an adult."

His eyes narrowed, and he scowled. With nostrils flaring, he said, "And yet you persist in acting like a child. Regardless, the fear of your near-death, the sight of that bite mark on your neck, and the learning of your corruption by that vile Vandiamante spawn struck me with a grief no father deserves to bear. Then you persisted in your lies about Ambrose. And now, I find you here, guarding this abomination."

He snarled the final world and leaped forward, slamming the barrel of his pistol into the alchemical flasks. They shattered, spilling their contents onto the table and floor. Karina shrieked.

"Why would you do that?"

Caspar pointed at the crimson serum oozing onto the floor. "Do you know what that is? That is how monsters like your precious Vandiamante survive when they cannot feast on sinful wretches such as yourself."

"She won't feed on me." Karina's voice was flat with a trembling undercurrent of building rage. "Marius broke—or almost broke—some central tenet of vampires, and she doesn't…" Karina paused, took a deep breath, and smiled, calming her voice. "She respects my body, my heart, and my consent, father. Something you never did when training became terrifying or painful. You will replace what you have destroyed."

"I will do no such thing. How dare you side with this monster after what her family did to ours? After she killed your cousin Severus."

Caspar shouted his words. Karina puffed out her chest and squared up to her father. "Gwyn didn't kill Severus. I did, because I saw him attack an innocent woman, kneeling atop a mass grave and mourning her murdered parents."

Garrus rushed between them and extended his arms. "Now, now. We don't need to yell. There are probably people sleeping in the rooms here. They look really nice. Karina, your outfit is quite fetching. Can't we just sit down and talk like the adults we all are?"

"Get out." Karina's voice was flat.

Garrus opened his mouth to speak, but the opening of the bedroom door silenced him. Everyone turned as a naked Gwyn staggered into view, rubbing her eyes as she muttered. "I can't wait to never have to day-walk again. Ugh, Rina, what's going on? I heard a cra—ash!"

Her words lifted to a scream. Gwyn's eyes widened, and her jaw fell slack as she saw both Caspar and Garrus Richter in the suite. As she moved to cover herself, Karina drew her pistol and shifted to place herself between Gwyn and her family. Gwyn hid behind the door, peeking out to see the commotion.

"Get out." A forceful resolution filled her words as she pointed her flintlock at her father's face.

Caspar snarled. "Naked? You were in bed with this whore after what Antonio Vandiamante did to—"

The clicking of the firing mechanism silenced him. Karina snarled with intensity equal to her father's. "What Antonio Vandiamante did was love Karolinya. I found her diary. She is the one who betrayed their love by siding with our family." Her words grew choked with sorrow as realization dawned. "And I did the same, but unlike Karolinya, I have a chance to make it right. The Vandiamantes killed none of our family and none we loved—until we attacked them in their home. We are the aggressors, father. We are the monsters. You may be too proud to seek forgiveness, but I am not.

"You may be my father, but Gwyn has showed me love and acceptance that you never have, that maybe you never could. I love you, father, but I can't agree with you. I, Karina Alyxandra Skejik, love Gwynarra Caoilfhionn Vandiamante. And you will not threaten her. Get out."

"It's not too late," Garrus said. "We could all sit down and talk this out. Right? Uncle Caspar, Karina, you two love each other. Karina, I know Uncle Caspar can be a bit harsh in his words and swift in his actions, but he does love the family. He loves you. And, Uncle Caspar, Karina sees the world differently than you—or even I—she is a girl, after all. And you're both kind of stubborn. Maybe if we just talked?"

"Know your place, Garrus." Caspar turned his attention to his nephew and barked an order. Garrus stood at attention and nodded, shame flushing his cheeks. Caspar turned his attention to Karina and held out the wooden stake. "I came to offer you my love and my forgiveness for your flagrant sinfulness. Atonement alone remains, Karina. Kill your whore and end that wretched line."

Karina nodded. Gwyn tensed. Her eyes widened. In the smallest voice Karina had heard come from the vampire's soft lips, she pleaded, "Rina?"

"It is what your mother would have wanted of you."

Caspar's voice was flattened, devoid of emotion. Karina froze. Why did he have to mention her?

"Mother," Karina whispered in a tone she formerly reserved for prayer. "What should I do?"

Karina's mind raced to her childhood. The only happy memories involved her mother, playing, snuggling, feeling that maternal love. She wanted her father's love and praise, but she always had her mother's love. That was never a doubt in her waking mind or a fear in her nightmares.

A lump formed in Gwyn's throat. Her trembling hands strangled the side of the door as Karina took the stake from her father's hand. Caspar beamed. Tears formed a hazy curtain over Gwyn's eyes. Karina turned to face her and made some gesture while mouthing words Gwyn didn't recognize. Karina tossed the stake into the air and caught it so her hand held the tip. Gwyn slammed her eyes shut.

Karina raised her arm and swung. Gwyn screamed. A grunt and then a thud sounded. Garrus screamed, "No!"

When Gwyn opened her eyes, she saw Caspar Richter lying on the floor. His chest rose and fell, but he did not move otherwise. Karina throw the stake onto the floor and pointed her pistol at her father. Her eyes blazed as she turned her gaze from him to Garrus. "How dare you profane her legacy! Garrus, get him out of here. And know that if any in the Holy Order of St. Arnulf Ironhand ever threaten Gwynnara Vandiamante again, I will burn the entire fucking order to the ground. Go."

Garrus nodded. "It was good to see you again, cousin. Best of luck." And with a series of heaves and false starts, he managed to scoop his uncle over his shoulder and carry him from the room.

Karina slammed the door behind them and then locked it. Trembling, Gwyn stepped toward her in small, tentative movements. The vampire's eyes were wide, and her jaw trembled as she tried to speak but found herself unable to produce sound.

Karina rushed toward her and wrapped the terrified vampire in her arms. Gwyn nuzzled against Karina's chest. Through the heavy movements of breathing, Gwyn heard Karina's heartbeat. The faintest of smiles slid across her lips, and she whispered, "My knight."

"You are safe now, my princess. I'm sorry you had to see that."

Gwyn shook her head. "No. I'm sorry you had to do that.

It hurts to lose family—in any way."

Karina smiled. She nuzzled Gwyn's face and kissed her forehead. "Aside from my mother and Garrus, you and Courage have shown me more love and genuine acceptance than my family ever has." Her gaze shifted to the coffee table. "I'll replace the equipment my father destroyed."

Gwyn looked over and surveyed the damage. "That's what the crash was. Replacing it will be no issue, but thank you."

Gwyn's smile grew broader. Her stomach rumbled, and a gurgle sounded from her throat. Karina brushed Gwyn's cheek with her thumb. "You're hungry."

The vampire nodded. Karina closed her eyes and took a deep breath. She exhaled, lifted Gwyn's gaze to meet her own, and said, "Then drink of me."

Gwyn hesitated. "Are you…are you sure?"

Karina nodded. "I am yours."

"Karina Alyxandra Skejik, as this will be the first time I have fed upon you, I must ask you one question. You are free to speak the negative answer, and you are free to demand the process of feeding end at any point. I will respect that wish. Now, do you consent to allowing me to drink your blood?"

Karina nodded. "I consent to that and more, should you desire to do so."

"That is a vague statement," Gwyn smirked as she spoke. Her voice grew huskier as she purred her next words. "Can't have that. Tell me what you want, what you desire of me."

Karina tensed. Her cheeks flushed, and she sucked in a breath. After swallowing hard, she said, "I…well…I've read in books that a vampire's bite is kind of orgasmic. So, I thought… well…maybe…you'd bite my inner thigh, and since you're down there you could…"

Karina paused and made a face that said, *You know*. Gwyn chuckled and stole a quick kiss, nibbling on Karina's lower lip as she pulled away. "What do I know? Say it."

"And I want you to lick the nectar from my flower."

Karina spat her words out with the haste of a child fleeing punishment. Without breaking eye contact, Gwyn smirked and then licked her lips. "You want me to slide my tongue between the lips of your pussy and give you more pleasure? Is that it?"

Karina nodded. "And then I'll do the same for you."

"As much as I desire both," Gwyn said, her hungry eyes locked on Karina's. "I must decline. What you just did for me—for us—was both noble and difficult. I do not want our first time together to be on such terms."

Karina's countenance fell and darkened. "But I thought—"

Gwyn smiled as she placed a single, slender index finger over Karina's lips. "I want you more than you can know, but my love for you blazes brighter than any selfish desires of mine." She wrapped her arms around Karina and kissed her neck. "We will make love, but both of us must be ready physically, mentally, and emotionally for the act."

Karina sighed and nodded. "Please, Gwyn, I love you. Let me still feed you."

"Do you still grant me consent to drink your blood?"

Karina nodded. "I do."

Gwyn asked, "Please, so as to not be any more tempting than you already are, is there another place from which you will allow me to feed?"

Karina paused in thought. With a tone of slight embarrassment, she said, "In training, we were taught vampires only fed from the neck or the inner thigh, as you were both predators and degenerates."

Gwyn chuckled. Her whispered words tingled in Karina's ear, sending a shiver down her spine. "We are predators, but degeneracy varies for each of us. I do enjoy a bit of debauchery on occasion. However, more to the point, I can feed from anywhere your blood travels. With the inner thigh off the table, I would suggest either the neck—which is a classic location—or your left wrist. You are right-handed, my darling, and I'd rather not injure your sword arm."

The neck. Karina's mind flashed to Marius' two-pronged blood extraction device. Her heart quickened, but she forcibly calmed herself. She unbuttoned the cuff on her left sleeve and rolled it up to her elbow. She turned her palm toward the ceiling and offered it to Gwyn.

Gwyn smiled. "Thank you."

The vampire took hold of her beloved's wrist with her soft, gentle hands. She kissed the flesh and listened. The blood moved with a trembling quickness. Gwyn licked her lips and allowed her tongue to circle the tips of her fangs.

Gwyn's fangs pierced Karina's flesh. Karina gasped. As Gwyn pulled back to observe the dark red blood flowing, she observed Karina's puzzled expression.

"Are you finished already?"

Gwyn chuckled. "Not hardly. Just checking on you."

Karina shrugged. "Marius' device hurt more than your fangs. I guess that's good."

"He intended to hurt you. I desire the opposite. May I?"

Karina nodded. "Yes."

Placing her lips over the bleeding puncture wounds, Gwyn sucked the blood from Karina's veins. There was a warm spiciness to it unusual in Atharian blood. The vampire wiggled and bounced as she drank. Karina gasped again, and then her gasps turned to moans with each successive suck. Her breathing quickened. Warmth built inside her, fueled by Gwyn's own moans and pleasant sighing.

After a short while, Gwyn pulled her mouth away, made eye contact, and gave the wound a single, slow lick. "That will coagulate the blood and speed recovery. Thank you."

Karina nodded while panting. "I love—you're welcome. I guess I tasted good."

Gwyn pulled Karina into an embrace and kissed her, allowing Karina to taste her own blood on Gwyn's soft lips. "Wonderful. Why do you ask?"

Karina chuckled. "You did that dance you do when you're enjoying your food."

Gwyn smiled. "I've not enjoyed the taste of blood this much in years. Now, let me draw you a bath and acquire you something to eat."

Chapter 16

A few minutes after fourteen bells on the following day, Honor Faern'doln and Xrissa Kosol arrived in Clérmontán. Thick clouds of charcoal gray blanketed the sky, hiding the sun from view. Amid the roaring whir of the occasional mechanomagical engine, the only sounds filling the cool, damp air were the sound of water drops falling from roofs and the footsteps of pedestrian boots on cobblestone. A spring fog rolled in from Myddean Sea after last night's shower. Even with the streetlights blazing at full power, the fog's thickness made it difficult to see more than a few feet ahead.

The pair, with SAAMy skittering behind them, asked for directions three times before finding themselves in front of the Moonlit Rose Inn. As they surveyed the exterior, Honor whistled. "Well, this place looks like one of those fucking Age of Stone temples my dumbass little brother used to be obsessed with."

"Age of Faith," Xrissa responded. "Courage sent me drawings he made of those Zyntarian temples when he was traveling. He's got a great eye for detail. I bet that wandvolver turned out to be amazing."

Honor smirked. "He's got good taste, but he's got no sense

when it comes to focus. Well, let's see what room this Silver Scourge paid for."

The two women squinted and shielded their eyes as the crystal chandeliers glowed with the light of noon of a summer's day. SAAMy's metal legs clacked as the automaton skittered behind the two women. They made their way to the reception desk where a tall and slender Snow Elf man with slicked blond hair looked down his nose at them. His voice was colder than the weather outside. "Welcome to the Moonlit Rose. The name on the reservation is?"

Honor's Edriu brogue thickened as she spoke. "Should be under Honor Faern'doln. The Silver Scourge said she reserved it for us and left the key here."

His eyebrow lifted, and his voice suggested doubt as he scanned the register. "Verily? Allow me to check. It does seem there is a reservation under your name and—what is this?" He balked in shock as he read the note beside the reservation. "Instructions for us to contact Hertogia Vandiamante in suite twenty-seven upon your arrival. One moment."

Using the call box at the desk, he called the suite. Karina answered, "Hello?"

"Yes, Hertogia Vandaimante, this is the reception desk."

"The Hertogia is in the bath. I am her protector. What is the message?"

The reception desk attendant said, "We have a note to contact her when Miss Faern'doln arrives. She is here. What shall I tell her?"

"Send them to their suite," Karina said. "We'll join them there in an hour."

"Very well. They are in suite thirty-one. Have a good day." He ended the call and returned his attention to Honor and

Xrissa. "You have two more nights reserved in suite thirty-one. The Hertogia and her knight will join you there in one hour."

He handed Honor the key. She smiled. "Thank you very much."

They ascended their stairs to their suite, which was identical to Gwyn and Karina's save that the central color was a pale yellow. Xrissa squealed and whistled. "This place is bigger than my first flat and my shop in Al'Adara combined."

Honor nodded. "My place while I was in the conservatory was as big as this one room. Wouldn't mind coming back here when I can enjoy it more." Her face darkened, and her voice fell as she stared out the window onto the cityscape. "I hope that idiot is okay."

SAAMy crawled onto the sofa beside Xrissa. His googly eyes bounced, and he whistled happily as she stroked the mechanical crossbow. "He will be. He has to be. Courage is smart enough to survive."

"I don't know." Honor shook her head. "Something about the way the Corvidiae described the place has me worried. And then the whole thing about the red king, a white queen, and the black knight. What the hell does chess have to do with this?"

An hour passed before Gwyn and Karina knocked on the door of suite thirty-one. Xrissa reached the door first and opened it. Seeing the pair in their traveling clothes, the Moon Elf smiled. "Hi! I'm Xrissa. This is SAAMy, and that's Honor. You probably figured that out."

Gwyn smiled. "So you're the baker we've heard so much about. I'm Gwynarra Vandiamante, and this is my knight and lover, Karina Skejik."

"You know about me?" Xrissa looked puzzled.

"Courage only speaks on three topics, his wandvolver, his family, and this Moon Elf baker who's the most beautiful and brilliant woman in the world."

Xrissa beamed. Karina bowed. Honor's face brightened. She pointed at Gwyn. "You're the one I spoke to, the Silver Scourge, white hair and a title. And the knight, wearing black. Guess we were supposed to find you two."

Gwyn and Karina tilted their heads. They sat in empty seats. Karina said, "What?"

"Sorry," Honor said. "Fucking Corvidiae riddle mentioned something about a red king's attack causing the black knight to fold and the white queen to weep. Whatever the fuck chess has to do with any of this."

"Oddly enough," Gwyn said. "A lot."

She and Karina explained their past to Honor and Xrissa. They contextualized it to include how they met Courage, their work for the Society for Afterlife and Arcane Research, and their falling out. Karina provided the details of the giant chess board atop the SAAR headquarters, which included red, white, and black armies. They ended by narrating their individual journeys after Bedwyr revealed the truth of Gwyn's identity to their reunion and reconciliation.

Honor exhaled and whistled. "Fuck, that's heavy. You two've got your own issues to work through, but you both seem to love my dumbass of a little brother. Neither of you got a riddle from the Corvidiae?"

Karina nodded. Gwyn shrugged. "No, but I did get a riddle from the Sythrokli Oracle with striking similarities to Rina's riddle. And we think we've got an idea of where he is. Rina?"

"Yes. Gwyn's riddle mentioned something about beneath a

black mountain of iron and living fire."

"Fuck! They told me to seek the place of iron's glow with fierce fires. You saying he's at a forge?"

Karina closed her eyes. "When I woke up, I was in a medical facility, I assume, in a black building in Iszenstadt on the southern end of the Shunkrir Peaks. It's an iron city, known for manufacturing. And while I was there, Marius said Courage was safe, because he had skills that damned vampire needed. Then I remembered Courage making a prosthetic leg for that physician we rescued, and it made sense to connect those dots."

Honor nodded. "It's our best guess. So, what's the plan? We take the rail straight there, break my brother out, and then...what?"

Everyone looked at Gwyn. And she felt the weight of their concern on her shoulders. She nodded in thought for a moment. "I need to make a call first, but if all goes as I hope, I suggest we take the rail to Dornbach and then hire a carriage to get us to Iszenstadt. We know the Crimson Fangs are watching our movement, so if they see us moving toward Iszenstadt, they'll increase their presence there. Dornbach would be the next rail stop closest to Florescia."

Xrissa scratched her white hair. "Why would heading away from the country Courage is in be good?"

Gwyn smiled. "Because the expectation is that I'm going home, and I was going home. They'll see your weapons and that walking crossbow thing and assume I hired you as guards. In Dornbach, we hire a carriage and then head to our destination. If my call goes well, we'll have transport to my home in Utrezzo."

"Yes," Karina said. She pointed at SAAMy. "What exactly is

that?"

Xrissa beamed in a manner similar to Courage's smile when he spoke about his wandvolver. "It's SAAMy, a sentient arcane arbalest machine. I built him myself. As you can see, he has a revolving cylinder of eight vials connected to the firing mechanism by a series of tubes. Each vial contains powdered Arcanyx crystals designed to to both enchant the crossbow bolts with specific energies to mimic certain magical effects, but I can also channel the few spells I do know through SAAMy, effectively extending the range of the spells to the range of the bolt. Additionally, he has sensor crystals connected to his mobilization apparatus that allow him to move independently or function as a standard repeating heavy crossbow. I built him before I left home, and he's kept me safe as I traveled before settling down in Al'Adara."

Karina nodded. "And the eyes?"

"They're cute."

Xrissa beamed and petted SAAMy. Gwyn chuckled. She rested her head on Karina's shoulder and said, "I can see why Courage talks about her all the bloody time."

Karina nodded. Xrissa's ears twitched, and she perked up. "He…he talks about me? Courage barely talks to me unless it's technical or to buy pastries."

Honor placed a hand on Xrissa's shoulder as she winked at Gwyn. "We'll work on that. Gwyn, please make that call."

Gwyn nodded and walked to the call box. She spoke the words *Sanktaria Estate* into the handset. A few moments later and a voice, a servant, answered. "Greetings and health unto you. Dominus and Domina Sanktaria are indisposed. May this one have the name of the caller?"

"Greetings and health unto you as well. I am Hertogia

Gwynarra Vandiamante, Sezara-elect of the Midnight Court. As Dominus Sanktaria heads the Regent Council, I wish to inform the Council I will be returning soon. One member of my entourage is delayed in Iszenstadt. I will arrive there shortly to collect him, and I formally request an armed escort collect us there. Myself, two Ashbourne, one Human, one Moon Elf, and my horse. An arcanist should accompany them to keep me apprised of the situation. There will be much to discuss before and after my coronation."

"Yes, Hertogia Vandiamante. I will convey your message. May the Way of the Blood flow with warmth and health."

The call ended. Honor's eyes were wide, and her mouth was open but silent. She pointed at Gwyn, but before she could utter a syllable, Xrissa said, "You're getting a crown? You're a princess?"

"I have avoided my throne long enough. My people need me, and Courage is one of my people."

Karina rose and wrapped her arm around Gwyn's waist. "One of our people."

Honor smiled. "My brother's a fucking idiot, but he's found himself some friends."

"Let's get Courage!" Xrissa shouted.

The four women spent the rest of the day preparing for their journey, purchasing first aid supplies, ammunition, magical reagents, and new alchemical equipment. Karina shaved and readied six wooden stakes. Xrissa assisted Gwyn in preparing more alchemic blood serum, including mechanizing the new alchemical equipment both to automate and to quicken the process.

Before they went to bed, Gwyn approached Honor. "I've got a small favor to ask, and if it's too much, you may decline."

"Look, you've taken care of my brother, and you're helping me find his dumb ass. What do you need?"

"I don't know magic, but you do. Would you mind sending a message to someone for me? His name's Mathias Greely. I just need to know if he's safe in the castle, and to let him know I'll be there soon."

Honor waved her hand. "No problem. Just have to think of how to word it within twenty-five words for the spell. Okay." She grabbed the small bit of copper wire she used to focus the energies of the Awtkha and cast the spell. "Mathias. Gwyn Vandiamante needs to know if you're safe, in her castle, and that she'll be on the way there soon. Twenty-five words to respond."

A few minutes passed before Mathias responded. "Oh. Hi. Twenty-five words? Well, I'm in the castle. Trying to clean the place up with this guy named Kiernan. Can't wait to see you."

Honor relayed the information, and Gwyn's shoulders relaxed. She smiled. "He's there, and Kiernan survived. That's good."

"Who's he?"

"A servant. When the Richters attacked, he helped me escape. I was afraid they slaughtered all of the servants. His safety bodes well for things. Thank you."

The four departed before the next dawn. Their travel route took them northeast to Dornbach. Heavy rainfall meant hoods to help conceal their identities. Finding a private carriage willing to take them to Iszenstadt took some time, but they were on their way by nightfall. Karina fell asleep, snoring as she rested her head on Gwyn's lap, and Xrissa curled up in the corner on the opposite side of the carriage.

She fell asleep after one bell in the morning.

"So," Honor said. "I had hoped we'd get a chance to talk without Xrissa, but the amount that Crimson Minotaur she drinks keeps her going for hours."

"Is that what's in that flask?" Gwyn chuckled. "I can see why Courage fancies her."

Honor nodded. "Since she moved to Al'Adara ten years ago. And you know how much he talks, right? He gets within ten feet of her, he clamps his jaw tighter than one of those C clamps he uses to hold things in place while tinkering."

They laughed. Gwyn said, "I got the sense she might want that changed."

"I get that too. It's one of the reasons I asked her to come along. That, and she's a burst of energy and sunshine. If I'm honest, I'm not sure this'll succeed. Wasn't from the beginning."

"But you had to try." Gwyn nodded. "We're going to try. We don't know their numbers, and we don't have a map of the facility. Our only assumption is they've locked him in the basement somewhere. And we know some of the resources at their disposal but not all."

Honor chuckled. "Look at you, acting like a general."

Gwyn smiled. She shook her head. "I was born an innkeeper's daughter, orphaned, and then adopted and raised to be a princess. After the Richters murdered my family for a second time, I ended up becoming a hunter. Hunters don't survive unless they know their quarry. After this, I hang up my sword and flintlock."

Karina stirred, groaned, and stretched. "Are we planning strategy at this hour?"

Gwyn kissed her gently. "No, my beloved. That will be

tomorrow as we near Iszenstadt. I'll say this, now that you're awake, this fight will be easier for me, as I won't need to hide my abilities and power. Now, the two of you should get rest. As should I, since I'll be day-walking tomorrow."

"Be certain to drink your potion tomorrow, my princess. I've seen your sickness during the day."

I thought I pushed through better around you, Gwyn thought. She nodded. "Two remain. And then, no more day-walking."

Chapter 17

While Gwyn, Karina, Honor, and Xrissa prepared to rescue Courage, the members of the Holy Order of St. Arnulf Ironhand trained to be ready for the next mission the Blessed Emperor tasked them to handle. Their training grounds, located both within the basement of and behind the family manor in Ullinburg outshone any facility used to train soldiers by the Grand Imperial Army. Dressed in their black leather uniforms, agents performed high level calisthenics and practiced hand-to-hand fighting and firearms marksmanship in the rear courtyard. And in the manor's basement, which now housed the Kriegsdieneryn provided to them form the Imperium Center for the Rehabilitation of Traitors, the order's arcanists summoned fiends and undead abominations into controlled combat rooms so agents could train to fight against their deadliest foes.

The Richter family manor, where the Holy Order of St. Arnulf Ironhand trained, sat just north of the city center of Ullinburg, a port city nestled within a small valley witin the Shunkrir Peaks and accessible only by ship or through dangerous mountain paths that have long served pilgrims seeking aid and blessing from St. Hurud. Located beyond the northern edge of the central market where, on this day as any other, traders and residents conducted business in both open air stalls and in the ornately painted wooden buildings that lined the square surrounding the old well. Beside the Richter manor sat the Grand Cathedral of Ullin's Heart, a massive structure of stained glass and stone built during the Age of Faith by King Ullin of Shunkris and dedicated to the Lord of Sky and Storm.

Between the high wall of the Richter family compound and the Grand Cathedral was a narrow alley, heavily shadowed and rarely traversed. Between the spires of the cathedral and the high gabled roof of the Richter family manor, only small patches of sunlight, not even large enough to attract a stray cat in search of a napping spot, dotted the cobblestones of the alley. Crates, barrels, and assorted refuse bins filled the shadows, forgotten and unseen by pedestrians. And shadowed by and hidden within this junk pile was a small, lead-lined iron box from which protruded a small antenna topped with an Arcanyx crystal inside of which swirled golden light.

The golden light's swirling intensified into a rapid blinking, and then the box exploded. A giant ball of blue flame, propelled by massive amount of arcane energy released by the detonation of the necro-evocation core within the box, shot outward from the alley. For miles around, stone structures crumbled, and wooden buildings, as well as all living beings within them, either turned to ash or perished beneath the crushing weight of falling and flying debris.

The spires of the Great Cathedral crashed onto the cobblestones of the central market square. The stain glass windows shattered into serrated daggers, slicing through the flesh of those praying within. Prayer, the choir's song, and the ancient pipe organ fell silent as the ancient monument to a people's faith transformed into a graveyard of once-hallowed dreams.

The flames danced across the gabled roof of the Richter manor. Those in the courtyard were spared suffering, dying in half a finger snap. Stones from the fence, the poles of the wrought iron gate, and beams from the manor itself flew in all directions, impaling some and crushing others. As the upper floors sank onto the ground floor beneath them, collapsing under the weight of the perfection of their artifice, the vegetation on the lawn dried and crumbled to dust, blown about by the gale wind of arcane energy.

The stalls in the central market ceased to be, their forms and contents vaporized, burned, or shredded. The few shoppers and traders in the market who survived bled from open wounds and watched as green and black pustules formed on their skin. Many gripped their throats, gasping for air, as their throats burned with a dusty flame and a hollow thirst built within them.

Groaning, weeping, wailing, and screaming cut through the silence after the explosion ceased. Death's reek, both fresh and ancient, filled the air. An icy chill, brought on by the explosion's swiftness that sucked the heat and life from the atmosphere, corrupted the haze of arcane energy, vaporized organic matter, and inorganic debris that floated and fell through the air.

And it was into this scene that the two dozen remaining members of the Holy Order of St. Arnulf Ironhand who trained and worked in the deep basement emerged when they ascended what remained of their home's grand staircase. Shock, fear, and sorrow paled their already fair faces. The oldest of them, Hanzlin Richter, a middle-aged man with thinning and graying brown hair and deep-set brown eyes sighed as he limped forward and surveyed the devastation.

"A mana bomb exploded," he said with a practiced calmness. "The blast survivors will be wrackghuls by sunset. Everyong activate the purification crystals on your goggles and grab your weapons." He lowered his head as a sigh of lamentation fell from his lips. "Aid those who can be saved, but have the unpleasant task of purging this city before the corruption spreads."

So they did, and it was at the end of this most unpleasant of tasks that Caspar and Garrus Richter returned from Clérmontán. When word of the city's devastation reached the rail driver, she relayed the message to Iszenstadt, requesting carriages be sent to collect the passengers, and then she halted travel. As the carriage containing the two men traversed the city streets, the experienced hunters stared in horror as they passed bonfire after bonfire where humanoid and animal corpses had been used for kindling.

The carriage stopped at the southern edge of central square. As the door opened, both men's eyes watered as the acrid smoke thrust the stench of burning flesh toward them. The remaining members of the family of monster hunters stood amid the blazing wreckage of the city, silent and mournful, bloodied and beaten after their task. Caspar limped toward them, and they turned and stood at attention.

"Hanzlin, what happened? The cathedral? Our home? The city? Why are the people burning?"

Hanzlin nodded. "An explosion, Uncle Caspar." He held out the remains of the necro-evocation core. "I found this, a mana bomb's necro-evocation core, in the the alley between our home and the Grand Cathedral. We healed and quarantined those who could be saved, but to prevent an outbreak of wrackghuls, we did what we had to do."

Caspar nodded. Garrus lowered his head. After surveying the ruins of the city and the family estate, Caspar asked, "Is this all of us that remain?"

Hanzlin nodded. "And Severus and Karina?"

Caspar shook his head. "Severus is dead. My daughter is lost to us. We will deal with her and that damned Vandiamante vampire soon enough, but we will need to relocate."

"We've got to leave soon. The necromantic energies from the blast will only grow stronger due to the deaths. If we remain past morning, half of us may be in danger of wrackghul sickness as well."

The elder Richter nodded, and then his comm ring illuminated. "Perhaps this will be of benefit to us." He flicked the ring and responded. "This is Grand Master Richter."

Kammherr Florescu, the Imperial Chamberlain, answered. "Grand Master, it is good to hear from you. Disturbing news has reached us in Sonnenburg. Is all well?"

"I am afraid not, Kammherr. I would rather not speak over such a line at present, as I am in the middle of what was Ullinburg's central market. Suffice it to say that the Grand Cathedral and our manor, along with much of the city, have been destroyed. It appears only fourteen of us remain, and due to the threat of corruption and wrackghuls, we will need immediate relocation."

"That can be arranged. I can have military transport routed to Ullinburg within minutes, and we need you in Sonnenburg, as a situation has arisen that demands your experience and involvement."

"Understood. Am I to leave immediately, or shall I wait for transport along with my family?"

"I will consult His Excellency. However, given the dual situations, it is likely you will wait. Regardless, direct your agents to prepare for pickup. Further communication will be sent once arrangements have been finalized."

Arrangements were made. Telling the passage of time was difficult for many with no church bells to toll the hour. Perhaps three hours later, as the sky darkened for nightfall, military transport vehicles arrived. The remaining residents of Ullinburg watched as the Holy Order of St. Arnulf Ironhand loaded up their remaining possessions, the monstrous Kriegsdieneryn, and themselves onto the transports and departed for Sonnenburg, leaving them to rebuild the city.

Two days later, Blessed Emperor Josyph Hapfsburgh assembled the remaining members of the High Holy Council to discuss two matters of great importance. Caspar Richter was the first to arrive. Marius Bedwyr followed shortly after him.

While they waited for High General Krank's arrival, Marius leaned across the half-moon table and asked, "Caspar, the news from Ullinburg saddens me, but is there at least joy to report from your conversation with your daughter?"

Caspar shook his head. "Ambrose, you have been a great friend these past few years, and you have shown my daughter more kindness, forgiveness, and mercy than any deserve. Yet, she persists in her sin."

"Shame." Marius nodded, keeping his tone sympathetic. "Though it may come too late, the truth will come to light, old friend. It always does."

The doors to the conference room opened, and High General Krank entered. He bowed to the Blessed Emperor, kissed his ring on the Blessed Emperor's trembling hand, and then took his seat between Marius Bedwyr and Caspar Richter. He said, "Forgive my tardiness, Your Excellency, gentlemen, but I have just received the most recent communique from Milmigua. And it is worse than I feared."

Marius' lips twitched as he tried to conceal a smile. Caspar turned to Krank. "Augustus, what is worse than you feared? What is happening? And why does the Indigo Coast concern us now?"

"And that," the Blessed Emperor said in a tone of forced strength as his coughing and trembling worsened. "Is why we have convened this council. High General, apprise Grand Master Richter of the situation."

The High General nodded. "I'll be brief. As you know, Caspar, over the past few months, there have been a series of random thefts of equipment and uniforms from various bases across the empire. Most had been of such a small scale, a handful of enlisted soldier uniforms or two or three rifles, that, while troubling, seemed of little note. And then they kept happening. Then, last month, with the efforts of your agents, we discovered that the thieves were Crimson Fangs, and they added destruction of armored vehicles to their crimes.

"Now, reports have come to us from media outlets in both our empire and throughout the independent city-states of the Indigo Coast that Imperial Army forces under the command of someone named General Coullinn have now captured Milmigua."

"I was unaware we had plans to expand to the Indigo Coast," Caspsar Richter said. "Logical to consolidate this part of the continent under our control, but it shocks me that this High

Holy Council was not made privy to that operation."

"You would have been," Krank said. "I would not launch such an operation without the approval of the Blessed Emperor and of this esteemed council. We ordered no such operation. Not only that, but no general in the Grand Imperial Army is of either Froamian or Edriu ancestry. It is my belief that the Crimson Fang have launched this offensive under the guise of legitimacy provided by the armaments stolen from our facilities. To make matters more problematic, word came today that Don Dijego de la Mancha, who fled the city with his entourage, and the rulers of the other city-states are en route to Sonnenburg to discuss the apparent violation of our neutrality treaty."

"Those will be most unpleasant negotiations," Marius said with the faintest hint of pleasure in his voice, which those present took to mean his joy at not needing to be present for them.

"They will be unfortunate," the Blessed Emperor said. A fit of wheezing followed by a series of deep, wet coughs followed. "While we await their arrival, Grand Master Richter, we recognize and offer our sympathy after the tragic events in Ullinburg, but we do have a request to make of you."

Caspar Richter nodded. "Thank you, Your Excellency. We wish we had information to put forward beyond the fact that someone detonated a mana bomb between our manor and the Grand Cathedral. To our knowledge, the impacts of the blast have been contained, and no wrackghuls have emerged. We are, of course, investigating the incident. What is it Your Excellency needs of us?"

"Your Excellency," High General Krank rose from his seat. "Military Intelligence is more than capable of investigating this matter."

The Blessed Emperor nodded once. "That they are. However, we believe that our Grand Army may be too close to this matter to investigate with haste and diligence. And before you say otherwise, the Holy Order of St. Arnulf Ironhand is more adept at contending with vampires than any in the Grand Army. Thus, not only will they be able to investigate the matter and provide us with evidence to present to Don Dijego and the others upon their arrival, but they will also be able to end these monsters occupation of our friend and neighbor."

"We will relish the opportunity to put the beasts down, Your Excellency." Caspar bowed as he spoke.

The Blessed Emperor smiled. He nodded. "And, High General Krank, we also request that you appoint Military Intelligence officers to investigate the incident at Ullinburg. Gentlemen, we trust your agents will communicate as appropriate, yes?"

High General Krank and Grand Master Richter assented. The Blessed Emperor then dismissed the High Holy Council. As Marius Bedwyr left the conference chamber, a feral and triumphant smile slithered across his face. *First Milmigua,* he thought. *And then to Whiteclyf.*

Chapter 18

The morning after the High Holy Council met to discuss the situation in Milmigua, the carriage containing the party seeking to rescue Courage Faern'doln neared Iszenstadt. The clocks chimed seven bells as the rising sun greeted them. Xrissa oiled SAAMy and tightened the bolts and nuts on his locomotion and sensation apparatuses. Karina cleaned and loaded both her flintlock and the Arcanyx-infused flintlock she took off her cousin Severus' corpse. Gwyn downed one of the potions to mitigate her day-walking sickness and then donned her red sunglasses.

Honor looked out the window and saw the Shunkrir Peaks rising in the north. She turned her attention back to her traveling companions. "What's the plan?"

Everyone again looked at Gwyn who said, "First order of business, we get a room. We'll discuss the specifics there. I was thinking the Miner's Rest would be ideal."

Karina lifted her right eyebrow. "The Miner's Rest? That's the quality of inn that my father would reserve for agents traveling. It's functional but not pleasurable."

"Exactly," Gwyn said. "The Crimson Fang know both what I am and who I am. The Moonlit Rose has long been frequented by Florescian nobility. I should have realized if they spotted me, they would track me there. That's one mistake I won't repeat again."

The Miner's Rest was one of the two Dwarven run inns at the base of the Shunkrir Peaks in Iszenstadt's Ironheart District, the heart of the mining, smithing, and gem cutting in the city. The exterior resembled a two-story home in the Polonishke style, an architectural tradition marked by walls of red and gold wooden tiles and curved trim on the gabled roofs that resembled the runners on a sleigh. Boisterous but not combative talking and loud music burst through the open door.

The interior of the Miner's Rest resembled more of a huntsman's lodge than a Dwarven tavern. Long communal tables of mahogany with half-log benches filled the common room. A trio of burly, bearded bards sat by the hearth playing a washboard, a fiddle, and a drum. Deer, elk, and boar heads were mounted on the stone wall above the hearth, and a pair of Dwarven twins with lustrous black hair, brown eyes, and gold-beaded beards slung drinks and food from behind the bar.

They approached the bar, and the taller of the twins walked over to them. His bass voice was boisterous and bright, and his accent placed him somewhere between Edrium and the Shunkri diaspora. "Welcome to the Miner's Rest. I'm Tavish Guffin and my brother here is Macarthur. Not often we get so many attractive ladies setting foot in here, but we've got what you need, even if you don't know what it is yet."

"I came up with the last bit," Macarthur chimed in with his honeyed baritone.

Gwyn laughed. "Thank you. We just need one room for the night."

"One room for the four of you? We can do that." He flipped through the guest register and ledger. "Let's see, two beds, yeah. We can put you up in room nine. That'll be five torbal."

Gwyn handed over the money and signed the name *Ayslyn Skejik* in the register. Tavish smiled and handed her the key, saying, "Here you go, Miss Skejik. Up the stairs, last door on the left. We got a communal stew on the hearth with fresh bread coming every hour. Complementary with the room."

Karina stiffened when the innkeeper said her last name but looked at Gwyn. Gwyn nodded, and the quartet made their way to their room. Once everyone had entered, Gwyn checked the hall and then locked the door behind them. "Now that we're here. The plan. Rina, you know the facility better than any of us. What can you tell us?"

Karina shook her head. "Not much. It's a black, windowless building. It's imposing, like a tomb almost. It's cold, and there are like medical bay rooms. Offices are on the upper floors. I think Marius has an office on the fifth floor. Didn't see more than maybe ten armed guards, but that doesn't mean there aren't more. I don't know where Courage was, if he's there, but I assume from all the riddles we've been given that he's beneath the ground. And there was a staircase descending and ascending."

"So, what you're saying," Honor said. "We break in, get into the basement, and find my little brother. Probably fight a bunch of vampires on the way."

Gwyn offered a solemn nod. Concern brought a frown to Karina's face. She squeezed Gwyn's arm. "You okay with this plan?"

Gwyn shrugged and shook her head. Two dark chuckles danced from her lips as she smiled a fang-baring smile. "For six years I've heard the question in sanctuaries from Sonnenburg to Ristarad, 'When…when will the Silver Scourge turn her blade on her one of her own?' And I avoided doing so, and now, as I prepare to put away the gun and the blade, the fears become reality. Fate goes as she must."

"Maybe you won't have to kill any?" Xrissa's voice was hopeful but uncertain of the veracity of her own words.

"'Prepare for shit. Pray for shine.' That's what our Da always said," Honor said.

Gwyn nodded, and then she went rigid as an unfamiliar voice entered her head. "Health and prosperity, Hertogia Vandiamante. I am Arcanist Mediciara. Per the Regent Council's orders, we are en route to your location. The line stays open."

Gwyn smiled. "Excellent news, Arcanist Mediciara. Keep arcane eyes on me, remain at a reasonable distance away unless requested. Will call when ready." She turned to her compatriots. "Our extraction squad is near. Rina and I need to change into our combat leathers and then, we retrieve our Ashbourne."

"How are we going to enter the building," Karina asked after she and Gwyn had changed. "I doubt they'll let us walk in—especially the two of us."

"I can take care of that."

Honor made a series of weaving gestures with her index and middle fingers, moving her focus from person to person while chanting. Gold and silver lights glinted and sparkled around the four of them, and the light then bent around them. Their clothing changed into the hunter green uniforms of the Grand Imperial Army.

Honor smiled. "There. Won't hold up to close inspection,

but it'll give us a bit of cover."

Their exit from the Miner's Rest garnered a few surprised expressions and whispers. A fifteen minute walk through the warm sunshine later, they reached the wrought iron gate and stone fence that bordered the foreboding windowless black building. Two armed guards met them at the gates. Both were Human men, and both smelled alive.

"State your business," one of the guards said.

Karina walked forward. "Site inspection. Orders by General Hamlish, Imperial Military Intelligence."

The guard who spoke to them looked at the other guard. The second guard checked a clipboard. He shook his head. The first guard said, "We've got no record of such orders coming through. Who are you."

Gwyn lowered her sunglasses to the tip of her nose. She stepped forward and made eye contact with both guards. Her eyes flashed from green to red to gold and back to green. The guards faces went blank. Gwyn said, "We're with Military Intelligence, as such, it's best if you kindly let us pass and forget you saw us."

The guards nodded slowly. They moved with a languid pacing and heaviness of action, as if they moved through water or snow. As they opened the gate, the first guard nodded. "Yes, ma'am. Go about your business."

Gwyn pushed her sunglasses up and smirked. The four women passed through the gate, and it closed behind them. As they approached the front door, Karina whispered, "You've never used your mind control on me, have you?"

"Not even when I wanted nothing to do with you."

Karina nodded in relief. The guards at the gate then opened the front door for them via a remote button. Beige walls and a white tiled floor greeted them as they moved through a long hallway. The air was cool and clean, smelling of bleach.

Gwyn's nose wrinkled, and she winced in disgust. She muttered in a hushed tone, "So, that's why the servants always cleaned during daylight."

"The scent of labor is too much for my princess' delicate nose." Karina whispered into Gwyn's ear.

The vampire narrowed her eyes, turned her head toward her smirking lover, and stuck out her tongue. Her grin destroyed any terror her mock glare may have evoked. Karina claimed Gwyn's mouth in a kiss.

"Come on, you two," Honor said. "Save it for later."

The lovers nodded. Gwyn chuckled. "I see interruption runs in the family. Lead on, my knight in black."

Honor rolled her eyes and shook her head. Karina led the party to the stairs. They passed a pair of armed Crimson Fang vampires who stopped to inquire as to their purpose. Gwyn flashed a parchment and reiterated the narrative about a facilities inspection. Xrissa added these armed soldiers could check with the guards at the gate, but upon seeing her tool belt and SAAMy on her back, they nodded.

One of the Fangs looked at the other and said, "Probably here to see the foundry." He turned to the party before adding, "Keep straight and head down to basement three. The guards will buzz you in. Careful, it's hot and a bit disgusting in there."

"Foundries are great!" Xrissa beamed as she spoke. "All that hot, molten steel being poured and shaped for use. The oil, the rubber, and the leather. The only smells that rival it are those of a bakery when it's time to make cinnamon rolls."

The Fangs eyed her suspiciously and nodded. "Right. Well, enjoy yourself."

Honor responded to his uncertainty and confusion. "She will. I'm sure. Thank you."

They made their way to the stairwell and descended. The air warmed progressively with each flight. When they reached the third basement level, sweat beaded and streamed from the foreheads of Honor, Xrissa, and Karina. Gwyn yawned and rubbed her forehead. It was damp. Her nose wrinkled from a familiar but unfamiliar stench.

Karina looked over. "Are you well? I assumed you being both a Snow Elf and *dead* that the heat would affect you worse than it would me."

"I'm not happy with the heat," Gwyn said. "I think my recent feeding and the potion for day-walking sickness have helped, but I am feeling fainty. The sooner we get Courage and leave this place, the better. I smell death, fresh and painful death."

The other women looked with concern. Karina exhaled. Vampires were known to have enhanced senses. How much death had Gwyn survived—or caused—to recognize freshness and suffering?

At the bottom of the stairs, they found a heavy, thick iron door with a comm unit attached to it. Karina pressed the button. When a voice emerged asking their business, she said, "Grand Imperial Army Military Intelligence. Here for a facility inspection."

"Facility inspection? We weren't notified of that."

Another voice said, "It's just like the higher ups, Damian. They don't fucking tell us shit."

"And you know MI," another voice called out. "They keep their cards closer to their chest than you do when you cheat."

After a moment of laughter and good-natured swearing, the first voice said, "You're fucking right. Hold on. I see you on the screens. You see that?"

There was an audible click from the door. "There, it's open."

The four women stepped into a square room where four men in Grand Imperial Army uniforms stood around a table. A series of screens showing the activity in different hallways filled one wall. Xrissa waved and smiled.

"Strange," one of the four said. "You weren't wearing those uniforms on screen. What is it, some kind of new arcanotech stealth uniform?"

Xrissa nodded. "Sure is. It's basically the same tech as a stealth field generator, but instead of generating stealth, it generates the image of a dress uniform. What it does is it takes the golden illusory strands of the Awtkha, bends them to match the angle of light coming from the nearest detected source, which then gets filtered through the Arcanyx crystal prisms on the device, which is a belt buckle, and then projects the desired image out onto the wearer. Sure, it doesn't hold to scrutiny yet, as you saw on the feed, but it does allow for keeping dress uniforms clean, pressed, and always ready for wear."

They nodded slowly. One of the guards pulled out a clipboard attached to what appeared to be a card reader. "Right. Well, just give us a second, so we can scan you in. ID?"

"Yes," Gwyn said. "Our ID."

"I got your fucking ID right here."

Honor's rapier flashed as its tip pierced the first guard's throat. Flintlocks fired, filling the air with smoke. Chairs crashed and shattered. The glass of multiple viewing screens hissed and cracked as bodies slammed into them. SAAMy crawled down Xrissa's back and fired a series of bolts into the chests of the guards. Karina flashed her silvered long knife and decapitated them. Their bodies turned to ash.

"That went well," Xrissa said, sipping Crimson Minotaur from her flask.

Karina shook her head. "Never needed ID before. The Holy Order's uniform was always enough."

"Well," Gwyn said. "We survived. Let's see if any of these screens will show us where Courage is."

Xrissa walked over and helped Gwyn work the controls to the viewing screens. The comm box flashed. Honor walked over. "Hello?"

"B3 Eyeballs, this is Central Comm. Everything okay at your location? High Control shows some of your screens shorted out but still picked up some noise."

"Uh, yeah," the Ashbourne said. "Fucking pistol fired off while cleaning it. Just that. We're all okay here. How are you?"

"We're sending a maintenance crew with the Assistant Director, just in case. Hold position."

"Negative," Honor said. "We're fine. We're all fine here. That's not necessary." She grabbed a flintlock and fired on the comm box. "Stupid fucking conversation. Hey, let's get moving. We're about to get company."

"We've found him," Xrissa said. "This way."

Weapons drawn, they raced through the door and into the Imperium Center's foundry. All four halted in their tracks and gasped as they saw the massive mechanical factory and mechanomagical workshop. Each woman shielded her eyes with her arm as humid heat and steam assaulted them. Molten steel poured from huge, heated cauldrons into smaller molds that moved along conveyor belts. The warbling vibrato of screams that could sour milk pierced the air.

Each woman gasped and said *fuck* as they all saw the foundry's purpose. Humanoids of all types lay naked and strapped to steel tables, their bodies connected to Health Preservation Units as black robed physicians in leather masks marked their bodies. Without anesthesia or magic, these physicians hacked and sliced into the bodies unable to die during this process, removing parts of the spine, the brain, one or more eyes, and the occasional stomach. Some amputated perfectly functional limbs. And through all of this, the HPUs pumped the bodies full of alchemical concoctions that prevented them from dying.

"What is this place," Gwyn asked.

"Ashfodell," Karina said with mournful silence. "This is what Ashfodell is."

"Let's find my damned brother and—"

A familiar voice popped into Honor's head. She smiled as Courage's voice, softer and more terrified than she had ever heard it, spoke. "Sister. Help. Trapped somewhere and chained to a wall. I've disabled magical dampeners, but I need help. Call Gwyn and Karina. One should come. Love."

After a chuckle, Honor replied loud enough her companions could here. "The cavalry will be there soon, you dingus. Stay put and stay alive. I love you, you big butthead. Activating scrying beacon."

The phsysicians and technomagi gave them a wide berth as they walked, weapons loaded and at the ready. They reached the heavy iron door. Honor pulled and found it locked. "He's beyond here, but the fucking door's locked. Of course it is."

"I can pick it," Xrissa said.

"But we've got to hurry," Karina said. "Remember, reinforcements are coming due to the altercation in the surveillance room."

"Xrissa," Gwyn said. "Can you have SAAMy sweep the area behind us for cover if anything comes?"

"Sure can." The Moon Elf nodded.

The vampire smiled. "Good. I'll get Courage. You get the lock open. Rina, Honor, you two be ready to take point as we make our escape."

"Yes, my princess."

"Fuck yeah. But how are you going to get in with the door locked."

"Watch me." Gwyn winked, transformed into mist, and slipped through the minuscule crack between the door and the floor.

On the other side of the door was a cell of pure white, save for the workbench in the center of the room beside a body chute, a simple cot in the corner, and a non-functional toilet beside the cot. The room reeked of sweat, blood, shit, and death. Arcanyx crystal shards were scattered through the floor. And chained to the workbench, walking around better now that power had been restored to his prosthetic leg was a gaunt and dirty teal-skinned Ashbourne.

He clutched his stomach. "Where is she? Honor said she'd be here soon, but how can she get here? How will she get through all the defenses and the guards and stuff? She's just one woman. It's not like she has an army. Ah!"

Courage jumped with a start as a cloud of mist swirled around him and then hovered on the workbench before transforming into the shape of a familiar vampire. "No army, just a princess, a knight, and a baker."

Courage hugged Gwyn tightly. "Fuck you don't know how

good it is to see you. A knight? A *baker*? You don't mean?"

"She's not Snow Elf pretty, but she is Moon Elf pretty." Gwyn laughed. She dropped onto the floor and took one knee. "They should've used something stronger than iron."

She grabbed the iron chain binding Courage to the desk and twisted it. She gritted her teeth and grunted. A few twists and bends later, the chain snapped. At that moment, the door screeched open. Honor raced forward and wrapped her arms around Courage, nearly suffocating him as they embraced.

"I thought I'd never see you again," both said to the other. And then Honor said, "Well, we're not out of this yet. Gwyn, what's the word on our getaway."

"Arcanist Mediciara," Gwyn said. "Are you listening?"

A moment passed. They moved toward the cell door. And then the Florescian voice returned. "We are outside the walls of Iszenstadt, Hertogia. We await your orders."

Gwyn nodded to the group. "Converge on our location. Stay outside of the black building's gated fence. Do not engage unless they fire first." Her attention focused on the group, she said, "We've got transport. Let's move fast."

They raced through the foundry, encountering no resistance from the technomagi and physicians there. In the surveillance room, they grabbed pistols and blades, ensuring everyone had weapons. They leaped up the stairs as fast as they could. Gwyn rushing to take point, as her vampiric celerity allowed for greater freedom of movement.

Bursting through the stairwell door and onto the first floor's hallway, the party's motion ground to a halt. Two armed vampires, two vampires whose attire suggested technomagical expertise, and then one hulking monstrosity stood before them. The creature had the body of an Elven woman with long purple hair. Her eyes had been replaced by Arcanyx crystal goggles. Armored boots and greaves covered her legs. Her left hand was a flintlock pistol, and her right hand ended in a rapier.

As everyone looked on horror, Gwyn gasped, "Assistant Director Mueller? What have they done to you?"

"I did that," Courage's head lowered, and he spoke in a whisper.

"Halt!" The armed vampires pointed their weapons at the party as they spoke. "Drop your weapons, and your deaths will be swift. Perhaps you won't end up like this traitor."

"She did nothing," Tears choked Courage's voice as he spoke. "She didn't deserve that."

"Let us end her suffering." Karina strode forward. She thrust her right arm into the air, and her thumb, index, and middle fingers on her right hand were extended vertically as she said, "Behold, the thunder of the Lord of Sky and Storm! Behold, and begone vile spirit, by the order of the King of Gods and men. Behold, you have—"

The automaton that was once Assistant Director Mueller fired a shot that grazed Karina's neck. Karina screamed. Gwyn growled at the vampires standing opposite them. "No divine mercy today. Death alone awaits you. Stake the hearts to put them in torpor."

She bolted forward and attacked the nearest guard. Honor lunged at the other soldier. Xrissa deployed SAAMy, activating a shielding apparatus to keep Courage and herself safe while she fired bolts and studied the Assistant Director. The technomagi took bolts to the hearts. They gasped and froze.

Karina wiped the blood from her neck and charged the guard fighting with Gwyn. Blades clanged against blades.

Flintlock shot staggered Human and vampire. Distracted by Gwyn's speed and flurries, the Crimson Fang vampire failed to see Karina's lunge. She buried her long knife to the hilt in the vampire's chest. Blood spewed from his mouth as he gargled his final breath before Karina removed the blade and slit his throat.

The other vampire pummeled Honor with a flurry of quick strikes. He punched her. He kicked her. She grunted. Blood dripped from her nose. The vampire licked his lips.

"I'll enjoy your taste before I give you up," he growled as he pushed his body against hers when she parried one of his strikes.

"Fuck you."

Honor tilted her wrist. The vampire moved to parry the telegraphed strike. Honor slammed her knee into his crotch. The vampire's gasp was an octave higher than expected. Honor ran him through, and Karina darted to her side and slit the vampire's throat.

Shot peppered the floor, sending Gwyn, Karina, and Honor scrambling.

"Karina, Honor." Gwyn barked her order. "Get behind that energy shield. I'll draw fire."

Gwyn fired her pistol at the automaton. The bullet shattered the left eye crystal. The creature spun and slashed at the vampire. Gwyn dodged. Using her celerity, she stuck and moved, keeping the construct off balance and away from her friends.

"What the fuck do we do against that," Honor asked.

Courage rocked back and forth, covering his ears with his hands. Tears flowed, and he breathed rapidly. In a trembling voice, he repeated the same sentences over and over. "This is my fault. I'm the reason we'll die. I'm sorry, Mum. I failed us all."

"I'm trying to observe," Xrissa said. "It's slow and powerful. Speed seems effective, but that won't last forever. I wonder..."

Pressing a button on SAAMy caused red and orange crystal dust to illuminate. As the dust moved through the tubes and into the flight groove. The metal bolt glowed with a white core. Xrissa fired.

As the bolt left SAAMy, it ignited into a small ball of flame. The flame struck the Assistant Director in the small of her back. She arched her back and uttered a hollow screech.

Her speed intensified, and she pummeled Gwyn with sword strikes and thrusts of her rifle arm. Gwyn dodged and parried what she could, but every third strike hit its mark. The vampire grunted and groaned. Blood flowed from wounds, but it soon healed thanks to her unnatural healing abilities.

"Okay," Xrissa said. "Fire's bad. Let's try ice."

"Don't use ice. Use electricity," Courage said. "I put the core in her. Overload it, and that should short her out. I think. That sounds right."

Xrissa nodded and changed tactics. Blue and yellow dust moved through SAAMy's tubes. Electric energy crackled around the bolt. She fired.

The bolt hit its target. The Assistant Director froze for a moment. Xrissa fired another electrified bolt. The automaton shook and trembled violently. Another bolt struck the automaton, and it trembled and then slumped forward. Gwyn walked up, shot the other eye socket out, and removed the head, allowing both the head and the body to slump onto the floor.

While the party fought their way out of the Imperium

Center for the Rehabilitation of Traitors, the extraction team approached the building. As they gained sight on the black building and its fence, a black carriage pulled by two black mechanomagical horses drove up to the wrought iron gate. Without a word, the gate opened for it, and the carriage passed into the gardens of the front courtyard.

At the moment the carriage stopped, the party burst through the front door. The carriage door opened, and Marius Bedwyr stepped from the carriage to see Karina and Gwyn fire cold iron shot into the guards at the gate. Xrissa fired two bolts from SAAMy, pinning the guards in place. Everyone stopped and stared at Marius. Courage hid behind Honor.

Marius bowed. "The queen who runs from her throne."

Gwyn flourished her small sword. "The prince who will never sit on his father's throne." He snarled, shame burning his cheeks as she said that. And then Gwyn narrowed her eyes and continued. "Let this, my *final hunt,* conclude our business on this day and forevermore."

Marius' bodyguards exited the carriage. Six armed Crimson Fang agents rushed from inside the Imperium Center. Gwyn's eyes darted from vampire to vampire. Karina tugged on her arm. Gwyn nodded.

Gwyn turned and led the party from the Imperium Center's premises. The extraction team, two carriages of white wood with golden trim and a golden bat on the door approached the party and opened their doors. Gwyn nodded, and everyone leaped into the carriages.

As they drove away, an older Human male in gold-trimmed robes of purple velvet, who was balding but with charismatic and fiery brown eyes, said, "Well, when you said you needed extraction, I did not anticipate the Hertogia would be breaking someone out of a prison."

"It's not a prison, Arcanist Mediciara," Gwyn said. "It was far worse. We'll discuss the matter once we get distance between us. Everyone, we're off to Florescia."

Chapter 19

Karina yawned as the sun set. The carriage in which they rode sped at a rate faster than she expected—even for mechanomagical conveyances. Reds, oranges, and yellows filled the sky as the sun descended toward the western horizon.

The vampires in the carriage were armed in a manner similar to imperial soldiers. They wore military weave uniforms that repelled blade and shot, and they carried both swords and flintlocks enhanced with Arcanyx crystal technology. Their faces were solemn and unemotional.

Gwyn kissed Karina's cheek. "Rest, my love. It has been a long day for us all."

"But you're awake, and I am your protector, especially while we move through imperial lands."

Gwyn smiled. She squeezed Karina's hand. "And so you are, but you do not have to bear that burden alone. The Regent Council has sent the Sezatorian Guard to escort us. You, my beloved knight in black, have earned a moment of rest."

"Maybe." Karina spoke through another yawn. "Once we pass Dornbach, I'll..." And then sleep overtook her as her head fell onto Gwyn's shoulder.

A few minutes passed with Gwyn running her fingers

through her snoring lover's hair before Arcanist Mediciara produced a bottle of blood-infused wine and poured two glasses. He handed Gwyn one and kept one for himself. Looking at Gwyn, he said, "Now that your Human is asleep, Hertogia—ah, I should grow accustomed to your new title, no? *Sezara* Vandiamante, would you tell me what you were doing in Iszenstadt."

Gwyn drained half of the glass' contents and then released a soft exhale. She nodded. "It's a long story, Arcanist Mediciara, but the short answer is I met Courage on my way home, but then someone named Ambrose von Harenheim requested my aid on behalf of the Society for Afterlife and Arcane Research. Courage volunteered to join me on that. Through that we met Rina here, and that is another long story we can delve into later should be absolutely necessary. Suffice it to say that we learned during our time working together that Ambrose was actually the vampire Marius Bedwyr, the last crown prince of Froam and the leader of a group of vampires rebelling against the emperor, the Crimson Fang.

"There was an altercation with an explosion. I was thrown from a window in Marius' office, and when I returned, Marius, Rina, and Courage were gone. Given the proximity of multiple members of the Holy Order of St. Arnulf Ironhand, I fled to Ristarad where I consulted the Sythrokli Oracle to find both Courage and Rina. The Oracle gave me an extended riddle about Courage being somewhere beneath the earth with fire and damnation. After that, I went to Rotzendam to aid Countess Sazkyeerts."

"Yes," the old vampire said. "She sent high praise for how you carried yourself and how you aided her people. It speaks well of your reign."

Gwyn blushed and smiled. "Well, before returning to Utrezzo, I decided to visit my parents' graves at Fáchrives. There, Rina saved me from being killed by one of the Richters—the first of two times she's saved me from that fate. We spoke and decided our best chance to find Courage was to Iszenstadt where the Crimson Fang vampires had kept her. During this time, Honor contacted me, and she and Xrissa joined us. And he was there, in a—and what I am about to describe—I'll just do it."

Gwyn drained the rest of her glass and then described what they saw in the foundry in detail. She described her physical senses of walking through the humid swelter, her revulsion at seeing the bodies—still alive—hacked to pieces and reformed into automatons of war, and the shock and sorrow of having to fight one that was once an ally and that when enraged could match a vampire's speed and strength. When she shot a quick glance at Courage for explanation, she saw his vacant stare that gazed through and beyond the carriage's wall. She nodded and returned to her own conversation, leaving him to process his experiences.

"To make matters worse for us all," she said. "Marius used some device on Karina's neck that mirrors our own bite marks before turning her over to Caspar Richter, knowing such an action would convince him I had done this to her. She did not consent, and while it was not a strict violation of the central tenet of our kind, the intent was the same.

"Also since the Crimson Fangs had imprisoned Courage beneath the facility where he kept Karina, we decided to break him out. As we reached the door, Courage managed to remove some sort of magical dampening device, allowing him to get word to his sister. After fighting our way out, we encountered Marius, but I chose to depart and ensure everyone's safety instead of confronting him. We don't know what he's planning, or what the empire is planning. I wanted my friends safe and away from imperial soil."

Arcanist Mediciara refilled Gwyn's glass and nodded. "Then we will not stop for rest until we reach the Sepulcher in Bellecairn. I will need to reserve an additional room for your additional entourage."

While Gwyn spoke with Arcanist Mediciara, Honor and Xrissa wrapped arms around Courage, who sat in silence. Honor leaned close to her younger brother and said, "So, Mum's doing okay. Whatever you said the Corvidiae, they've given her time. She's stable."

Courage nodded. His voice was a breath's volume above a whisper. "What day is it?"

"I think it's the seventeenth of Kieliah," Honor said.

Xrissa nodded. "For another few hours at least."

"I've got thirty-eight days left then. Fuck. I need to go back."

"What the fuck do you mean go back?" Honor's eyes widened "They had you chained to a fucking table. They were doing horrible things to people there. They might have done that to *you*. No, you're not going back there. The fuck is wrong with you?"

"Mum. I've got to go back." Courage's hands trembled, and his voice warbled as he spoke. "The red king. I've to kill the red king."

"Red king?" Honor threw her hands up. "There's a red king somewhere in Iszenstadt. The white queen is cradling the black knight's head on her shoulder. What kind of fucked up chess game have you gotten yourself involved in?"

Courage fell silent. He curled up into a ball, placing his feet on the seat and drawing his knees into his chest. He buried his face in his knees.

Honor sighed. “Fuck, Courage. I didn’t mean to yell at you. Why do you have to go back to the red king?”

“That’s what they want. Him. Something about a stolen name and an avoided fate. I’ve got to bring it to light. I guess they want him dead. I’ve got to be there and do it.”

“Courage Anders Faern’doln.” Honor’s utterance of his full name drew everyone’s attention. Karina awoke, confused as to what she heard. He shrank into the seat.

Honor sighed. “Look at you, terrified after what you went through—and rightly so. And you look like you’ve been starved or only given enough food and water to keep you functional. If you go back right now, they’ll kill you. And no one here wants that. There’s time. You just said you’ve got like forty days.”

“Thirty-eight days. That’s when the moon will be at the same phase it was when we were in Sonnenburg.”

“That’s over a month away, Courage,” Xrissa said. “You can buff up, make another wandvolver so I can see it in action…” She paused and wrapped her hand around his. “And we can plan before we do it.”

“What are we doing,” Karina asked, yawning. “Why are you going to Sonnenburg, Courage?”

“I’ve got to expose Marius for what he is, probably kill him too.”

“Be careful, young Master Faern’doln,” Arcanist Mediciara said. “Speaking of killing a vampire in the presence of the Sezatorian Guard is unsafe, even if you intend no harm to their Sezara.”

“Shit,” Courage said. “I didn’t mean nothing to him,

whoever he is."

"He's me." Gwyn smiled, raising her glass.

Courage's eyes and index fingers moved as if he were performing a calculation. He gasped. "That's a feminine form. You're a lady vampire. You're the white queen!" He pointed at Karina. "Does that make you the black knight?"

Karina nodded. Honor threw up her hands. "Would somebody fucking tell me what kind of fucked up godsdamned game of chess you're all fucking involved in?"

Gwyn shrugged. "I don't know if we know. All I know is that Marius is the son of the last kind of Froam. The Richters killed his father when the empire conquered Froam. He was sent to the same orphanage as I was, was adopted by an aristocratic vampire family, and started his rebel group of vampires sometime after that. My guess is he wants revenge and his father's throne. I don't know any more about him than that. Rina, what about you?"

Karina shook her head. "I learned what you know only when he revealed it himself. We always assumed the Fangs were building to a rebellion, but their seemingly random actions never seemed to amount to anything other than a… distraction. Wait!"

Karina paused for a moment, and then she said, "Marius, under his alias as Ambrose von Harenheim, is a member of the High Holy Council."

"And…and…and he had the real Ambrose turned into one of those things he calls the Dieneryn, the Servitors," Courage said. "He showed me what happened to him as part of a threat to get me to work on his project."

"So he is close to the Imperial Throne," Arcanist Mediciara said. "I know what that implies."

Everyone nodded save for Courage. The Ashbourne tilted his head to the side. "You think he wants that throne...oh! The identity he stole was a Council member."

"And the Fangs' activities, which never seem focused on one thing. They've stolen uniforms, weapons, bombed bases, and stolen food to give to the lower classes—but that's a rarity. They've been distractions from his move to be at the Blessed Emperor's side."

Arcanist Mediciara chuckled. "And here I thought Atharian politics were less strategic than Florescia's.

Karina turned to Gwyn. "But why you? You're clearly the white queen he's moving against. Weren't you leaving the empire when he asked for your aid?"

Gwyn nodded. "I was. I knew his name before we met him in his office only because he tried to anger me at a sanctuary, and the barkeep said his name was Marius. As he left, he said we'd meet again. That was the only time I met him before we did together."

"He clearly sees you as a threat," Honor said. "Jealousy, maybe. After today, I doubt he's warmed up to you either."

"No." Gwyn sipped from her glass. "Preparation will be necessary. Arcanist, can we perhaps send some of yours to Al'Adara to collect Courage's family, and anyone close to Xrissa, and bring them to Delfia or Utrezzo?"

"Mum's sick," Courage said. "She can't make this trip."

"With a fixed location," the arcanist said, "we could perhaps use teleportation spells. Is there a direct threat against them?"

Gwyn shook her head. "Part of me wants them safe in case the Fangs retaliate. Part of me wonders—and this is my own ignorance of sanguimantic healing—if our blood physicians could help her."

"We've tried physicians," Honor said. "We've tried fucking wizards. And prayers from priests have done nothing. What makes you think Florescian doctors are better than those in Al'Adara? We went to the most respected and expensive doctors there. It's a fucking center of learning where people come from around the world study science and alchemy."

"Sanguimantic ministration is not a traditional subject taught at *mortal* universities." Mediciara emphasized mortal to convey meaning lost in the discussion's emotional heat.

"What the fuck is that supposed to…" Honor paused.

As realization dawned on her, Courage finished the sentence. "But Mum's not a vampire."

"But she does have blood," Gwyn said.

Arcanist Mediciara nodded. "I cannot say with any certainty, having performed no examination of said patient, but if it is a possibility you have not yet exhausted, our medical practice would be no more invasive than any normal blood draw. The choice remains with your family."

Courage and Honor looked at each other and shrugged. Honor said, "You'd still have to keep those promises you made to the Corvidiae, or this won't amount to shit."

Courage nodded. "I know, but you'd offer this to us?"

"A queen protects and cares for her people." Gwyn smiled. "You may not be vampires, but you are my people. Xrissa, what about you?"

The Moon Elf woman tapped her nose and looked at the roof of the carriage as she thought. "My family's all in Preania over in Granith, but maybe I could accompany your people there so I can check on the shop and give my staff some instructions and a raise for handling things while I'm away. Someone's got to keep Courage fed so he regains his strength."

"Yeah, someone's got to keep me fed—wait. I can feed myself, and Gwyn's got to have a cook or something."

Gwyn and Honor looked at each other and smiled. Gwyn said, "I know Kiernan is still alive, but I don't know about the remainder of our staff. Besides, as Sezara of the Midnight Court, I demand the privilege of tasting these legendary cinnamon rolls." She turned to Arcanist Mediciara. "Begin the process once we arrive in Utrezzo and while arranging affairs for my coronation."

He nodded. "As you desire, Sezara."

Chapter 20

"Really? The place we're stopping at for the morning is in a cemetery? What type of bad writing cliché is this? Stop! The mausoleum wall is right there. You're going to crash this carriage into—oh. It's an illusory wall. This place is gorgeous."

Courage Faern'doln's tone shifted from sarcasm to fear to surprise and awe as he spoke. The Sepulchre was indeed located within the oldest cemetery in Bellecairn's Cathedral Heights, an older district on the city's western edge marked by Tshípogothic architecture. Crumbling buildings, rusted gates, uneven and cracked cobblestone pavement, and flickering street lamps desperately clinging to the last gasp of arcane energy marked the districts edge.

The cemetery itself was a monument to the city's transformation from ancient to modern times. A wrought iron Tshípogothic fence with glaring and growling gargoyles atop the corner posts formed its border. At the edges were ancient standing stones with runic inscriptions marking the earliest graves in the area. After passing through the rusted iron gates, one entered the Grove of Reflection, a small tree-bordered flower garden with benches for quiet contemplation. A few hundred tombstones flanked the garden on either side, and the massive mausoleum and chapel with its ornate stained glass rose windows stood in imposing silent solemnity against the back wall.

After disembarking from the carriages in the livery area, Hertogia Gwynarra Vandiamante and her entourage entered the reception hall. This large and luxurious chamber had high ceilings with ornate crystal chandeliers. Sumptuous burgundy and gold wallpaper adorned the walls, and the furniture for guests to sit while awaiting their rooms, their conveyances, or their guests were made of the finest mahogany with leather, velvet, and silk upholstery. On the wall to the entrance's left was a massive hearth kept ever burning that a small cauldron of spiced oil might perfume the chamber with seasonal scents.

Through two arched doors of stained glass opposite the hearth was the sanctuary's bar area. Mostly empty at this hour of the morning, save for a few day-walkers, this dining facility boasted a long mahogany bar with comfortable leather chairs adorned with golden accents. Large Arcanyx crystal lights nested in the wall behind stained glass windows washed the dark, smoky interior in a kaleidoscopic array of colorful light. A quick glance suggested the bar carried over two hundred varietals of blood-infused wine and spirits, illuminated by crystals set to pulse in time to a relaxed heart rate.

While Arcanist Mediciara acquired the rooms, Gwyn and her mortal entourage sat around one of the coffee tables. Gwyn sank into Karina's arms and sighed in contentment. She then dismissed the Sezatorian Guard, allowing them to gain sustenance at the bar and with blood dolls, should they desire. The guard bowed and took their leave. Gwyn, Honor, and Xrissa all yawned in rapid succession.

Courage leaned forward, eying the lovers with suspicious

curiosity. "So, did you always know she was a princess type person when you started calling her that?"

"Of course not," Karina said. "I was mocking her for being introduced with a title." After a pause, Karina shrugged and added, "Somewhere along the path, it became more flirtatious."

"Neither of you possessed any subtlety about that," Courage said. "But you two had a pretty violent fight. How'd you go from that to this?"

Gwyn looked up at Karina and nodded. Karina sighed. "Well, all of us went through different things. Marius convinced my father Gwyn had corrupted me, which given my past indiscret—"

Gwyn placed a finger on Karina's lips. "That was not an indiscretion. You were young and in love, a love he did not accept then and will not accept now. That is his sin. Love is blameless."

Karina smiled. "It will take some time to accept that."

"And I offer all the time in eternity." Gwyn bit Karina's lower lip and pulled her lover in for a kiss. After breaking the kiss, Gwyn said, "Now, back to the story."

Xrissa sighed. "Love leads to marriage. Marriage leads to weddings. Weddings lead to cake. You'll need a baker. I've never baked with blood before. Can vampires taste food?"

"I've got ninety-one more years of being able to taste food, Xrissa. After that, no."

"So the wedding has to be soon. Got it!"

Karina swallowed hard. "We'll discuss that later. Anyway, after Father threw me out, I headed toward Froam and then Florescia. I needed to apologize to Gwyn even if she refused me anything beyond that. Something happened, and I ended up being granted an audience with the Corvidiae in front of the Lord of Sky and Storm's grave, and when the audience ended, I was in a swampy area where I saw—well—my cousin Severus pointing his pistol at Gwyn. I shot him."

"Oh, that's harsh," Honor said. She then ruffled Courage's hair and said, "I know I call my brother a butthead and an idiot all the time, but if I had to shoot him—even when he's being an ass—or anyone in my family, that would be fucking horrid. Sorry."

Karina nodded. "I didn't realize who was involved until I drew closer after shooting him. Then, Gwyn and I talked for several days, and a few events later, we kissed and made up."

"That's right," Gwyn said with a knowing smile. "It takes a lot of courage to speak openly and honestly with the woman you love, hiding nothing, and keeping no secrets."

Courage narrowed his eyes and stuck out his tongue for a brief moment. Then he nodded and smirked. "I did prod you two along as best I could. I'm glad to see my hard work paid off. You can thank me with a wedding invitation and the largest piece of cake."

Everyone laughed. Courage was the first to fall silent. He looked away, beyond Gwyn, into the night. His voice was soft. "You're a queen. You got your knight back. Why'd you come after me?"

Gwyn sat up and leaned forward, offering Courage a sincere and compassionate smile. "You're my friend. You disappeared shortly after the explosion. The comm ring ceased to function. I was worried, and if I have the power to alleviate suffering, then I will at least try to do so. You'd have been out sooner, but oracles and death goddesses love speaking in cryptic riddles."

"Thank you." Courage nodded. Fear and sorrow darkened

and weakened his voice as he said, "I thought I would be turned into one of those things."

Honor rustled her brother's hair. He glared at her and growled. She chuckled. "You think I'd let that happen to you, you butthead? You last contacted me when you were on your way to Schwarzfeld. I gave you four days before I started tracking your location, and when I couldn't even ping you on this entire fucking plane, I went to Madame Atoel."

Courage balked. "That dizzy old witch is a bit of a space flier. Why would you go to her?"

Honor slapped the back of Courage's head. "Because she's good at what she does, and because I was worried about your dumb ass, you dingus."

At this point Arcanist Mediciara returned with the keys to the various rooms. "Here you are. The rooms are through that door and down the stairs in the basement. Sezara, your Guard will work in shifts stationed outside your door, as we trust your Human companion will be able to protect you should the need arise."

"Without fail." Karina wrapped her arm around Gwyn.

The elder vampire nodded and continued. "As to the needs of the mortals, you may order food and drink in the restaurant area, but be certain to specify mortal fare, lest you get a drink infused with blood. Beyond that, I trust each of you has the knowledge and ability to behave appropriately, given you are all reflections of our sezara."

After another yawn, Gwyn rose from her seat, shot Karina a pointed an knowing look, and then took hold of Karina's hand. "Come on. You may have napped in the carriage, but the beds here will be far more luxurious than my shoulder."

Karina rose, and the two of them made their way toward

the descending stairs. As they passed by Courage, Karina patted his shoulder. "It's good to see you safe."

Gwyn rustled his hair, eliciting an annoyed groan, and said, "Don't do anything we wouldn't do before you turn in." She turned to Honor and Xrissa, adding, "Would you two make sure he eats something? All of you, eat something."

They nodded, and the two lovers descended to their suite. Polished mahogany planks formed the floors in the spacious, high-ceilinged guest rooms, and ornate tapestries from the twelfth century in the Age of Arcanum lined the stone walls. Woven into their fabric were nocturnal scenes of bats flying through the moonlight and wolves howling at the moon. Black velvet curtains hung from the massive four-poster bed. An ever-burning fireplace crackled in the stone wall opposite the bed.

"The hearth will offset the cold," Karina said as they undressed for bed.

Gwyn nodded. "We'll have one in our room at my home. All the rooms have them to aid the servants, any mortal guests, adopted children, and lovers."

"Mortals die," Karina said, sitting on the bed and removing her boots. "I'll die after I grow old, hopefully. You won't change."

Gwyn sat beside her lover and placed her pale hands atop Karina's olive-toned ones. "What worries you?"

Karina shook her head and sighed. "What if...what if I don't become a vampire and you tire of me?"

Gwyn kissed Karina's cheek. "I had similar thoughts when I learned the Vandiamantes were vampires. I can tell you this, from the moment they adopted me, I was a Vandiamante. Never did they allow me to want for or doubt their love, my belonging with them, or that we were family. When the time came for me to decide my path, the only fear I had at that moment was the fear of being alone. Never once did I fear they would cease to love me if I chose to remain mortal. And, Karina Alyxandra Skejik, I Gwynarra Caoilfhionn Vandiamante, Sezara of the Midnight Court and Hertogia in the Royal Court of Florescia, make the same promise to you. Never will you want for love, affection, and care from me. Never will you feel pressure to become as I am. That transformation must be your decision alone. I will love you and walk beside you regardless of the path you choose."

Karina nodded and smiled. Gwyn wrapped her arms around her lover, and the two women breathed in each other's presence. They undressed, kissed, and went to sleep.

After Gwyn and Karina left the reception area, Honor rose and said, "Well, we should get something to eat and then head on down to sleep."

"That sounds like a good idea." Xrissa patted her rumbling stomach as she spoke.

She rose and walked beside Honor. Courage nodded. "I'll be there in a few. Just order me like a sandwich or something with cabbage and potatoes."

He remained seated, his gaze focused on something unseen in the distance. Xrissa nodded to Honor. The older Ashbourne nodded. "Alright. I'll get you something. If I finish eating before you join me, we'll bring it to the room for you. I love you, little brother."

She patted his shoulder before walking to the restaurant and bar area. Xrissa chugged her flask to the point the magic struggled to refill the Crimson Minotaur quickly enough. She sat beside Courage. "So, both Gwyn and Karina praised your wandvolver. I wish I could've seen it in action."

Courage nodded once. "It blew up. I miscalculated."

"But it worked, and you're smart. You can make it better next time, for your next adventure."

Xrissa kept her voice hopeful, but Courage's response were devoid of hope. "Doubtful."

"But what about your next treasure hunt? The letters you send are always so exciting, and your face lights up when you get to share all you've learned about a piece of history."

Courage sighed. "I've got to focus on Mum—wait. You look forward to hearing about that?"

A moment of confusion washed over Courage's face. He turned his gaze from the distance and searched Xrissa's smiling face. She nodded and brushed some loose strands of hair behind her ear. "Your face lights up like the candles outside in the Bazaar Plaza and the Zahra Oasis during the Midwinter Light Festival. There's joy, excitement, hope, and pride in your words, in what you did, and in what it allowed you to learn. You always know the right time to send a letter or to visit the shop to brighten up either a boring or a bad day. And maybe there's a bit of jealousy too."

Why did Xrissa say that last bit? Why is she blushing? Genuine confusion filled his words. "Jealous? What? How? You're successful. You're an amazing baker, and let's not even talk about the fabulous machines you use throughout your shop. If you want to travel, why not just go somewhere, like you are now?"

Xrissa sighed and shook her head. "Honor's right. You are the most brilliant dumbass in the world. Every letter you send, every visit into my shop where we talk machines and you your adventures delving into ruins, I bounce in excitement, both to hear everything have to say and then in the hope you'll ask me to join you on your next one."

Courage blinked. She didn't mean that in *that* way. Did she? "But it's dangerous."

"I'm not helpless. I have SAAMy and a few fighting skills I picked up in Preania."

The automaton stirred at the mention if its name. Its eyes jiggled and spun. Courage laughed. "So you do. It's dirty and musty."

"So was my shop when I bought it. I survived that."

Courage nodded. "Fair point. Does that mean…" He paused and tensed every muscle in his body. "Does that mean you want to travel with *me*?"

"Yes!" Xrissa threw her arms up as she exclaimed her desire. "I hear from this vampire princess you've been traveling with that you talk about me all the time. When you're home, you come by the shop every day, but unless we talk machines or your adventures, you kind of sit at your table in silence."

Courage lowered his head and swallowed hard. His voice was soft and soaked in anxiety. "You're the reason I chose my virtue name. I wanted to work up the courage to talk to you and tell you how pretty, smart, talented, and amazing I think you are."

"I think you're pretty amazing, smart, and handsome." Xrissa batted her eyelashes and grinned.

Courage blinked. A sheepish grin tiptoed across his face. "You do?" Xrissa nodded. And then Courage asked, "What do we do now?"

Honor Faern'doln slammed two cardboard boxes onto the table in front of Courage and Xrissa. "You take these boxes, and you get your asses down to our room, you dingus. You two need to eat something, and then we're going to get some sleep. We've got a long ride ahead of us."

Chapter 21

Marius Bedwyr slammed the door to his office on the top floor of the Imperium Center for the Rehabilitation of Traitors. He growled, snarled, and screamed in anger. With a single hand, the vampire lifted one of the wood and leather chairs and hurled it toward a wall. The chair splintered as it crashed into the shelves, sending books careening onto the floor. He stalked over to his desk, pounded his fist onto the corner, and then sat in his chair, resting his face in his hand that trembled with rage.

A moment passed and his bodyguards as well as the three members of Central Comm slunk into the office. They kept their gazes focused on the floor as they approached, halting only when Marius spoke.

"How? How in all of Ashfodell did this happen? I leave for only a few days and not only does someone break into our facility, but it's that damned Florescian cunt and her Richter bitch. And not only that, but how do they manage to abscond with my captured little technomagus and kill one of the finest and strongest Kriegsdieneryn we have manufactured to date? Well? Answer me!"

The vampires in his office focused their gazes on anything but the snarling, flared-nostril face of their leader. Marius snapped a fountain pen. Black ink bled over his hands and desk. With a growling shout, he hurled the broken pen at the nearest vampire, who dodged it.

"We're…we're not entirely certain, Sir." One of the members of Central Comm responded. "They set off no alarms until an incident on B3 where we heard background chatter including the firing of several rounds of shot. We contacted the B3 watch station, and upon receiving an odd message from what we now know to be one of the perpetrators, sent a maintenance team along with the Assistant Director to ensure the safety of all our technomagi. None of them were harmed, and their work was not disrupted."

"Well that's fucking brilliant, isn't it?" Marius rage had yet to subside. "They just walked all the way to the end of the foundry and broke the damned Ashbourne from his cell. How? Only two keys exist, and I keep both of them."

"Our investigation, Sir, indicates the lock was picked somehow. And the chain keeping the Ashbourne in his cell appears to have been twisted off, somehow."

Marius leaped over the desk and grabbed the throat of the speaking vampire with a single hand, lifting him a foot off the floor. "It was bloody steel chain. Yes, it was too thick for him to break or to do anything to with the tools provided to him, but a single fledgling vampire bitch was able to snap it. Did you forget about her?"

He slammed the vampire into the floor. The vampire grunted and shook his head. "No, Lord Marius. Also, the magical dampening crystals had been removed and shattered. As such, we suspect that allowed the Ashbourne to potentially get word of his location to his friends."

"Impossible," Marius shrieked, causing the five other vampires to shoot each other concerned glances. Marius growled a deep breath and returned to his chair. "Unless someone told him where he was being held, he had no knowledge of that."

Another one of the Central Comm vampires spoke up. "The only thought I have on that, Sir, is once he sent a message, another with more experience in arcane magic could perhaps locate him."

Marius clenched his fists and pounded his desk. "And the Assistant Director? How did they overcome her? She was designed to be strong enough to kill a vampire."

The three Central Comm vampires looked at each other. The one who spoke first said, "It seems they overloaded the power core. Surveillance footage shows that one of them had a crossbow-shaped automaton empowered by multiple types of Arcanyx crystals. Shall we send agents after them, Sir?"

Marius narrowed his eyes. "Did you not see the carriages they ran toward? That bitch is headed to Florescia under the protection of the Sezatorian Guard. And I need the bloody Richters to—wait." A feral, hungry smirk snaked across Marius' lips. "Do you have footage that clearly shows Karina Richter among the number of those who assaulted our facility?"

"I'm fairly certain of it, Lord Marius," the third and final Central Comm vampire said with a nod.

"Be certain that little bitch is present and visible." Marius tapped his fingers on the desk and sighed. "The High Holy Council meets again in three days once the agents Caspar Richter sent to Milmigua return with their findings. The day I leave, I want evidence of her involvement in a break-in to assist a prisoner in breaking out of our rehabilitation facility leaked to the papers, especially the *Sonnenburg Daily*. We may need to quicken our pace. Now go, all of you."

"Yes, Lord Marius." All five vampires spoke and bowed in unison before they departed.

Once they left, Marius glared at his map for moment. Begrudgingly, he moved the white queen and the black knight to Delfia, knowing that would be their destination. As he stared at the map of what would become his empire, his thoughts drifted from topic to topic. The Crimson Fang strike team that conquered Milmigua had already fled into the coastal caves beneath Whitclyf, and they were prepared to launch their attack there tomorrow. Given the diplomatic scandal brewing, imperial forces had pulled back from the southern border and were, in general, hesitant to show a serious presence beyond the empire's center. But the northern part of the empire, what was happening there?

Marius pushed a button on his desk. The map behind him spun around, revealing a massive comm screen and box unconnected to imperial comm lines. He pressed a button to flag the Czarnenburg cell of the Crimson Fangs. A moment passed before the call was answered, and the cell's leader, a burly Human vampire with long blond hair, hazel eyes, and a thick handlebar mustache answered, speaking in a fluid northern Atharian accent. "Lord Marius, what may I do for you—and for us?"

"Hello, Ivyn," Marius said. "What is the situation in Czarnenburg?"

"In general? Well, the Laughing Death continues to ravage Old Town, and it's spreading into the Market and Hillfront areas as well. The clergy are speaking about punishment for sinful lifestyles. There are some quack physicians touting clean eating as a cure. Oh, and the fucking constables have been purging any in Old Town they catch showing any symptoms. Been a few riots, and we've helped the rioters a bit under table."

Marius nodded. "Change that. Be overt. I want my Fangs to break into storehouses and steal food to bring to the residents of Old Town. Any constable setting foot in that district after sunset becomes food. Spread the word. Let all know that the Crimson Fang protects the people."

Ivyn nodded. "Yes, Sir. Think we have enough in the cell for this? Or should we recruit?"

Marius smirked. "Let them come to us. If any start praising, saying they wish they could thank us or something similar, approach them in secret. And then turn them. Understood?"

"Yes, Lord Marius."

Marius ended the call. He repeated the same instructions to the leaders in the Tircienburg, Zamekstadt, and Dornbach cells. With the Grand Imperial Army hesitant to act, and the Holy Order of St. Arnulf Ironhand weakened and focused elsewhere, the rise of the Crimson Fang would have no opposition within the Atharian Empire.

Two days passed, and the Crimson Fang vampires acted upon Marius' orders as he traveled again to Sonnenburg. Heavy rains slowed his travel by a day, and during his travel, he tested the power levels and distance of the control remote override master switch implanted in the Kriegsdieneryn. He smiled.

I wanted to enjoy this process more, Marius though as his carriage drove through Sonnenburg's northern gate. *But with that damned bitch on her way to Delfia, I have little choice. I was hoping Caspar's daughter would kill her, and then I could rally the people behind us as we avenged one who protected them from the monsters that were almost as terrifying as the abominations now seen fighting at the Richters' command.* He twirled the small remote in hand and smirked. *Well, that's why we built this little insurance device to assume control of the Kriegsdieneryn and implant a false memory within the eyes of any Ofhani with him. I may have lost that little Ashbourne, but I doubt he knew what we had planned for those devices.*

Thick, dark clouds shaded the streets of Sonnenburg from the afternoon sun as Marius Bedwyr's carriage sped past the alms beggars outside the gate, splashing them with standing water as the wheels rolled over the cobblestones. As the carriage slowed to a stop, Marius turned to his bodyguards and said, "Remain with the carriage. I need to appear alone for this to work."

"Yes, Lord Marius," one said.

"If you are certain, Lord Marius." Upon receiving verbal confirmation, the second bodyguard nodded. "Yes, Sir. As you wish."

Marius grabbed his briefcase and descended from the carriage. The Imperial Palace guards saluted Marius, recognizing him as Lord Ambrose von Harenheim, and he nodded to them as they opened the palace doors. As he walked along the green velvet carpet of the Grand Promenade, he noted the statues he would enjoy toppling the most when the empire belonged to him. The mirrors lining the walls in the Hall of Reflection required him to negotiate his placement relative to others walking, engaging them in conversation while raising his briefcase to block the side of his face, and moving with a speed swifter than a Human's average so all mortals he passed assumed he had a reflection.

Once in the Imperial Receiving Suite, the servants directed

Marius to the Imperial Throne Room. The room was a vast and imposing rectangular chamber with a high vaulted ceiling adorned with a fresco depicting the rise of Emperor Albrecht Wartheimer, the Great Liberator, from the moment he received the Lord of Sky and Storm's blessing and pulled the Sacred Sun Sword from the stone which now sits beneath the Imperial Throne to his war to liberate the Athars and the Polonovs from Romatruski rule to his uniting of the warring factions under his banner to form the nation of Athar, which he ruled as emperor. The vaults supporting the ceiling rose from stone walls punctuated with tall, arched windows. The gold and crystal chandeliers hanging from the ceiling illuminated the chamber with technomagical light mimicking the noonday sun. Two rows of white marble columns topped with intricate carvings rise from the polished red oak floors.

A gold-trimmed carpet of green velvet extends from the door to the Imperial Throne, located atop a dais at whose center is the legendary sword from which Albrecht removed the symbol of the Blessed Emperor's choosing. Encrusted with diamonds, topaz, and citrine stones, the golden throne blazes around the seated emperor, granting him the appearance of a god rising from the sun.

Rows of wooden benches with green velvet cushions, identical to that upon which the Blessed Emperor sat, flanked the throne. Here, the imperial family, the High Holy Council, and other honored guests sat during ceremonies. Portraits of previous emperors adorned the wall behind the throne.

After kneeling before Blessed Emperor Hapfsburgh and kissing his ring, Marius shook hands with High General Krank. Marius scanned the room and then chuckled. "This may be the first time I've arrived before Caspar."

"Grand Master Richter will appear before us shortly," the Blessed Emperor said. "The rains that slowed your travel did the same for him and his entourage."

"Finally, we'll know what happened in Milmigua." High General Krank glowered. "I need to know who to court martial for treason."

Marius nodded. "Yes, and none too soon, as the delegation from the Indigo Coast arrives in two days to demand answers of us."

Marius and Krank spoke on cordial terms for the next few moments until the doors to the Imperial Throne Room opened on the announcement of Caspar Richter's arrival. Marius reached into his pocket and flipped the power switch on the remote control device. The vampire's thin lips curled in a lean and hungry smile.

Two agents of the Holy Order of St. Arnulf Ironhand flanked their Grand Master. Behind the three men were a dozen Kriegsdieneryn. Three Ofhani Searchers, disembodied heads surrounded by two crossing wheels covered in eye-shaped Arcanyx crystals, floated in the air, their eyes scanning in all directions. Walking behind the humans were three Zerafi Scorchers and six Malaki Grunts. The hulking Scorchers had a faceless iron mask adorned with spikes covering their faces and six arms that ended in flamethrowers that hurled Zyntarian fire gel at their targets. The Grunts had the most humanoid appearance, with bronze armor covering their muscular bodies. Their arms, however, ended in rapid-fire repeating muskets and an assortment of bladed weapons.

Caspar Richter bowed low. "Forgive me, Your Excellency, tardiness was not our intent, but we come with important and urgent news that will bring glory to the empire."

Marius slid his finger over to the second switch. The crystal eyes of the Searchers flashed for a brief second. Marius smiled. The Richter entourage stepped forward and stopped at the base of the dais.

As Caspar ascended the dais, Marius slid his finger onto the control override switch. Caspar kissed the Blessed Emperor's ring. Marius flipped the switch.

Emperor Hapfsburgh nodded. "Grand Master Richter, what word do you bring us from your search of Milmigua?"

Caspar descended the dais and kneeled before the Blessed Emperor. "Your Excellency, when we arrived at Milmigua, we found evidence of the Crimson Fang presence, but those damned vampires had departed the city, leaving a populace terrified of our presence."

As the Grand Master of the Holy Order of St. Arnulf Ironhand continued his debriefing on the mission and their findings, the six Malaki Grunts raised their musket arms and fired on the Blessed Emperor. Everyone looked on in horror, but Marius, using his vampiric celerity, pushed Emperor Hapfsburgh to safety, taking a pair of musket shots in his shoulder and arm in the process.

Grunting, Marius produced the control device from his pocket and pressed the control override button once more. "Halt!"

The Kriegsdieneryn stopped their attacks and stood at attention. The two Richter agents activated their comm rings and relayed the message that the Kriegsdieneryn had malfunctioned. The Imperial Guard, their weapons drawn, surrounded the three Richters, who raised their hands to show they meant no threat.

Marius and High General Krank assisted the Blessed Emperor in standing. His eyes were widened, and the old man's chest heaved as his heart thundered within it. Marius whispered into the Blessed Emperor's ear and then said for all to hear, "Your Excellency, the Kriegsdieneryn have never malfunctioned before. That so many moved in unison is suggestive of something far darker that I fear not name."

"Your Excellency," Caspar Richter pleaded. "This is nothing more than a malfunction. You must believe me. I will have my nephew Hanzlin examine these automatons, and the truth of my words—words even Lord Ambrose von Harenheim spoke—will come to light."

The Blessed Emperor hobbled to his throne and sat. Looking over those assembled, he said, "It saddens us to say this, Grand Master Richter. High General Krank, we must request you perform the unfortunate and mournful duty of taking custody of these three men and of examining the Kriegsdieneryn we have entrusted to their control. Grand Master Richter, you and your agents, are now under arrest. Guards, take them away."

Two days later, all twenty-six remaining members of the Holy Order of St. Arnulf Ironhand stood, shackled and unarmed, before the Blessed Emperor, a battalion of imperial soldiers, and the remaining two members of the High Holy Council. To the side of the Emperor was a large crystal viewing screen. The air was thick and heavy with the solemnity and fear of the moment.

Sorrow soaked the Blessed Emperor's face. He raised his right hand and said, "Our investigation is complete. We will not waste time, but we will present the one piece of evidence that saddens us the most. Lord von Harenheim, explain what we are about to see."

Marius nodded, practiced sorrow on his face. He walked over to the screen and switched it on. "Yes, Your Excellency. Military Intelligence recovered the following memory taken from the Ofhani Searchers. My technomagi and I had discussed altering their recording circuits so they could be switched off, but it appears our indecision has aided this investigation. Here."

He pressed a button, and a scene began to play. In the basement of the Richter family manor, Caspar Richter and several agents were seen modifying the cores of the Kriegs-dieneryn. The Richters grumbled, and Caspar argued this never happened. The Blessed Emperor ordered him to remain silent.

The scene continued, and all heard Caspar Richter state in a loud and clear voice to no opposition but uproarious agreement, "Performing the duties of Military Intelligence is beneath us. Our sacred task is to find and remove Ashfodel-lian threats, and we should be hunting the Crimson Fangs and that Vandiamante whore aligned with them. Shame that the Blessed Emperor fears to lift the Sacred Sun Sword against our true foes. He is weak, but with these tools, we can free the empire of all vampires, end the treason of those disloyal to the Lord of Sky and Storm, and destroy that last Vandiamante who corrupted my poor daughter, Karina."

"Your Excellency," Caspar pleaded. "This is a mistake. That never happened. I have never wanted to oppose you."

"And yet," the emperor said. "You have done such a thing to us. During our investigation, the *Sonnenburg Daily* posted a story complete with clear daguerreotype images of your daughter Karina, wearing the Holy Order's uniform, assaulting Lord von Harenheim's rehabilitation center for traitors. This incident, the memory on the Ofhani cores, the report of your daughter's actions, and your lack of bringing any justice to Milmigua have both called into question your loyalty to this empire and your devotion to your sacred task.

"We have no choice, and though it pains us to say this, say it we must. Caspar Richter, we find you guilty of treason and heresy in conspiring to assassinate the Blessed Emperor of the Atharian Empire. The Holy Order of St. Arnulf Ironhand is to be disbanded. Caspar and Hanzlin Richter, we sentence the two of you to be impaled on stakes and to have your corpses displayed in Cathedral Square until such a time as nothing remains but your bones. To the rest of you, we will show this mercy. You are exiled from this empire. Choose this day where you will go."

The Richters stood in stunned silence. Garrus raised his hand and said, "May we go to Florescia?"

The Blessed Emperor nodded. "Guards, see them to the border with Florescia, and remain there until you are confident they will not return. Take the damned to their prison cells."

The Imperial Guards escorted the Richters to their destinations. Blessed Emperor Hapfsburgh turned to Marius and Krank. "You two are the last members of our High Holy Council who have remained loyal. For that, we thank you. Lord von Harenheim, as the divinely ordained genius behind these creatures of atonement, we request you form a task force to serve as a replacement for the Holy Order."

Marius dropped to one knee. "You honor me, Your Excellency. However, I must decline, as such a task seems better suited to Military Intelligence than to my research staff."

"Nonsense, Lord Ambrose," High General Krank said. "I

concur with our Blessed Emperor. Military Intelligence is up to the task, but your creations could perform the more unpleasant tasks once assigned to the Richters without moral reservation. As long as each strike team included a technomagus or two who had those control devices you had to switch them off if they malfunction, none would succeed in opposing His Excellency's will."

The Blessed Emperor smiled at Marius with compassion and sympathy. "We know of your deep friendship with Caspar Richter, and we know this must grieve you most deeply. However, we do ask this of you as our faithful servant. Do consider our request."

Marius paused in thought. After a moment, he sighed. "If it is your will, Your Excellency, I will depart and begin work."

"Go with our blessing."

Marius bowed and departed the Imperial Throne Room. Before departing for Iszenstadt, Marius Bedwyr paid a visit to Hessiakraft Gaol. Black stone walls topped with razor wire towered over all but the central tower, which loomed over all beneath it with a burning crystal eye. Armed guards patrolled the walls, their eyes ever tuned to the prisoners in the yard where prisoners lifted, moved, and broke stone boulders the size of their bodies.

Narrow walls of stone, arranged in a labyrinthine pattern, filled the cell blocks within the central tower's three basement levels. The halls were narrow and devoid of all but the barest artificial light. Cold, damp, and stale air filled the cell floors, and no Arcanyx crystal devices provided relief or ventilation. Using his rank, Marius was granted access to Caspar Richter's cell, which was more cramped and sparse in its furnishings than the one provided to Courage in Iszenstadt.

Stripped to a pale gray prisoner's uniform, shackles around his ankles bound Caspar Richter to the back wall of his cell. When Marius entered and the thick iron door had closed behind him, the old man hobbled toward him, falling to his knees, and begging his old friend, "Ambrose, it's good to see you. You have to believe we're innocent."

Marius smirked and nodded. "Oh, I believe you. I do."

Caspar smiled. His eyes looked toward the ceiling. "Praise the Lord of Sky and Storm. You'll speak to the Blessed Emperor on our behalf? Please, help him to see the truth."

"Oh, I can't do that, old friend. I'm afraid I can't do that."

Caspar's face darkened in fear, confusion, and betrayal. "But why? Are we not friends? You have done nothing but kindnesses for my family, even showing mercy to my daughter."

"Ah, yes, that. Ambrose von Harenheim died several years ago when he became the first prototype of the Dieneryn." Marius smirked, baring his fangs in full view of the old man. Marius bowed. "Please, allow me to introduce myself, given the name Owaiyn, son of Cinnsealach Ó Lonagáin the last High King of Froam, slain by Grand Master Vladislav Richter when the Atharian Empire conquered my nation. Carted off to St. Hiltegardt the Open-Armed Orphanage, I was tortured and beaten until the Bedwyr family adopted me, and my adoptive father gave me a family and education if he was distant and unemotional. You know how wealthy vampire families are, no? Well, he was killed, and I changed my name to his middle name, Marius."

Caspar fell backward and gasped. "You cannot be speaking the truth. Ambrose, you are not this vampire traitor who terrorizes our good citizens."

Marius smirked and laughed. "But I am, old friend. I am the leader of the Crimson Fangs." He produced the silver pendant with six golden Arcanyx crystals he wore around his neck. "A life's aura pendant, simple magic that can fool the powers granted you arrogant shits by your fucking god."

Caspar's voice trembled. "If you are Marius Bedwyr, then my daughter…my Karina…"

"Spoke nothing but truth to you, Caspar." Marius rushed forward and grabbed Caspar Richter by his throat. Pinning the old man to the wall, Marius growled the rest of his words. "You fucking monsters took everything from me: my family, my home, my crown. Now, I will return the favor."

Marius released Caspar, and the old man grunted as he fell to the floor. Marius walked to the cell door, stopped, and said, "I look forward to your execution. Shame your daughter won't be there to witness it."

Marius Bedwyr left the cell, and as the door slammed shut, the light flickered, leaving Caspar Richter in darkness.

Chapter 22

As the sun rose on the day Blessed Emperor Hapfsburgh disbanded the Holy Order of St. Arnulf Ironhand, the carriage caravan escorting Hertogia Vandiamante to her home rolled onto the narrow cobblestone streets of Utrezzo. Gwyn had fallen asleep on Karina's shoulder, and as she cradled her sleeping lover, Karina looked upon the city outside. Tall buildings of white stone and red brick flanked the streets for the first few blocks, but as the carriage wheels clacked further into the Monte Verde district, the streets opened to lush, open-air botanical gardens, parks with marble fountains, and spacious villas.

Moving into the central market, Karina saw vendors selling fruit, vegetables, silk clothing, leather goods, art, and all manner of toys and diversions from within their colorful canvas stalls. Musicians, singers, jugglers, and dancers milled about the streets, sitting on corners, and performing in the hopes someone would toss a few coins into their hats, buckets, or instrument cases. Citizens and travelers of all ages and social classes walked freely, dined at restaurants, and enjoyed the street performers, and Karina noted she saw almost none of the city's constabulary.

The carriage turned north and made its way to the Hertogial

Quarters, a district marked by lavish villas and opulent and gilded buildings. The carriages ascended a winding mountain path, and the bumps on the carriage caused Gwyn to stir. She whined, flung her arm around Karina, and returned to her death sleep. Karina kissed her forehead. Was she dreaming this? Karina could have sworn she saw Gwyn smile in her death sleep.

Honor observed Karina's wide eyes and open mouth and asked, "Guess your new home's not so bad, is it?"

Karina stiffened her posture. She chuckled and blushed. "I guess not, but I've never been outside of the empire before. There are wealthy citizens here handing food to peasant children. That…that would never happen back home."

Her voice trailed to sadness as she reflected on this observation. Honor nodded. Before she could speak, Courage jumped in. "Travel has a way of changing perspectives. I've learned so much through my travels from ancient ruins, libraries, and labs that it's sometimes hard to look at home the same way."

Karina nodded. As she thought about this, one of the Sezatorian Guard said, "You get to wake Sezara Vandiamante, Human."

"Me?" The vampires nodded. Karina poked Gwyn's cheek and spoke in a gentle voice. "Wake up, my princess. We're almost to your castle."

There was no response, save for vampiric chuckling. Karina tried again, poking harder, but she earned no response. She sighed. "What am I supposed to do? Gwyn, wake up!"

Nothing. Courage leaned forward. He spoke in a loud voice. "You remember the first time you two shared a room and this happened?"

"Yes, Courage. I don't know what we did to wake her. She just woke up."

Karina's voice increased its volume. Courage nodded. "Exactly. But we were talking when it happened."

"I remember. We were arguing about the fact that I thought she was dead, but you said she was in a deep sleep."

Gwyn yawned. She blinked a dozen times and then opened her eyes. Speaking through a series of yawns, she asked, "Why are you two loud enough to wake the dead?"

The vampires laughed. Gwyn looked at Karina confused. Karina pointed at the Sezatorian Guard. "They told me to wake you, since we're almost at your home."

"Home?" Gwyn's face lit up. "We're home? Why didn't you kiss me awake? You won't always have Courage to yell at."

Karina sputtered. "I didn't think that would work."

"Yeah," Courage added. "That only works if you've got skin as white as snow, which you do, hair as black as coal, which you don't, and lips as red as blood, which you also don't."

"You haven't seen my lips right after I've had fresh blood." Gwyn crossed her arms over her chest and swung her legs across Karina's lap.

"I have," Karina said. "They are quite red. And you did that adorable happy food dance you do when you enjoy your meal. I'll try to kiss you awake the next time."

"The next time I have to day-walk," Gwyn said. "I hope that's either not for a long time or it involves you and your flower."

Karina blushed as the white stone of the castle's gatehouse and outer wall came into view. Two towers staffed by human soldiers hired by the Regent Council flanked the portcullis in the gatehouse. As the carriages neared, the soldiers raised the portcullis, allowing the carriages to pass into the spacious courtyard. Military training grounds, a maze of manicured hedges, a garden of vibrant seasonal flowers and trees, and a massive water fountain shaped like a winged cat spitting water from its hissing mouth.

Instead of a keep, the castle itself was a massive, white marble Florescian villa. Tall towers with crenellated roofs stood guard on the four corners of the edifice. Tall, arched windows lined the walls of the rectangular building built around two smaller, central courtyards. Seven steps ascended from the front courtyard to the massive double doors leading into the Vandiamante castle.

Two figures stood before the doors were two figures. The first, a short, bald male with pointy ears and ratlike features, Karina recognized as the Nozy Mathias Greely. A tall Sun Elf man with shoulder-length black hair streaked with gray, a narrow and angular face, and green eyes. His black frock and vest paired with his gray trousers reminded Karina of the servants. He was probably a butler or something.

Gwyn's eyes lit up, and a smile burst across her face. As the carriage stopped, she pushed the door open and rushed from the carriage. Karina and the Sezatorian Guard scrambled to follow her. With a shout, Gwyn raced toward the servant, wrapped her arms around him, and burst into tears. He reciprocated the tears as he embraced her.

"Kiernan," Gwyn said. "I feared you were dead. When I learned you survived. How?"

The older Elven male smiled in a grandfatherly way as he rested his hands on Gwyn's shoulders. "And I might have been, Mistress Gwynarra—forgive me, *Hertogia* Gwynarra—were it not for the decades spent among the Black Jester's

Traveling Troubadours..." His smile faltered as he surveyed Gwyn's appearance. "You have cut your lovely hair so short."

Gwyn nodded. "It was necessary to survive. I see you've stolen Ylfredo's wardrobe. Are you now my estate steward?"

He bowed. With a chuckle and a shrug, Kiernan said, "Someone had to care for this estate until you returned to us. And now here you are."

Mathias received a hug as well. "Yeah, Mister Valfrido introduced himself as the venerable steward of the Vandiamante estate. It was a tense meeting—not as tense as when you pinned me to the wall in St. Hiltegardt's—but still tense."

"Yes, Hertogia Gwynarra," Kiernan said. "As I said upon apologizing to young master Mathias once he produced your letter, having an unexpected squatter in this estate was unacceptable. He has proved a good companion and a good steward as well."

"So, it's only the two of you here?"

Kiernan nodded solemnly. "It is."

"That will change, Sezara," Arcanist Mediciara said. "Now that you have returned to us, we will staff your estate to your satisfaction. Now, if you will excuse me, the Sezatorian Guard will remain with you and your mortal entourage. I must return to Delfia to prepare for your coronation. We shall send the carriages for you shortly before sunrise two days from now. Farewell."

"Do not forget to make the plans to bring Honor and Courage's family over. I know Xrissa said she wished to teleport with your team for her own purposes."

"I'm going too," Honor said. "That way Mum and Da know this is all above the table."

"We will begin preparations," Medicara said. "I suggest

contacting them if you are able so they may begin packing."

"We can do that," Honor said. She turned to Gwyn. "Thank you."

Arcanist Mediciara bowed once more. He returned to the carriage, and the carriages drove away.

"I'm going with you too," Courage said.

Honor narrowed her eyes and shook her head. "No, you're not. You need to rest and be as far away from Sonnenburg as we can get you for now."

"Listen to your sister, Courage," Gwyn said. "I promise we'll all see Marius again, probably sooner than we'd all like. But mortals are fragile, and you've been through a lot. Besides, you can help me get your family's rooms ready while they move. You know them better than I do."

Courage sighed and nodded. "Fine. I can do that."

Karina had stayed back a few paces during the conversation, but once the carriages departed, she moved beside Gwyn and wrapped an arm around the vampire's waist. Kiernan's eyes darted between Karina and Gwyn. He lifted an eyebrow. "Someone I should know?"

Karina balked and sputtered. Gwyn chuckled and looked up at her with a smile. "Rina, I've met your father, and I promise my venerable estate steward will not be as difficult of a person to impress as he was. Kiernan, this is my knight in black leather, my beloved, Karina Skejik."

She paused and sent an inquisitive glance to Karina, asking for permission. Karina sighed and then responded with a slow nod. Gwyn shifted position to stand between her beloved and Kiernan. Then Gwyn said, "Because we both know this fact will come to light, she is the disowned daughter of Caspar Richter—disowned for protecting me from his attack."

Gwyn emphasized the last phrase and shot Kiernan a knowing look. He snorted but smiled. His attention turned to Karina, and he gave a shoulder-level bow. "Welcome, Miss Skejik. I trust this will not play out the way Antonio's love for Karolinya Richter did."

Karina swallowed hard, and Gwyn sighed in an audible, dramatic fashion. Karina shook her head. "I won't allow it. Besides, I don't think my father wants anything to do with me."

"Well," Kiernan said. "You all must be exhausted from the journey. Welcome, allow me to show you to the guest quarters. Hertogia, unless you desire your old rooms, I have prepared the master suite for you."

Gwyn paused. "The master suite? But that's where Grandfather—oh, I'm the Hertogia now." She nodded. "You've prepared it? How?"

Kiernan smiled. "Well, I redecorated the room based upon the furnishings that were in your old chambers. Since your rooms were largely undisturbed, I moved your possessions into the master suite and, as such, redecorated based upon that color palette." Kiernan noted Gwyn's distant expression, and after a pause, he added. "If you wish for new furnishings, that can be arranged."

Gwyn smiled. "Forgive me. My mind wandered to the way things were. This will be fine, but Rina will get a say in the decor as well. And we'll probably transform Grandfather's study into a room of her liking."

"I'm going check out the kitchen! We need breakfast. Bye," Xrissa exclaimed as she burst through the group and entered the castle.

Kiernan spun from Gwyn to Xrissa to the open door and

back to Gwyn, a puzzled expression on his face. "I did prepare some of Hertogia Gwynarra's favorites, as she is still young enough to enjoy them."

Courage chuckled. "Well, we can snack on that while Xrissa makes cinnamon rolls. She's downed three flasks of Crimson Minotaur in the past hour. You won't stop her."

"And I only hope I'm allowed to eat one," Gwyn said, taking Karina's hand and leading her into the castle. She paused as she crossed the threshold, shrugged, and added, "Since I'm only Snow Elf pretty."

"I didn't mean it like that," Courage said.

"Yep," Honor said, tussling Courage's hair to make him growl. She laughed. "You are a genius little brother. G-e-n-i-a-s-s. Come on, let's message Mum and Da."

Gwyn led Karina through the castle, starting with the narrow entrance foyer. Gold-trimmed tiles of white marble lined the floor. Full-length portraits of each vampire who held the title of Hertogius or Hertogia Vandiamante decorated the side walls, flanking the central arches leading to the external hallway around the villa. Gwyn led Karina through the glass door at the far end, which led to the first of the central courtyards.

A glass and stone fire pit, surrounded by wooden seating formed the central feature of this courtyard. Gwyn wrapped her arms around Karina's left arm and smiled. "The rear interior courtyard, through that hallway ahead, was mother's private flower garden. But this one was a family space. Every night at midnight, we'd have musicians, jugglers, and storytellers entertaining in this courtyard while the blood wine flowed and where food was prepared for those of us who could taste. We'd sing, dance, laugh, and play until dawn."

"Perhaps we'll continue, or I guess revive, the tradition." Karina kissed the top of Gwyn's head.

She shook her head. "Maybe we'll do something different. You've mentioned your mother reading stories to you, maybe we'll invite some of her people. They can teach me how to honor your blood. This is your home too, for as long as you remain here."

"You would do that for me? I haven't seen any of her people since I was small. Where—how would we find them?"

"We'll ask. That's how. And yes, I would do that for you. After all, you'll learn to tolerate, or perhaps even enjoy, the debauchery of the Florescian court. Now, come on. Kiernan is showing Honor and Courage to their rooms. Let me show you to ours, so we can freshen up, and then we'll descend to the dining hall for breakfast, which hopefully will include these legendary cinnamon rolls."

While Gwyn and Karina freshened up in the the master suite, Kiernan led Courage and Honor to the guest suite. He opened the varnished oak door inlaid with intricate filigree carvings of roses and thorny vines. Inside was a large sitting room whose white marble walls framed in golden trim. Gold, red, and black paisley rugs lay atop the oak floor boards. Warm gray and black leather furniture filled the room, arranged in a crescent around a coffee table and opposite an ever-burning hearth.

"The bath is through the door on your left," he said and pointed. "And there are two bedrooms and a small study and library through the hall on your right. Should you need to communicate, there is a comm box in each of the bedrooms. The button with the coat of arms of a scarlet wildcat holding a golden fasces will summon me should you need that. Breakfast is prepared. I hope your friend has found her way to the kitchen?"

Courage nodded. "She owns a bakery. She has a keen sense for where kitchens are."

Kiernan nodded and smiled. "A professional. Then the kitchen should be safe."

"She might even automate it to make things easier on you, since it's just you and all."

He snorted. "After I take your bags to the larger of the two bedrooms."

"We can take them," Honor said. She reached to grab the the bags from Kiernan, and her nose perked at his cologne, which smelled of bergamot, cedar, and rosemary. "Didn't exactly pack a lot for this trip. Guess we'll need to go shopping."

"We can arrange for a carriage to take you into Utrezzo. I would suggest we summon a tailor this afternoon to take your measurements for your coronation attire. It will be a rush job, but nothing Gabrini can't handle."

"But you're the only one here." Honor tilted her head and leaned forward slightly. "Who will drive us then?"

"I'm certain Hertogia Gwynarra can manage without me for a few hours. Besides, she may sleep during the day as was always her custom." Kiernan then gave them directions to the dining hall where he had laid out the breakfast for them. After that, he said, "Now, I will give you privacy while you freshen up, rest, and anything else you need to do."

As he closed the door behind him, Honor said, "He seems nice."

Courage shrugged. "Seemed okay. I'm just looking at this room. I thought our room at the Sepulcher was big, but this place is fucking huge. There's like five rooms in this suite.

Think there'll be enough room for the family?"

"This place is fucking huge. Let's go give Mum and Da a call. With a call box, we can talk as long as we want."

"You know how to use one, right?"

Honor glared at her younger brother. "Fuck you, you butthead."

"Genius. Said it yourself."

"And I spelled it a-s-s, because you're a right fucking ass."

Courage curled up in the armchair beside the table atop which the call box rested. Honor sprawled on the sofa adjacent to that table. She grabbed the receiver and spoke their father's name, Owaiyn Faern'doln, and pressed the sending button. When he answered, she said, "Hello, Da. It's Honor, and I've got my dumbass little brother Courage beside me."

Courage pushed the button that switched the call from a handset call to a speaker call while turning his nose up at his sister. He then said, "Hi, Da. How are you and Mum?"

"It's good to hear from you both," their father said. "Courage, your sister worried us with her frantic departure to find you. Is everything okay? Your mother stabilized, so we assumed all was well."

Courage chuckled nervously as he ran his fingers through his hair. "Well, about that. Kind of why we called. See, I kind of started tagging along with this monster hunter named Gwynarra Vandiamante, and we met up with this vampire hunter named Karina Richter. Then the Society for Afterlife and Arcane Research hired us to check out some hauntings and stop the ghosts from hurting people. Long story short, Gwyn turned out to be a vampire princess, and Karina's the daughter of the man who killed her family. But Karina got kicked out of the family for not killing Gwyn, even though she did try, but now they're together and in love. That's a whole other long story. Anyway, we made a powerful enemy of this other vampire named Marius. He locked me up, and so Xrissa, Gwyn, Karina, and Honor—I guess—rescued me. Now we're in Gwyn's castle in Florescia, and—"

"What the family genius is trying to say, Da," Honor placed her hand over Courage's mouth. He mumbled protestations as she continued. "Get everyone packed up with clothes and toys and such. I'll be there in a day or two along with some vampire arcanists to teleport the entire family to the cast—ouch! You fucking bit me, you little shit."

"That's what you get for interrupting me, you butthead."

Owaiyn laughed. "Your bickering will warm your mother's heart. Do you really think this is necessary?"

"We don't know, Da," Honor said. "But Gwyn doesn't want anyone getting hurt. Apparently this Marius is a fucking piece of work. She also thinks the vampire blood healers might be able to do something for Mum's condition. It's worth a fucking shot."

Owaiyn remained silent for a moment while he mulled over the request. Then he sighed. "This is a lot, and you're not giving us much time to prepare."

"We know, Da," Honor said.

"Yeah," Courage chimed in. "Marius lives in Sonnenburg, which is a lot closer to Al'Adara than anywhere in Florescia. Please consider."

"There are seven of us here, you know," Owaiyn said. "I doubt your brother Tairyn will want to uproot his family, but I'll talk to your mum and be in touch."

"Please, Da," Honor said. "Please do. I love you all."

"I love you all too," Courage said.

"And we love you. We'll talk soon, kids."

Almost three hours later, Gwyn and Karina descended from the master suite, hand in hand, and entered the family dining room on the second floor in the rear half of the castle. The Sezatorian Guard followed them. Gwyn's eyes bulged, and a smile burst across her face as she saw the massive amount of food atop the gold-flecked gray marble table. Karina pulled a chair out for Gwyn, and the vampire leaped onto the table grabbing a handful of sausages, fried potatoes, and black pudding.

Kiernan appeared from the kitchen door and cleared his throat. Gwyn looked up from the reverie of eating, a thick link of sausage in her mouth. Kiernan folded his arms over his chest and narrowed his eyes. "A Florescian lady sits in her chair and asks for food to be passed to her. You know this, Hertogia Gwynarra."

With a sheepish grin, Gwyn nodded and sat in the chair Karina had pulled out for her. She held up her plate. "I would like sausages, rashers, balck pudding, potatoes, crepes filled with strawberries and hazelnut cream, toasted bread with cinnamon butter, the fluffy quick bread, and the mushroom and pepper frittata." She batted her eyes at Kiernan and added, "Please."

"That is better. Our sezara must mind her manners." Kiernan took her plate.

Karina chuckled. Gwyn turned to her and asked, "What's so funny?"

She shook her head. "I've never seen this side of you. You've always been composed and proper at the table, aside from the little dance you do when you enjoy your meal."

Gwyn shrugged. "I like good food. And you're in for a treat. I've only ever seen you eat porridge, but trust me, try things."

Kiernan set Gwyn's plate before her. He then turned to Karina and asked, "Miss Skejik, might I inquire as to your preferences?"

"Same as me, but no black pudding. She needs to try things that aren't porridge." Gwyn said.

Karina sipped water from the crystal glass. "Maybe smaller portions. That a lot of food."

After serving Karina, Kiernan sat at the servant's table to eat. Gwyn looked over and said, "Kiernan, main table, please, and I won't listen to a lecture about tradition. You eat with us, as one of us, and the others when they get down here."

He protested, but Gwyn remained resolute. With a nod, he took his plate and glass and joined and sat at the family dining table. Gwyn smiled. Everyone jerked their heads toward the kitchen door as the clanging of metal bowls and maniacal laughter emerged. Kiernan rose from the table as the door swung open, and Xrissa Kosol burst into the kitchen with two dozen cinnamon rolls the size of an adult Human's head atop the silver tray in her arms. She had tied an empty flour sack over her head to serve as her toque, and even though she had donned one of the floral aprons the servants used when cooking, flour and butter covered her clothing and her skin.

"Cinnamon rolls are ready!"

Xrissa danced around the table, placing a cinnamon roll on the bread plate for each place setting then placing the tray on the table. The warm and almost autumnal, yeasty, and sweetly spicy aroma of the cinnamon rolls wafted through the air. The Sezatorian Guard remained motionless, but a keen observer would have noticed each of the guards' noses twitching as they smelled the rolls.

As she sat at the table, she swigged her flask. "Didn't have the chocolate I normally use. It was so bitter, but I think I adapted the recipe well enough. Enjoy."

Gwyn reached for the roll, and as her fingers touched the sticky glaze, Kiernan cleared his throat once more. Gwyn narrowed her eyes and pursed her lips, but she picked up her knife and fork, cut a small bite, and chewed. The earthiness of the toasted walnuts, the sticky sweet tanginess of the sugar and cream cheese glaze, the warm autumnal spices, and the molassess-drenched cinnamon and sugar filling, and the bitterness of the chocolate burst through her taste buds. She threw her head back against the chair, moaned, and then danced in her seat.

"So, you liked it," Xrissa asked.

"I've only seen her moan like that and dance once when eating," Karina said.

Gwyn planted a brief, sugar-sweetened kiss on Karina's lips and then said, "This is on par with your blood, my love, but I think you'll enjoy this more. It's so delicate, sinful, and decadent." She turned to Xrissa. "I see why Courage loves these and you. These are phenomenal. And they're so huge."

"I like them big." The Moon Elf beamed. "And I'm a huge fan of adding fresh nutmeg as well as hints of cardamom and clove. The warmth and homeyness of those spices wafts outside my shop's door and sells the rolls for me."

"Cinnamon rolls!" Courage's voice bellowed as he pushed past Honor, ran into the dining room, and grabbed a cinnamon roll. He shoved it into his mouth and sighed in happiness. Without removing the pastry from his mouth, he said, "These are fucking fantastic as always, Xrissa.

They spent the remainder of the day asleep. At sunset, Vincenzyo Gabrini arrived to take the measurements of all the mortals present and to get a sense of their personalities so he could design clothing both appropriate for the coronation and fitting for their personalities. Courage and Gwyn began planning the spaces for the Faern'dolns, should they join everyone in Utrezzo.

True to his word, Arcanist Mediciara returned the following day with a team of arcanists. Gwyn led everyone to the basement where what remained of the temple dedicated to Zanguis, the Ashfodellian Princess and the first vampire, once sat. The space had been cleared after its destruction during the raid, but it would serve the purposes of today's magical working. The arcanists slit their arms and drew intricate circles of bloody runes onto the stone floor. They chanted a lengthy incantation, and the runes sprang to life, glowing a blazing cerulean hue.

Arcanist Mediciara turned to Honor and Xrissa. "The circles should take you to the Faern'doln house. Once you have gathered everyone, their belongings, and performed your tasks, return through the circles my arcanists will draw. The return circles will take you to the Sezarian Estate in Delfia. There you can rest as Hertogia Vandiamante prepares for her coronation. Safe travels."

"Thank you for this, both you and Gwyn," Honor said.

Gwyn smiled. "Welcome to the family. You and yours will always have home and protection in my lands."

"Seems your six years abroad have taught you what makes a good sezara," Kiernan said.

Gwyn blushed. Everyone said their goodbyes, and Honor and Xrissa stepped through the circles and disappeared in a flash of blue flame. The team of arcanists followed them. The glowing runes faded and then disappeared. Those who remained made final preparations before taking the carriages to Delfia.

Chapter 23

Three nights later, Gwyn and her attendants sat in the boudoir of the Sezatorial Estate in Delfia. Silk wallpaper of a pale creamy pink silk on which dark seafoam green leaves had been painted covered the walls. Oil portraits of former sezaras and the wives of the former sezars adorned the walls. White and gray marble statues of three nude women, the legendary Graces Pazientzia, Grasi, and Mitzercordia, stood in three of the four corners. The bed frame, bookshelves, seating, armoire, dresser, and vanity were all made of birch painted a creamy white, and all the cushions were covered in chambray and seafoam silk. A pink crystal rose stood atop the coffee table. Its warm glow heated the rose-scented oils that perfumed the cool chamber.

Dressed in a lace-trimmed white dressing gown, Gwyn sat on the stood before the vanity as the six vampire women serving as her attendants laid out her coronation attire, did her makeup, fixed her hair—not that her short, asymmetrical bob took required much attention beyond washing, drying, and brushing. While they readied her for her coronation, they caught her up on all the latest gossip in the court.

"Did you hear that Hertogius Allighyeri is planning a masquerade ball? I can't wait to see what he wears!"

"I think I'm going to start wearing my hair like his consort. You know, for a mortal, her fashion sense is divine."

"Well, I heard that he got that consort pregnant with another little dhampir."

"You, Sezara, must be careful with that handsome mortal of yours. Rumors fly faster than a bat on espresso."

"And did you hear about the Marcieza Billamonti?"

"No, what?"

"Well, that little succubus has been poaching from all the families in the Regent Council. She's going to get staked if she isn't careful."

Gwyn smiled, nodded, and laughed as she responded in a practiced show of interest, which had become harder to fake after six years of not needing the skill. As the gossip turned more personal, a knock at the door drew everyone's attention. Gwyn nodded. Nothing happened.

"Oh, I have to grant permission." Gwyn straightened up. "Enter."

The door opened, and one of the attendants stepped into the room. "Sezara Vandiamante, there are several foreign Ashbourne and one Elf who wish to speak with you. Shall I tell them to wait until after your coronation?"

"Let them in."

"But, Your Majesty, there are *men* among them, and you are in your dressing gown."

Gwyn narrowed her eyes and pursed her lips. Her tone remained flat. "They will not see me undress. If they are who I believe them to be, then they're a family—my extended family now. Let them in."

"As the sezara desires."

The attendant bowed and left. Gwyn rolled her eyes

and sighed, muttering to herself. "I suppose I should grow accustomed to this formality."

The door opened again, and the attendant returned. "Sezara Gwynarra Vandiamante, I present to you the Faern'doln family of Al'Adara."

The attendant stepped to the side and seven teal Ashbourne and one Snow Elf woman who appeared to be in the middle of her five hundreds entered. Courage resembled his father, but his father's black hair had silvered at the temples. Courage also got his button nose from his mother. The Elven woman was lovely, but her pale blue eyes showed both a love and an exhaustion only those with chronic illness understood. She was slender—even for a Snow Elf, and her white hair had become ethereal and translucent. Aside from Honor, the five younger children, three girls who inherited their mother's hair and twin boys who looked just like their father must have at their age, huddled behind the adults.

Gwyn rose and bowed. "Welcome. It pleases me that you accepted my offer. This estate is mine when I travel to Delfia for courtly business, but once we return to Utrezzo, my home is your home. Courage's family is my family. Speaking of Courage, where is he?"

"Xrissa's wrangling him and helping him get changed for the ceremony. I'll probably join them once we leave here. I wanted to introduce you to everyone, and Mum and Da wanted to thank you for your hospitality. So, this is our da, Owaiyn Faern'doln, and this is our mum, Marlenya. Starting with the oldest of the girls here, we have Sofia, then Yvelyn, and then River."

"Are you really a vampire," River asked.

Gwyn laughed. "I am."

"Are you going to drain our blood and turn us into your slaves," One of the boys asked.

"Yeah." The other boy chimed in now. "Can you turn into a bat?"

"River, Elyas, Fyrgis," Marlenya scolded them. "Those are such inappropriate questions to ask of someone who has shown us and your brother Courage great kindness."

Gwyn waved her hand. "It's fine. I've had far worse questions hurled my way. To answer them, no. I am not going to drain your blood. Drinking mortal blood without consent is one of the greatest sins my kind can commit. And no, I cannot turn into a bat. I turn into a cat. Welcome again, and Marlenya, it is good to see you after all Courage has said of you."

"He spoke of my illness, I'm certain." She said.

Gwyn nodded with a sympathetic smile on her face. "But he also spoke of you with such love, and seeing that you too are a Snow Elf makes it so much more fun."

Honor laughed. Marlenya tilted her head to the side. "I don't follow."

"When Courage first spoke of Xrissa, he assured me he wasn't flirting with me, because I'm 'only Snow Elf pretty' and not 'Moon Elf pretty' like she was."

Owaiyn slammed his palm into his face. He shook his head. "That boy is brilliant with history and with machines, but when it comes to talking to a woman, he's as dumb as any other man."

Marlenya sighed. "My Courage is a sweet boy, but like his father, he can be an ass."

"Been saying that all his life," Honor said.

"Are any of you attending the coronation," Gwyn asked.

Owaiyn shook his head. "Afraid not, Miss. It may be morning for you, but it's getting close to the kids' bedtime."

The children stomped their feet and whined. The girls begged to stay up and see the pretty dress Gwyn was going to wear. Gwyn smiled and shook her head. "Listen to your parents, children. They love you, and I promise there will be plenty of time to see all of my pretty dresses. Sleep well."

"Thank you again, Miss Vandiamante," Owaiyn said.

"Yes, thank you." Marlenya smiled as she spoke.

Honor led her family from the Sezara's boudoir. Gwyn smiled. One of the attendants handed Gwyn a glass of wine, which she drank before they helped her into her multiple layers of underpinnings and then the gown for her coronation.

The coronation of the Sezara of the Midnight Court took place in the Grand Cathedral of St. Lilit the Bloody Clawed, which was attached to the Sezarian Estate. Massive pillars of black marble supported the soaring ceiling of the long nave. Stained glass windows depicting St. Lilit's miracles and prowess lined the walls. Backlit by Arcanyx crystal sheets, they cast colorful light upon the black stone floor. Crystal lanterns floated and moved beneath the ceiling, moving to form the night's constellation patterns, and their flickering resembled the twinkling of stars.

The air was cold, not uncomfortable for mortals but noticeably so. Censors wafted the rich, earthy, blood-soaked incense blend favored by vampires worshiping Zanguis. Statues of the Princess of Ashfodell lined the walls of the nave.

The choir sat at the western end of the nave, behind the altar, raised the altar's dais and separated from the ebony pews by an ebony screen inlaid with intricate carvings of the moon and nocturnal animals. They chanted their a cappella hymn praising the Blood Princess for her gift of immortality. Standing in front of the screen and behind the altar were the Archbishop of Delfia, dressed in his red velvet robes, the Regent Council, and the eldest member of each noble house represented by the Midnight Court.

The organist played a thunderous D major chord, silencing the choir for a moment. All seated in the pews rose as the choir began singing the processional hymn "Glorious Soul of Eternal Night." The double doors to the cathedral opened, and the processional began.

Torch bearers adorned in the red, black, and gold uniforms of the page boys of centuries past led the way, walking three steps ahead of the sezara and her attendants. Gwyn followed, wearing a gown of white silk and a silver brocade designed to mirror the image of the moon in its fullness. The gown's scooped neck connected to a diamond-encrusted, collar of white lace that rose to Gwyn's chin; the lace's pattern matched that of the lace sleeves that came to a point on the back of Gwyn's hands and were secured by a silver ring worn on her middle fingers. The attendants who assisted Gwyn dress carried her train.

Gwyn's left arm entwined with Karina's right. Her hair had been slicked back in the pompadour style Gwyn loved. She wore black trousers with a red satin stripe along the outside, riding boots, and a white tunic. Over the tunic, she wore a ceremonial obsidian breastplate and a tabard displaying the coat of arms of House Vandiamante. An ornate longsword hung from her belt.

As Gwyn and Karina reached the base of the dais, they

stopped. The Archbishop of Delfia said, "Our Great Mother Zanguis, Princess of Blood and Fire who will one day reign in Ashfodell, you have appointed Gwynarra Vandiamante to be our Sezara. Grant her the wisdom and strength to fulfill the duties appointed to her."

The chief of the Regent Council, a gaunt Human male vampire with a face resembling an angular crescent moon and no hair beyond a tuft behind each of his ears then said, "We, the representatives of the vampires of Florescia, do hereby acknowledge Her Majesty as our rightful sovereign and pledge fidelity and honor in your service. I now present unto you the symbols of your authority."

He walked forward and stood before Gwyn. He then handed her an orb of pure Arcanyx crystal encrusted with diamonds and emeralds and a scepter of silver topped with a moonstone the size of a fist. He bowed before her and returned to his position as the Archbishop then anointed Gwyn with fragrant and sacred oils.

When the men nodded, Gwyn recited her oath twice. "I, Gwynarra Caoilfhionn Vandiamante, do solemnly swear upon my name and my family's blood that I will be faithful and bear true allegiance to the vampires of Florescia. As their sovereign, I will defend them to the utmost of my power against all enemies, foreign and domestic. I will uphold the laws of both the Midnight and the Mortal Courts that no harm may come to any of our kind, according to their respective laws and customs. By the power of the gift of Zanguis, this I swear."

The chief of the Regent Council stepped forward, holding a crimson velvet cushion atop which sat a silver crown encrusted with diamonds and moonstones. Gwyn kneeled, and the chief of the Regent Council and the Archbishop placed the crown on her head. The representatives of the noble houses then came forward and handed Gwyn the silver sword of office, a curved blade bearing the name, The Fang of Zanguis.

The Archbishop then turned to the crowd. "Noble houses, honored guests vampiric and mortal, we present to you, Sezara Gwynarra Vandiamante, long may her nocturnal reign be."

The crowd chanted, "Long may she reign," until the Archbishop again silenced them by raising his hands. "It is my understanding that Her Majesty has business to conduct this evening."

The crowd murmured and whispered in surprise. Gwyn ascended the dais and turned. With a smile on her face, she looked over the crowd and then focused her gaze on Karina. Authority and power filled her voice as it reverberated through the cathedral. "Karina Alyxandra Skejik, on our journey here, you swore that you desired to be our loyal knight. Does that promise hold true on this night?"

Shocked into silence, Karina hesitated for a moment before hastily nodding. "Yes, yes it does."

Gwyn nodded. "Then kneel before us and take your oath."

Karina kneeled before Gwyn. The crowd fell silent. This was unusual at a coronation, but it was not unheard of.

"Do you, Karina Skejik, swear to uphold the tenets of honor, of loyalty, and of chivalry, defending us, your sezara, with all of your strength, all of your heart, and all of your life?"

"I swear it."

"Do you swear to protect the weak and the innocent, bringing justice tempered with mercy?"

"I swear it."

Gwyn drew the Fang of Zanguis from its sheath. The flecks of diamond within the silver blade glittered in the light from the chandeliers. Then repeat this oath after me.

Karina nodded. "I, Karina Alyxandra Skejik, do hereby swear to uphold the ideals of honor, of loyalty, and of chivalry. I will be courageous and stalwart, always championing the cause of justice tempered with mercy. Never will I back down from a challenge. Always will I be loyal to my queen, serving her with honor."

Gwyn tapped the blade on Karina's right shoulder, then her left, then her right again. With a flick of her wrist slid the blade under Karina's throat, lifting it to meet her smirking gaze. Gwyn winked. Karina blushed. And then Gwyn said, "Before Zanguis, your Sezara, and those assembled in the Midnight Court, we pronounce you Donna Karina, our loyal knight."

The crowd applauded. After the Archbishop led those assembled in a final prayer and presentation of the Sezara, Gwyn, Karina, and her attendants receded from the Grand Cathedral. Once they had returned to the Sezara's suite within the Sezarian Estate, the crowd departed from the cathedral.

Chapter 24

Karina took Gwyn's hand in hers, and Gwyn led her back into the bedroom. In the soft light of the crystal candles, they kissed. And as each deepened the other's kiss, adding hunger to desire and need to hunger, the sezara helped her knight undress. Gwyn moaned into Karina's mouth as their tongues danced. Karina's chest rose and fell as her breathing became more ragged. Her eyes widened in desire.

As the pajama top fell to the floor, Gwyn ran her hands along Karina's muscular stomach and arms, kissing the olive skin and teasing her lover's nipples with her thumbs. Karina moaned. Gwyn slid her arms under Karina's armpits and wrapped them around the Human woman's muscular shoulders. She nibbled on Karina's ear. The Human gasped. Gwyn chuckled and trailed nibbling kisses down Karina's neck and along her right shoulder.

Gwyn pushed Karina onto the bed. She pulled the pajama pants from Karina's legs, slid out of her own dressing gown, and then crawled on top of Karina. The shadows from the velvet curtains accentuated the muscles on Karina's thighs. They twitched, and Karina gasped as Gwyn placed gentle kisses on them.

Karina spread her legs, making it easier for the slender vampire to slide between them. Gwyn looked up. "Do you still consent to this?"

"I do."

"Then let us begin."

Gwyn crawled up on top of Karina before offering a teasing kiss that ended with the vampire's tongue brushing the edge of Karina's lips. Gwyn straddled her knight's chest and trailed nibbling kisses down her neck and shoulder. Her small, soft hands kneaded Karina's small tits. A series of moans mixed with quick, sharp gasps escaped Karina's lips as Gwyn's hands groped her flesh mounds, her index fingers and thumbs twisting and pulling her nipples as they moved.

Gwyn kissed her way down to Karina's right breast. She sucked the nipple into her warm, wet mouth. Karina's eyes rolled back briefly. A long, ragged breath warbled from Karina's lips. She begged for more. Her back arched, and she wrapped her arms around Gwyn, her hands holding the vampire's head close to her tit. Gwyn held Karina's nipple in her mouth, allowing her warm, soft tongue to gently circle the aroused nub. Warmth built within Karina's core.

Continuing to suck and nibble on Karina's tits, Gwyn slid a hand up the soft thickness of Karina's inner thigh. She slid two fingers into her lover's warm, wet pussy. She thrust her fingers in and out with haste. Karina's hips bucked against the vampire's fingers. The heat building within Karina's core raged as Gwyn stoked the flames with her mouth, tongue, teeth, and fingers.

"Yes, please." Karina's words were ragged and guttural as she begged the vampire to continue. A whimper trailed from her lips as Gwyn stopped all action.

"Yes, please what?" Gwyn teased.

Karina panted. "Yes, please, my sezara."

Gwyn chuckled as she returned to her ministrations. While sucking Karina's nipple deep into her mouth, the vampire mumbled the words, "That's a good knight."

Sweat beaded on Karina's forehead. Her breasts heaved, and her hungry eyes begged Gwyn to continue. The vampire sat up, her legs straddling Karina's hips. She licked her lips and kneaded her own breasts for a moment. She looked down at Karina. "Once again, I must ask if you consent to my feeding from your inner thigh."

Karina nodded. Her black hair fell loose from her gelled pompadour. She blew it aside. "Yes, take me, drink me, please."

Gwyn leaned down and ravaged Karina's lips with her own. As she broke the kiss, pausing to suck on Karina's lower lip, the vampire purred, "I intend to."

Gwyn kissed her way from Karina's lips down the center of her body. When she reached her furry mound, the vampire inhaled Karina's spiced musk. Gwyn purred and licked her own lips. She slid down on the bed and then kissed her way up from Karina's knee as her lover whimpered and begged for more potent attentions.

When she reached Karina's pussy, Gwyn ran her nose up between her labia, brushing over her clit. Karina gasped. Gwyn chuckled. She licked Karina from ass to clit in slow, steady strokes. Karina groaned. Her hips ground against Gwyn's face, and she clutched Gwyn's black hair in her hands.

Gwyn slid up and focused her tonguing on Karina's engorged clit, making slow, rhythmic circles around the nub. Karina begged for more. Gwyn slid two fingers inside

Karina's pussy, moving them in and out in wavelike motions timed to her tongue circles. Karina panted. Her back arched, and her hips ground hard against Gwyn's face. Waves of heat radiated from her core.

Karina's legs trembled. Her moans came short and quick. Gwyn slid her face to the side and sucked on Karina's inner thigh. Her pussy clenched around Gwyn's thrusting fingers. Karina's body quaked. And then Gwyn bit. Her fangs pierced Karina's thigh. A sharp pain jolted through her body. Karina screamed. And then, as Gwyn lapped the hot blood tasting of earth and warm spices, waves of pleasure replaced the pain. Karina's eyes rolled in the back of her head, and a guttural rattle formed a contrapuntal melody to her spasmic moaning.

Karina panted. Her legs twitched as the pleasure slowly subsided. Gwyn kissed the bite marks on Karina's inner thigh. She crawled beside her lover, kissed her, and rested her head on her knight's shoulder. They shared a kiss.

Gwyn whispered. "Stay on your back."

Gwyn sat up and then straddled Karina's face. She hovered over her lover's face. Karina smelled the sweet, earthy scent and saw the glistening wetness of the vampire's sex. She licked her lips. Gwyn rolled her hips, dipping her snatch close to, but never connecting with, Karina's lapping tongue. A begging whimper escaped Karina's pouting lips. Gwyn smirked.

The vampire lowered herself. Karina's greedy tongue lapped the sweet, musky juices. Gwyn ground her hips, soaking Karina's face, and moaned as the woman's nose and tongue flicked her engorged clitoris. Purring groans escaped her lips. Karina's hands slid up the sides of Gwyn's body, cupping and kneading her pale round breasts. Gwyn moaned.

The city clocks struck four bells, but Karina's ears heard

only her lover's gasps, cries, and moans. Gwyn ran her fingers through Karina's hair, massaging her scalp. Karina moaned into Gwyn's crotch. The vampire gasped as the vibrations tingled her clit. Pressure built inside Gwyn's core. Moans quickened. Hips rocked. Legs trembled.

As the pleasure intensified, Gwyn shoved Karina's face into her needy pussy. She rode Karina's face hard, soaking the hunter with her wetness, until her orgasm exploded. Waves of pleasure washed over Gwyn's body, as a deep, guttural moan warbled with a thick vibrato down three octaves into a low, satisfied growl.

Gwyn collapsed onto Karina. Sweaty and satisfied, they shared a long, deep kiss.

Chapter 25

The morning before Gwynarra Vandiamante's coronation, the top story on the front page of the *Sonnenburg Daily* read, "Emperor's Left Hand Purges Sonnenburg of 'Disloyals.'"

The city of Sonnenburg was shaken to its core last night as the Emperor's Left Hand, a newly-formed police force led by Lord Ambrose von Harenheim, conducted a series of raids on the homes of members of the aristocracy, the Lord Mayor, and the City Parliament. The raids used grotesque automatons known as the Kriegsdieneryn and were reportedly carried out in response to reports that these individuals were plotting to overthrow the Blessed Emperor.

The Left Hand's agents reportedly arrested two dozen people, including the Lord Mayor Hauke Gollwitzer; several city councilors, including Finn Wald, Branik Pizk, and Murana Masur; as well as several members of the nobility, including Lord Ianwarin Haufbauer, the Grand Master of the Grand Order of Printers. Lord von Harenheim stated that the detainees were taken to an undisclosed location, where they will be formally charged, arraigned, and tried. Some eyewitnesses allege others, including servants and children, were executed on site.

The Blessed Emperor has, as of yet, declined to comment on the raids, but his supporters have praised the Left Hand for its actions, calling it a necessary step to protect the empire from its enemies. Kammherr Florescu told the Daily, "While many are afraid of the Left Hand, its force is necessary to remove those who threaten the Blessed Emperor's safety and, by extension, the safety of the imperial citizens. Those who have committed no treachery have no need to fear."

The raids, the latest in a series of crackdowns on dissent against the Blessed Emperor and his High Holy Council, have caused widespread fear and uncertainty in Sonnenburg. Many people are wondering who else might be targeted by the Left Hand, and what the future holds for the city. In recent months, the government has also arrested and executed journalists, academics, artists, playwrights, and religious leaders who have been critical of the regime. Less than one month ago, students protesting governmental censorship were executed and had their bodies left to rot in the streets.

The crackdown has raised concerns about the state of freedom of expression in the empire. Some critics who spoke on condition on anonymity have accused the Blessed Emperor of becoming a tyrant, while others have warned that the country is headed for a dictatorship.

Only time will tell what the long-term consequences of the raids will be for the city of Sonnenburg and for the Atharian Empire. However, it is clear that the Blessed Emperor is determined to crush any opposition to his rule.

Yleon Friedberg grunted as he slammed his copy of the *Sonnenburg Daily* onto the varnished red oak bar within the Rusty Blade, one of the oldest pubs in the city. The silverware, the plate containing the remains of his breakfast, and the stein of coffee clinked and sloshed against the wood from the force of the Human's hit. A few patrons looked over, saw Yleon's sun-leathered fist tremble as it strangled the newspaper, shook their heads, and returned to their own breakfasts and conversations. A man sat in the corner, coughing.

"What has you so riled up, Yleon?"

Yannick Weidte, the bartender, walked over while cleaning smudges from a rocks glass. Yannick was tall Human and sturdy of frame, with his wispy blond hair pulled into a ponytail and tied with a purple ribbon. Strong wax kept the curls of his handlebar mustache even and stiff.

Yleon's brown eyes met Yannick's blue ones as Yleon held up and waved the newspaper. "Have you see this? This isn't our empire anymore. And who in Ashfodell is this von Harenheim? Never heard of him until a few weeks ago when that society he led got raided. Then we find him on the High Holy Council. Now, he's in charge of some police force using..." He pointed to the image of one of the Malaki grunts before adding, "These *things*."

Yannick blinked twice and scrunched his face in disgust. A shiver slithered down his spine. "They're creepy and almost human but not quite. I don't know. Look, the Blessed Emperor receives the word of the Lord of Sky and Storm. He wouldn't approve of this if it weren't divine will."

Yleon snorted. "As if the man who ordered the High Exarch's execution would listen to a god."

"You forget," a Sun Elven man at the end of the bar said in almost conspiratorial tones. "You forget the High Exarch plotted with the Crimson Fangs to kill the Blessed Emperor."

"Says who?" Yleon lifted his hands. "The only witnesses

were Grand Master Richter, and he's been arrested for treason and plotting to overthrow the same Blessed Emperor, High General Krank, and this Lord von Harenheim. And the only one to have spoken publicly is von Harenheim, who also happened to save the Blessed Emperor from the Richters alleged attempted coup. You ask me, it's all too convenient."

Yannick watched as the coughing man's cough worsened to the point he just got up and left. Yannick nodded. "And that, Yleon, is why no one of sense gets their political commentary from men shouting into the air at a bar."

Yleon nodded and returned to his breakfast. The day in Sonnenburg flowed as normal for the majority of citizens. They went to work, took their lunch break, and then departed as they clocked out for their shift's end. Many went to a second job after work. Some went home to cook or receive a home-cooked meal. Others went to a pub or a restaurant for supper.

As the sun descended toward the western horizon, a crowd gathered at the King's Feast, one of the more upscale dining establishments in Sonnenburg. Though it was one of the oldest pubs in the city, its proximity to the imperial palace led to its transition from the comforting, hearty fare of the home to an upscale reimagining of Atharian cuisine, all served under the gentle, flickering glow of Arcanyx crystal candles.

Soft baroque chamber music played over the crystal speakers, forming an ambient background noise to the hum of conversation happening at the tables. And then three beeps interrupted the music. The conversation died down as an announcement came across all speakers in the restaurant and throughout Sonnenburg. "This just in! In a raid on the Rusty Blade Public House, the Emperor's Left Hand arrested Yleon

Friedberg yesterday on the grounds of fomenting treason. Friedberg is a nutrition supplement manufacturer who, in recent days, has been outspoken in his opposition to the recent crackdown on dissent, going so far as to suggest that Lord Ambrose von Harenheim is orchestrating events to seize power from the Blessed Emperor himself."

The diners returned to their meals as the music returned. Most conversations returned to normal, but a handful discussed the news of the afternoon.

"Of course, it happened at the Rusty Blade," one man said with a bemused chuckle. "Those sorts of people would congregate there."

Another man leaned over from his own table to ask, "Have you been there? No? Well, I did once, and a fight broke out over a game of billiards. How gauche."

"Really," the first man said. "Is it any surprise that neighborhood would produce those who speak ill of our Blessed Emperor?"

"Not in the least." Now a third man joined the conversation. "So many who've blamed the empire for their poverty come from that district. If they would only lift themselves by the straps on their boots, work longer hours, and thank their employers for the opportunities given them, they would raise their station."

"We can't really blame them," the first said. "They lack the mental and moral capacity to be proper citizens. They don't recognize the blessings His Excellency bestows upon them. Really, they should be bound to their work stations like machines."

The second man chimed in. "Perhaps the technomagi could build machines to replace them. Seems far more efficient."

The conversation continued in that fashion, with the wealthy and influential men discussing those living in the cramped spaces of the Industrial Quarter as lesser beings.

The sun set, and the crystal street lanterns illuminated the streets of Sonnenburg. Within the cramped spaces of the Industrial Quarter, a district of narrow, uneven streets with broken cobblestone, the lights flickered in uneven intervals, casting long long, menacing shadows that flitted about the night. The reek of industrial waste filled the air with a bitter fog, as the mechanomagical purification system merely contained the stench within this district.

Amid the flickering of lights and the gawking conversations of passersby, the staff of the Rusty Blade continued with the cleanup after the day's raid on their establishment. The windows had been shattered. A battering ram had smashed the door. The jagged remains of bottles, glassware, and plates lay strewn about the charred, blood-splattered floor. Only an hour earlier had the cadaver farmers had come and taken the bodies slain in the chaos.

As he swept up the last of the glass when twenty-one bells tolled, Yannick Weidte wiped the sweat from his brow. Leaning on the broom, he said, "There, almost done. Shit! We did not need that. I'm sorry, everyone, but depending on how long repairs take, we might be closed for a month—maybe longer."

Ilsa Gehrzh, a young blonde server who spent the last hour tossing the broken and charred remains of furniture into the rubbish dumpster, walked over and asked, "Guess you should've reported Yleon this morning or something? All he did was bitch and moan, didn't think it was that big of a deal."

Yannick shrugged. "I agree. He had his breakfast and left

for work. He came back for lunch, as he usually did, and then they burst through our door with those...*things*." Yannick shuddered. "The pictures in the *Daily* were disturbing enough, but seeing them in person was horrifying."

"The fuck were those things," Kresnik Ristovic asked, throwing the mop onto the floor. "They looked almost Human—like they were at one point but had machines grafted onto them."

Ilsa turned to Kresnik. "You know what I heard? I heard they were human—criminals—and becoming these things is their punishment."

Kresnik shook his head. "Impossible, Ilsa. No one would agree to that. They have to be corpses taken by the cadaver farmers. The Blessed Emperor is a holy man. He wouldn't allow such things to be done to the living. Still they are terrifying."

"They wouldn't stop unless that one agent with them commanded them. They are destruction. Who could oppose such a force?" Ilsa shuddered.

Yannick held up his hands. "Alright, you two. I don't need either of you getting arrested by the Left Hand. Whatever the story is, let it be over tonight."

While the staff of the Rusty Blade cleaned up their restaurant before an unfortunate closing, a group of St. Aquitom University students gathered in the private gathering room upstairs at the Snake and Whistle, a pub frequented by students. Once all had gathered, Benyamin Schneidemann, a tall and lanky young man with a mop of chestnut hair and round spectacles sitting on the bridge of his nose, locked the door behind them. As the pub owner's son, getting the key was easy for him. He then went around the room and closed all of the shutters on the windows.

He looked around the room and nodded. "We're all here and safe. No one was followed?"

The three assembled shook their heads. A young woman with wavy ebon hair and piercing sapphire eyes, Anya Zelymski, said, "We're students, Benyi. Everyone knows we come to this pub. No one would think anything of it."

Benyamin nodded. "I know, but after what happened today at the Rusty Blade, I don't want to take chances."

Everyone sat around a round table at the center of the room. In addition to Anya and Benyamin, two others joined in the planning. Klara Winters, a petite blonde with a bright smile who had only recently turned eighteen, sat to Anya's left. And then there was the oldest of the four, Otto Zezzler, a tall and muscular man with a shaved head and a red goatee.

"Anya," Benyamin said. "Ready to start?"

Anya nodded. "We all saw what happened earlier today, right? Or at least we read about it in the Daily's evening update? Someone needs to do something about this. The empire's always had its problems, but with the Emperor's Left Hand and those things—those Kriegsdieneryn—silencing anyone who even so much as question what's going on."

Otto snorted. "Kriegsdieneryn. What are they planning for, a war? With whom?"

"Haven't you heard what happened in Milmigua?" Klara leaned closer to Otto. "They're clearly headed to the Indigo Coast for the port cities."

Benyamin pushed his glasses against his face and nodded. "That would make logical sense. Take the coast, before pushing into Florescia, so the war is only on one front. The only question is, why now? We've had a non-hostility treaty with each of the city-states on the Coast for four centuries. Why now?"

Everyone shrugged. And then Anya said, "I don't know if we'll ever truly know. So much is going on in secret, but we have to do something."

"But what?" Benyamin ran his fingers through his hair and brushed his unruly bangs out of his face. "What can we do? The Grand Imperial Army is too powerful, and those *things* made from the twisted remains of *people,* are too strong."

"We can't give up!" Klara clenched her fists as she spoke. "We have to keep pushing for changes to benefit everyone."

"Easier said than done, freshman," Otto said. The High Holy Council, the only people the damned emperor listens to, keeps shrinking. That's what's scaring people. Right now, it's just the emperor, the High General of the Grand Imperial Army, and the head of the Left Hand. If the emperor dies, one of them could ascend, and that would make Ashfodell look like the Summerlands."

"So what do we do," Anya asked. "We can't lead a revolution. We don't have the resources or the training."

Otto shook his head. "No, but do have some guns, swords, axes, and other weapons. And we can improvise other things, like stuffing oil-soaked rags in full bottles of booze and setting it on fire. We can also rig up some low-grade explosives in pots filled with gunpowder and nails. We're not helpless."

Klara shifted nervously in her seat. "Are you proposing we fight?"

"We may have to, freshman."

Benyamin sighed. "Otto's right, I'm afraid. And yeah, I'm afraid. It probably won't be our choice. The emperor has used the army to break up student protest before, so now any protest might become a fight. It's not about what we want, but what we have to prepare for."

All nodded in resignation and understanding. The four continued their planning late into the night. After planning, they went their separate ways, each looking over their shoulder as they returned home to prepare.

The next evening, the evening update of the *Sonnenburg Daily* had the following headline on its front page, "Student Protest Turns Violent, Emperor's Left Hand Seeks Leaders."

The Emperor's Left Hand continued its march to squash dissent for imperial policy within the capital city today. Earlier today, students from St. Aquitom University gathered in the university parade grounds to protest the use of force against dissenters.

Without stated provocation, the protesters produced muskets and fired first into the air and then into the crowd. The city's constabulary responded in truly heroic fashion, many sacrificing their lives to protect unarmed civilians from the mob of angry students.

Several students engaged in acts of domestic terror by throwing either flaming bottles of alcohol or homemade explosives into the crowd as the constabulary pushed back against their unfocused rage. Eventually, the rioters dispersed, running through the narrow alleys of the quarter to avoid pursuit.

At the time of this issue's release, the Emperor's Left Hand has promised to investigate the incident, using all powers and authorities at their disposal to find the leaders of this riot and bring them to justice.

The incident is the latest in a series of crackdowns on dissent by the Emperor's Left Hand, raising concerns about the current direction taken by the empire. Some observers have warned that the government is becoming increasingly authoritarian and that the people's right to dissent is being eroded.

Lord Ambrose von Harenheim, Imperial Director of Emperor's Left Hand, has issued the following statement. "We have no interest in stripping honorable, law-abiding citizens of their rights. However, when those same citizens turn to acts of terror and rage, we must enforce the laws as they are written. We are committed to protecting the good citizens from those troublesome elements who would seek to undermine the nobility and stability of our glorious empire."

The Sonnenburg Daily will continue to update coverage of this event as information becomes available.

Chapter 26

As the clock struck twenty-two bells in Delfia on the night after the protest outside St. Aquitom University, Sezara Gwynarra Vandiamante stood before the armoire in her private suite in the Sezarian Estate. Wearing only her white linen stays and bloomers, she searched through the assorted selection of dresses purchased on her behalf based upon the clothing left behind in her bedroom in Utrezzo Her left leg bounced and trembled as she searched through the couture collection. A sighing growl escaped her lips.

Karina moved to stand behind Gwyn, wrapped her arms around the vampire's waist, and brushed her lips against Gwyn's pale neck. "What frustrates you, my darling?"

Gwyn smiled as she leaned into the embrace. She then stretched out her arms and gestured to the rack of elegant and beautiful dresses. "This."

Karina surveyed the clothing. "You have quite the assortment of dresses and gowns that would be fetching when draped over your body. This is a problem?"

"Yes." Gwyn sighed. "No, but yes. It's just that it's my first meeting with my advisory council, and I don't know what to wear. I need to project grace and charm but also strength and power. Look at this one."

She grabbed a green silk gown with a scoop neck, gathered waist and a full circle skirt. Beads of smoky green crystal formed a line of fringe that extended from the neckline to the bust line.

Karina nodded. "Yes, it's lovely. And I would love to dance with you while you wear it."

"Exactly." Gwyn shouted. She flinched at her own volume. "Sorry, didn't mean it to come out that loud. I'd love that too. But it's a fucking ball gown. How the fuck am I supposed to be regal wearing it? Also, the gold stitching at the waist will clash with my silver crown."

The vampire sank into her mortal lover's embrace. Her lower lip protruded in a pout. "I'm not ready for this. I haven't been trained for this."

"But you knew this day would come, did you not?"

Gwyn nodded. "Three maybe four *centuries* from now. And with everything that's happened in the last few weeks—and with everything that might happen in the next few—I'm…I'm scared."

The dress fell from Gwyn's hand and crumpled onto the floor. Gwyn spun around and curled up onto Karina. The Human's strong arms held the vampire tight as she sobbed, her body trembling.

I should say something, Karina thought. *But what? I've only had brothers, and treating her like they treated me and I treated them didn't work the last time I tried it.* She lifted her eyes toward the heavens for a brief moment. *Lord of Sky and Storm—anyone—help?*

Karina's heartbeat and Gwyn's sobbing were the only sounds audible for a few minutes as Karina held Gwyn close to her chest. Karina nodded, her cheek brushing Gwyn's temple. "I wish I had an answer for you. I doubt you want me to suggest an outfit. Gowns aren't my strong suit, as I'm certain you've gathered. I'm here to hold you now, and I'll be right outside your meeting chamber."

Gwyn's green eyes were glassed over by her tears. She smiled up at Karina, and Karina brushed the tears from Gwyn's cheeks. "You really are my knight in black leather."

"Until the day I die, my sezara." They kissed.

Clutching Karina's tabard tightly in her hands, Gwyn sighed. "I wish you could be beside me—especially given recent events—but tradition dictates a consort may not sit in the meeting."

Karina nodded. "The only way to change that would be marriage, correct?"

Gwyn nodded. "When the time is right. When things settle down. I hope they'll settle down."

"The situation with Marius Bedwyr concerns you, doesn't it?"

Gwyn sighed. "That's really why I wish you could be by my side. You know the empire better than I do. My concerns with a member of the emperor's council will pose diplomatic issues for us and our court. And it means we can't avoid him during diplomatic visits, should they become necessary."

Gwyn's voice trailed to silence, and she looked away as she spoke. Karina wrapped her arms around Gwyn, holding her tightly for a moment. Once she released the hug, she looked into Gwyn's eyes. "You're regretting sparing his life in Iszenstadt."

Gwyn buried her face in Karina's chest and nodded. "I shouldn't. I gave him a chance to end this business between us, but if he's on the emperor's council, this business will be discussed—somewhere, somehow. I will need to explain to my advisers what happened." Tears formed in Gwyn's eyes once more, and she trembled. "Rina, I don't want war. He'll have the empire's army, and we'll only have my people."

Karina held Gwyn close. Karina felt her heart pound in her chest and her breath quicken as Gwyn's fear radiated toward her. "I don't think either of us want that, my love."

"And you," Gwyn sobbed into Karina's chest. "Your family is there. You'd—no, I wouldn't allow you to fight them. It wouldn't be fair."

"I am sworn to defend you, my beloved sezara. Aside from perhaps my cousin Garrus and the young children, the rest of my family would not hesitate to attack you. But we will respond to that incident should it become necessary. As much as I enjoy you close to me, you must dress for your meeting."

Gwyn nodded and then chose her dress, and together they left the private suite and walked to the Sezatorian Council Chamber. After discussion, Gwyn donned a burgundy dress with a high collar fastened by three moonstone-covered snaps, sleeves that puffed at the shoulders and tapered to a fitted cuff with the forearm tight against the body and held steady by eight moonstone-covered snaps, and a gored skirt that brushed the floor with a light touch.

The Sezatorian Guard opened the twin oak doors, granting them entrance into the chamber. As they crossed into the chamber, the members of the Council rose and bowed. Karina pulled the large chair at the table's head out for Gwyn to sit, and once she sat, Gwyn nodded, signaling for Karina to depart.

Gwyn recognized the faces of her advisers, but she given

the distance she put between herself and Florescian vampire society over the past six years, names had been forgotten. The chair of the Regent Council, Hertogius Toscio Sanktaria, an elderly man who resembled a portly friar and who dressed in a black and silver brocade frock with a cream waistcoat over his white shirt, introduced the rest of the Council.

The handsome Human man with dark hair and green eyes on Gwyn's left, Hertogius Alceste Duca of Flevignano and Inquisatore Grande for the court of Sezar Chiampi, wore an elaborate suit of schloss green adorned with gold embroidery. Next to him was the red haired Wood Elf Dominius Damaso Federici of Grachtovia, appeared to be in the early decades of his two hundreds. He wore cutting edge fashion fitted to his slender figure. The next to be introduced was a distinguished and short Gnomish man, Hertogius Ottavyo Pezzyllara of Bollanzano. His beard covered his black suit, and his mustache was wider than his shoulders. And next to him was Contezza Chiara Vivona-Forte of Delfia. This slender Human woman had long dark hair and piercing blue eyes. Her amber dress, while elegant and expensive, was of a style popular three centuries prior.

Servants poured blood-infused wine for each vampire at the table and then departed through a servants' door. Once only the Sezara, her advisory council, and the members of the Sezarian Guard stationed within the room were present, Hertogius Toscio Sanktaria said, "First, I speak on behalf of myself, the Regent Council, and the Sezarian Advisory Council, in saying it pleases us, Sezara Vandiamante, that you have ended your exile and returned to us."

The table voiced their polite agreement. Gwyn smiled. Dominius Federici added, "And without having murdered one of our own kind while on your violent little jaunting."

Gwyn nodded. "We came close on more than one occasion, once due to lack of information provided to me and once due to the other vampire's actions. And yet, we have managed to protect our own at all times." She sipped her wine. "Now, this is not a social gathering. We assume there is business to discuss, and we would like to be briefed on events in Florescia relevant to our people and our interests before we bring forth the matters we have to discuss with this esteemed council."

As it turned out, the Regent Council had effectively maintained the policies Sezar Vandiamante had instituted before his murder, which meant most of the meeting was spent briefing Sezara Vandiamante on those policies. Of those policies, the only one needing discussion was the need to increase the Sanctuary Support Tax as a result of an increase in manufacturing costs of alchemic bone ash used in preservation of the blood serum infused into the alcohol. Negotiations on how much to increase the price required almost a full hour of debate, leading to an increase of seventeen djykel per vampire.

"That will fly like a bat with a broken wing," Dominius Federici said.

Contezza Vivona-Forte leaned toward Gwyn and whispered, "And though you and I negotiated the men down from twenty-three, the proclamation will have your name on it. There will be dissent."

"Yes." Hertogius Pezzyllara chuckled. "And given the lack of a legitimate heir or even a Sezar at your side, you and your little pet Human will be the talk of the courts—especially as state visits near." He turned his gaze to Hertogius Sanktaria. "Tell me, Toscio, when will the delegations from the Zyntarian

Isles arrive?"

Hertogius Sanktaria nodded and sighed. "Three weeks, but the delegation from Amydzeen has pushed forward their visit. It seems they had early knowledge of our Sezara's return. They will be here in ten nights. Ottavyo does make a good point, Sezara. Your grandfather had a Sun Guard, but he did not share a bed with Ser Baltyrico. Have you given thought to a marriage?"

Gwyn narrowed her eyes as her gaze bore into the dark eyes of Hertogius Pezzyllara. "Karina Skejik is not our pet. She is a mortal. We have never demonstrated deception of that fact, and she is our lover. We have also never denied that fact."

She straightened her posture in her chair and allowed her gaze to shift from person to person. Her Froamian brogue strengthened as she spoke. "As to the question of a considered marriage—fuck this regal formality—Karina and I will discuss the matter when it becomes appropriate. We have only just professed our love to each other, and accepting what I am, given my penchant for day-walking, wasn't easy for her." She wagged her index finger, adding, "And I will not fucking tolerate any suggestion that I marry another for political reasons. Grandfather married for love. Father married for love. I will marry for love."

"And that, dear Sezara," Hertogius Flevignano said as he leaned forward. "That leads to the question of your lover's ancestry."

Gwyn tensed. She nodded once. Before she could speak, Hertogius Pezzyllara finished his colleague's thought. "Yes, she has the look of a Putnici, and a surname unknown among the aristocracy here. A foreign consort is one thing, a mistress fine, but to wed a commoner would—"

"Be a tale worthy of telling until the end of time," the Contezza added. "The poeti will sing songs of this love against the odds for centuries to come of the adventuring queen and her foreign peasant lover. Fated to be together, they defied the odds set by opposition of birth and fell in love."

I don't think she's that much of a peasant, Gwyn thought. *Given who her father is and all that. Better not say that.*

Gwyn smiled and blushed. "Yes, something like that. There are two issues I wish to discuss with you, as they may become issues with which we must contend in the near future."

"And they are," Hertogius Sanktaria asked, raising a bushy eyebrow.

Gwyn spoke in an even tone. "As your sezara, *our* desire is to open Nozies, granting them full participatory rights. We know—yes, we know—that our word will not grant them access to the world of mortals, but as the mortals have a long history of hunting our kind, it benefits us to protect all of our kind."

"The sewer rats?" Hertogius Pezzyllara growled as he spoke. "What else would you do, give space to the bloody Zernachs?"

"They have suffered much in their mortal life," Gwyn said.

Zernachs were the rarest of vampires, being cursed into immortality as a result of dying by suicide while on sanctified ground. As a further punishment, the gods forced their eternal form to display evidence of their mode of death. While the Nozies had a feral, ratlike form, the Zernachs bore evidence of how they offended the gods, which terrified many who beheld them.

Gwyn nodded and continued, "As have many of us, ourself included. We will not increase their sorrows by exiling them from our society. Gaining their trust would be more a challenge than gaining that of the Nozies. That is a conversation we are willing to revisit at a later date, but we desire the issue to be one you consider."

"And the other?" The Contezza bounced and giggled. "Oh, it's been ages since any of our rulers began by bringing forth issues of concern."

Gwyn smiled. "During our years as a hunter of monsters, as we have already established, not once did we slay one of our own kind. As my wandering came to an end, a man named Ambrose von Harenheim contracted both my lover and I, along with the young Ashbourne named Courage Faern'doln, to assist with a matter. During that time, we learned he was a vampire named Marius Bedwyr and the leader of a group of rebels, revolutionaries, or something like that, called the Crimson Fangs."

Gwyn then spent several minutes explaining what he was doing in Iszenstadt, how he tortured and enslaved Courage—and probably others, and how he was a member of the Blessed Emperor's High Holy Council. The council's facial expressions displayed the path from bemusment to shock to abject disgust as she spoke. Gwyn paused, and then she said, "Marius also used a puncturing device to simulate a forced bite on the neck of our Karina before turning her over to Caspar Richter with the insinuation that we forced ourself upon her. We thank Zanguis Karina still lives.

"However, if he is willing to do that, then we must ask ourself what he is willing to do. Given his proximity to the Blessed Emperor, we wish to warn this esteemed council that dealings with Marius will be inevitable and likely strained. We also have concerns that his Kriegsdieneryn will be assigned to the Holy Order of St. Arnulf Ironhand in another assault on our home and then on the rest of our people as the Atharians march westward."

"This is concerning news the Sezara brings to us," Hertogius Sanktaria said.

Dominius Federici waved a hand to the side. "Part of it is no concern to us with the recent news from the empire."

"What news is that," Gwyn asked.

"Have you not heard, Sezara?" Federici leaned forward. "Caspar Richter has been executed. The *things* you described under his control both attempted to assassinate the emperor and recorded his plans to take the throne for himself. It was this Ambrose von Harenheim who saved the emperor's life. The Richters' once *holy* order has been disbanded in shame. They will no longer concern you."

"And as to your other concern," Hertogius Pezzyllara added. "The Atharian Empire has not moved to expand in two centuries. Were they so desirous of our lands, they would have done so."

Gwyn nodded through a jaw clenched to avoid displaying shock. When the meeting adjourned, she burst through the doors, grabbed Karina's hand, and dragged her along. Gwyn hissed, "Come. We need to talk."

Karina blinked and followed. The Sezarian Guard walked after them, each the vampires shooting concerned and confused glances at the others. Keeping up with Gwyn's vampiric celerity was not easy for her, but Gwyn returned to her private suite. She slammed and locked the door behind them.

"Did I do something wrong," Karina asked.

Gwyn paused, stiffened, and then winced. "Shit." She raised her hands and exhaled. Her eyes met Karina's terrified eyes, and Gwyn shook her head. "No, you did nothing wrong, my love, but please sit down."

Karina nodded and then sat in one of the plush armchairs. She rolled up the sleeve on her shirt. "What's wrong? Was the meeting stressful? Do you need to feed?"

Gwyn rushed into Karina's lap and wrapped her arms around her lover. "I'm not hungry, but thank you. Yes it was. And what's wrong? News came from the empire."

"Okay, bad news? Is Marius on the offensive?"

Karina shifted. Gwyn scrunched herself into the chair beside her lover. The vampire exhaled. "Maybe. I don't know. What I did learn is your father has been executed for treason. His Kriegsdieneryn attempted to kill the emperor, and Marius saved the emperor. The Holy Order of St. Arnulf Ironhand is no more."

Gwyn watched Karina's expression. Karina displayed no emotion. She nodded in slow, deliberate nods. "Father would never have betrayed the empire. He was set up. Someone framed him." Her voice sped up and developed a tremble as she continued. "Gwyn, my father wasn't the most loving person to me throughout my life, but he wasn't a traitor. He would never do this. Those things—Courage worked on them—He'll know what happened. What about my family? Garrus? Are they dead too?"

Gwyn shrugged. "All I know is that the Holy Order of St. Arnulf Ironhand has been disbanded and that your father was executed. I'm sorry."

Karina laid her head on Gwyn's shoulder. Gwyn wrapped her arms around her Human lover. And then the tears came.

Chapter 27

B*reaking News! An Emperor's Left Hand special forces unit led by Constable Stefan Fleischler has tracked down and arrested three of the four leaders of a student protest that took place last week in Sonnenburg in response to the perceived use of force against those accused of dissenting with imperial decrees.*

The three arrested students are Benyamin Schneidemann, 21; Anya Zelymski, 20; and Klara Winters, 17. They are all being held Hessiakraft Gaol, and are expected to be charged with heresy, treason, and inciting a riot.

The fourth leader sought, Otto Zezzler, 22, was killed in the altercation that took place during the arrest. Zezzler was shot by a member of the Emperor's Left Hand when he resisted arrest and fired on imperial forces.

The protest last week was the largest student demonstration in Sonnenburg in twenty-three years, and the second in the past year alone. Hundreds of students took to the streets to protest the growing concern of increased use of force by the imperial government. The protest was peaceful at first, but it turned violent, necessitating intervention by the city constabulary.

While the Blessed Emperor has given no statement directly due to his recent illness, Kammherr Florescu has condemned the protest, reminding all imperial citizens that the Blessed Emperor's policies come to him from the Lord of Sky and Storm himself. Thus, violent opposition to imperial decree is, by default, both treason and heresy to the faith.

The Sonnenburg Daily will continue to follow this story as it continues through trial and sentencing.

The morning after that evening update to the *Sonnenburg Daily*, two days after the Sezara of the Midnight Court of Florescia met with her advisers, Florescu waited outside the Blessed Emperor's bedroom in Imperial Apartment wing of the palace. He paced from wall to wall in front of the ornate mahogany doors with gold fittings, wringing his hands and muttering about someone being late even for a Froamian. The Imperial Guard stood motionless as they observed the Kammherr's movement.

A few moments passed, and the Kammherr spotted Marius Bedwyr approaching at an even pace with a physician's satchel in his hand. "There you are, Lord von Harenheim. Do you have the serum?"

Ambrose patted the left breast of his charcoal morning coat. "Of course. His Excellency fares no better this morning?"

Kammherr Florescu shook his head. "His physician left an hour ago after giving the third blood transfusion in the past two days. The concern now is that His Excellency has developed either laughing death or the crimson plague. He hopes the latter, as it develops at a slower rate."

The crimson plague was a blood disease resulting from exposure to contaminated miasma arising from cracked Arcanyx crystals leaking their magical energies. These energies seeped into the body through the lungs and then poisoned the blood. It shared early symptoms with both

Veigt's laughing death and the common influenza. The crimson plague differed from the other two as it transitioned to its later stages, when disorientation grew into delirium and huge red pustules grew from nodes where the miasma had clotted the blood into large cysts. Left untreated, the cysts burst, spreading the contagion and causing the infected to bleed out.

Marius nodded. He forced a frown to his face. "Unfortunate. I have the serum you requested I prepare."

"Then administer it."

Marius smiled. "Will you accompany me?"

The Kammherr shook his head with great vigor. "You know how I feel about the sight of blood. We trust you, Lord von Harenheim."

"And I value that trust more than you know." The Imperial Guards opened the doors, granting Marius entrance into the Blessed Emperor's bedroom suite.

After passing through the sitting room, more Imperial Guards opened the door to the emperor's private bedroom. Like the rest of his personal suite, a heavy cotton cretonne featuring red flowers with green leaves covered the Korylean birch wall panels of the spacious bed chamber. Nine coffered panels covered the ceiling, and the Atharian eagle stood proud in the central medallion of each coffer. Golden frames containing mirrors, portraits of the Blessed Emperor as a young man in military dress, and religious icons adorned the walls. With the exception of the carved oak four-poster bed, the room's furniture was made from the same imported wood as the wall panels.

The air, warmed by the gold-leafed hearth of white marble, reeked of thick incense smoke. Marius wrinkled his nose.

His Excellency had not bathed in days, and the stench of his diseased body needed to be concealed. Marius smiled. The emperor was farther along than anyone—including Marius himself—suspected.

The Blessed Emperor rested in his bed, coughing and wheezing were the only signs he was awake. Marius walked across the ornate Kalamashi rug that covered the birch panels on the floor. He closed the gaps between the heavy green velvet curtains draped over the windows.

The Blessed Emperor's skin would have been more pale than the silk sheet beneath the green velvet comforter were it not for the jaundiced pallor sickness had given him. His chest trembled as it rose and fell at a slow, uneven pace. The candles in the room flickered. They were the only light, as the mechanomagical light sources had been removed as a precaution.

Marius sat in the chair beside the bed. He reached into his coat pocket and produced a flask-sized Arcanyx crystal glowing with pale green and swirling black energy. A single crack the size of a thumb nail tarnished the crystal's natural perfection. Marius slid the crystal between the mattress and the bed frame, placing his right hand on the emperor's arm as he did so.

With a sputtering cough, Blessed Emperor Hapfsburgh opened his eyes and turned toward the person who touched him. "Lord von Harenheim, we did not hear you arrive. Why did no one announce your presence?"

Marius bowed. "None wished to disturb your rest, Your Excellency. I've come with a serum to aid in your healing."

The emperor offered a weak smile. "You are one of our most loyal and devoted subjects, and yet, you refuse every honor we offer you. Why?"

Marius opened the physician's satchel. "I am but a foreigner brought into Your Excellency's empire. I wish none to think of me as anything but a loyal citizen. You do me great honor, and I feel blessed by the honors and accolades you bestow upon my humble self. Now, you rest, and allow me to minister to you, Your Excellency."

The emperor nodded. Marius tightened a cloth around the emperor's arm just below his elbow. He then produced a syringe and a vial of a small red liquid from within his satchel, pierced the vial with the syringe's needle, and drew the viscous liquid into the syringe. After a quick search for the cephalic vein, the vampire pierced the Emperor's skin. The Blessed Emperor gasped from the briefest moment of pain, but Marius remained undaunted as he pushed the serum into the vein.

As he finished, Marius licked his lips as he bandaged the wound. "There, Your Excellency. You should be stronger by morning."

Four wet, hacking coughs burst from the Blessed Emperor's lips. He turned to make eye contact with Marius. "Thank you, Lord von Harenheim. Please, allow us to reward you without argument for your service."

Marius smiled as he surveyed the glazed eyes of the emperor. The vampire's eyes flashed briefly, and he said, "I would ask nothing of you, Your Excellency, but if you see us as truly worthy of honor, we will accept the honor thrown at us as a tribute to the imperial glory of your empire."

The Blessed Emperor nodded. "Yes, we know this to be true."

They spoke for a few moments before Marius Bedwyr

kissed the Blessed Emperor's ring and departed. On his way out of the palace, he gave instructions to Kammherr Florescu to allow the emperor to rest before visiting him. As his carriage drove toward the Silver Dragon, Marius smiled at the decaying bodies of Caspar and Hanzlin Richter impaled on wooden stakes just outside the gates to the palace grounds.

The next morning, the *Sonnenburg Daily* had a single article on the front page, "The Atharian Empire Mourns the Death of Blessed Emperor Josyph Hapfsburgh, Ambrose von Harenheim Named his Successor."

The Atharian Empire begins mourning today following the death of Blessed Emperor Josyph Hapfsburgh. The emperor passed away in his sleep in his bedroom within the Imperial Palace in Sonnenburg. He was eighty-seven years of age.

The imperial physician, Dr. Elias Fischbein, stated the cause of death is the crimson plague, a disease caused by magical energies seeping from cracked or improperly shielded Arcanyx crystal technology.

The Blessed Emperor's age had shielded many from recognizing his suffering, leading those close to him to fear he had developed a rapid onset variant of the infectious condition.

Even though recent events have marred his reputation among some population segments, Emperor Josyph Hapfsburgh was known for his wisdom, his compassion, and his dedication to his people. He will be deeply missed.

Kammherr Florescue announced that Lord Ambrose von Harenheim, the director of the Emperor's Left Hand, will succeed the late Blessed Emperor Hapfsbufrgh. Lord Harenheim was a relative unknown until a few months ago when he illuminated the treason among the researchers within the Society for Afterlife and Arcane Studies. His dedication to research that both improved the lives of imperial citizens and offered absolution to traitors earned him a place on the High Holy Council. His coronation will take place in three days.

The was a wise and compassionate ruler who dedicated his life to the service of his people. He will be deeply missed, but his legacy will live on.

The Atharian Empire mourns the passing of Blessed Emperor Josyph Hapfsburgh, but it also celebrates his life. He ruled over the longest period of peace and economic growth the Atharian Empire has known. His memory will be cherished for generations to come. As such, a week of mourning has been declared in preparation for the late Blessed Emperor Hapfsburgh's funeral at noon on 15 Kieliah at the Grand Cathedral of St. Victus.

The night that news release went live, the crowd at Sonnenburg's vampire sanctuary, Sheridan & Bram's, was ecstatic with the news that the next emperor would be a vampire. As the blood-infused alcohol and the fresh blood from the dolls flowed freely among most of those seated in the rich mahogany furniture and hearth-warmed chamber that resembled a Froamian pub, one table in the back, populated by three vampires whose traveling cloaks were lined in crimson.

The three vampires sat and drank, shaking their heads. One, a tall and broad-shouldered Human male with curly red hair named Rhys Gryphith slammed his stein of red ale onto the mahogany table. "Can you fucking believe it?"

"Keep your voice down," a pale Elven woman with platinum curls framing her face and cascading down her shoulders and over the curve of her breasts hissed. "We don't need to start a bloody scene."

"Nyssia's right, Rhys," the other man, Pádraig O'Devlin, a short and stumpy Dwarf with brown hair and a scar over his left eye, said. "But we both agree that this whole situation is bullshit."

"It's not what we joined the Fangs for," Nyssia Quynlevyn said as she sipped her wine. "Thought we were going home, getting our country back."

"It's what Marius fucking promised us," Rhys said, downing half of his stein.

Pádraig nodded. "Aye. We all thought he meant it when he said he was going to sit on his father's throne again. Now, here he is, getting ready to take over that damned imperial throne. It's like he's becoming one of them bloody Atharians."

Nyssa sighed. "He always talked about sitting on his father's throne, wearing his crown—*our* crown, and now this. Did Marius ever intend to free Froam from Atharian rule?"

"This could be our chance," Pádraig whispered. "Once Marius gets the crown, do you think he'll send the army to stop us from throwing the Atharians out? He'd never do that."

Rhys shook his head and stared into his ale, hoping the red liquid would provide the answers it never provided mortals. His voice slumped with defeat and resignation. "I don't know—not anymore."

Three days passed, and as eleven bells tolled from the tower of the St. Victus Grand Cathedral, the hour to crown the new Blessed Emperor of the Atharian Empire drew near. The coronation would not begin for another hour within the cathedral itself, but all citizens lined the streets leading to Cathedral Square on this sunny spring day to witness the grand procession beginning with a military parade.

The procession began with the Grand Imperial Army's marching band striding north from the St. Hurud Imperial Army Base. The steel plates on the heels of their jackboots clicked in time as they performed "The Sky Blessed Our Emperor" as they walked.

Imperial citizens stood on the sidewalks. Some waved flags bearing the Atharian Eagle. Others cheered. Veterans saluted the military as it marched. And still other covered their ears from the noise, rolled their eyes, or sipped from flasks or bottles.

The Grand Imperial Army followed. One hundred thousand soldiers marched in the Atharian step wearing their dark green dress uniforms adorned with golden epaulets beneath gleaming breastplates of polished steel that reflected the sun's light in a glorious display of the Lord of Sky and Storm's might and grandeur. They displayed no emotion and paid no heed to the crowd as they marched, rifles over their shoulders and swords hanging from their belts.

The Emperor's Left Hand and their five thousand Kriegsdieneryn followed. The not-so-secret police of the Atharian Empire all wore black wide-brimmed hats, uniforms of black-leather accented by gray wool, and sunglasses with red crystal lenses. The Ofhani Searchers hovered above the other Servitors as the Zerafi Scorchers and the Malaki Grunts trudged along the path directed by their handlers. The Kerburi Wall-Breakers were the last of the servitors to march in formation. These headless monstrosities waved their warhammer arms as their battering rams comprised of three preserved heads with their eyes and mouths sewn shut protruded and retracted in rhythm with their steps.

The black-robed faculty of St. Aquitom University and the white-robed clergy serving in the St. Victus Grand Cathedral proceeded after the military. Wearing their ceremonial attire, they chanted the hymns to the Lord of Sky and Storm. Side by side, their movement created the impression of a massive phalanx, split between the darkness of ignorance and light of wisdom.

The green and gold imperial carriages, pulled by massive chestnut brown Clydesdales followed. Inside them were the major participants in the imperial coronation. As the carriage containing Marius Bedwyr entered Cathedral Square, another smile crossed his face as he passed Caspar Richter's lifeless remains.

His carriage stopped right before the gates to the palace grounds. The Imperial Guards formed lines on each side of the carriage door and then raised and crossed their swords in the air. One by one, the participants in the ceremony stepped from the car and onto a gold-trimmed carpet of red velvet. Marius Bedwyr, dressed in a white robe covered by a gold-trimmed cloak of red velvet, emerged last.

From the Cathedral Square, they proceeded into the Grand Cathedral itself. Marius shivered as he stepped over the threshold, but his smile broadened as he passed through the gold-flecked white marble apse. Per tradtion, he stopped at the statue of each saint, kneeled, and offered a short prayer prepared by Kammherr Florescu.

Censors wafted the rich, sweet, earthy incense blend through the cool air as the castrati choir chanted hymns in their angelic voices. Given the High Exarch had been stripped of his title due to treason and no other cleric had been appointed by the previous Blessed Emperor, Kammherr Florescu assumed all the duties of the various functionaries for this ceremony. As a result, he donned white robes trimmed in gold with a green stole draped over his shoulders and stood behind the altar adorned with an orb, a crown, and a sword. Two Exarchs, adorned in white and gold, flanked the altar.

As Marius reached the base of the dais upon which the altar stood, he paused. Kammherr Florescu, said, "Our Great God in Elysium, the Lord of Sky and Storms who watches us as we toil, as we travel, and as we travail, you, in your sacred and infinite wisdom have appointed Ambrose von Harenheim to guide us through the years to come, blessing him with the wisdom, courage, and strength to fulfill the duties appointed to him as our Blessed Emperor.

"I, serving today as representative of both the sacred and secular authorities of the Atharian Empire do hereby acknowledge His Excellency as our rightful sovereign, ordained by the Lord of Sky and Storm himself, and pledge fidelity and honor in your service. I will now present unto you the symbols of your authority."

Taking the sacred objects, he walked forward and stood before Marius. The Kammherr then handed him a skull-sized orb of pure Ziderite, a golden metal found at the center of a meteorite that crashed to the ground before the feet of Albrecht Wartheimer to signify divine grace in his most glorious battle to liberate and unite the peoples of the empire. He bowed before Marius and returned to his position as the Exarchs stepped forward and anointed the vampire with sacred oils, causing him to wince and grit his teeth through the pain.

When the Kammherr signaled, Marius recited his oath twice. "I, Ambrose Friedrich von Harenheim, do solemnly swear upon my name and my honor that I will be ever faithful and bear true allegiance to this most sacred office of Blessed Emperor. As the sovereign of the Atharian Empire, I will defend it to the utmost of my power against all enemies, foreign and domestic. I will uphold the laws of this empire with great fidelity and pass swift but wise judgment on those who run afoul of those most sacred bonds of social unity. This, by the authority and might of the Lord of Sky and Storm, I swear."

Kammherr Florescu and the Exarchs stepped forward. The Kammherr held a green velvet cushion atop which sat a golden crown encrusted with diamonds and emeralds. Marius kneeled, and the three men placed the crown on his head. Kammherr Florescu then handed Marius the golden sword of office, scabbard of which contained a key to the true sword wielded by the Blessed Emperor in times of struggle, Albrecht's Sun Sword.

The Kammherr then turned to the crowd. "Nobles and honored guests, we present to you, Blessed Emperor Ambrose von Harenheim. Long may he reign."

Marius smirked as the crowd chanted, "Long may he reign" and "Hail, Emperor von Harenheim!"

Chapter 28

On the morning of Marius Bedwyr's coronation, the remaining members of the Richter family awoke in the beds of the rustic rooms they rented in Solegno's Forest Haven Inn. The rooms weren't large, but they were larger than the spartan dwellings afforded them at the manor, and the beds were soft. The cool air in the rooms smelled of the oak and pine used in their construction as well as the trees in the Ardbri Forest to the town's east.

Solegno was a small fishing village on the southern tip of Hoarfrost Bay. For many travelers, this quaint town was either the first stop on their path into Florescia or their last stop before setting foot into the once-independent nation of Edrium, now a vassal state of the Atharian Empire. As such, many of the residents spoke Floresci, Edriu, and Atha with varying degrees of fluency.

Garrus woke before the others in his family, and after he prayed, shaved, and dressed, he descended into the lobby and walked to the attached restaurant for breakfast. He had lost weight on this trek, as the Atharian soldiers allowed little rest on the forced march that began once they reached Dornbach. After receiving his first espresso and ordering a meal, he waited in anticipation for the large farmer's breakfast he had ordered.

After the server left his table upon taking his order, a local man at the table next to his leaned over. The man was tall and slender, with thinning gray hair and a trimmed beard. "Forgive me, son, but your accent is Atharian. Are you heading home for the coronation?"

Garrus sputtered on the strong, bitter drink as the man said those words. Garrus shook his head. "Sorry, did you say coronation? What happened?"

The man nodded. "Seems your old emperor, Hapsfburgh—I think, died of crimson plague. Haven't even buried him yet, but they're crowning some guy named Ambrose. I don't know his last—"

"Von Harenheim," Garrus muttered. His face fell and darkened in sadness. "Of course, it's him."

The man nodded in thought for a moment. "Yeah, I think that's it. You know him?"

Garrus shrugged. He shook his head and replied, "Met him a few times, but I don't know him that well. My uncle did. But I'm on my way to Utrezzo. Will I be able to make it today?"

The man nodded. "By tomorrow morning if you walk or take a horse. You can get there by early evening if you hire one of the carriages over at Allighieri's Livery."

"Thank you. I'll talk with the rest of my family when they get up, which should be soon."

But it wasn't soon. Garrus was able to finish his breakfast, which consisted of a mushroom, onion, and pepper quiche and half a pound of cured and pan-fried pork belly. Having no other plans, they purchased rides from the carriage service and then departed.

Two carriages of varnished pine ferried the twelve remaining Richters on their journey. As they traveled, some members of the family prayed. Others read books. A few looked out the windows. Ludwig Richter, a tall man with tufts of white hair just above his large ears, stared at the nervous expression on Garrus' face.

Ludwig's voice was dark and deep. "Has your confidence in your *plan* dissipated, Garrus?"

Garrus ran his fingers through his chestnut hair and sighed. "I don't think so, Uncle. I just hope it works."

Ludwig snorted. "You know who rules Utrezzo, don't you? You know what we did there six years ago. You were among our number there."

Garrus forced a smile onto his face. He nodded. "That's why I'm nervous."

"And what, Garrus, do you think we will do? Walk into that castle and request sanctuary?"

Garrus shook his head. "No, Uncle Ludwig. We'll go in there, and we'll ask for forgiveness, and if she's willing to hear us out, maybe we'll ask for sanctuary."

While the last remnants of the Richter family traveled to Utrezzo, Courage Faern'doln, Honor Faern'doln, Xrissa Kosol, and Kiernan Valfrido gathered in the spacious kitchen within the Vandiamante castle. Honor and Courage sat in the breakfast nook the servants often used for morning coffee. Courage had a full mug of espresso, a quarter of one of Xrissa's speical cinnamon rolls, and an assortment of mechanical parts laid out before him. Honor sipped her steaming cup of espresso and watched her brother work.

"Your coffee's getting cold, Courage," Honor said.

Courage paid no heed as he drilled holes into a curved piece of titanium that he had lined with a special arcanoweave fabric mesh designed to keep his arm cool and to absorb residual magical energies. Once he had drilled the holes, he screwed gear tracks into place, and once he had done that, he placed the sliding doors into the titanium. With the crystal flame torch, Courage then soldered the wiring in place, connecting the power source to the gears. He tested it, and the sliding doors slid along the track, opening. He smiled and took a bite of the cinnamon roll.

"I said your coffee's getting cold, butthead."

"That's nice, sister," Courage nodded.

His attention remained focused on the new version of the wandvolver. Courage increased the power in the torch and then welded the curved door atop the gauntlet, which contained the power mechanism and six wands, charged with specific spells. This time, Courage kept the wands that produced a telekinetic hand, provided healing and purification, detected magical energies, and fired arcane bolts. He added one wand that produced a bright light from radiant, holy energy. The sixth wand was an arcane jammer, designed not to counter magical spells but to jam technomagical currents and force devices to power down.

Honor smirked and grabbed her fork and stabbed what remained of Courage's cinnamon roll. Before her tines pierced the pastry, Courage pulled the plate out of the way. He looked up from his work, glared at his sister, and took a bite. Through a mouth full of the gooey, sweet, and soft pastry, Courage asked, "What the fuck is wrong with you? Taking food off someone's plate. You've graduated from butthead to disgusting slob."

"Slob?" Honor laughed. "Your bedroom always qualified

you as a slob."

Courage swallowed and sipped the espresso. "Oh, that's cold. Anyway, I'm no slob. My room is cluttered with parts for projects."

"And how many of them have you actually completed, you butthead?"

"More than the number of instruments you've given up on playing." He took another bite of the cinnamon roll and returned to his project.

While Courage worked and while he and Honor continued bickering and teasing each other, Xrissa explained the automated machinery she installed in the kitchen. While she sipped Crimson Minotaur from her flask, Kiernan asked, "So, all I will need to do is to place the ingredients here, press this button, and then watch to ensure nothing malfunctions as it cooks?"

"Exactamundo. And this red button on the counter will submerge the machinery into the space below, giving you an easier surface to clean. Also, the blue button next to it will activate the self-cleaning crystals, so you don't have to spend time cleaning. Also, if you build up the staff, you can do it the old fashioned way."

Kiernan chuckled. "That will be Her Majesty's decision, but as I get older, I do appreciate the assistance this will provide. And you said this is how you power your bakery?"

Xrissa nodded. "Sure do. I've got some great staff who are about to get another raise when I get back, but I don't see why I shouldn't make their lives easier, right? But I mechanized my baking process when I started to help me out. Made it easier for me to work the front of house and build relationships with my customers." Xrissa smiled at Courage and raised her voice as she added, "When they actually talk to me."

Courage looked up and then lowered his head, blushing sheepishly. "I tried. You're just so pretty it scared me."

Xrissa giggled and brushed her hair in a dramatic fashion. She sat on the counter and crossed her legs. With a teasing sigh, she said, "Shame I have these intimidating Moon Elf features. Maybe if I were nothing more than a plain Snow Elf."

Courage hid his face in his collar. "I didn't mean it that way."

Everyone but Courage laughed. Xrissa hopped onto the floor, skipped over, and kissed Courage's forehead. Kiernan followed over and freshened the siblings' coffee. Honor smiled. "Thank you. I could've gotten that."

"Yes," the estate steward said. "But it is my pleasure to serve the guests of House Vandiamante. And, did I hear correctly that you play musical instruments?"

Honor nodded, but Courage spoke first. "Yeah, she's a really good musician. Writes her own songs and went to conservatory and everything. She can sing too…when her head isn't stuck up her butt."

"Fucking idiot. You're lucky we all love you sometimes." Honor sighed and shook her head. She turned back to Kiernan and said, "Yeah, I'm damned good at the violin and the lute. I'm not bad at the dulcimer."

Kiernan smiled. "It has been years since we have had music in this house. Her Majesty has her harp, but I've not heard her play since before her departure all those years ago. We have many instruments in the conservatory. Perhaps you will grace us with song while you remain here."

Honor nodded. "I might. I'll see what you've got."

True to her word, Honor spent much of the day tuning and practicing. As the sun descended toward the west and the clocks chimed for seventeen bells, Sezara Gwynarra Vandiamante and Donna Karina Skejik strolled into the castle's armory. Suits of steel, titanium, and obsidian armor stood against the walls, and racks containing an assortment of weapons, including longswords, rapiers, sabers, pikes, halberds, spears, pistols, rifles, longbows, and crossbows lined the walls. Holding her smallsword and flintlock in her hands, Gwyn walked to the back wall where Kiernan had placed a plaque bearing the inscription, *Gwynarra Caoilfhionn Vandiamante, the Silver Scourge,* on a golden plate.

With a nod, a sigh, and a wistful smile, Gwyn placed her weapons on the rack beneath the plaque. "That part of my life is over. The White Queen is born as the Silver Scourge dies."

Karina wrapped her arm around Gwyn's waist. The softness of the red velvet gown felt nice. "Are you certain that putting your weapons away is the path to walk?"

Gwyn nodded. "I never wanted to be that, but the choice wasn't mine initially. Adventuring, hunting monsters, all of that served to teach me lessons I hope will guide me as a queen who protects her people. My place is not on the battlefield any longer, I hope."

Gwyn turned to face Karina and threw her arms around her knight and lover's neck. Karina brushed Gwyn's lips with her own in a quick, gentle kiss. She said, "And should the day come when you must return to battle, I will stand before you. I am your shield, and I am your sword."

Gwyn smiled. "And you are my heart. I have no doubt in that you will be at my side when I need you."

They kissed again, and the armory door opened. Kiernan

cleared his throat and said, "Forgive the interruption, Your Majesty, but you have Atharian visitors waiting for you in the Receiving Room."

Gwyn lifted her right eyebrow. "Visitors? I don't recall any official visits on my agenda until next week when the Amydzeenian delegation arrives."

Kiernan turned his gaze to Karina. "Mistress Karina's family requests an audience."

"My…*family*?" Karina swallowed hard, and her hand gripped the hilt of her sword.

Gwyn reached back and grabbed her weapons from the wall. Kiernan raised his hand. "I do not believe your weapons will be necessary, Your Majesty. While there are twelve of them—"

"Twelve of them?" Karina's eyes widened as she spoke. "Father never sent more than two on a mission unless…"

She turned her gaze toward Gwyn and saw her lover's jaw tremble as she stared forward with wide eyes. The vampire clutched her weapons tight against her chest in a manner similar to a child clutching a beloved stuffed animal while recalling a nightmare. Karina slid her arm back around Gwyn's waist and held her close.

"As I was saying," Kiernan said with a sigh. "They appear to be out of uniform and unarmed. They submitted to an inspection performed by your guards. Her Majesty's weapons will be unnecessary."

Gwyn tightened her grip on her sword. She closed her eyes and forced a deep breath into her lungs, which she held and then exhaled. With a steeled expression on her face, Gwyn opened her eyes and said, "Tell them we will meet with them in ten minutes. A queen must prepare, and guests who arrive unannounced must learn manners."

Karina swallowed hard. Kiernan bowed. Before departing, he said, "As Her Majesty commands."

Ten minutes later, the twelve members of the Richter family waited in the receiving room. The anxiety from their shifting about in their seats or milling about without aim on the red and gold rugs atop the white marble floor warmed the cool air. The golden filigree on the cream silk wallpaper glinted in the light of the crystal candles sitting atop three-pronged golden candelabra held in golden sconces shaped like women's hands. Murals depicting the triumphs of the honored ancestors, such as when Damianyo Vandiamante weathered the sun's angry glare to lead the Florescian army to victory against Ostijanese forces in the Battle of Bollogrein Fields.

In addition to the twelve Ricthers, Courage, Honor, and Xrissa sat on the cream silk cushions of the walnut furniture. Though terrified of the Richters' presence, Mathias Greely stood behind Courage and Honor. The kept one hand on a weapon, and SAAMy stood ready at Xrissa's feet, his googly eyes pointing at the Richters. All but two members of the Sezarian Guard stood behind the guests, their hands on their firearms and hatred blazing on their faces.

Kiernan entered pushing a cart containing tea and pastries. As he poured the tea into cups and passed them around, he said, "Miss Xrissa provided the lovely pastries, and the tea is stronger than milk but not as strong as coffee. I hope it is to your liking."

Ludwig Richter growled a sigh. "How much longer must we be kept waiting?"

Kiernan served everyone, leaving Ludwig for last, and then

said, "Her Majesty and Mistress Karina are on their way. It is not our tradition to keep guests waiting, but it is proper etiquette for guests to announce their intention to visit when coming from a foreign nation. Have a cinnamon roll. It might sweeten your disposition."

Garrus snickered as House Vandiamante's estate steward flicked a plate overflowing with cinnamon roll into Ludwig's hands. Kiernan left with the cart. A moment after he left the room, the remaining members of the Sezarian Guard strode into the room and announced the imminent arrival of Gwynarra Vandiamante, Sezara of the Midnight Court, and her first knight, Karina Skejik. The use of Karina's mother's name hurled waves of fear through the Richters, concerned as this change could mean she would not ally with them.

Shortly thereafter, Sezara Vandiamante entered with her crown sitting atop her head and the train of her red velvet gown flowing behind her. The traveling clothes Karina purchased in Clérmontán served as Karina's day wear, and she strode beside Gwyn, their arms locked at the elbows. As they sat in the two remaining chairs, Kiernan entered with a glass of wine, which he handed to Gwyn before departing again.

Gwyn sipped her wine in silence, holding the glass in front of her mouth until the selfish smirk that danced on her lips finished its movement. She set the wine down and placed her hand atop Karina's. Gwyn smiled at the Richters and said, "Well, we must admit your unheralded and uninvited arrival during our waking hours comes as quite the surprise. However, we welcome you to our home and hope that once you depart you will leave some of the happiness you bring."

"Cut the crap, vampire," Ludwig screamed as he leaped

to his feet. Karina responded in kind, extending an arm to protect Gwyn. The guards behind him thrust the butts of their rifle stocks into his shoulders, and Garrus assisted in pulling him down.

Garrus shushed Ludwig. "Stop it. It's a standard greeting in Florescian aristocratic circles. She's being polite." Ludwig grumbled as he crossed his arms. Garrus sighed and turned his attention to Gwyn. He ran his hand through his hair and chuckled. "Sorry about him. He can be a horse's ass at times. Thank you for seeing us—and for not having us shot on sight."

Karina returned to her seat but narrowed her eyes as she focused her attention on Ludwig. Gwyn nodded and smiled. "Your fate, as you are on Florescian soil, is as yet undecided. Tell us, given the history our families share, why have you come?"

Garrus tensed and sucked in a deep breath. Karina leaned forward, placing one hand on her knee while readying her draw. Garrus exhaled and then said, "First, it was brought to my attention by my cousin Karina there, by your side, that our family's hatred of you may have begun with faulty information and that the feud was, more or less, one-sided."

"It was not faulty information," Karina slammed her fist on the chair's armrest. "Garrus, everyone, it was based on a lie. Antonio Vandiamante did not kill Karolinya Richter's betrothed. He was her betrothed. He told her who he was. He was honest, and she betrayed him to our family's hatred for things deemed unholy. Her diary should be in the library at home. Go read it."

"That's not possible, Karina." Garrus' voice softened. "Someone set off a mana bomb beside our house. There's nothing left but ruins, and the same is true for most of

Ullinburg. Plus, we were kind of exiled and have nowhere else to go."

Karina sank back into her chair. Her voice was soft as she spoke in hushed tones. "Destroyed? That's what the Corvidiae showed me."

Courage's ears perked up, and he lifted his head. "That's what the thing we found in the orphanage was for. Why are you all looking at me funny? I told you it was a device that converted emotional energy into arcane energy and sent it somewhere. Those kids' suffering was being used to charge that bomb. Oh, damn."

"But I brought that there," Mathias said. "Mister Ambrose said it would help keep the other children happy by siphoning their fear away from them."

Gwyn smiled as she looked at her childhood friend. "It's not your fault. Ambrose von Harenheim, whom all in this room now know as Marius Bedwyr, lied to you. He used your desire to protect those who suffered as we did in St. Hiltegardt's to his advantage in a bid for revenge on those who took everything from us. And so, now that he has his revenge, the Richter family is homeless and exiled, we ask once more, what brings you to our home this night? It is curious to us that you are unarmed."

Garrus nodded slowly. "When the late Blessed Emperor disbanded our order, Uncle Caspar and Hanzlin were sent to prison to await execution, and we were exiled. We were escorted, shall we say, to the border and told never to return. Look, um, Miss Sezara Vandiamante, we know you don't owe us anything, but we came with—well, *I* had two goals in mind for coming here.

"The first is forgiveness. We don't deserve it after killing your family. All of us before you now, unarmed and unarmored, helped kill your family. Some of us are old enough to have helped kill your birth family. And I'm starting to wonder how much of our information has been filtered to Uncle Caspar through this Marius Bedwyr for his own purposes. You don't have to forgive us now—or ever—and we certainly haven't earned it. But when I saw Karina point her gun at Uncle Caspar's head to protect you, I figured there must be something special there I didn't know about. She's never stood up to Uncle Caspar like that—or at all—ever."

Gwyn and Karina shared a glance. Karina nodded, and Gwyn smiled. Gwyn turned to Garrus. "We have heard your first request and shall take our time to consider it. However, we must ask if the emperor who exiled you has died, as you have suggested, why do you not return home?"

"Fair point, yeah." Garrus nodded. "We were in Solegno this morning when I learned that Blessed Emperor Josyph Hapfsburgh had died, hasn't been buried yet, and today Ambrose von—er, Marius Bedwyr—was crowned as the new Blessed Emperor. So, we can't go home. That's our second request. We don't come as enemies. I wish I could say we came as friends, but that wouldn't be honest. We need help. We beg your forgiveness, and we beg you grant us sanctuary."

Gwyn turned to Karina. "What do you think, my love? These people share your blood. They have admitted to crimes against both a noble house in the Florescian court and against the ruling house of our Midnight Court. For their crimes, the expected punishment is not death but forced servitude as thralls. Shall we enforce our laws, or shall we show mercy to those who would not even show mercy to you?"

The Richters all lowered their gazes. Karina nodded and

exhaled in anxious contemplation. These people were her family. She loved them. They loved her. Well, *Garrus* seemed to care about her. The others put duty and tradition over caring for her when Marius turned her over to her father after simulating a bite and insinuating that Gwyn was responsible.

Karina exhaled once more and then said, “My presence causes enough gossip in your court, my sezara. I fear my family’s presence would undermine your authority.”

“We have considered that, yes. Are you then suggesting execution or servitude?”

Each of the Richters’ faces paled. Their eyes widened. Hearts raced inside their chests. Breathing quickened. Many fidgeted in their seats. Gwyn’s smile bared her fangs.

Karina sighed. “May I speak freely, sezara?”

“We grant you that, always.”

Karina nodded. “We saw what kind of servitude Marius employs for people who betray him, and if you punish them by turning them into thralls, he’s right. You’re just like him, and you prove all the horrible things my family said—that I said to your face—about your family are true. They don’t have to stay here, but please don’t kill them.”

Gwyn nodded with a neutral, disinterested expression marred only by the slight twinge of a proud smile curling up from the corners of her lip. She sipped her wine to hide the smile until it subsided. She remained silent for a moment. “We will make this offer to the family of Donna Karina *Skejik*. We do not permit you to remain in our castle or upon our grounds, as the last time you arrived without invitation, you performed terrible violence against our family. However, we will not have you escorted back to Atharian soil to face a punishment you may or may not have earned for alleged treason against the emperor. We will write a letter of introduction to Sezar Ciampi on your behalf. With this letter, you will travel to Delfia where you will present yourself to him. By his decision, we will abide."

Karina released a breath she didn't know she was holding as Gwyn rendered her decision. Garrus nodded. "That is more than fair and generous. Thank you. Oh, and the cinnamon roll is really tasty."

Gwyn smiled. "Now return to Utrezzo for the night. We will send the letter tomorrow evening."

The Sezarian Guard escorted the Richters from the receiving room. Gwyn turned to Karina and exhaled. Karina said, "That was merciful. You worried me."

The vampire nodded. "Forgive me, but I should have discussed it with you prior. They are your family, and should things continue for us, I want you involved in my decisions. Besides, given how few of them seemed concerned when your father threw you out of your home, I was hoping they'd squirm a bit more than they did."

Karina chuckled. "But they brought news I wish were untrue."

Gwyn nodded. "Aye. Fucking asshole is the new emperor. I'm sure we'll be expected to attend the old emperor's funeral. I just hope this was his endgame."

That night, an unnamed editor at the *Sonnenburg Daily* toiled in preparation for the release of one fateful headline in the morning's issue: "Blessed Emperor Decrees Mandatory Conscription for the Poor."

In a move to bolster the Atharian Empire's already robust defenses against threats from neighboring nations, Blessed Emperor

Ambrose von Harenheim has declared mandatory conscription for all males fifteen-years-old or older from families earning below 1,200 torbal per year.

The decree, issued only an hour after yesterday's evening release hit the presses, states that all able-bodied men must report for military service for a period of six years. Women from these families who are unmarried by their seventeenth birthday will be drafted into the medical corps.

The emperor's decision has been met with mixed reactions. Some people believe that it is necessary to protect the empire from its enemies, whoever they may be, while others argue that it is an infringement on their personal freedom continuing the moves made by his late predecessor.

In a prepared statement delivered to the Sonnenburg Daily *by Kammherr Florescu, the emperor said that the decision to impose conscription was not taken lightly. He said that the empire is facing a growing number of threats, both from within and without, and that the Lord of Sky and Storm wills him to take the necessary steps to ensure its security by removing the idleness of the poor and gifting them with a path out of poverty.*

The mandatory conscription, which should impact nearly three hundred thousand families, is to begin immediately.

As the editor finalized the copy, he ran his fingers through his silvering hair and exhaled. "If people thought the protests were bad before, shit's only going to get worse from here."

Chapter 29

As the clock struck midnight after his coronation, Marius Bedwyr waited in the lavish apartment on the top floor of the Imperial Palace. Seated in the largest of the leather chairs in the sitting room, he sipped a glass of blood-infused wine while reading the latest progress report from the Imperium Center for the Rehabilitation of Traitors. His sword of office lay on the table beside him. A recording of Cassandra Arenfroi's "Rondo of Ash and Bone" played in the background. Three firm knocks, one slow and two rapid in pace, sounded against his door.

Marius looked up from his reading. "Enter."

Three men entered his chamber wearing the black uniforms of the Emperor's Left Hand. At the center and two steps in front of the other two was a young-looking man with jaundiced olive skin, greasy black hair, and a cold sapphire right eye. He walked with an uneven gait, as his left leg was a finger's width shorter than his right leg. The other two had arcanist's hoods sewn into their uniform jackets and pulled over their heads so as to keep their faces hidden. The three saluted their emperor, and he nodded in return.

"Lord Marius," the man, Kasymyr Pyrkl, said. "The Blood Wolves have replaced the guards outside your chambers for this shift. All is ready for your descent into the Sacred Armory—if you are certain that is necessary."

Predatory undertones colored Marius' paternal smile. "Our dear, loyal Kasymyr, it is necessary. Were you not the one who brought us word of the grumblings amongst the oldest of the noble houses? Given their concern that we permitted the abbreviated coronation ritual to be performed without any meaningful representation of the Church and that we did not descend into the armory to lift that blasted blade from its scabbard, we must determine if the blade will allow we to wield it."

"But Albrecht's Sun Sword boasts a blade of pure divine energy, and given that you—that *we*—are—"

"We are aware of the blade's nature, our child, and of our own. Were the choice fully ours to make, the blade would be destroyed in the fires of Ashenfell. However, until such a time as the nobility cease their incessant prattling about tradition and appearances, we must maintain the appearance of a respectable, normal Human. You do understand, don't you?"

Kasymyr nodded. "Yes, sire. Soon, we will return home and no longer need to hide."

Marius smiled. "But we promise you, my loyal child, you will be rewarded in this, our empire, for your service. Once High General Krank meets his end, you will replace him as the High General of our Grand Imperial Army."

Does he no longer have intentions of returning to Froam, of freeing our home from imperial rule? Kasymir knew better than to voice such concerns when Marius was even the slightest bit aggravated. Instead, he smiled and bowed. "Thank you, Your Excellency. Shall we head to the armory now?"

Marius set down the report and curled his fingers around the scabbard of the ceremonial sword of office. As he rose from his chair, he said, "That is, after all, why you have been summoned."

The Sacred Armory was beyond the catacombs beneath the Grand Cathedral. After passing through the gold-adorned white marble interior of the church and descending a narrow staircase, the four vampires stood in the dark, reverent silence of the catacombs. The air was cold and damp, illuminated only by flickering Arcanyx candles and perfumed by the scent of sweet incense that masked the decay from the skeletons stacked in niches carved into the gray stone walls. Some were ancient, dating to before the unification of the empire, and some were more recent. All had skulls that faced the passages, giving the illusion of the dead watching the living, or the unliving, who passed by their resting place.

The small slime cube who patrolled the hallways, keeping them free of dust and vermin, paid no heed to the vampires. They too chose to ignore the semi-sentient cleaner. The pre-imperial mosaics depicting the great saints of the faith remained in tact, cleaned with love by the same slime who now slid along the floor, devouring a rat that had scurried into its path. The only sound within these darkened halls were the echoes of the vampires' boots.

Another narrow staircase spiraled down at the end of the catacomb corridor. Mud bricks fortified with bone formed these stairs. Legends told that these were the bones of heretics slain by the Holy Order of St. Arnulf Ironhand during the Age of Faith, and recalling those legends made the vampires smirk as they recalled bringing low that once holy order. Centered on the eastern wall of the landing beneath the stairs were two doors of white marble.

Marius turned a ruby on the scabbard of his sword of office, and a small panel in the scabbard slid out, revealing a key. He took the key and unlocked and then opened the doors to the Sacred Armory. Three sarcophagi belonging to Albrecht the Great Liberator, St. Victus the Light-bringer, and St. Arnulf Ironhand rested on a dais against the far wall. Blessed weapons from the previous ages, greatswords, axes, maces, flails, and spears, hung in display cases on the walls. But, rising from a hunk of white marble carved to resemble the stone from which Albrecht originally drew the blade was the golden scabbard containing the Sun Sword of the Blessed Emperor.

As the vampires strode into the hall, Kasymyr marveled at the inspired masterful craftsmanship that went into making the scabbard. Legend said the scabbard was gold-wrapped kelerite, a metal found only in meteors that crashed into Eilofoht during solar eclipses. The metal had been shaped into a scabbard etched with holy sigils protecting it and its wielder, lined with soft leather on its interior, and then wrapped in gold and encrusted with rubies, diamonds, and topazes. Two halves of a blazing golden sun formed the guard that flanked the white leather-wrapped grip whose sun-shaped golden pommel held a blazing diamond. When drawn by an emperor blessed by the Lord of Sky and Storm, the blade blazed with the fires of the sun, blinding those who opposed the emperor and causing all unholiness to flee his presence.

Damn, Kasymyr thought as he exhaled. *For something with such terrifying power, it lies dormant, no more dangerous than a corpse. And yet, its energy still radiates and warms the air here.*

Marius, on the other hand, strode to the dais. He smirked,

running his hand along the sarcophagi, at the corpses of those who would revile and slay him had they the opportunity. He paused before the sarcophagus containing St. Arnulf Ironhand. He wrapped his fingers around the carved throat and smiled. "Oh, Arnulf, how does it feel knowing those your sainted little band of heretic hunters once brought low have now risen and strangled the life from your devotees?"

"Lord Marius," one of the Crimson Fang arcanists said. Once he turned and acknowledged the request, the arcanist continued, "We should not dally in this place for too long. Draw the blade."

Marius nodded. A cocky smirk adorned his face as he strode to the sword housed in stone within the Sacred Armory. His fingers curled around the grip with the graceful, serpentine slither. Marius winced. The holy energy within the sword heated the grip, and as he tightened his hold on the sword, his own undead flesh burned.

The emperor's nostrils flared. The heat searing into his hand intensified. Sweat formed on his brow, something that had not occurred in over two centuries without illusory magic. The arcanists focused their gaze on the sword, making notes during the process. Kasymyr shifted his gaze from the sword to Marius and back again, his jaw opened in shock and concern.

With a shout of pain, Marius released his grip on the sword. He winced and grabbed his hand. One of the arcanists examined the wound, and Kasymyr hissed in sympathetic pain, turning his head from the bubbling and blistering flesh.

"This was not unexpected," Marius said. "Though it is painful. It will heal, correct?"

Both arcanists nodded. The one examining his wound said,

"In time, Lord Marius. I would recommend dressing the wound and wearing gloves to avoid suspicion."

"Once more," Marius said. "Kasymyr, did you bring the gauntlet as instructed?"

"Yes, my lord." Kasymyr handed the steel glove with full finger articulation to the emperor.

Marius winced as he slid his blistered hand into the gauntlet. Stabs of pain jolted his hand. He flexed his fingers and then grabbed the sword's grip with enough force to strangle a horse. The sacred energy pulsed again, warming the air and the gauntlet. This pain was tolerable, and yet, grunt after grunt, pull after pull, the blade refused to leave its scabbard.

With an enraged roar, Marius released his grip. He hurled the gauntlet against the wall of the armory, screaming, "Arcanists, do your bloody fucking job."

Kasymyr clenched his jaw and remained silent and unmoving as the two arcanists flanked the sword and its stone. Each drew a bit of blood from their arms and began weaving incantations in a gruff, guttural language. The drawn blood thinned into a crimson web that surrounded the sword but could not touch it. The blood web pulsed and glowed, and the sword trembled as the arcanists' continued chanting. Marius stepped to the sword, victory in his eyes, as the hilt lifted two inches from the scabbard's opening.

White light exploded from the blade. Thunder roared, hurling all four vampires against the chamber's walls. The sanguine web turned to dust and fell to the ground.

Marius leaped to his feet, roared, and punched the nearest wall. Grabbing the nearest weapon display case, he hurled it onto the floor, screaming, "What the fuck was that? Why did your magic fail?"

The arcanists scrambled to analyze the dust. One said, "I'm not sure, Lord Marius. The enchantments on the sword, the divine energies that legends say create it, make it stronger than our magic. It appears to be too holy for any of us to handle."

"We could," the other arcanist said. "And theory dictates this should work, but we could corrupt the sword, weakening its holiness enough you could draw it from the scabbard."

Marius rushed the second arcanist, grabbed him by the throat, and lifted him from the floor. "Then fucking do it. I don't care what it costs. I don't care who has to die, how many infants you must sacrifice, how many souls you must damn. By Zanguis, I will draw that blade before I send my empire's army against Florescia and that Vandiamante cunt for giving sanctuary to the last of the fucking Richters."

With another roar, Marius threw the arcanist against the floor before storming out of the armory. Kasymyr released a fearful breath, nodded, and then followed after his emperor.

To Be Concluded...

About the Author

Rebecca St. Claire is a Qualitative Research Consultant. She has a background in medieval literature and linguistics, focusing on the Germanic and Celtic traditions. When not working or writing, she spends her free time playing *Dungeons & Dragons;* screaming at the bosses in *Bloodborne* (or playing other video games); reading fantasy, romance, and gothic fiction; and cuddling her three cats.

You can connect with me on:

https://cursingravenbooks.com

Milton Keynes UK
Ingram Content Group UK Ltd.
UKHW021034200524
442968UK00016B/1204